Drayton and Mackenzie

Drayton and Mackenzie

Alexander Starritt

SWIFT PRESS

First published in Great Britain by Swift Press 2025

1 3 5 7 9 8 6 4 2

All rights reserved

Copyright © Alexander Starritt, 2025

The right of Alexander Starritt to be identified as the Author of this Work has been asserted in accordance with the Copyright, Designs and Patents Act 1988.

Printed and bound in Great Britain by CPI Group (UK) Ltd, Croydon CR0 4YY

A CIP catalogue record for this book is available from the British Library

We make every effort to make sure our products are safe for the purpose for which they are intended. Our authorised representative in the EU for product safety is Easy Access System Europe, Mustamäe tee 50, 10621 Tallinn, Estonia gpsr.requests@easproject.com

ISBN: 9781800755260
TPB ISBN: 9781800755567
eISBN: 9781800755277

To Stella

"There is a tide in the affairs of men
Which, taken at the flood, leads on to fortune"

I

All his life, James had found things too easy. So far, he'd only really known one thing: the arbitrary, rule-bounded competition for grades. Before his A-levels, he trained with the total absorption of an elite athlete. In the maths papers, he even ratcheted the bar a few notches higher: the rules said you weren't allowed to leave the exam room in the first twenty minutes, so he tried to finish by that mark. In the first of these maths papers, he reached his personal finish line with eighteen seconds to spare. There was a moment of exhilaration. But as the pleasure and tunnel vision of racing receded, he suddenly understood that he would now have to leave the exam room alone, while the rest of his class stayed inside together.

Each time he hit this mark in the subsequent exams, it made him sadder. At least after the summer there would be Oxford. The big league. He deferred the disappointment of the present by looking ahead. And he arrived there assuming he would have to sprint constantly just to keep up. But in tutorials he watched other students admit they hadn't read "that particular chapter" or just look blank and terrified when the tutor was talking. Others confidently embarked on theories that quickly leaked and foundered, or they just kept clinging to the last idea they'd read about.

Practically no one, not even those struggling, seemed to simply put in the forty hours of weekly study that the tutors recommended. From the snatches of their conversation he overheard, they were using that time for club nights and sports matches. James couldn't understand them. He found that forty hours was hardly enough to master the basics.

But most bemusing were those who seemed to intentionally trip themselves up — because it showed that they were a free spirit, or glamorously troubled, or too popular for secondary reading. They seemed to think it was interesting to be bad at things. They didn't seem to understand that being bad at things was the default. Almost everyone since the dawn of time had been bad at almost everything. It was simply the world operating as expected. It was like if you let go of an object and all it did was drop inertly to the ground. Far more remarkable if, when you let go, it began to fly.

His tutorial partners found him aloof, stand-offish, arrogant. His tutors thought him enigmatic: usually a student this brilliant would eagerly accept their invitations to join the little informal gatherings they hosted with interesting alumni. James said he couldn't spare the time from working. But surely – *surely* – that was a lie. Meanwhile, James lived in fear. Because the only students he knew were the handful that the timetable paired him with, it was entirely possible that in other tutorials there would be dozens of people far better than him. He studied like he had for A-levels, as if pursued by a rival who had no weaknesses and never tired.

The only extra-curricular activity he tried – just for the first term – was rowing, since it was a bona fide irreplicable Oxford experience and not, like the student newspapers and debating societies, just a sandpit version of real things for grown-ups. In later years, when he was the subject of articles and interviews, he was often asked whether it was true that one of the others in the boat with him was Roland Mackenzie. Yes, it was true. James didn't notice him at the time.

Instead, he was thinking about undergrad essays, which he'd realised with a sense of disillusionment were merely a technique, a form to be learned like Shakespeare learned the sonnet. All you needed was three facts and confidence. Point, counterpoint, conclusion. Thesis, antithesis, synthesis. It was very Hegel. And once he saw this, he saw it everywhere: Parliament, the law courts, *Newsnight*. The two raucous sides of the House; the two sharply antagonistic barristers; prosecution, defence, judgment; one side, other side, vote.

He supposed he'd been naive to think of university as concerned with intellect. Maybe it was different at postgrad, but at this level, Oxford was just an elementary course in information-processing, a training school for Britain's future lawyers, politicians and administrators. You skim-read the sources and hastily produced an opinionated synopsis. Of course, it made sense. Society needed administrators far more than what his tutor had called "a rare original response" to Spinoza. It didn't occur to him that since he'd quickly learned the essay form, he could have tried to employ it for something with value of its own. He could only see the test and not what lay behind it.

In the end-of-year exams, he came first by miles, his result an outlier in the distribution, far above the girl in second. His beefy imagined opponent, up close, turned out to be stuffed with straw. It hurt so much he had to lie on the carpet of his childhood bedroom, gritting his teeth until it passed.

He fell into a lethargic slump. After the summer, his essays became perfunctory. His Comparative Government tutor asked if he was alright. He stayed in bed all morning eating Jaffa Cakes and reading sports biographies. So as not to have to keep renewing it, he stole from the library a life of the Czechoslovakian distance runner Emil Zátopek. At the 1952 Olympics in Helsinki, Zátopek won gold in the 5,000 metres, the 10,000 metres and the marathon – a feat unlikely ever to be equalled.

Zátopek had never run a marathon before and didn't know how to pace himself, so he ran next to the world record holder, Jim Peters. After a pitilessly quick first nine miles in which Peters tried to break him, Zátopek turned to Peters and asked how the race was going. Peters, in astonishment, tried to trick Zátopek by saying the pace was too slow. Zátopek accelerated and was gone. Peters didn't finish.

James loved that Zátopek had been born with less raw speed than his rivals. And he was born poor. So he worked harder than anyone before him had realised was humanly possible. He ran in snowstorms to toughen himself; he ran carrying his wife on his back. When his day job as a conscript in the Czechoslovakian army prevented him running his sets, he climbed the fence into Prague's athletics stadium and ran at night. Performance-enhancing drugs were invented to let other athletes survive training like Zátopek.

There was a quote in the book from Christopher Chataway, an Olympian himself and one of Roger Bannister's pace runners for the four-minute mile, who said, "For me and many others, it was simply more than we could stand." Sometimes this floated up to James's conscious mind when he was buying a sandwich or walking to the library – "simply more than we could stand" – and he smiled with joy. Imagine what Zátopek could have achieved if he'd been born with first-class talent *and* worked that hard.

He climbed out of his despond by imagining that he was competing not against the students around him but against the best student from every cohort back through Oxford's nine centuries. No one could ever know how well he scored against them, but that only made the contest all the purer.

Then it was James's final year. A job fair on a drizzly November afternoon. It was 2004, and the financial crisis hadn't happened yet. Companies had come to offer a ladder up into the decision-making class, the top ten thousand who collectively made history rather than having it inflicted upon them. The talk among the students was about how much more competition there was than in their parents' time. After the crisis, they would consider themselves lucky for having made this leap before it hit.

James went to the job fair expecting each recruiter to pitch the merits of Zátopekian devotion to his particular calling. He wanted to ask the civil servants how many years it took to become head of a proper department like the Treasury or the Foreign Office. And how would they compare the deep background power of the bureaucracy with the trivial attention-seeking but ultimate say-so of the politician? Was it better to be cabinet secretary for fifteen years or prime minister for five?

But the fair wasn't like that. It was in a big bare room, like a school assembly hall, that was used for conferences. They'd set up two rows of desks facing each other to make an avenue of high-paying jobs. Each desk had company-branded pens and USB sticks. They had tall, free-standing posters, like Japanese battle flags, with pictures of smiling models pretending to be account managers and investment analysts. There were some noticeably less glossy stands for the graduate fast track at Tesco's, the police and the NHS.

A hundred years earlier, the jobs might have been to administer part of a West African country or help run one of the great concerns – jute, shipbuilding – that catered to the Empire. But now most were for the professional services that since the 1980s had proliferated from the margins to the centre of the economy. Asset managers, consultants, lawyers, PR, a discreet caste of British men in blue suits, who, rather than attempt the risk, heartbreak and occasional glory of trade or industry, lived safe and comfortable on the steady flow of fees. For them, London was a kind of Switzerland, except with better restaurants.

The students meandered around these displays in sports kit or pyjamas. To James, it looked more like a Home Counties labour exchange than a search for vocation. He examined leaflets hamming up the exclusivity of joining the "Magic Circle" or the "Big Four". The only one that appealed was a KPMG poster that exclaimed "Tax needn't be taxing!" It had a picture of what looked like real accountants white-water rafting in brightly coloured helmets. At least they were honest that accountancy was dorkish. He took a brochure. Perhaps tax *would* be an interesting window into the nature of things.

As he ambled around, he said hi to people he'd seen in college, and they said hi back. But he didn't know anyone at the fair or beyond it who he could be sure he'd see again after graduation. He was explicit to himself about this failing. He diagnosed that it was partly because he hadn't joined the extra-curricular clubs. Of course he'd rowed in the first term, just to know what it was like, but that was it.

Partly also, he assessed, the problem was his personality. His younger sister Cleo, who was in her first year at Cambridge, knew how to talk to people at parties without turning it into a seminar. James didn't. This was a weakness he intended to work on, because it sometimes allowed a pale rind of loneliness to grow around his days. He had some ideas for how to become a charming raconteur, along with getting a six-pack and learning either Russian or Arabic.

Years later, when journalists asked him for the story of his life, his memories of university would feel constrictive, as if he were thinking himself back into a too-small jacket. Not particularly dreamy Oxford days. But since these interviews were just a way of broadcasting his messages, he didn't mention it.

He was looking for the Civil Service desk when someone politely touched his elbow. It was a recruiter, only a few years older than him, maybe twenty-six, quite short, with a slight paunch already. He was dressed as an Oxford type, in a midnight-blue velvet jacket and a bow tie striped in the college colours, with gold cufflinks in the shape of his employer's initials, an A and an O. James didn't imagine this guy had been wearing velvet jackets before he got to Oxford. It was a persona handed down by institutional tradition, like slang in the army. Now he was peacocking with it to draw in fresh graduates. He had a friend with him, another recruiter, more normally dressed in a grey suit. Evidently the straight man in the relationship.

The first recruiter shook James's hand and said, "Hello there. James, isn't it? I'm Will, from Allen & Overy, the top firm in the Magic Circle. And this is Hatch, who's doing really well at a plucky outfit called – what's it called again, Hatch? Freshwater?"

A handshake from Hatch. "Hi, James. Steve Hatchett. I can tell you that at Freshfields we do a lot more business than they do at A&O. If you like the sound of three years writing gas contracts from a satellite office in Uzbekistan, Will's your guy. But I can't imagine you want to go to Uzbekistan, do you?"

Hatch had teed it up for him to say something like "Not if I come back dressed like that" or "I hear Freshfields would be lucky to get some business in Uzbekistan."

But James didn't have the knack of banter. And actually he would quite like to go to Samarkand, to see the tomb of Tamerlane. He said, "Sorry, but why are you talking to me? I mean, out of everyone?"

"Right, right," said Will. "Good question. Well, this isn't my first rodeo, you know, so I just asked Big Eddie: who's the number one student you've got in this cohort, because that's all I'm here for."

James glanced around and spotted his tutor, Professor Lawton – Big Eddie – who was worldlier than most of his colleagues and had come to the recruitment fair to make sure the right people met each other. He was loitering on the edge of the room, leaning against the wall with his gorilla's shoulders straining against his hairy tweed blazer. His fists were in the blazer's pockets, jingling whatever he kept in there.

Big Eddie was one of the ideas men behind the early years of the Blair government. Recalibrating the engines of capitalism to drive social justice, like motors driving a flywheel, was the subject of his books. No more violent, twentieth-century-style ideological conflict, no more class war, capital versus labour, left versus right – but a third way. It was said in college that he'd run out of new thoughts to feed into the insatiable political machine and was hardly ever in Number 10 any more. But he knew what it was to sit on those sofas in Downing Street with Blair, Brown and Alastair Campbell, and decide the fate of the country. James hoovered up whatever he could glean from him.

Will said, "He was our tutor, too, oh, a fair few years ago now. Hatch and I were tute partners back then. Eddie says you're a shoo-in to come first in the year for PPE. Is that right?"

In the way they ogled him, James thought he detected, beneath the pleasant smiles, a tinge of hostility. He'd noticed before that people who considered themselves high achievers could turn lumpen and resentful around him.

He said, "Someone always comes first. If you got the fifty stupidest people in Britain to sit the exams, one would come first. The only thing you're beating is other people."

They laughed as if he'd joined in. Will said, "Too true. Most of the profession are utter buffoons. Like this one right here." The two of them laughed again, very happy to be together on this jaunt to the old alma mater. They felt very grown up. "But that naturally makes it all the easier for a clever chap like you to get ahead. For clever chaps, it's easy-peasy."

James, feeling that familiar disillusionment, said, "I'm not really interested in a walkover."

The recruiters glanced at each other, clearly both deciding at the same time that he was a bit of a dick. But Will didn't let his bonhomie falter. He wholeheartedly agreed: "Of course! You wouldn't want to be bored. And it's not boring, is it, Hatch?"

"Course not." Hatch judiciously wobbled his head from side to side. "To be fair, you obviously have to do some legwork at the beginning, same as everywhere."

James was becoming very aware of the room around him, the milling students, the musty smell of rain-dampened hoodies. Outside, the sun had sunk below the ceiling of cloud, and there was an orangey-red glow on the windows. He felt that if he moved at all, even just his finger, the whole room would stop and turn towards him, and he would be at the centre of a silent ring of masks. He could hear himself getting haughty as he said, "So what you're saying is I should choose the law because the competition are idiots and the work isn't more boring than anything else?"

Will said, "No, no, no," and the jovial expression dropped from his face. "I can see we've come at this from entirely the wrong angle. I apologise. Hatch and I have probably known each other too long to be allowed to talk to other people. So let me give you the brass tacks: we'll pay for your law conversion, and we'll match any salary here."

Hatch broke in: "We'll give you that, plus BUPA and a relocation bonus for moving to London."

Will countered: "We don't do health insurance until you're a bit more senior. But someone like you'll be up there in no time. And you're not going to need it, are you, until you're older. Hatch, be honest, have you ever actually used it once, apart from your annual check-up?"

Hatch couldn't help smiling just a little. He said, "It's the peace of mind. I might develop something."

Will couldn't help himself either: "Like what? Crotch rot? Your chat'll have to get a hell of a lot better for that to happen."

They both disintegrated into laughter again, and James thought: Maybe it's time to get out of this smug little country and go to America. He tightened with the perennial fear that he should have studied computer science.

Will was saying, "Sorry, James, sorry. That was childish. Now, we're having a little invite-only soirée this evening. Why –"

Hatch interrupted again: "We've laid on a much better spread than they have. If you go to —"

James held up a hand to stop him. He had to get away. "Listen. Thanks." He inadvertently turned down his mouth as if giving them bad news. "But, well, no thanks. Good luck with the law." He gave them a nod and walked away.

Will came a few steps after him and threw his final hook: "If you're thinking you should shop around for a better offer, there isn't one. We'll match any salary here. Once you've done the round of the others, come back and talk to me. Will Cambourne, Allen & Overy!"

The idea that there was nothing more than this — that the best England had to offer was Will Cambourne — drove James out onto the drizzly street. The last of the daylight was going out overhead, and he stamped along with his thoughts in a jangle. The wet roads were hissing with passing cars. Small-town rush hour in narrow streets. Everyone hurrying to get out of the rain. A few postgrads huddled together outside the cinema, their umbrellas a multicoloured testudo. Some homeless men were taking shelter under the high portico of the Taylorian library, like primitives living among the ruins of ancient Rome.

As his thoughts began to cohere, he cheered himself up by imagining that he would dedicate every minute of the rest of his life to a single sacred cause: the downfall of Will Cambourne. He'd join Allen & Overy and quickly become Cambourne's boss. He'd pretend to be Cambourne's friend, feeding him enough titbits to keep him walking deeper into James's maze. Then he'd have Cambourne's promotions be passed over, his raises be meagre, his every project inexplicably fail. And finally, when Cambourne was broken, held together only by dependence on his loyal friend James, now head of the company, James would bring him into his enormous office at the top of a skyscraper and say, "Will, I am the architect of your destruction." In that moment it would be revealed that all his seemingly random and disconnected actions had actually served one sole purpose.

Having reached that pinnacle, James's mind started to wander back down towards its everyday paths. The rain had saturated his curling black hair, and dirty rainwater trickled down past his ears. His dad claimed that the hair was the genetic legacy of a Spanish sailor cast ashore from the Armada. It wasn't impossible. In winter his skin went grey rather than white. And his dad's family was from East Anglia, so . . . maybe.

For now, however, he was wet, his woolly jumper was damp and he wanted to sit down. He trudged towards college. The way back felt much longer. He let himself in through the door cut into the big front gate.

As he stepped through, he saw Cambourne on the quad. He was standing under an arch beside the college bar, regaling some undergrads whether they wanted to be regaled or not. Alert despite his apparent easy-breeziness, he spotted James and saluted him with a plastic tumbler. He broke away from the group, walking backwards to finish what he was saying, then swivelled and headed for James.

By a decade later, when many people wanted James's attention, he'd learned how to give a frictionless brush-off. For now, his impulse was to flee. He could reach his door, punch in the key code and be gone. But with his young person's self-importance, he decided that running was beneath him. So he gave a reluctant wave and let their paths cross.

Cambourne hailed him as soon as his voice could reach. "James! Good to see you again, old man. Let me shake your hand."

James let his rain-wet hand be moved up and down. From close by, he could see that Cambourne's eyes were watchful. Cambourne said, "Good to see you again. Very good. Now listen – oh, can I get you a drink? There's a few grand behind the bar. Champagne? Whisky? I'm not sure I'd drink the cocktails, personally, but they make them." James said nothing, and Cambourne's tone shifted. "I know you don't like the chit-chat, so I'll tell you the heart of it." He moved closer and went on confidentially. Another layer of performance. "The reality is, it would be a real feather in my cap, personally, to bring in the man who comes top in PPE. Biggest fish in the bag. And that gives *you* a lot of leverage."

He paused for James to say something self-deprecating. But James just said, "Um, thanks for the interest."

Cambourne grinned. "I get it. I really do. You want to play each firm against the others, bid up your price. Makes perfect sense. But let's skip to the end of that process. We'll max out every salary increment so you'll be in the hundred-grand club by the time you're about twenty-five or -six. Even I'm not getting that yet, and I've already bought a two-bed in Shoreditch."

James felt as if he and Cambourne were speaking different languages. He said, "Do you even like working there?"

"Love it. Never been happier."

James peered into Cambourne's face but found no sign of whether that was true or not.

Cambourne again became confidential. "Can I just say, I'm sure you think I'm a vulgar materialist for talking so much about cash."

He raised his eyebrows at James, who, caught out, shook his head and denied it. "No, no."

Cambourne could see he'd got his man. The most talented recruits often wanted to wax lyrical about the meaning of life before they signed the contract. He'd done it himself. "It's okay. And you know what, if your life's mission is to cure cancer, go for it. That would be much appreciated. But if you're like everyone else, and you want a job that's intellectually stimulating and gives you a nice life – or a *very* nice life – this is it. It's not the temples of bloody Mammon. It's that when you're forty you don't want to live in a grimy flat with five randomers off the internet. Or you want to be able to go with your friends when they rent a villa in Ibiza. Or one day you'd like your kids to have some decent schooling. That's what it's actually all about."

James tried to imagine himself renting a villa in Ibiza with his friends. He said, almost apologetically, "But isn't it just a bit . . ."

Cambourne raised his eyebrows again, making James feel rude.

James rushed on: "Okay, if you work forty hours a week –"

"Ha. I'd love to only work forty hours a week."

"Okay." James blushed. "Okay. But as a baseline, that's about a hundred thousand hours' work before you retire. Imagine what you could accomplish if you put it all into one thing. And what are you putting it into? A flat in Shoreditch?" James was embarrassed for him.

Cambourne nodded deeply, as if this were making him think. He said, "Really interesting stuff, James. You've obviously taken the philosophy part of the course to heart. We should talk more out of the rain. The upstairs room's booked at the Blue Boar, the one with the private entrance." Cambourne thought he had his fish on the line, and relaxed into his spiel. "We've spent like drunken sailors on the spread, but I don't think there's anyone actually there. We could go over, have a few snifters and put the world to rights."

With the lucid certainty of all his ideas, James suddenly knew what he was going to do. Not giving Cambourne any further attention, he turned back the way he'd come and strode out of college. Before the door fell shut behind him, he could hear "Bit abrupt, old bean. But great! I'll see you in the —"

The door clunked into the gate and cut him off.

James felt calm and clear-headed again. He walked quickly to the homeless men under the high arch of the Taylorian. Arranged on the steps around them was their constant luggage of plastic orange Sainsbury's bags, rucksacks and sleeping bags. Most of them he'd seen around, selling the *Big Issue*. A lanky, skinny ginger man with a wispy mouth-beard was said to be a former professor of philology.

James was a little intimidated. The homeless men seemed more hostile and unpredictable now they weren't begging for change. But he thought of the young Julius Caesar telling the pirates who'd kidnapped him: let me go or I'll come back one day and have you crucified — which he did. James said: "Excuse me."

An older man, expecting bullshit, wearily said, "What?"

"I thought you might want unlimited food, drink and a warm place to sit down. Upstairs at the Blue Boar, the side entrance. A law firm has paid for a feast, but there's no one there, so it'll all get thrown away if you don't take it. They might come back at some point and kick you out, but if you want it, it's there."

Most of them looked at him. The philology professor seemed to be in a dream. Another one, quite unfriendly, said, "What's it to you?"

"Basically, I think they're a bunch of wankers, and they'll be pissed off if you take all the stuff that's meant for posh boys in velvet jackets and signet rings."

"But you're a fucking posh boy."

"Maybe so. But it doesn't change anything I've just said."

His parents were academics, not poshos. And it was normal in revolutions for the rabble to be roused by a breakaway member of the bourgeoisie. Lenin's dad was a civil servant. "It's up to you. Good night."

He started walking back towards college, and the same one shouted after him, "Oi! Posh boy! Come back."

Still walking, he called out, "No. But if someone stops you, my name's Will Cambourne. That's Will. Cambourne." With that, he left them, sauntering now, laughing occasionally and smiling up into the drizzle. He imagined the tramps stuffing themselves with Bollinger and prosciutto. Good luck to them. His heart was light. It was as if he'd restored balance to one small corner of the universe. As if he'd taken the random trajectories of human lives and arranged them into a satisfying tableau: "The needy at the tables of the rich." From disorder, a shape. From chaos, meaning.

Roland never knew about the careers fair. To him, it was only another unread poster among the continual flowering of coloured paper on the cork noticeboards. What he was looking for he wasn't going to find in some dry workshop about "Using the internet for research". He didn't know the people who went to those things.

And anyway, he was more than fully occupied – with his weekly essay crisis and with his friend Emily's plan to hire a narrowboat and throw an all-day tropical party while puttering up the river. Roland was trying to buy enough sand to turn the foredeck or whatever it was called into a beach. On the afternoon when James was at the fair, Roland was at a builder's merchant on the edge of town where one of the staff had got caught up in this silliness and was whizzing him around the yard in a mini-forklift.

But afterwards he read about the fallout from what James had done, in *The Times* and the student newspaper, *Cherwell*. A crew of hobos had got into some empty corporate feast and had what sounded like the party of the decade. *The Times* had some weighty comments to make about the responsibilities a privileged university owed to the town it lived in. But Roland paid especial attention to *Cherwell* because he felt a kind of paternal benevolence towards it.

For a few months, he'd been passionately involved. He wore a newsman's costume of long shabby coat over a sweat-stained white shirt, with a tie pulled to one side. To his slightly bemused friends and at parties he talked with winning enthusiasm about the importance of the news, and he had a brief, news-themed romance with the deputy editor.

The highlight was having sex under her desk. There were A3 proofs strewn around, and they started trying to throw each other off their rhythm by reading out random sentences in seductive whispers. He put his mouth to her ear and moaned, "Bust up at bus stop."

But after a while, the whole news thing started to feel a bit thin. He couldn't get excited any more about other people reading words he himself barely remembered. So he joined a drama group instead. He still sometimes went to the after-edition drinks. He affectionately felt that the paper stayed attached to him in some way, like an ex-girlfriend.

There was a rumour that it was James who'd turned a gang of tramps loose in a corporate drinks party. Roland thought it was the funniest, most incongruous thing he'd ever heard. He knew James from first term, when they'd both tried rowing. They went out on the river before breakfast while the boaties tried to evangelise them that early starts and gym sessions were a fun way to spend university.

It was surprisingly moving to be on the water at dawn, with the river flowing soft and cold beneath him. White mist rising off its dark surface. The long light boat slipping past reeds and meadows. He liked the quiet and the regular creak-dip-pull, creak-dip-pull, and the eightfold pattern of the blades dipping in time. His heart got so full up with this feeling that he had to tell the others about it. And then the officious little cox would start shouting, "Roland, you're out of sync!" or "Sharpen it up, Roland" or some other boatie bullshit that he wasn't into.

James didn't seem the kind of guy for shenanigans. Not a particularly gifted athlete but good at rowing because he had the classic attributes of a high-achiever: follows instructions, goal-oriented, willing to be bored. Roland had none of those qualities, and didn't want them. The more the cox told him off, the more he turned against rowing. It was actually kind of totalitarian, a Nazi sport, all about subsuming the individual into an eight-legged collective organism, like a pond skater. And he wasn't going to be anything's leg.

He quit in a late-night email telling them to keep their goose-stepping jackboots off his face. In the morning, the angry boaties, a man down, banged on his locked door. Roland pretended to be asleep until they went away. They got over it and even presented him with a flimsy little trophy at their end-of-term party: "Least likely to make the Olympics". They meant it as a peace offering, and that was how he took it. They weren't a bad bunch – just dorks with muscles. One of them, bending over outside and bracing a hand against the wall while she spewed, was wearing a T-shirt that said "Today I will do what you won't, so tomorrow I can do what you can't." Not exactly party vibes. But any kind of strong attitude impressed him, and for a moment he was lost in admiration.

James was at that party. Roland remembered him boring someone about the module choices for next year. When the drinking games started, with everyone capering and stripping as the boys and girls swapped clothes, James pointlessly won a few rounds out of ingrained competitiveness. He didn't seem to understand you were trying to lose. Then he was too drunk and outside throwing up with the others, not having visibly enjoyed himself at all.

And now this. Roland loved it. With a great sense of his own wisdom, he thought that *American Psycho* was dead right: it was always the tightly wound keen-beans who eventually ran amok. They came a bit loose, and, next thing you knew, they were chopping up prozzers with an axe. He should watch it again this afternoon. Christian Bale was *such* a good actor.

Roland had a sort-of friend called Stefan whose poster-plastered bedroom was near hall and whom Roland often visited while he was waiting for lunch to start. An earnest, obsessive Austrian, he kept his curtains drawn and was always going on about the layers of meaning in *Seven Samurai*. He wore Japanese manga T-shirts, and his ambition, which he and Roland regularly plotted out, was to astonish Oxford with a stage version of something called *The 47 Ronin*, for which he was only forty-six ronin short.

Roland's other friends said Stefan had what they called yellow fever. Apparently, he kept hitting on the insular Asian maths girls. He'd invited Susie Teoh, who was Malaysian, to the Chinese restaurant near the roundabout, and she'd reported him to the dean. It was also widely agreed that he was a foot fetishist.

Stefan had discovered that the Japanese mafia had a website. There was even an email address: info@yamaguchi-gumi.com. Together, Roland and Stefan composed an email. Calling themselves "students" was too small-fry, "professors" a bit of a stretch, so they said they were "scholars at the University of Oxford". Because the Yakuza saw themselves as heirs to the samurai, Stefan and Roland said they were researching the survival of traditional values in contemporary Japan. And since they needed some reason for writing, they asked whether they could come and visit.

A few days later, Roland was summoned to Stefan's bedroom by SMS message. Stefan refused to say what it was about until, after stoking as much anticipation as he could, he announced what Roland had already guessed. "The Yamaguchi-gumi have written back. And they say yes! Shit, Roland! Can you believe it? They say they want to contribute to the West understanding Japan better. Isn't this completely crazy?"

Somehow Roland wasn't surprised at all. He just felt a door slipping off its latch, waiting to be pushed open. From the bed where Stefan had instructed him to sit, he sprang to his feet and yelled, "Let's get moving! I'll pack a bag!"

Stefan stared at him in critical bewilderment. "What are you talking about? We can't go anywhere. We're in term time. Unless you want to go to Tokyo for the weekend."

Roland sat back down. "No, no, of course not. That was stupid."

Stefan took on a slightly exasperated tone. "No, Roland, you're not stupid; you're just not practical."

Roland was startled. A second ago, we were adventuring to Japan, now I'm not practical. In a few days, he'd think: Fuck Stefan.

In the meantime, he wondered whether it was true. To be fair, he hadn't thought about it being term and so on. He said, "You're completely right" and held up both palms in surrender. "Tokyo. Too far for term time. Got it." He made the okay sign.

"I can't believe they wrote back. What an incredible story. Maybe we'll be able to keep the correspondence going. Like a Yakuza penfriend. Wouldn't that just be, like, totally unbelievable?"

"But we could go in the Christmas vac, couldn't we? That's only a couple of weeks away, isn't it?"

Stefan looked uncomfortable. "I suppose, yes, theoretically. It's three weeks away."

Roland sprang up again. "Fantastic! We'll go in the vac! That'll give us time to learn some phrases and get some Japanese clothes."

"But don't you have the same dissertation deadline as me?"

"I don't know."

"The first day of next term."

"Come *on*." There was more to life than dissertations.

"Roland, my family goes to my uncle's in the mountains over Christmas. We go every year, you understand. Or –" Something occurred to him, and with sudden urgency he said, "Roland, have you already finished your research?"

Roland had not finished his research. It wouldn't have been precisely accurate to say he'd started. But now there was the prospect of Japan. He sat down to think, then got up again. He stood for a few seconds in silence, articulating. Then he threw his arms out wide and said, "We've *got* to go. We've *got* to. This is . . . this is . . . an *opportunity*, a big opportunity. Do you think we'll ever get invited again, ever? We won't. We should go now. Today. But we can go at the end of term if you want. Okay, that's fine. But let's just go."

Stefan said, "Well, no, listen, Roland. It's difficult because –"

Roland interrupted. "If you don't want to come, that's your choice and I'll respect it. But I don't understand. I thought you were totally mad for this Japanese stuff. Kurosawa, these posters, the Asian girls. This whole thing was literally your idea."

Stefan had been becoming increasingly shamefaced, and now he flicked over into irritation. "I know what you're implying, and I do not have yellow fever, which is very, very racist by the way. And I can't explode my dissertation just to chat with some probably uneducated petty crook about his views on the world. What's he going to tell us anyway? How to steal someone's wallet?"

Roland laughed because what Stefan was saying was so terrible. "Fine. But I have to tell you, this is *the worst* decision. *The worst*. And obviously, if you change your mind, I still really want you to come."

The Yamaguchi-gumi crime syndicate arranged for him to meet a representative they called Tanaka-san in a certain bar in Tokyo just after Christmas. Roland wanted to fly immediately after the end of term, but his mum persuaded and ultimately bribed him to wait until Boxing Day.

This was their first Christmas in England since Roland was a toddler. His dad was an engineer in the oil industry. The sun had stained his hands and forearms as if with tea. He still wore his high-performance wraparound shades on rainy days in Guildford. From more than two decades of postings to expat compounds in Egypt, Oman and Qatar, he'd reached a fearsome amateur standard of golf and tennis. After 9/11, he started wondering whether it was time to leave the Middle East. And then his Arab colleagues kept questioning him about why the Brits and Americans were destroying Iraq. He was no longer simply an expat, like the Dutch or the Italians; he was a Brit. So they'd moved "home".

With the enthusiasm that Roland had inherited, he was adapting a house in a commuter village near Guildford to be self-sufficient in energy. It wasn't finished yet, so they had Christmas in a rental. A new-build box for living, not so different from the expat compounds. In exchange for sticking around till Boxing Day, Roland's mum transferred him enough money for two weeks in Japan, on the condition that he finish his dissertation before he left.

At the gate in Heathrow, he was thrilled that most others in the boarding queue were Japanese: real Japanese people, lots of them, with Japanese faces and straight black hair and shiny clothes and colourful trainers, as if the double doors at Gate B9 were the actual entrance to Japan.

On the plane, he brought out *The Chrysanthemum and the Sword*, a book Stefan had recommended, and found his place. He'd already read a couple of others upstairs in his bedroom while he was supposed to be writing his thesis: *Shōgun*, about a real English sea captain who washed ashore on Japan and became a samurai; and *In Praise of Shadows*, about why Western crockery was white and hospital-bright while the Japanese preferred the layered depths of dark lacquer. He'd caught the romance of an alien culture and started to feel that he wasn't just going on a holiday but on a journey to somewhere utterly different, dislocating himself in space to open up the gap for some profound insight.

When the plane's lights were turned off, Roland clicked on his overhead spot to keep reading. Around him the dim cabin slept and sighed while the white pages shone in his lap. The book was about trying to isolate a kind of operating system of Japaneseness that could explain Japan's infinite phenomena – the crazy game shows, the Mitsubishi factories and the raked-gravel Zen gardens – from a finite set of rules.

Roland felt like a lone acolyte peering into sacred mysteries. With the wastes of Siberia far below, and a breathing, sleeping Japanese woman in the seat beside him, he experienced a great calm happiness. With every rotation of the four jet engines outside in the cold night, he was being carried closer to the truth. As he read further and grew sleepier, the images started to swim: horned battle helmets, cracked pottery repaired with gold, medieval dildos made of green jade – and he was asleep in his seat.

The feeling that he was trembling on the brink of some great insight intensified when he was actually walking around Japan. Or rather it felt as if everything around him – the dinky taxis whose drivers wore white cotton gloves, the shocking glass modernity of the cityscape, and the quiet, almost rural-looking backstreets behind his hostel – as if all this were trembling with meaning and might at any time dissolve into some great revelation.

He had a few days before he was due to meet Tanaka-san. On the first, jet-lagged, he clicked awake at quarter to five and couldn't get back to sleep. He pulled on yesterday's clothes and crept out of the dorm. The common room was silent and chilly in the half-dark. It had a framed photo of Mount Fuji and a jaunty sign reminding residents to wear flip-flops in the showers. There was a cartoon flip-flop with googly eyes and a mouth, saying "Healthy feet are happy feet". Beside it was a smaller Mrs Flip-Flop, saying: "You can buy me at reception." So Japanese.

Roland didn't have flip-flops and last night had unknowingly gone into the shower barefoot. He'd definitely been seen. Pretty much the opposite of the exquisite Japanese politeness he'd been reading about. He would apologise as soon as there was someone at reception to apologise to.

With this, another thin stream of worry started flowing: he really hadn't done a very good job on that dissertation. And he was actually slightly relying on it to pull up his other marks. His plan, before all this, had been to go totally monastic over Christmas: knuckle down, get serious and write an amazing dissertation to bring his average back up. But it would be such a waste to come to Japan and spend the entire time fretting. The right thing was to block out those thoughts for now, recharge and really smash it when he got back.

He helped himself to some paper from the printer at reception, sat down next to the hostel's home-made binders of tourist info, and started drawing up a schedule of cultural visits. National Museum – yes. Imperial

Palace — yes. He'd got lucky: New Year's was one of only two annual days that the palace was open. Fish market — yes. Design museum — definitely. He had to get his head around *kintsugi*.

He'd been through almost everything when the hostel began to wake up. Groggy backpackers shuffled down the stairs yawning and rubbing their eyes, and headed into the courtyard for a tai chi lesson. A very skinny Japanese teenager in asymmetric clothes and a single dangling earring came in from outside. He put his bag down behind the reception desk and switched on the overheads. To Roland he said, "Jet lag?"

Roland stood up and resisted the urge to bow. "Yes. I've been up for a couple of hours. I just got in last night. From England."

The Japanese kid didn't take up the invitation to get acquainted. He just said, "You want breakfast?" Like in the stereotypes, the R in breakfast was somewhere between an R and an L. "We got American cereal, breakfast bagel, Danish pastry."

"Do you have any Japanese breakfast?"

The kid laughed. "You are in Japan. There is Japanese breakfast everywhere. In the hostel, we got foreign breakfast. Apple Jack, Cheerios, Reese's Puff."

Roland wavered. Going out onto the frosty street to search for an authentic breakfast seemed a lot for his first day. The kid saw him wavering and said, "You are jet-lag. You need to eat. Bring your stomach to Japanese time. Then have Japanese breakfast tomorrow."

Roland gratefully agreed. He paid a mysterious quantity of yen for a portion of Cheerios in a miniature Tupperware box, a portion of milk in an even more miniature Tupperware cylinder and a round yellow token, like the discs in Connect Four, to put in the coffee machine.

First on his schedule was beating the crowds at the National Museum by arriving when it opened. But as the Cheerios slid down into his stomach, drawing in the blood supply, his limbs grew so heavy. By the time he finished, he was so drowsy that it was all he could do to rinse his bowl and stumble back upstairs to his dorm.

As he wrapped the single duvet tightly around himself, he realised with a jolt that he'd forgotten about the flip-flops. But he pulled on his eye mask and slept till mid-afternoon. Neither that day nor on any other did he make it to the National Museum, nor to anywhere else on his list.

That first afternoon, he told the Japanese kid, "Look, I know it's not a big deal, but I went into the showers yesterday, and I'd just arrived – but I know that's not an excuse. Now that I've noticed, I can obviously see there are signs literally everywhere. And it *totally* makes sense. Like, verrucas and stuff."

A girl who was sorting through flyers at the other end of the desk, setting aside those that gave a free drink on entry, noticed him.

The kid was both bored and confused. He said, "You want to make complaint about the showers? You have problem with your feet?"

The girl's eyes shut for a moment with suppressed laughter.

Roland said, "No, no, no. I'm just saying, yesterday, I went into the shower with bare feet."

The kid frowned and said, "No, you must to wear flip-flops. You must to read the sign."

The girl let out a high-pitched sound like *hmmm*. Roland noticed her lovely warm tanned skin and her blonde hair pulled back into a ponytail. He caught her eye. She lifted her eyebrows, and he smiled.

He told the Japanese kid, "Look, sorry. I'm making way too big a deal of this. But I don't want to be rude. So, sorry. This is really stupid. I've made a mountain out of a molehill."

The girl said, "Can't be too careful. Healthy feet are happy feet."

They both laughed, and then they were talking. Roland said, "This is ridiculous. I don't know how I've got so tangled up in it."

"Do you need some help? It really seems like buying footwear is too much for you."

The Japanese kid's eyes slid down and to the right, to where his phone was sitting on the desk behind the counter. With one hand he flicked up the flip screen and started reading his messages.

Roland and the girl kept talking. She was from New Zealand, from Dunedin, called Harriet. She was travelling around East Asia with her friend Jenny, whom she called Jinny.

Roland explained what he was doing there. It took her a few seconds to take this in. She said, "So, wait, this Tanaka guy's like an actual gang boss?"

"Umm, I don't know if he's a boss or how the, like, promotion system works. But, um, yeah, as far as I know."

"And you found his email address on the internet?"

"That's right. Well, my friend did. He's obsessed with Japan. Or, to be honest, he's got a thing for Asian girls. And samurai stuff."

Harriet, incredulous, started grinning awkwardly. "Hold on. Are you sure it's not a wind-up?"

A trapdoor opened under Roland. "What?"

"I, like, hate to say it, but it just seems, you know, *weird*, don't you think, that this crime lord has his email address on the internet and then you just email him, and he says: sure let's go for a drink?"

Roland said, "Oh my God." He put his hands on his face. "Oh my God. I literally never thought of that. And I've come all the way to Japan."

Harriet, cringing from this awkwardness, blew out her cheeks. "Umm. You know. I'm sure it's on the level. I literally don't know anything about it. I'm sure he's a real crime lord."

Roland said, "Can you imagine! Can you imagine if it's just some ten-year-old who's made himself a Yakuza website."

The Japanese kid's eyes flicked up at the word *Yakuza*, but he went back to his messages.

Harriet said, "Are you, like, okay about this? I'm so, so sorry if I've ruined your trip."

"No, no, not at all. If he's a real crime lord, great. If he's a ten-year-old, then, okay, you fucker, you got me. And I'm just having a random holiday in Japan. Which is kind of awesome."

Harriet mimed her head exploding, and said, "Oh jeez, this is too good. You've got to tell Jinny. We're going to get some noodles and then check out these bars. Want to come with?"

In the fast-food noodle bar, Roland told his tale again, and Jenny laughed so hard she had to bury her face in Hattie's shoulder until her shaking subsided. When she was done, she dried her eyes on her sleeve and said, "That's the best thing I've heard on this entire trip."

Afterwards, they took their flyers to noisy bars full of foreigners, and went from one to another until the places began emptying out and there was grey light in the sky. From there, they slid into a routine of staying out till morning and sleeping through the days. Each afternoon when Roland woke up, he was full of horrible sour guilt about the National Museum. He swore himself complicated promises that he would wake up earlier tomorrow. If he didn't, his punishment would be an extra day in the library when he got back. Two extra days; three . . .

But at night he was lifted by a kind of elation. Even just when driving around Tokyo in the dark back seat of a taxi, his thigh and arm against Harriet or Jenny, looking out, the fluorescent street scene reflecting on the window and playing across his face. Neon, costumes, space glitter.

One evening, they drove over the Rainbow Bridge bending through the night sky. From its arc he could see hundreds, maybe thousands, of illuminated skyscrapers standing up out of the plain that Tokyo was on and marching on over the hills around it. Compared with this, every capital city in Europe was just a murky little medieval toytown.

A thought that had been growing since he arrived in Japan enphrased itself: Oh, we in Europe aren't actually the height of civilisation. No one ever told me.

There was a calm delight, as if someone had raised the lid of the box Roland was living in. The roof was no longer cardboard but infinite and starlit. The world was so much larger and stranger than he could have guessed. He saw himself seeing these things and thought: This is really living. I'm going to remember this forever.

He wasn't wrong. More than thirty years later, when his daughter visited Japan, most of his mental image had faded to black, but he could still see a few wisps of fluorescent pink light, and he still possessed the remembered feeling of a night long ago.

Eventually, inevitably, Roland and Hattie slept together, giggling and shushing each other under his too-small duvet in the dorm. They undressed clumsily in their body heat, with legs or arms sticking out into the colder air. He was skinny, but she was so lean he could see the shapes of the muscles running up her side, and she was so hungry to be touched that when he did it was like she was being electrocuted through his fingers.

It turned out that Tanaka-san was a real crime lord after all, or at least a criminal of some degree. But he seemed surprised that Roland was the person who had come. They met in a street like a narrow canyon with a jumble of flashing signs suspended above it. Amid dangling bags of candyfloss and racks of "I ♥ Tokyo" T-shirts, there was a door and a grey-haired bouncer with a paunch slumping against his black T-shirt.

Inside was a quiet whisky bar. Deep shadows, dark wood, just like *In Praise of Shadows*. The bar was empty, and Roland imagined it had been emptied for them. The man who must be Tanaka-san was on a stool at the bar. The barman was waiting as far away as possible at the other end. Otherwise, there was no one except two more bouncers hunching and smoking in a booth in the back corner.

Tanaka-san was in his fifties, and his face was saggy and pouchy under the eyes, the skin a tired grey-brown. It was incongruous above his neat suit, which gave him the slim figure of a much younger man. Roland wondered whether he had the swirling, elaborate full-body Yakuza tattoos, but only his face and hands were visible. A white cuff gleamed as he put his tumbler down on the bar.

Tanaka-san said, "You are the professor from Oxford?"

Roland smiled broadly, failing to hide his discomfort. He said, "Um, not a full professor yet, unfortunately. The whole tenure thing, you know. Just an, um, scholar for now." His ingratiating smile wasn't returned. "I'm very interested in Japan, in Japan's traditional culture, which I know that the, um, the, um . . ." – he realised he didn't dare say the word *Yakuza* – "I'm so grateful to you, really I am, for talking to me about it."

Tanaka-san stared at him. Roland kept his smile on, but it felt ever more rigid. He couldn't believe he'd come wearing trainers and a hoodie. Maybe he should say one of his Japanese greetings. As he tried to arrange a phrase in his head, Tanaka-san motioned Roland to take the stool beside his. On the reflective black bar was a square white ashtray with two butts squashed into it. Next to it was a pack of Mild Sevens with a clunky steel lighter on top.

Tanaka-san said: "You like whisky?"

"Oh, yes, thank you very much. That is, I don't know anything about it, but yes. My mum's actually from Scotland. Near Inverness."

Tanaka-san looked over his shoulder and nodded at the barman, who brought a bottle and a second tumbler. While he poured, no one spoke. Roland wanted to say *domo arigato* but his courage failed him, and he whispered, "Thank you."

Tanaka-san lifted his tumbler and said, "*Kanpai!*"

Roland had done a lot of this with Harriet and Jenny. He said, "*Kanpai!*" and lifted his so the glasses only just touched. He took a suitably appreciative sip of the precious stuff.

Tanaka-san knocked his back, made a *hrmmm* noise and lit a cigarette. "So," he said. "What are your questions?"

Roland hadn't prepared any. He'd imagined a chat and a few drinks: him and Tanaka shooting the shit about life as a samurai outlaw. He hadn't read anything about the Yakuza because he'd assumed Tanaka-san would tell him. He began talking while trying to think of something to ask. "Yes, okay. I'm very interested in the, you know, principles, the anthropological principles that – I don't know if you've read this book, *The Chrysanthemum and the Sword*? It's amazing. I just read it actually. The army, in the war, the American army, asked this woman to write a book about the Japanese, to help them understand the enemy."

He ran out of words, and in the quiet that followed, Tanaka-san said, "I have not read this book."

"Oh, okay. Well, no. Why would you? You're Japanese!" Roland grinned feebly. "It's got this great story about doing callisthenics, um, in the war, to keep the spirit high. Like star jumps and stuff." Roland mimed a star jump, stretching out his legs and arms, and balancing on his bum.

Tanaka-san again looked surprised.

Roland said, "I'm not explaining this very well. A lot of it is about shame, about, am I pronouncing this right, *haji*?"

Tanaka-san's eyebrows lifted. "You want to know about shame?"

"No, no, no. I mean, well, yes. But shame and honour, the honour code, you know."

Tanaka-san nodded that he'd understood and made a pronouncement: "Honour is very important. The most important. We learned this from samurai."

And that was it. He didn't say any more, just looked at Roland as if that was the last word on the subject. Then said, "Do you have more questions?"

Roland managed to string it out a little longer. He would blabber until he hit on a topic, then ask, "And what do, um, you think of that issue?"

Tanaka-san would nod and reply, "Yes. The Sengoku Jidai was a time of many wars in Japan." Or "Japan and the West have much to learn from each other."

Finally, Roland gave up, and appealed to Tanaka-san's compassion. He said, "I'm sorry, I really haven't done this well. I should have prepared more specific questions. I feel so stupid. I've, well, I've *wasted* your time. And if I'd prepared better, we could have really got into the heart of it."

No part of Tanaka-san softened. He said, "It has been a very interesting conversation. Thank you for coming to visit Japan. I hope the West will reach a better understanding of our country."

He paused for Roland to respond, and Roland said, "Yes. Yes, thank you so much for meeting me. I'm just sorry, yeah I'm really sorry. And yes, I hope that people in the West start to really get what Japan is all about."

Tanaka-san nodded and began moving him along. He stood up off the bar stool, said "Please" and motioned Roland towards the back exit. Terrible crushing embarrassment and shame. *Haji.*

Roland didn't know whether it was ruder to gulp the last of his whisky or leave it behind. So he gulped while Tanaka-san watched. Then Roland gabbled his thanks again and inadvertently dipped his head in a hasty sort of bow that went unacknowledged.

They went out the back, onto an alley cluttered with bins, cardboard boxes and tall metal cages on wheels. A few waiters and line cooks in dirty kitchen uniforms were smoking cigarettes and chatting on their breaks. As Tanaka-san and Roland walked towards the main street, every one of them put his hands to his sides and bowed. Following a half pace behind, Roland thought: Oh God. Oh God. I am such an idiot.

It was more or less his last experience of Japan.

He'd run out of money. Hattie and Jenny had said goodbye with a kiss and a smile and taken the train to Kyoto. He changed his flight and went back to England early. On the plane, he winced and twisted in his seat, clutching his face. The blabbering. The seated star jump. Unbearable.

He had to undo, to make up for, to make good. As soon as he got home, he'd email his tutor and switch to Japanese.

JULY 2005

On a warm Oxford morning, just before lunch, the sunshine was bringing out the honey in the stone, and the colleges were resting in their summer hush. The undergraduates had taken their racket home with them, and the streets were peopled only by drifting sightseers.

Big Eddie – James's tutor – carefully manoeuvred his bulk onto an ancient Dutch bicycle. He was starting to sweat under his tweed blazer and he regretted not leaving it in his study. He cycled very slowly down to the Exam Schools where the undergrads' results were posted. At the noticeboards, he said hello to other tutors there on the pavement. The traffic grumbled and belched behind them – an undignified setting, he thought, for something so momentous in these students' lives. Though maybe it was fitting that after they'd had their three allotted years inside the cloistered sanctums, the final act should be out here, on a busy, ugly road with air that tasted of exhaust fumes, below the intimidating cliff front of a formal building now closed to them forever.

He took out his notebook and began writing down his tutees' marks. Every year, he emailed his students their results so they wouldn't have to wait for the indefensibly tardy letter from the university. Other professors were stooping and bending to find the names they were looking for. But his first name was at eye-height. First place: James Drayton. No surprises there. And by a landslide. Eddie was proud of himself but checked that impulse. James would have come top under any tutor. Nevertheless, in some profound way he was satisfied: that excellence existed, that amid the scrabbling and blundering of most students, some few could make it so simple.

In summer term, he sometimes moved the tutorials for his favourites onto a picnic blanket in the parks. There was usually cricket going on and, even though Eddie didn't follow sport, he noticed the rare difference in sound when someone struck the ball sweetly: a clean thock, the ball rising, the tutees involuntarily glancing across, spectators smiling and shielding their eyes to follow its path upwards.

A few shots in a long match. A few students in a long career. Maybe this evening he wouldn't gossip in the SCR; he would go back to his rooms, open a bottle of the good burgundy and savour this mixture of satisfaction and melancholy. He'd let himself remember the days, in the 1970s, when he, Eddie, was new and bright, flying upwards like a cricket ball with the world laid out before him.

He went back to his notebook until someone said, "Hi, Eddie."

It was Margot, a philosophy don in his college, thin, sharp, teasing, fun. They sometimes overlapped on students, her teaching them philosophy and him politics. She was a bit younger, in her forties, and he used to think she was a bit loopy in the Oxford way. But he'd realised the loopiness was only at the front of her mind, like a little illuminated stage with props and speeches. Hidden in the dark around that was the rest of her intellect, like a vast auditorium with thousands of eyes watching and thinking. She was dressed in some type of patterned ankle-length skirt. Afghan? Kazakh? She had a thing about Central Asia. In winter she wore a brown Afghan hat like an upside-down Yorkshire pudding. With his heightened sense of the passing years, he was conscious that life was coursing through her female body.

She said, "Aren't you hot in that blazer? Haven't you noticed it's summer? You're not getting absent-minded, are you?"

He laughed and said, "I am actually. Too hot, that is. I should have left it at college." He lifted the heated tweed away from his shirt.

"Well, don't take it off now. You must be sweating like a pig. You've got to get some new clothes, Eddie."

He enjoyed being prodded. Most people only wanted to talk to him about Blair and Iraq. He said, "We can't all dress like Azeri tribesmen."

"Whyever not? I think you'd make a very nice Azeri tribesman. I can just see you squatting on some hillock on the grassy steppe, ruminatively smoking your pipe and watching the goats."

"Sounds lovely. How have your goats done this year?"

"Not too bad, in the main. Only one disappointment. Roland Mackenzie. Ever come across him?"

Eddie shook his head. "No. Not a PPE-er, is he?"

"No. Physics and philosophy. Clever boy, actually. And very likeable. Gave me an incredibly lavish gift at the end of his first year, then I think forgot for the next two." She was amused. "The bloody little fool's gone and got a 2:2. Only student in the year not to make the cut."

Eddie grimaced in commiseration. "Ah. At least it won't have too big an effect on your average, will it?"

"Oh, the average, the average! If the Warden wants to fuss me about the league table, so be it." She snapped her fingers as if exorcising a minor devil. "But he wasn't even that lazy. Not appallingly lazy. No lazier than half of them. The midpoint of the laziness bell curve. And more sincerely interested than most. Just very distractable. He came to me on the first day of Hilary and asked if he could switch to Japanese."

Eddie let out a big belly laugh. "Wonderful."

"Yes. Can you imagine what that bitch Aiko would have said if I'd suggested it."

Eddie nodded and murmured, "Hmm." Since he got to play politics in the big world, he didn't in college. Margot noticed his non-reaction and, feeling slightly exposed, quickly said, "What about you? How've you done this year?" She looked past him. "James Drayton. First place! Chapeau, Edward. The Warden will invite you to high table before the week's out."

"Ha, yes. I do like those little breadsticks."

"Breadsticks? They'll be giving you champagne! Top of the year. PPE. The Warden will want to show you to the donors. Let them see we're a first-class college deserving of more cheques."

"They're boring, aren't they, the donors?" Eddie remembered an irritation. "Last time I was there, I had one who kept telling me I should retire from teaching political philosophy because Labour and the Tories are exactly the same these days. It's just management and efficiency, blah blah blah. I was sitting there thinking, I don't tell you to retire from being a petrochemicals magnate just because you're a fucking moron."

"That was very polite of you, Eddie. The Warden will be most grateful for his new Chair in Petrochemicals. But seriously, old thing, well done you. Top of the year."

"Donors." Eddie shrugged it off.

"You may like to recall that I taught young Drayton a paper in first year."

"I'll make sure you get the credit."

"I remember him. Very bright. Read everything. Love a student like that. Makes the others seem worth it. What's he doing now? Is he staying on?"

"No, um, he's gone to McKinsey." Eddie raised his eyebrows. "Management consultant."

"Oh no! How could you let him?"

"It's not for me to tell him what to do. And, to be fair, I think his plan is to treat it as training, learn about business, and then move on to something else, maybe politics."

"They never do though, do they? Once they've got those corporate mega-salaries."

He sighed. "No, not usually. Oh, well. A rare mind harnessed to making the rich marginally richer. All in a life's work, eh?"

"Oh, Eddie, don't be sad. I can't bear it. Listen, my friend's early-modern music group's having a recital tonight. Why don't you come? They have a viola da gamba."

"Thank you. That's very kind. But I'd rather be a management consultant." He looked at her dead on, appraising how she would react, and said, "How about this? I happen to get some pretty mega fees myself for my political consulting. Why don't I use them for something worthwhile and take us to Quod for dinner? We can get dressed up in something lighter than tweed, have champagne, oysters, steaks, burgundy, whatever they've got, and enjoy what we can while we can."

"Oh, Eddie, you *are* sad. I'd love to, but, as I said, I do have this recital tonight I promised I'd go to, and it's not as if they attract huge audiences to these things."

Eddie again inclined his heavy head. "Of course. Every seat counts, as we say in my field."

Something passed through Margot like a deep breath. A mutiny against routine, a desire to not always know how every evening was going to end. She shook her head and said: "Ohhhh, you know what? They'll be having recitals till I die. They'll forgive me for skipping one, eventually. I'd love to come for dinner, if the offer's still on. It's a marvellous idea."

James didn't see Eddie's message until that evening, when he had a chance to check his personal Hotmail. He was sitting at the desk in his hotel room, wearing that day's shirt and boxers. Salt had soaked into the collar and was chafing his neck. The skin of his thighs stuck to the plasticky seat. His suit jacket and trousers he'd hung up to keep sharp, as recommended in a memo for new McKinseyites.

The room was on the top floor of the Hilton DoubleTree in Milton Keynes, a city he liked far more than his parents' jokes had led him to expect. A planned city! He'd like to plan a city. The warm evening light was making his room glow, and he wanted to go and see the roundabouts. But he had a ream of Tesco sales data to tidy up before morning. At some point soon he and the others would order room service.

Automatically, he checked his email. There was the weekly circular of updates on McKinsey alumni. Someone had become chief adviser to the governor of Basra; someone else was now CEO of Foot Locker. Then Eddie's message. Finals results. First place. Big margin. Warden delighted. Initially he reacted no more than he would have to a booking confirmation email. The expected had occurred. But it felt inhuman not to celebrate at all. Education complete. The years from four till twenty-one.

He stood up and silently lifted his fists above his head. Keeping them there, he walked into his bathroom, twisting sideways to get through the door. In the mirror, he saw a white shirt he'd owned since sixth form, plaid boxers riding up, black hair on his pale thighs – and expressionlessly shook his fists. Then he went back to his chair and opened the next batch of data.

But after a few minutes, he broke off to read Eddie's email again. The final paragraph was, "For what it's worth, I'd say from my own experience that an exceptional result in finals can take years to recover from. For me, certainly, it was a bit of an albatross around my neck. If you'll forgive some advice from a former teacher who wishes you well, in my view the crux is to keep always in mind that the reason you fill up a car with petrol is not so that you can get a high score on the fuel gauge. Your degree has, I hope, tanked you up with what you need to roar out of the garage and off into the wide world. Exams are only a measure of the thing; they are not the thing itself. In themselves they are fairly meaningless. I don't mind admitting I envy you a little, young man, so go forth, says I, and don't look back until you're old and comfortable."

To James, this sounded like the kind of high-minded sentiment tutors were honour-bound to impart to students. But a chilly, immobilising sadness began to creep over him. Apparently the person who'd come second wasn't even close. And "meaningless"? That hadn't hurt at first, but now a bruise was rising towards the skin.

He tried to re-immerse himself in his job. It was sort of interesting, like a long *New Yorker* article on some unimagined niche – how Big Pork moves pigs around America. It was the grand strategy of corporate empire-building. At Tesco HQ, they were walking around like they'd just come up with the Industrial Revolution and were about to conquer India. Their brainwave was to set up a site on the web where you could buy anything: earplugs, washing machines, golf clubs – anything – and have it delivered with a couple of clicks. They would obliterate the high street and replace it with a giant warehouse that was already going up outside Reading. The richest corporate superpower of the twenty-first century would be Tesco, and the men and women of the Tesco high command would be as kings.

James's part in all this was to meticulously cut out and paint one jigsaw piece among thousands. He had to discover which Tescos were already selling lots of non-groceries, like irons and DVD players. It wasn't quite what he'd done at Oxford – *Can the law be both just and compassionate?* Or, *What is the use of debt in society?* Nor was it easy to see where he could distinguish himself: you either fetched the information or you didn't.

At Oxford he'd experienced the calm meditative purity of exertion in thought. That wasn't required here. This task wasn't designed to stretch or test him. What was wanted was merely toil, methodical and repetitive. The answer didn't need to be imagined, only assembled. The number of Tesco shops he had to check was 2,116.

For a little while he enjoyed the mental puzzle of figuring out how to construct the answer his bosses wanted. In the morning he was going to present his findings to Tesco's top executives. He was curious to see how sharp they were, after a career of flogging lettuce. But he resented that he'd have to stay at his laptop most of the night. At Oxford he never stayed in the library past four p.m., studying only when his mind was fresh.

He couldn't see how it made any difference to Tesco's grand plans if he gave his presentation on Friday instead of tomorrow. But his manager insisted. It was irritating to be subject to someone else's arbitrariness. It was just a culture of performative zeal. McKinseyites were supposed to be the shock troops of capitalism, sacrificing themselves to smash through problems. James was supposed to be eagerly hurling himself into the fray. But he couldn't quite get himself geed up.

Where to apply was something he'd decided by writing Oxford-style essays in favour of six professions – the others were law, finance, civil service, diplomacy and academia. Somewhere there was a pantheon that housed Emil Zátopek and Julius Caesar. You stood at the bottom of a mountain and saw several paths winding upwards. The trick was to choose. He selected McKinsey not for love of sales data but because it seemed to lead all the way to the top.

Without knowing it himself, he was immersed in the belief that he had a certain quantity of potential to be fulfilled. As in GCSE physics, a certain inborn amount of potential energy to be converted into motion. It was as if life were a high-jump contest and, given his genes and background, there was a theoretical maximum height he could reach. His purpose was to leap as near as possible to that perfect score.

This was a peacetime philosophy, the individualist product of a society that hadn't felt threatened since it won the Cold War. There was no need for anyone to put on a uniform or dig for victory. The twentieth century had conclusively settled the question of how a society should be organised: liberal democracy, free markets and personal self-realisation. Even the Russians and Chinese had hauled down the red flag and realised they'd rather have a nice time than a world revolution. Even the Irish had settled their eight-hundred-year vendetta, simply because no one wanted it any more. It was possible for someone to write an essay called "The End of History?" and for everyone to understand just from the title exactly what he meant. Ideology already felt as quaint and romantic as medieval disputes about the nature of angels.

With this peace came a loosening of constraints, an unparalleled tolerance of how others lived their lives, an assumption that most quarrels were only misunderstandings – and also a marked tendency to navel-gazing, to the invention of problems, a certain ennui. For many more Brits than would admit it, the 9/11 attack on America – a few weeks into James and Roland's final year of school – came as a much-needed stimulus. The two boys from James's school year who joined the army did so because war in Afghanistan might be the last great adventure before the world succumbed entirely to soporific contentment. It was an unawaited stroke of luck that those swivel-eyed jihadists didn't realise they were living in the modern age.

For James, there was no sense that expanding Tesco's sales onto the web was what the human race urgently needed. It didn't have to be. This was a ladder. And yet: he'd come first in the most prestigious course at the most famous university in the world, and he was sitting here in his boxers copying and pasting the item code for ironing boards. It didn't feel as if he were ascending to greatness.

*

McKinsey certainly tried to make him feel he was being initiated into the global elite. His onboarding was at the so-called McKinsey Alpine University, an old-world grand hotel up a mountain in Austria. It was the first time since childhood that he'd flown British Airways. He learned that he was the only one in the cohort not to have already joined the Executive Club. One of the others brought him into the club lounge as a guest. He pictured himself and his family always sitting not in the nice quiet lounge with everyone else but in the horribly noisy airport concourse like a bunch of clueless rubes.

Kitzbühel was also the first time he'd been inside a high-end corporate hotel room. On family holidays, his parents had taken them to self-catering farmhouses in the Pyrenees or to stay with old friends in a white-washed apartment in Portugal. This room had a shredder for destroying sensitive documents; a shower that massaged his skin rather than merely pouring water onto it; and a bed of hitherto unimagined depth, like falling backwards into treacle.

On the bedside table was a single book: a three-hundred-page cloth-bound volume by Marvin Bower, the man who'd taken James McKinsey's small company and laid within it the foundations of something that considered itself unique. That he hadn't given his own name to the Firm was somehow more ideal, more McKinsey. Like the consultants who came after him, he pulled his strings in discreet anonymity; he was the cardinal and not the king, the all-powerful servant who would not have wanted his face stamped into the coins.

James had heard a lot about Bower and "the McKinsey way", as if it were a major school of philosophy. Tao for capitalists. But he almost felt he was missing something. One apparently classic Bower precept was that all good information can be presented in a bullet-pointed list, and that all good lists have three points. There must be more to it.

In the breaks between sessions, the novices sat in breakout pods in the hotel lobby, a cross between a chalet and a conference centre, with cowbells and flipcharts. Through the windows they could see the Alps in sunshine and shadow. Most recruits were hopped up on how special they were, and what they talked about was McKinsey. It was repeated that McKinsey invented the barcode, that McKinsey had reorganised the White House; that McKinsey oversaw the reconstruction of post-war Europe. The executives plodding along in other companies were ordinary footsoldiers; McKinsey were the Marine Corps, the janissaries, the Varangian Guard. No one talked about money. This had appealed to him before he applied, this idealism.

His plan was to make more friends than he had at uni. He'd bungled at the start of Oxford. Now the scores had been reset to zero. The group embrace of stories about Bower and McKinsey gave him a chance to be honest and real, to show himself – and incidentally to show that he could demolish false notions with the best of them.

In a breakout pod between sessions, he spoke up and said, "Don't you think there's a bit of a cult of personality going on with Bower? Isn't everything in the book actually quite obvious? They're clearly just trying to build a mystique around the Firm, I suppose so they can jack up the prices and indoctrinate the employees – you know, us."

No one seemed to want to join him in this. Their instructors kept telling them it was a hallmark of McKinsey's unique intellectual culture that even the lowliest analyst could challenge the CEO. But a Singaporean guy called Aaron just said, "I don't know. I don't think it's really a big deal. I just wanted to pick up on something Marco brought up earlier about having organised thoughts . . ."

And the conversation moved on.

Later, Aaron, who was as intrusively friendly and upbeat as a Jehovah's Witness, started talking about the Jesuits – another elite cadre, along with the Marines, that McKinsey was regularly compared to. Aaron, who'd probably been to a Jesuit school or something, said the Jesuits were a civilising force. They compiled the first bilingual dictionaries for Asian languages, chose solitary lives of constant travel and risked martyrdom for their mission – you could see the parallels with management consulting.

This was in itself attractive to James, but his powers of argument had been engaged, and he didn't know better than to debate for the pleasure of debating. He said, "The Jesuits believed they were serving a higher cause. They didn't go to Asia just to increase parchment sales by ten per cent."

"McKinsey has a higher cause."

"Like what?"

"To increase prosperity and show society how to advance. I'm from Singapore, right? When we got independence, Singapore was a . . ." – Aaron shied away from a curse word – "It was a Third World slum. People literally lived in tin shacks. And now look at us. We'll soon have a higher GDP per capita than UK. Sorry!"

"Sure, but who here honestly believes that McKinsey exists to further the advancement of humankind?" James looked around the faces of the little group. No one wanted to be part of this weirdly hostile dispute. The Jesuits? Literally: what? James suddenly wished he could skip this footling team stuff and just be assigned his work.

From then on, he found he had nothing more to say in the breakout chats. He was silent, too, in the morning, when everyone spread their copies of the *FT* across white tablecloths. Pastry flakes and spots of coffee spattered the pale-pink sheets. The recruits pointed out McKinsey alums in the high positions they hoped to one day occupy themselves: William Hague, former head of the British Conservatives. The head of HSBC. The head of Volkswagen. The head of LEGO. There was usually one person who couldn't resist saying: "You know Chelsea Clinton's working in the New York office?" They had breakfast debates about Jeff Skilling, who was soon to go on trial. He'd been sent by McKinsey to advise an oil and gas giant, Enron. Skilling took over, made Enron the most celebrated company in America, and then blew it up. Some recruits said he'd lost his grip on the values set out by Bower; others that he was a latter-day Icarus.

James stopped listening and filled his belly with free breakfasts. He didn't need to love the Firm or be friends with everyone. The Firm was a kind of training. And McKinsey was undoubtedly a higher league than

Oxford. If Oxford was a school for civil servants and bankers, McKinsey was a school for their bosses. From here he could go on to do a couple of years at the Number 10 Policy Unit. Or something interesting at Google. It was all good training.

But on the evening that Eddie sent him his results, alone in a hotel room, with his bare thighs sticking to the chair, he couldn't quite remember what all the training was *for*. He tried to carry on with the Tesco data but couldn't get his gears to engage. He stood up, stretched his hands and jumped to frog-splash onto the starchy duvet. The room-service menu was on the nightstand. Getting to order whatever he wanted still felt like being a kid in a movie. He and the other juniors on the study – Aaron, whom he knew from Kitzbühel, and Eleni, a glamorous shark from an Anglo-Greek shipping dynasty – had got themselves into a jokey test of strength. The loser was the first to crack and admit they were hungry, the least committed to their labours. James had yet to lose; he just ate biscuits and crisps until someone called.

But he lifted the grey handset to his ear and dialled Aaron's room. He heard "Hello, Aaron Jumabhoy" in placeless international English.

"Hi, it's James."

"Ohhhhh, burned-out already?" Aaron loved this joshing.

"Yeah . . . I need to eat. I think I'll be doing an all-nighter."

"Strong. Very strong. So they gave you crappy data?"

"It's all there. It's just a mess."

"Sorry, man. But I guess that's why they pay us the big bucks, right? Do you know what you want?"

"The burger, thanks."

"No problem! I'll call Eleni."

James pulled on a matching navy-blue hooded tracksuit. He'd bought it after seeing that the hotel had a gym. He still intended to get a six-pack. The equipment was a marked step down from Kitzbühel. It was strange to have opinions about the quality of hotels.

Aaron's door was propped open with a black shoe. He was sitting at the round table where they ate every evening, in his after-hours uniform of a Ralph Lauren jumper with a shirt underneath. Their disagreement about Jesuits had given him a liking for James. He kept wanting to talk about Francis Xavier's arrival in the Moluccas. He truly did believe that McKinsey's mission on Earth was to guide humankind into productive technocracy.

They nodded at each other and James sat down, opening his laptop. Aaron had his headphones in, and James could hear Bryan Adams' "Summer of '69" leaking out of them. For a few minutes they worked without speaking. James was gradually figuring out the optimal sequence of keystrokes for his copy-and-pasting. Did you really need to come first in your year at Oxford to do this?

Aaron finished his slide, sat back in his chair and took out his headphones. Shifted his round tortoiseshell glasses up out of the way, massaged the indentations on either side of his nose. "Eleni said she'd come over in a couple of minutes."

"Okay." James carried on copying and pasting. He had 827 stores to go. Then he'd have to make slides for a presentation. He hadn't paid much attention to the insultingly basic training in PowerPoint.

Eleni and the room service arrived at the same time. With the certainty of someone used to staff, she directed the waiter to put the tray on the bed while the boys cleared space on the table. James went awkward when she matter-of-factly passed the waiter a fiver. The waiter grinned with surprise and, as he took it, said, "Don't mind if I do."

Eleni had mentioned going to see friends in New York for a long weekend — something extraordinary to James, who'd never flown anywhere for a weekend. Like Aaron, who'd worked in the Singaporean government, she was a few years older than him. She'd done a PhD in biochemistry, which she assured them was going to be a "huge deal" without really being able to explain why. Her black Mediterranean hair, pulled tight and clipped to the back of her head, was gleaming from the shower. She too was dressed more smartly than James: heels, tight jeans, a fresh white shirt. Wrapped around her shoulders was a grey pashmina.

James was a little intimidated. He feared that she could see facets of his personality that he couldn't see himself. Because this feeling didn't have any other mode of being understood, it registered as attraction.

They pushed aside the computers and files, and lifted the steel cloches off their plates. Eleni was having a chicken salad. Aaron was having grilled chicken with steamed broccoli. James started ferrying the burger up to his mouth without really tasting it.

As Eleni was arranging her laptop, she said, "So, James. I hear you're pulling an all-nighter."

He sensed an opportunity to impress. "It's not a big deal. The data they gave me's just not in very good shape."

"Yeah, Aaron said they fobbed you off with crap."

James blinked. "It's not crap. It's all there. I can do it easily."

"I'm sure you can. But you shouldn't have to. You can't let those little dweebs take advantage."

In James's degree, whenever something extra was needed, the solution was to reach deeper into himself. But here the problem was other people. His equivalents at Tesco were practising a kind of civil disobedience. They suspected – correctly – that he knew less and was paid more than them. It was dawning on them that, despite the many wonderful compliments they'd been given on their grad scheme, even their own bosses put a lower price on their work than on McKinsey's.

So, when he asked for the data, one of them told him, "McKinsey's so much faster than us at everything; it might be quicker if you guys, you know, found it yourselves." James didn't know what to do next. They'd finally given him the data that morning, the last possible moment before a fuck-up would be obviously their fault. So now he had to copy and paste at night.

He didn't have the energy to defend himself, and just told Eleni, "Yeah, I suppose I'm not used to it yet. Until now, it's just been me and the books."

Eleni nodded, accepting that, then got cross: "Those little fuckers. Slow-rolling you. They'll do it again."

"It's really not a problem. I can easily get this done by tomorrow. Easily."

Eleni shrugged and said, "Yeah, of course."

They carried on at their laptops as the room started to smell of burger grease.

Eleni said, "Actually, if you're clever about this, it's a lucky break." James and Aaron looked at her. "We're supposed to like, *butter them up*, aren't we, the clients. But sometimes they *can't* be buttered. And then we have to play hardball. This is an opportunity for you to show you can do that."

James realised Eleni was playing the game of career advancement at a far higher level than he was. And she was right. His onboarding instructors had obliquely warned that sometimes when you made landfall in a client company, proffering coloured beads to the unsophisticated natives, some "liaison points" could be "consistently less helpful". In that case, you just had to "buckle up" and "push through". In other words: keep shooting till they see reason.

Eleni said, "You're lucky. Most of us only get to show we're capable of doing our jobs."

"Yeah, you're right. That is what I should do." But he wasn't fired up.

Aaron noticed and said, "It's quite a brutal thing for your first study. If you want, we can swap presentations, and I'll do it. Mine's almost finished."

"No, no. It's okay. Thanks, though. I can do it."

Eleni said, "It's all you need to make yourself stand out from the crowd."

James thought: But I already stand out from the crowd! For an instant, he was about to let slip that he'd just come first in his year. But his pride saved him from that. With the operatic despair of a twenty-one-year-old, he suddenly felt that everything was for nought; that all striving and talent ended up in the grave; that no matter how strong and true you hit a ball, it still eventually dropped into the mud.

He'd come first in his year at Oxford, and all it had got him was this: sitting in a hotel room in a tracksuit, looking out the window at the last light of a day of his life passing away forever.

He got up and said: "I can't really concentrate. I'm going to carry on back in my room." But once he got there, he didn't carry on. He'd cobble something together in the morning. He just lay on the prickly sheets with his face in the pillows, sobbing quietly in case they could hear him through the wall. The streetlights came on. He sobbed until he felt light, hollow, translucent, like an empty glass, with every thought and emotion poured away. And then he slept.

After reading his own results email from Margot, Roland came down in a state of shock to his parents' bare kitchen. Even though they'd been in this place for months, it still looked like a temporary rental: bland kitchen units edged in bright wood, and no pictures except a black-and-white photo of trams in some old-time town put there by the estate agent. His parents had moved so often they'd lost the knack of making things homely.

But this house had tall French windows onto a temperate suburban garden. His parents, after two decades in desert countries, couldn't get over how green it was. So much grass, so much vegetal growth, everything so supersaturated with water. Someone had told them there was a colour called "English Green", as of grass after rain. Now whenever they saw anything at all greenish — a Range Rover, an M&S shopping bag — his dad would cry out, "Oh, Lorna, English Green!"

Roland's mum had moved the kitchen table in front of the open French windows. The radio was chatting away, and in one of the neighbouring gardens someone was playing ping-pong. She had her glasses on and was studying some schematics that she'd unfolded across the table. When she noticed him, she said, "Hello, sweetheart. Don't distract me. I'm trying to understand the damage your father wants to do to our new garden. He wants to put his blessed pipes under the flowerbeds, and he's adamant they won't need digging up when they go kaput, but of course they will. There are turkey sandwiches in the fridge if you're hungry."

Her voice, like the contents of her fridge, was mishmashed Scottish-American. After decades among expats, she ordered Miracle Whip and radioactive-green Mountain Dew from a specialist American food store in Holland Park.

Roland didn't say anything, just let how he was feeling appear on his face. She carried on studying the diagrams then glanced up and exclaimed, "Oh my God, what's happened? What's the matter?" She was on to him right away, pulling him into a hug. Because she was so much shorter, he had to bend forward to be embraced. Without moving his arms, he put his face down on her shoulder.

She sensed that it wasn't as bad as her first thought; the parental panic subsided – no one was dead. With her free hand, she moved her glasses onto the top of her bob. "Okay, shush now. Tell me what's happened. Is it a girl? One of the girls from that group who came down? Zoe? I could see you liked her. I liked her, too, but I did think maybe she was a bit –" She caught herself in time, and just hummed the words she was going to say.

Roland mumbled into her shoulder. She said, "What was that? Tell me again please, angel."

He lifted his face and said, "I said, it's not a girl."

"Then what? One of your friends?"

"No, no. I got my exam results."

Now his mum was stricken. "Oh Jesus, Roland." She grabbed him by the shoulders. "What have you done? Tell me."

He closed his eyes and said, "I got a 2:2."

She let out a long-drawn "Ohhhh." Then, "You stupid boy. How could you?"

He mumbled, "I'm sorry, I just –"

She cut him off. "Yes, yes. There'll be time for your sorries later. Sit down and let me think."

He sat in the chair in front of her diagrams. Pretty much no one got an education as good as his, and he'd wasted it. What an entitled prick. He put his face on the table and closed his eyes again. The edge of a diagram tickled his cheek.

His mum was still standing where she was. She remembered something else and said, "Oh, think how Mr Bishop is going to take this."

Mr Bishop was head of physics at the international school in Cairo. Displaced and lonely, he seemed to show any colour only when refracted through his pupils. It wasn't obvious how he'd ended up there. Inevitably, there was speculation, sometimes malicious, that he was secretly gay and had come to North Africa for the boys. The mums at the expats' club hushed down any public mockery, but sometimes, when they'd had some wine and were feeling permissive, they let these jokes bubble up into view, because Mr Bishop was pitied, and so he was sometimes laughed at.

He ran a physics club where they froze old socks in liquid nitrogen and programmed a toy car to steer itself round an obstacle course. The end-of-term treat was to climb up a wobbling ladder through a hatch and out onto the school's flagstone roof. Around them were cables, antennae and the whirring crates that housed the air conditioning. Beyond their flagstone raft, Cairo's sand-coloured jumble of roof terraces and clothes lines spread out to every horizon.

They fired bottle rockets up into the scorching blue dome over the city. As Roland stood there squinting, shielding his eyes because he'd forgotten his sunglasses, he imagined that, with enough fuel, their repurposed washing-up bottles could escape the air bubble in which the planet bobbed like a frogspawn in jelly.

That was why he studied physics, along with philosophy. Mr Bishop rang him on the morning of each A-level exam to make sure he got there. And now, through sheer selfish fecklessness and ingratitude, Roland had failed everyone who'd ever helped him. He raised his head off the table's surface and banged it back down.

His mum said, "Don't do that, sweetheart. You're going to need every brain cell you've got." She put a hand on the back of his head, as if to stop him doing it again. Then, with a kind of shudder, the initial shock and anger passed from her. She laughed, took his head in both hands and planted a kiss in his hair. She said, "Oh, you bloody idiot, you'll be fine. I didn't even go to university, if you can believe such a thing. And I've seen a lot more of the world than just stacking shelves in the Inverness Co-op."

Roland made an inchoate sound.

"Are you saying something or just groaning?"

Another animal sound.

"What was that?"

"Groaning."

"Hmm. Okay. But can you take your face off my schematics, please? I still don't really understand how this contraption works. Apparently, it's always warm underground, but how warm can it really be? I mean, when someone digs a grave it's not like a bloody oven, is it?"

Roland rolled his head sideways so his mouth was free. "It's got a heat pump."

"What?"

Roland groaned.

"Come on, you. Don't forget we paid for that education of yours."

Roland closed his eyes and said, "It's like a fridge in reverse. The liquid goes round the pipes and, like you said, brings the warmth back." He cheered up very slightly. It *was* quite clever. "That warmth is enough to warm up this other liquid which evaporates into gas. And then when you compress the gas, it heats up, like, a lot. It's like when you pump up a bike tyre, and the pump gets hot in your hand. It's the same effect."

His mum said, "Okay. And where on this diagram is the pump then?" She put her glasses back on and bent forward to inspect the sheets. But then she realised something and said, "Oh God."

"What?"

"Your father's going to be so angry with me. I gave you that money to go to Japan. And you fannied around instead of doing your work."

"I'm so sorry, Mum."

"Oh, shut up, shut up." She fussed him out of the way and folded up the diagrams, then muttered, "I'm going to have to sit through your father's wretched Formula One, and go and stay at your grandparents' for a whole bloody week. You're coming with us, you hear me? And you're going to spend quality time with them every day. Hours and hours of it. So much they barely remember you have a mother."

While she was muttering, she was thinking.

She gave him another kiss on the hair and said, "Here's what we're going to do, darling boy. When your father gets home from tennis, you're going to tell him a good plan for what you're going to do next. And in exchange, I won't throw you out on your ear. Does that sound fair to you?"

Roland's exam result had set in motion some conveyor he couldn't control. Already he had less choice than before. He wailed, "But I don't have a plan!"

"Of course you don't! You haven't started yet. But you listen to me." She double-tapped a fingernail on the tabletop. "I'm not going to have your father more hurt by this than is absolutely necessary. And I'm not going to spend the rest of my time until I go stone deaf hearing about whether we should have let you go to Japan or not. So, when he gets home, you're going to say, 'I got a disappointing result in my finals, but don't worry. I've thought about how to make something worthwhile of my life, and I've got a good plan, which is . . .' and then you say what the plan is. Alright?"

Roland nodded. This did seem fair. He must make amends. And more importantly, he and his mum were now on the same team. He jumped up, full of purpose, and said, "Okay. How long have I got?"

She looked at her watch. "He's playing with one of the pros, which he likes. So he'll try and play longer than he should, until his back starts to hurt. It just depends if the pro has another slot free. So you've got either an hour and twenty minutes, or twenty minutes."

Again Roland said, "Okay." He nodded and clapped his hands together, psyching himself up. Something occurred to him. "One thing I could do – maybe I shouldn't mention it, but actually, yes. Japan has something called the JET Programme. It's really serious. Like, *really* serious. The government pays for it. And then it'll completely make sense that I went to Japan that time, because I'm getting really serious about Japanese."

"And it's a language course?"

"No, no, no. Much more than that." Roland was slightly making this up. "You go to the best unis in Japan and you learn much better Japanese than most Westerners ever do. You also get introduced to all kinds of people. You learn the whole culture. You become, like, a bridge between Japan and the West."

"Right. And how long does it take them to turn you into a bridge?"

"I think it's two years. Maybe three. Yes, I think three."

"And the Japanese government pays for this? Because you've already studied philosophy, and now you want to study Japanese. It's not exactly engineering, is it?"

"But you meet all these high-up people, so you can, you know, do business between Japan and the West. And yeah, the government pays for it."

"Sweetheart, are you really going to become an international businessman? What are you going to do, import Toyotas to Guildford?"

"I could do. It's all maths. And if I spoke amazing Japanese and knew the Toyota people, why not? And anyway, it's not just about business. You're meant to be able to interpret each country to the other." Roland was growing into the idea.

Lorna took a few pensive steps around the table and looked out into her safe and lovely English garden. She said, "Well, of course it sounds like a good thing when you put it like that. But three years? Are you sure? It's a long time at your age."

Roland tried to pause and think this through, but a great surge of adventure was already carrying him away. In his mind's eye, he saw again the Rainbow Bridge in Tokyo, the mile-long arc of lights bending across a city so modern and vast that the cars drove on a floating ribbon through the sky. He felt again the sense that some profound understanding had eluded him, something that trembled on the brink of revelation and fell back. The tiny drinking cups, the pebble gardens. He said, "I'd love to go. I would really, really *love* to go."

"Well then. Japan."

"Japan."

"Really really?"

"Really really."

"Well. Terrific. What a terrific idea. It'll be such an adventure. And you really want to go?"

"I really want to."

"Terrific. C'mon then, let's celebrate. Terrific. Fetch some prosecco from the fridge. Oh! It'll be so fascinating."

Roland was getting happy. The exam results didn't matter in this bigger picture. As he opened the fridge door, he began to tease his mum. "What were you going to say about Zoe? You said you did maybe think she was a bit . . . a bit what?"

"Careful, you."

"So, how cross do you think Dad's going to be with you?"

She laughed and said, "Bring that wine here so I can box your ears."

When he did, she affectionately pulled his earlobes and patted him on the cheek. "You won't remember, but your father went to Japan when you were little. He had a job in the Russian oilfields on the . . ." – her finger sketched compass points in the air – "*east* coast, opposite Japan, for a couple of months. He went to the northern island, whatever it's called. Honshu?" Roland didn't know. "Or is that the main one? Anyway, they have these tribal people. You should ask him about it."

"Oh, yeah. I read about them. I think they're called, um . . ."

"You'll be an expert in all this soon enough." Her thoughts had moved on. "I've never really got to East Asia. We had a few months in Malaysia once, just before I was pregnant with you. Oh, Roland, you ratbag, you're giving me itchy feet. You better not make my nice new house and my nice new garden feel all small and retired and old-fartish with your tales of travelling about. We haven't even finished it yet."

"No, come on, you'll love it. Going to the tennis club fundraiser when I'm in a Zen temple on Mount Fuji."

She pretended to cuff him across the head. "Zen temple, my rear end. You'll be in your classroom hitting the books. Now, let's drink the prosecco in the garden before you go and write an apology letter to Mr Bishop. Come on, chop-chop. Pour two glasses. I'm going to need mine filled right up."

He popped the cork and poured, inexpertly letting foam rush up the necks of the glasses.

"Maybe your father and I will come visit you. You better hope he's had a good tennis lesson. Oh, I'm so jealous. Japan! And I thought Cairo was far away."

*

Unfortunately for Roland, it turned out that the JET Programme's deadline had passed months before. The next round of applications began in December. He wouldn't be able to actually start for more than a year. In the interim, he decided to teach himself Japanese while doing something else.

He'd discovered that JET stood for Japan Exchange and Teaching. You taught in a school, and he could of course teach English elsewhere too. He applied for a job about forty-five minutes after finding out about JET. He wanted to maintain a sense of momentum. It proved to be a path of no resistance: innumerable Asian schools wanted cheap English teachers.

Two weeks later, he was interviewed in the offices of Teach English Abroad (UK). They had a distinguished address, in Knightsbridge, but inside it was messy, ex-institutional and neglected, like a school that was closing down. Some rooms were stripped of furniture, and empty but for loose piles of teaching materials left on the floor. Everything was branded with squirmingly bad Teach English Abroad TEA pots, to suggest some refined old-fashioned Englishness. To Roland, who'd been to the best international school in each country his parents lived in, and then Oxford, it was funny that such ramshackle places existed.

He was interviewed by the head of TEA (UK), Mrs Thomas, a scratchy and harassed woman in her forties who was evidently holding the operation together. He was waiting outside her office when she hurried jerkily down the corridor. Once in earshot, she said, "Mackintosh?"

"Um, Mackenzie."

She carried straight on into the office, saying, "So sorry. Do come in. Take a seat." She arranged herself. "So, you're about to go to university, and you want to do some teaching first. Is that about it?"

"Sort of. I've actually already been to university. Just finished about, um, roughly six weeks ago. I was doing physics and philosophy, and my thesis was —"

She interrupted. "Good. Yes. Sorry. I had you confused with someone else. You haven't come out of order, have you?"

"Um, no. I don't think so."

"Good." She recited a spiel about TEA (UK)'s exacting standards. When he was overseas, he would be representing everyone back in London. This talk had probably once been intended to inspire but now came across as accusatory, as if Roland had already decided to ignore it. Once she was done, she asked some interview questions and, while he answered, rummaged through her files.

Roland carefully confined himself to topics he could talk about with unfeigned eagerness, like his interest in learning a non-European language. His sincerity caught Mrs Thomas's attention, and she relaxed a little, leaving the paperwork alone. Then, as he went on, she grew impatient. Finally, she interrupted again and said, "You'll do fine, you'll do fine. You've passed, you're in. You'll be a credit to the organisation, I'm sure."

Roland said, "Wow! Just like that?"

She almost smiled, and said, "Yes. Just like that."

There was something else. She flicked her biro onto her notepad, sighed with discontent and said, "Piece of advice. You've got real interest. That'll take you a long way – maybe too long a way. My advice to you is this: just because you live in, say, Thailand and speak excellent Thai and have Thai friends, that doesn't make you a Thai. And it never will. Do you understand what I'm driving at?"

Roland didn't really. But he felt that this was serious for Mrs Thomas and respectfully lobbed her a softball question: "So what's the answer? Stay at home?"

"Ha. No. No. It's this." She picked up her biro again and twiddled it between two fingers. "Talent has its own . . . its own stickiness. So does curiosity. Don't get stuck unless you want to be." She lifted her eyebrows as if they both knew what she was talking about. Roland nodded and, out of sympathy, pretended to take this in.

When he went back to the TEA (UK) offices for a month of perfunctory training, which his parents paid for, Mrs Thomas singled him out for chats. There was something about him that attracted teachers. At lunchtimes, she invited him to walk to Tesco with her to buy sandwiches. She always said they could discuss the course on the way. Instead, she dropped many hints about her own youth.

In the lessons, he read laminated sheets about how to teach and scored a hundred per cent on the multiple-choice quizzes that followed. When his month was up, Mrs Thomas gave him a certificate attesting he'd passed the training course "with distinction". A few weeks after that, in September, the season of new endeavours, he set off from Heathrow. Not back to Tokyo but to the remote desert town of Nagaur, in Rajasthan, India.

For a few weeks after he arrived on the bus from Jaipur, his chugging narrative of himself — his exams, his parents, his beginner's guide to Japanese characters — went quiet. The town's presence flattened him. He was turned outward, absorbing the place.

Nagaur wasn't one of the great cities of northern India, a Mumbai or a Delhi, with numberless crowds in ceaseless circling motion. It was small, shabby, reddish-brown and low-rise. There was a rough old fort with a ruined palace at its centre. It sat unguarded; the roads were too bad for tourists. Outside the fort's open gates was a loud market square. But away from that, the town wasn't busy. Every evening, night poured into the streets as if from a jug, filling them up with rich, warm blackness. Here and there, a dangling electric bulb cast a glowing sphere under the awning of a cigarette kiosk.

Roland liked it. The warmth reminded him of Cairo. So did the garbage by the roadside, and the call to prayer warping and crackling through the mosques' loudspeakers. A comfortable sense that things were less orderly than in England. On windy days, the sky thickened into turbid orange as sand blew in off the desert.

He was living in a breeze-block annexe around the back of the headmaster's house. Beneath the white paint, the walls were raw concrete. The headmaster was about thirty, very skinny, with bony cheeks and wrists. Every day he wore the same black suit and waistcoat. Roland was the only other teacher, and he ate dinner with the headmaster and his wife every evening.

On the flat roof was a grubby white plastic garden chair where, after lessons, he could smoke Gold Flake cigarettes and watch the market. Most of it was just people prodding alien vegetables. But sometimes wrapped-up tribesmen rode into town on undulating camels, to sell embroideries and buy mobile phones. There was a holy man with grey dreadlocks who crawled back and forth wearing only a loincloth and an expression of wordless rage.

Roland saw no other outsiders. There was no through traffic because, beyond Nagaur, there was only more desert and the closed border with Pakistan. At night, the stars, in the dry air, looked like sharp bright granules. Unlike in Cairo or Oxford, he had the sense that no history had ever happened here. There were no blue plaques. It was just people living. This struck him as very profound.

One evening after dinner, he was smoking on the roof when he saw a fire on the wall of the old fort. There was a basic shrine up there. He heard drumming. Silhouetted figures passed in front of the flames. Roland felt very far from modern life, and the romance of the past swept him up. He imagined he was in an adventure story about the Raj, a junior administrator out of his depth in a far-flung district. Pale fearful faces at night. Unexplained rituals. The country never really under control. The real India, deep India, on which the Brits had barely left a mark.

The small libraries of the expat country clubs where he'd grown up majored in tales of the imperial heyday. The siege of Cawnpore and the Birkenhead drill felt far closer when you were sitting in the Katameya Heights Country Club than they did in the mother country. There was lots of derring-do overseas. Scott and Shackleton. Field Marshal Monty and the Desert Rats. Victorian heroes with their stiff manners and their soppiness. Gordon of Khartoum, who went out to face the Mahdi's army armed only with a rattan cane, and was cut down.

Roland's parents had been to Khartoum for a weekend. As a boy, he'd daydreamed about serving as a red-coated officer of the Raj, gravely wounded and yet leading his outnumbered highlanders into the withering fire of the enemy's jezails.

It had to be said that Nagaur wasn't much like all that. More to the point, Nagaur was Indian, and he was learning Japanese. He had nothing against India. But you couldn't just substitute one Asian culture for another — as if he were some inverted xenophobe who would fall for anything exotic because on some level they were all the same.

Dinner was in the headmaster's house, where the breeze blocks were lightly disguised by the embroidered tribal cloths nailed to the walls. The headmaster made conversation with the guest while his wife texted her sisters. The food was served by a maid, a stout woman in her fifties with a thick grey plait hanging down her back. Roland could see her midriff in the gap at the side of her sari, and he gazed in fascination at a roll of soft brown flab.

The headmaster was used to his untrained English auxiliaries being nervous about what the hell they were going to do with the pupils. At the first few dinners, he kept telling Roland that his mere presence was a "tremendous learning bonus". He insisted, "If you had not come from Oxford, the younger children would not have any teacher whatsoever at all."

He waited until Roland realised that an answer was expected, and hurried to say, "Yes, yes, no teacher. I understand."

The headmaster nodded and went on. "They would not have any help with their English. They would not have any help learning their three Rs: reading, writing and 'rithmetic." Roland pretended to enjoy this play on words. "Now, they are very lucky. They have not been taught by an Oxford man before. Oxford is the best university in the world, is it not?"

Roland tried not to think of his 2:2, looked the headmaster right in the eye, and said, "Yes. Oh, definitely."

The headmaster seemed to want to ask more about it, but was too conscious of his dignity as headmaster to be openly curious. He himself had attended the Teacher Training College in Bikaner, though he didn't graduate. The framed certificate next to the school's entrance was a confirmation of enrolment. He just said, "Excellent. Very excellent. So don't fret. Teaching is not difficult. Isn't that right, Nihal?"

His wife looked up from her phone. She smiled at Roland and said, "Yes, don't worry." She pronounced it *vurry* and wobbled her head in the Indian way. "Everyone gets used to it very quickly. And for the children, it's as my husband told you: it's a *tremendous* learning bonus." Roland accepted this entirely. If the alternative to him was a zero, anything he did was above and beyond.

It all happened in a single room across the street. The headmaster taught his class in one half of the room while Roland taught his in the other. As Roland spoke, he heard the headmaster's Indianised English in the gaps between his own sentences.

The kids — Roland had about twenty, between five and ten years old — were likeable and seemed happy. They chatted too much, and sometimes the headmaster came onto Roland's side to punish them. He'd escort a kid outside onto the street and hit him hard across the knuckles with a wooden ruler. Roland glumly wished this wouldn't happen but couldn't seem to do anything about it.

Roland read them stories and had them draw pictures of what they'd heard. He asked them up to the blackboard to do sums. Sometimes they read aloud from a set of tattered workbooks whose pages had been softened and stained by countless fingers. It was very frictionless. No effort, no problems. Roland stood in more or less the right place and delivered more or less the right words.

Aside from those few untaxing hours, he was free to live however he wanted. Mainly, he sat on the rooftop smoking.

One evening the headmaster was in a jovial, pepped-up mood. He seemed on the verge of breaking into laughter. After Roland had been wondering for a while what this was about, the headmaster leaned towards him across the table, gave him a deep, brother-to-brother smile and said, "I am hearing that you love to go up onto the roof and see the hustlings and bustlings in our town."

Roland nearly laughed as well. "Yes. Yes, I have. It's interesting. I like to see what's going on."

The headmaster was nodding his full agreement, wanting Roland to say more. When Roland stopped, he lifted a skinny brown finger and said, "Nagaur is a very interesting town. We have the palace. We have the fort. A very interesting town. You are the first teacher who goes on the roof every day. You are not too hot?"

"Oh, no, no, not at all. I wear a baseball cap. And I've got my sunglasses. And, um, I lived in the Middle East, in Cairo, for a long time, so I'm used to it."

The headmaster was nodding as if this were all great stuff. "Yes, yes. The pyramids." He lifted his finger again and said with emphasis, "You must tell tourists from England to visit Nagaur."

"Oh, I will. I definitely will."

The headmaster was delighted. The next day, two older boys from the headmaster's class, Niraj and Arjun, both about fourteen, came up to the roof and asked to join him. Roland guessed the headmaster's idea was that they could practise their English while keeping him company. He'd rather not have done any overtime, but with the two boys watching a little shyly for his cue, he shot out of his chair and said, "Of course, of course, come on up."

They'd brought magazines, back issues of *Men's Health India*. Niraj had also brought an ancient black umbrella duct-taped to a metal pole. The boys set it up on a triangular base next to Roland's plastic chair and opened the makeshift parasol. With respectful care, they adjusted it until the pointy-edged shadow was centred on where Roland sat.

But Roland realised *they* didn't have anywhere to sit. They were planning to squat on their haunches. There was no way he was going to sit while they squatted beside him, like some imperial panjandrum with his native attendants. He said, "No, no, no," and moved the chair away. The boys didn't insist but took on an air of consternation. As they watched, Roland squatted where the chair had been. He understood he should still take the shady spot, out of recognition for their efforts. But he gestured for them to squat beside him and said, "Come on. We can swap after a while." He felt like he was turning into a cultural bridge again.

The boys reluctantly got down either side of him. They came as close as they would have to each other, and he got the tang of their bodies. After about a minute, Roland's knees were on fire, and stripes of pain were running down his thighs. He said, "You two stay there," and with relief sat down on the dusty rooftop. He lit a Gold Flake and pretended not to see the boys glancing at each other.

After waiting as short a time as politeness would allow, Niraj said, "So sorry, sir. We must go now."

Arjun echoed what they'd tacitly agreed. "Yes, we must go now. Thank you, sir."

The next afternoon, when Roland came up the stairs, the headmaster's maid was sweeping the rooftop. She'd already cleaned the litter of plastic bags and other crap out of the roof's edges. As she was finishing, the boys arrived with two chairs from the schoolroom. The three of them sat in a row, with Roland mostly in the sliding shadow, still wearing his sunglasses and his Katameya Heights Golf & Tennis baseball cap. Roland tried to learn Japanese, and the boys studied *Men's Health India*, hunching over each snippet of an article like Muslim boys memorising the Qur'an. Sometimes they gazed enviously at his Gold Flakes, but he refused to give cigarettes to children, even nice ones.

After a few days, they relaxed and asked him questions: did he like India? Was it very different from England? Did he like their school? They'd never been as far as Jaipur. After a few more days, they lost some more self-consciousness and peppered him with the questions they actually wanted answers to: did he work out? What kind of music did he like? Was he married? Did he have a car? Roland tried to be a good person for them to talk to, like an older brother.

One day, Niraj brought a borrowed Discman preloaded with a CD they wanted him to hear. As he sat there with the headphones on, the two boys expectant, he realised the music was a pop ballad from the '90s boyband Westlife. Roland started laughing. The boys laughed too. He said, "This is Westlife, isn't it?"

They both beamed. Niraj said, "Yes, Westlife. You know them?"

"Oh yeah, yeah. I remember them." Roland was still laughing, and the boys were thrilled. It occurred to him that the headmaster's scheming wasn't wrong: they were good company.

The book Roland carried up to the roof was M. B. Jansen's *The Making of Modern Japan*, which the back said was "The capstone of Jansen's work as America's foremost historian of Japan." Every time he carried it up the steps, he thought: A book is a thinly sliced block of wood, so how is this book lighter than a block of wood? Is paper less dense than the wood it's made from?

After some chit-chat with Niraj and Arjun, his conscience would eventually force him to announce that it was time for reading. He lit a Gold Flake and tried to focus. But the sentences warped in front of his eyes. No meaning came through. It was difficult, sitting on the rooftop in Nagaur, to believe in the reality of the Tokugawa shogunate.

Sometimes he tried vocabulary instead. There were three separate scripts. He stared at pages of glyphs as if they were abstract art. When not at the school, he had no obligations, and the hours often passed slowly before dinner. Yet, as the weeks went by, he didn't successfully memorise a single *kanji*.

There was one contented and productive week when he drew up a timetable of language-learning, with daily targets and weekly reviews. But the day after he'd finished this, he didn't start the learning it prescribed. He gave himself a week's grace to get ready, and adjusted the timetable accordingly. But on the appointed day he didn't open the textbook. Instead he hid the timetable deep in the security pocket of his suitcase.

If Roland and James's positions had been reversed, if it had been James trying to learn Japanese in India, he would have managed it. He would have blocked out his surroundings and coerced the symbols into his brain. But Roland didn't share that streak of zealotry, the conquistador's readiness to disregard the appeal of the external world as he stamped himself into it. Instead of learning how to politely introduce himself to a Japanese person, he watched a box set of *Friends* that a previous teacher had left in the bottom of the rickety wardrobe. This was what your twenties were meant to be like: a band of pals getting into scrapes in the big city. He would have that in Tokyo for sure, but with the extra twist of foreignness.

The application deadline for JET was rushing nearer with alarming speed. There were pages of questions and several essays to write. Roland hadn't started. The single term he'd signed up for here in Nagaur was already halfway through. The headmaster was asking if he had any friends from Oxford who might like to take over. He felt as if he'd only just arrived.

As he lay in his bed, sweating and watching Ross and Rachel lob jokes back and forth, his thoughts alighted ever more often on the kids themselves. Niraj walked an hour and a half to come to lessons. That did shove a little spike of guilt into Roland's ribs. Especially when he was half-assing it, which he always was. Niraj had invited him to come and meet his family. Roland had promised to find a day when he could take a break from his studies.

He started to wonder what Niraj could do with some real teaching, some real education; at what speed he could learn if instead of being taught by Roland he had someone like Mr Bishop. Roland began trying a little harder with his class. He didn't notice that he was avoiding the headmaster's questions about finding someone for next term.

II

AUGUST 2007

For the first time since university, James and Roland's paths through life — one drawn in straight lines, the other squiggled and meandering — began to cross.

It was one of those warm quiet afternoons when London forgot it was a rainy trading post on the periphery of Europe, and imagined it was not so different after all from Rome or Barcelona. James's cohort at McKinsey were in the pub near their office, and there was a demob feeling in the air.

The Red Lion was in shadow, but the sunshine was slanting down to hit the pavement and wall opposite. The young analysts, with their jackets off, took their drinks from inside and drifted across the road to the hot strip of sunlight. They were just off Jermyn Street, an old-London enclave unknown to the tourists one street away on Piccadilly. There were hereditary tailors, members' clubs and an antiquated-looking strip club with a wrought-iron gas lamp above the entrance.

James's intake had fulfilled their initial two-year contract, and many were leaving. Like satellites, they'd spun once round the Firm to build up speed and were now slingshotting off into deep space. The Firm encouraged them to leave and found yet more McKinsey colonies inside other companies. Soon they would be in another job and indentured to someone new but, right then, they tasted the freedom of departure. In this interval, they were beholden to no one. Those who'd flirted for the past two years suddenly began sleeping together.

James pushed on shoulders and elbows to get through the happy crowd. Not for the first time, he was out of tune with the mood. He'd come straight from his performance review and was looking for Eleni.

They never met away from the office and had no expectation they ever would. But while they were at work, talent recognised talent.

Someone shifted aside to let James past, and there was Roland. There was a brief lag before James's brain connected to the right file of information. Roland looked very different: as tanned as a surf instructor, sandy hair gone light, very skinny. He was dressed in grubby cream-coloured linen pyjamas, which stuck out among the black and white of London office wear. He had a pint and cigarette in one hand, and his other arm was slung around the shoulders of a guy James didn't know. Seeing him was a surprise. But to James, Roland was nobody in particular, and he carried on.

For Roland, it was less surprising. Since he'd got back, all he'd done was see people from the past. Anything familiar gave him a hit of happiness: the Boots at the airport; the bored, narky voice of the security announcements; the neat moderate furnishings of England. He was amazed to discover there was a new £20 note. And it was purple! On the empty mid-morning bus out of Heathrow, he sat up behind the driver and chattered the whole way to Guildford.

To him, James looked stressed and unhealthy. His big handsome head was puffy and yellowish, and the beginnings of a belly pressed against the front of his shirt. He didn't seem to be having a good time. And Roland was having so much of a good time, he wanted everyone else to as well.

James found Eleni in the sunshine, listening to voicemails with her face turned upwards and her eyes closed. On the window ledge behind her was a glass of white wine and a pack of Marlboro Lights. She had a pint for him. When she saw him, she lifted it with her fingertips, trying not to get beer on her hands, and held it out.

She said, "So it went badly?"

He kept her waiting while he drank, then nodded once. He stared at the advert in the blanked-out window of the shirtmaker's behind her. A man in a hoodie skateboarding. Why? When the faculty of speech came back, he told her, "They said what they always say."

"Not quite meshing."

"Not meshing, not fully engaged, etcetera."

Eleni could feel the negative energy crackling off him. "Did they say anything else?"

"Oh, apparently they sometimes wonder if I'm really trying."

"And did —"

James talked over her. "If you can do the work without really trying, you'd think that would be a good thing." Eleni didn't like to be talked over, and she performatively waited to hear if he had more to add. He said, "Sorry I interrupted you. And yes, obviously I understand that ability's not the question. It's *engagement*." He rolled his eyes. "What the fuck do they want me to do? Organise a team dinner at my house? Yes, I see, that is what they want. It's not enough to do my actual job at least as well as anyone else."

Eleni had been ready to offer a sympathy routine but, since it didn't seem to be required, she moved on. "Did they say anything about next steps?"

James gazed up to the distant sky. A pigeon high above made a banking turn and caught the sunlight on the back of its wings. He said, "They think it would be a good idea for me to consider exploring other avenues of career development."

Eleni went so tense she was almost shaking, and jabbed her finger at him. "James! You need to do something about this right now. Or" — she dropped her voice — "they really absolutely will kick you out."

James couldn't speak. He went to take another gulp of his drink, and Eleni grabbed his forearm to stop him. "Okay. The first thing you're going to do is —"

"I know what you're going to say."

"Why haven't you done it then?"

"Eleni, I'm never going to be the most popular guy at McKinsey."

"No, you're not, but if you were just averagely likeable, you wouldn't be having these problems." It was probably true. Eleni's own review was basically just her presenting a list of demands. "You can find, like, a *mode* that makes sense to people. For example: my thing is that people find it surprising I'm so pushy. And while they're being surprised, they usually do what I've asked. And after they're done being surprised, they're like, 'Oh, Eleni's so pushy, ha ha, you better give her what she wants or she'll bite your head off.' It's not rocket science."

"So, what? You think I should be pushier?"

"No. You would come across as arrogant and everyone would hate you. Maybe your thing is that you have no social skills so once people expect that, they'll let you get away with all kinds of stuff."

"Okay, but I'm not –"

"I'm not finished." Eleni was so exasperated she was quietly shouting at him. "You could use the fact that they're probably going to kick you out. That's a narrative right there. Reach out to some partners and say you've seen the error of your ways. Something's clicked. Now you get it. The lost sheep wants mentoring. This is so obvious. I don't know why we even still need to talk about it."

James hadn't expected failure to be so gentle. There was no mention of disappointment, no telling off. The HR people made supposedly flattering references to his "undoubted skills". With seamless, implacable cordiality, they talked as if it were merely a matter of "fit". His being there was an honest mistake. The Firm had ordered the wrong part. There was no opportunity for him to struggle. The struggle had been over the previous two years and somehow, bafflingly, he'd never got a grip on it.

There was enough cash in his account to move to a cheap country – an ugly corner of Sicily, perhaps. He'd get a routine job where no one would look for him, maybe gutting fish on a boat that paid cash in hand and didn't leave an electronic trail. Over a couple of years, he'd learn Sicilian, and with his black hair and his complexion, he could probably start to pass for a local. He would abjure all ambition. He would never strive. He would never act on his natural tendency to rise. He wouldn't save his wages to buy a stake in the boat. He wouldn't gradually buy out that first boat and then take out a loan on a second. He wouldn't over decades become the boss of the Messina fishing fleet. He would just lie quiet, like someone in witness protection. James Drayton, who'd been sacked from McKinsey after two years, would disappear completely.

But he was still young, and this was only the first real defeat his pride had suffered. His weariness was still outmatched by fury. He did not pause to consider whether the HR people were right, or whether McKinsey was still the right path upwards. He refused to lose. His mind, in desperation, grasped for the problem-solving patterns of thought that McKinsey had trained in him:

1. He needed something drastic enough to be a game-changer.
2. His people skills weren't good enough to provide it.
3. Ergo, he had to use his one competitive advantage: analysis.

He said, "Actually, with the stuff we've been looking at" – he and Eleni had been seconded to an oil and gas company in Aberdeen – "I've got an idea for a deep study of where the sector is going."

Eleni started shaking her head.

"I don't think anyone has realised that shale is going to create a massive price crash. And because –"

She cut him off. "That's a terrible plan. How many oil-price forecasts do you think get published every day? There's literally an entire industry whose only job is to do that."

James didn't say anything. Rather than argue fruitlessly, he drank his drink and looked around. They could hear the muffled sounds of traffic on Piccadilly. Reflexively he checked his email and scanned the alumni circular: someone had become John McCain's deputy campaign manager; another was now chairman of the Halifax.

After a few minutes, they began talking about whether Eleni would join the family shipping business. Her uncles said they would come up with an interesting job for her. But working for them could mean envelopment, suffocation, a permanent end to upward progress. The company hierarchy was fixed by how much of it you owned. She would always be subordinate to her uncles, and in time she'd be subordinate to their children. But you could move a lot of levers in the real world if you went – in one jump – from analyst to director.

They were strategising when Roland came over. He'd become a bit more smelly and dishevelled and was radiating contentment. He reached out a hand and eagerly said, "James! Hi! I don't know if you remember me. We were in the same college." He splashed his hand over his heart. "I'm Roland."

James warily shook the hot, damp hand. Unhappiness made him rude, and he said, "Of course I remember. We rowed in the same boat."

Roland smacked himself too hard on the forehead. "Of course! So stupid of me. Oh, that was so fun, wasn't it? Going on the boat. The misty mornings." He registered Eleni, and said, "Oh, I'm so sorry, I'm Roland. Me and James were at uni together." After shaking hands, Eleni put hers in her pocket and wiped her palm on the lining.

Since James didn't offer anything but just glared at him, Roland bumbled on. "James, I just saw you and" – he laughed – "I remembered that time you sent those homeless guys into that corporate recruitment thing. That was *so funny*."

James's temper flashed out. "Did you come over just to remind me of that?"

Roland lifted his eyebrows. "Oh, I'm sorry. You guys are obviously in the middle of something, and I just came and crashed your conversation. Sorry! Great to see you, James. And great to meet you, um . . ."

Eleni, despite the fact he'd just forgotten her name, couldn't allow herself to be quite that bad-mannered. She said, "No, no. We were just chatting. Tell us more about yourself. Why are you dressed like that? Have you been on a gap year?"

Roland was delighted by this sign of welcome and yelled: "YES!"

Some of the others glanced over.

"I've been teaching in a school in a tiny town in the middle of the desert in India for two years. I was actually only meant to be there for a couple of months. Well, actually, I was meant to be in Japan, but – oh God, it's a terrible story." He'd been telling this to everyone he met, embellishing it with haplessness and whimsy. He launched in. "Basically, I got a 2:2 in my finals."

James said, "You got a 2:2?" It was like announcing he had erectile dysfunction.

"Oh yeah, I totally fucked it." Roland clasped his head with the hand that wasn't holding his pint. "The reality is, I just didn't do the work, and so I didn't know the stuff. You know, that's the reality, isn't it?"

In James, the pain of failure was soothed a little. "So, you ran away to India?"

"Yeah, I guess I kind of did. To a place called Nagaur, in Rajasthan."

"Was it interesting?"

"Yeah, in some ways it was kind of absolutely incredible. I wasn't a very good teacher, but" – Roland shrugged, lifting his hands – "I had this one pupil called Niraj, who just . . . it's not like he's some undiscovered maths genius, but if he had ten years of real school his life would be completely different. I was only meant to be there for a term but, you know."

James, like so many others, was drawn to him. He made mishap seem so commonplace, so normal and non-threatening. Eleni asked, "So how come you came back?"

Roland breathed in deeply, to signal that this was the knotty part of the tale. "Well," he said, "I realised – and I know this is selfish – but I kind of realised that either I could stay there forever, or not, you know? I mean, it wasn't like in the first year I'd help twenty kids and in the second year forty, and in the third year sixty, and so on. It was always going to be just twenty kids. And out of them, only one or two could really benefit. It's just not, it's not –"

"Scalable," said Eleni.

"Exactly! Teaching isn't scalable."

James said, "So what's your plan now?"

"I don't know really. Everyone's telling me I should come work at McKinsey, but I don't think they'd take someone with a 2:2."

With that, James was back in his internal funhouse. He barely noticed when Roland returned to his friends. He must come up with something so brilliant it was irrefutable, like the obliterating ultra-white light of a nuclear bomb. His mind worried at it like at a jigsaw where all the pieces are the same colour, turning his hunches round and round to see if they combined. Roland was forgotten.

James stopped going to the after-work drinks on Fridays, his only social contact. He simply didn't have much disposable time: from Sunday evening to Thursday evening, he was up in Aberdeen, advising Welltec, a company that built robots for oil wells. Fridays, he was in the London office for training he'd probably never need. Then, on Friday at five p.m., he was free, and his real work began.

Instead of going to the pub, he walked back to his parents' house in Canonbury. He paid out those fifty-five minutes from his pinched little purse of time because his brain performed better if he let it go soft before changing track. When he arrived home, he went straight up the stairs to his dad's study. He kicked his tight shoes off under the desk and tossed his suit jacket onto the armchair, reckless of wrinkles. His notes were in the drawer his dad had cleared for him. Then he flexed his toes and began turning his jigsaw pieces round and round. He paused for sleep, meals, meditative trips to the bathroom and a bath on Saturdays.

His parents had lived here since they were PhD students. It was a tall, narrow townhouse, with curving window seats, corniced ceilings and lots of stairs. They bought it with their PhD stipends and a renovation grant from the council, which was trying to bring middle-class people into the area. When they arrived, the neighbourhood was dingy and violent, the brick house fronts still velvety black with the soot of factories shuttered decades before. On their street lived squatters, an IRA man and penniless war widows on peppercorn rents.

Since then, they'd been part of the generation for whom no toil nor thrift was as financially significant as buying a house before the boom. In many years, the house earned more in value by sitting there than they did by going to their jobs. Given their relatively frugal habits, it afforded them a life unconstrained by money.

For them it would have been inconceivable – a joke, even – to become a management consultant. Because their university days were before

Thatcher deregulated the City and made careers there irresistibly lucrative, none of their clever friends went into finance. They were diplomats, spies, writers, politicians, academics or barristers. When James said he was joining McKinsey, his parents frowned and worried and tried to be understanding. His dad solemnly told him, "I'll support you in whatever you do." Despite his explanations, they ultimately believed the only possible motive was some misguided and servile interest in the activities of the rich, the career equivalent of *Forbes* magazine.

His dad was a music scholar who wrote about how the classical tradition reached its final flowering in Leonard Bernstein. His mum was an economic historian specialising in why Britain's industrial might withered to nothing in the 1970s and '80s. On their walls were framed posters from exhibitions they went to before James was born. In the downstairs loo, in an act of brazenly false modesty, was a typewritten note from Bernstein to James's dad, thanking him for "hearing so clearly". Above the bath was a shelf of books chosen for reading in the tub: the *Paris Review* interviews, Auden's account of his trip to Iceland, Nabokov's essays on Russian literature. In the guest bedroom were shelves of books on German and Japanese industrial policy. Crammed in here and there were author copies of his parents' books translated into Swedish (his dad's) or Korean (his mum's).

James, ensconced in solitary concentration, in a room dedicated to the life of the mind, felt his hulking fears shrink back to their rightful size. What intelligent person could seriously get wound up by the diktats of some corporate HR team?

Outside the window was a green canyon – the hidden strip of gardens between two rows of houses. The vast shaggy head of an enormous tree – a beech? – filled the airspace in front of him. It seemed a solid mass, but when the breeze ran through it, the leafy multitude bunched or split like a shoal of fish. Watching the complexity of thousands of translucent green objects in continual motion – and the sunlight projecting their swirling shadows onto the lawn below – his future at McKinsey seemed too trivial to contemplate.

As he worked, James felt unusually fresh and lucid, like a distance runner who'd been cooped up inside too long and was back out on the road. He should have been fatigued, but on Saturday and Sunday mornings he snapped awake before the alarm, his mind already up and moving. He felt lighter, stronger, more awake, than he had since finals. Using his biro as scalpel, he delicately separated the layers of causality that determined the price of oil. In that question lay the entire intricacy and sum of the human world. It was the invisible net that connected the heat in his parents' radiators to Shia militias planting roadside bombs in Iraq; to Texan roughnecks figuring out how to extract shale oil; to millions of Chinese people buying their first car and European countries passing laws against carbon emissions.

There was also the oil market itself, which was self-aware, skittering up or down in response to its own expectations and regularly panicked or elated by the mob psychology of traders.

It was the hardest problem he knew. The questions were as numberless as the leaves outside. Whether Iraq would disintegrate was only one leaf. The prospects for China were another. No human could encompass them all, but sometimes their aggregate movement could be patterned and predicted. His theory was that shale fracking would succeed. That would make America the third big producer of oil, alongside the Russians and Saudis. That new glut would, according to the law of supply and demand, crash the oil price. Within, say – he picked a number – five years.

But gradually the feeling grew that this wasn't quite it. For all his rigour and audacity, it didn't quite strike that clean, satisfying note in his head, the sound of something big and important being understood at once. He could maybe point out some consequences of a price crash: Kremlin aggressive, Middle East turbulent, less interest in green stuff. People thought their lives were about what they read in newspapers, but James was beginning to believe that all those happenings were merely the surface phenomena of something deeper: the cross-currents of history, of which two were technology and economics. But Eleni was right: people were always predicting the oil price would go up or down.

On the Sunday evening flights up to Aberdeen, to his job at Welltec, his brain was swollen and sensitive in its cranial case. He could neck three complimentary G&Ts in the hour-long flight. The gin helped. He kept his eyes closed, and the white noise of the engines throbbed dully through the seats. His thoughts were shallow and diffuse.

Unexpectedly, they often drifted towards Roland. What he imagined was a blur: colours, noise, clichés of India. He was too drained to experience surprise, but it was true that since university Roland had chalked up one run on life's scoreboard and James hadn't. It was only helping kids, but still. Maybe James could ask him about it.

It was interesting about teaching not being scalable. You could carry one kid up the hill to better prospects, but then you just had to trudge back down for another. It was too Sisyphean, too crude a slog, to do for long. It must be possible to invent, to improve ... and particularly in India, where the schools must be rubbish. The Chinese next door had been at the same level as India when James was born; now they had tech giants and space lasers. Why not India? Why weren't their schools better? A classic conundrum for the puzzle-solving minds of management consultants.

On the flight, sitting with his eyes closed, James made the near-weightless decision to figure it out.

The next Friday, he gathered his thick sheaf of notes on the oil price, carried them down to the kitchen and stuffed them in the bin. His parents found them later and wondered, hoping but not saying, not wanting to jinx it, but giving each other meaningful looks: maybe McKinsey would soon be no more than a learning experience.

When he went back up to his dad's study, James was crushed by tiredness. He was twenty-three and hadn't slept with a girl in this calendar year. The HR people had emailed, still unassailably cordial, to set a date for his leaving the Firm. For a while he stared blankly out the window at the green mass of swaying leaves. He wasn't willing to leave the desk, and watched *The Wire* on his laptop for two days straight.

The following weekend, enough energy had trickled into the reservoir for him to begin. Once he did, he could feel that this was a better subject.

Like a straighter toss for a tennis serve, it let him reach further and hit harder. Which he did. By Saturday afternoon, some fourteen hours into reading through Google and the McKinsey intranet, he was sure he understood the future of India. After the complexity of oil, schools seemed very straightforward. The crux was that each school was given too meagre a ration of cash: enough to keep going but not enough to improve, like scraping the last blob of jam across too big a slice of toast.

The answer was to take funding away from the destitute, hopeless areas and give it to the promising ones. There'd be complaints, of course, but it was better that some succeed than that all stagnate together. You'd choose cities where a supply of better-educated workers could jolt the local industries into a higher gear. As those industries sped up, they'd pay more taxes into the local schools and colleges, and so, onwards and upwards, the virtuous circle whirring round and round like an accelerating engine.

The Chinese had built one colossal engine to power their country's rise: manufacturing for export. India might be able to turn some of its cities into an IT engine, a pharma engine, a petrochemicals engine. With a dozen of those whirring away, you might be able to lift a billion people very slightly off the ground.

As for so many previous Englishmen, it seemed so simple to alter the destiny of India. The material stuff of the world, matter in the form of pencils, schoolrooms and human bodies, was susceptible to reason. Facts were facts. They could be comprehended and orchestrated, even from a quiet study four thousand miles away. He was content – despite the HR people, and despite Eleni believing he'd given up – because he knew, certainly, absolutely, independent of anyone's opinion, that he, like Roland, was doing something that contained a single grain of inherent worth.

His picture of the country he assembled out of numbers. Each city got a score for its roads, how often its grid blacked out, the distance to the nearest container port. Then exam results. Economic growth. Whether the local industry was favourable (pharmaceuticals) or unfavourable (textiles). Early one Sunday morning, while his parents were still asleep, he finished typing these scores into his spreadsheet. He pasted in the formula to combine the rankings. Excel computed for half a second and then printed the winning cities into a new column.

Number one city: Surat, on the coast, a few hours north of Mumbai. This region, Gujarat, was where the fuel for India came ashore, ferried from the Middle East on a fleet of tankers. The biggest refinery ever built was there, turning oil into feedstocks for plastic, ink, paint, fertiliser. And for obscure historical reasons, a local sect, the Surati Jains, controlled the global trade in new diamonds. Last of all, the regional premier, a guy called Narendra Modi, was considered sound. Okay. Made sense. This was where India should build its finest schools.

James went outside into the garden, where the early-morning air was cool and the grass dewy under his bare feet. The enormous tree loomed over him, its outer leaves rippling. It looked like a great green brain with electrical signals running across its surface.

For a few days afterwards, he was at peace. He showed his report to no one. One day he might send it to Roland. Freed for a while from the overhanging whip of ambition, James discovered curiosity. He walked down to the Tate Modern to see paintings by a Brazilian artist he'd never heard of. Back up in Aberdeen, he surprised his colleagues by asking them about themselves.

Eventually, his contentment waned. HR were getting quite insistent that he should reply. He looked around on Google for organisations with an interest in Indian schools. The Department for International Development allocated grants there. He printed the report on his dad's screeching printer and put it in a manilla envelope. He could hardly be bothered to write DFID's address on the front but did so, and sent it off.

Chris Mapother, a still young but demotivated partner at McKinsey, pushed thoughtfully out of the slowly revolving office door. It was the end of the day. He should be going to a client dinner but instead he was heading to the Tube, and home.

His wife Kitty, who was at Deloitte, had been offered a job as head of their Madrid office. It was certainly possible for Chris to move to McKinsey España, a low-stakes backwater run by slim, elegant hidalgos with a penchant for leather – boots, gloves, briefcases – who all seemed to be related to each other.

It would mean accepting he'd never reach the very top. He still had a comparatively ample amount of time to get there . . . But he imagined his troublesome lower back loosening in the warmth, some knot in his core relaxing. No more physio at lunchtime. His boys could grow up bilingual. Tanned, too. Indefinably Hispanised. He could become slightly Hispanised himself. Maybe he'd start wearing hats. He'd spare his boys the stress of London school entrance if he could. Kitty had to let them know by the end of the week.

Chris wandered along Jermyn Street, where gym-fit men and women in flattering office clothes were streaming out of hedge funds and overtaking him as they flowed towards Piccadilly. Black cabs and a huge, boxy, silvery-grey Roller shuffled along nose to tail. From behind him, someone called out, "Chris!"

He didn't hear and carried on.

"Chris!"

This time it reached him.

"Chris, hang on." It was a colleague, another youngish partner, Solomon Chen, who said, "You heading to the Tube?"

They walked together and Solomon asked, "Did you ever work with Sophie Cox?"

"Don't think so. She was one of ours, right?"

"Yeah. Good egg. Went to the Civil Service. She's at DFID now, and she just emailed to say she's been sent some kind of proposal on spec from an analyst on your team."

Chris stopped. "*What?*"

"I know. It's super-weird. Something to do with funding schools in India."

"But . . ."

Hedge-funders were stepping around them on the pavement. Chris felt tricked somehow. His own juniors doing things behind his back. "Who the fuck sent it?"

"Some kid called James Drayton. Who is he?"

"Oh, Jesus."

"What?"

Chris motioned his head, and they carried on walking. "He's the one – do you remember, a couple of years ago, a new recruit at Kitzbühel stood up and explained to everyone that the McKinsey way was a cult of personality around Bower and really it's no more than smoke and mirrors."

"That was him?"

"That was him."

"Ah." Solomon grinned and said, "I mean . . . is he totally wrong?"

Chris didn't take that up.

"So what's he like?"

"A pain in my ass is what he's like."

They reached the mouth of the Tube, on the corner of Piccadilly Circus. Like a drain it was sucking in torrents of office-clad people from every direction. The crowd rushing down the steps was so thick that Chris and Solomon had to push out to one side and stand in the entrance of a bank.

Solomon went on. "Sophie was asking if his analysis was solid."

"Yeah, there's no problem with that. He's a clever kid. But we're actually kicking him out because he's such an awkward bastard. Doesn't want to be a team player. I'll call him tomorrow and tell him he's done."

"Oh, no. No, no. Don't do that. Because, umm, the thing is, they want to do it. DFID."

"*What?*"

"Yeah, I know. Apparently they've got this real pain point around showing that the money they spend actually has an effect. And he's come up with some metrics they can use. They want us to build it out and advise them where to allocate the cash."

Chris couldn't speak. He was a proper person. He was a partner at McKinsey, for Christ's sake, only in his forties, and the universe was trying to play some prank on him.

Solomon said, "Yeah. Crazy. When was the last time an analyst brought in a contract? It's not huge money, but even so. I'm sure we'll be able to sell them some more stuff as we go along."

"So, we can't get rid of him."

"Well, ultimately . . . I hadn't really thought about it. Ultimately, I guess it's up to you. But it'll look pretty off if we take this contract and then say we've sacked the guy whose idea it was."

Chris thought: That's it. I'm going to Spain.

III

In this way, three years slipped almost unnoticed into the past. James and Roland's possible destinies, the protean turmoil within them, resolved into a small number of almost-solid shapes. The open field before them on the day they left university narrowed into a forking path. James would never study law or be elected to Parliament. Roland would never learn Japanese. They would never become MI6 agents in Afghanistan or sail the Pacific or prospect for diamonds in Angola, or any of the other lives at the outer edges of the possible.

Three years before, they'd been like marbles dropped onto the apex of a domed roof: they could have rolled in any direction, sent one way or another by the slightest dent or bobble in its surface. But now they'd started rolling down, even if only a few inches, picking up speed, and to go back to the other possibilities already disappearing behind the top of the dome, they'd have had to run against gravity.

That autumn, in 2007, McKinsey took in an enlarged cohort of recruits to keep up with the boom-time expansion of its business, and Roland scraped in. The HR woman who rang with the news wanted to impress upon him how lucky he was. He was an "outside-the-box hire". In her experience, candidates with unconventional CVs could sometimes offer new perspectives. The Firm was all for "cognitive diversity".

Roland knew the deeper reason he'd been accepted. When his interviewers asked for examples of when he'd encountered a challenge, he spun them colourful Indian tales about camel salesmen and the furious fakir dragging himself through the streets of Nagaur. The three middle-aged men on the panel brightened up out of the boredom of interviewing. There were a few chuckles. One interrupted to say, "I actually travelled round Rajasthan and the rest of India for a few months before Oxford. You'll know it much better than me now. I drank so much of that syrupy Indian whisky. Oh, what's it called?"

"There's one called Bagpiper. Or Royal Stag?"

"No, no. It was, argh, sorry – Officer's Choice! Ha! Really sweet rotgut stuff. They've got epaulettes on the branding. Funny, really, that that kind of empire nostalgia still has a big market. You could get it everywhere that wasn't dry."

For a couple of minutes, Roland sat quietly, wearing a friendly expression, while the panellists talked about countries they'd visited in their youth. By the time their attention came back to Roland, he guessed he had the job.

When he started at the office, the partner who'd travelled in Rajasthan sought him out a couple of times in a wistful mood, to talk about something he couldn't name, some feeling that evanesced even as he brought it out.

But while Roland and James each navigated his little course, on the other side of the Atlantic a storm was picking up. It began in dozens of unremarkable places at once. Rather than moving through water and air, its element was money. In flimsy new housing developments in Florida and in beaten-down towns in Wisconsin and Ohio, whole streets' worth of homeowners were defaulting on their mortgages. They'd kept up with the payments for the first two years while they were still on the hope-inducing introductory rates. But now the rates were going up. Some families packed what would fit in the car and flitted their houses at night. Others stumbled on from month to month through the rising flood, falling in, hauling themselves back out and finally, exhausted, surrendering to a force far greater than themselves.

These unpayable mortgages had been so profitable for banks, and there were so many of them, and they were supposedly so safe, that the banks packaged them up into little bricks. These bricks became the foundation for ever more fantastical structures, the invisible arches and flying buttresses of high finance; the tasteful marble-clad foyers, the rooftop helipads, the towers of Wall Street. Because the banks expected to have so much cash coming in, they let credit flow into everything. Companies were always hiring; restaurants were opening; people felt prosperous and were always spending, which made everything go even faster. But the bricks were rotten. And as they cracked and split under the weight, the banks began to crumble.

JANUARY 2008

When Roland joined McKinsey, he was thrilled to imagine himself as a faceless corporate drone. He got his first credit card, went to Selfridges and bought a suit like Patrick Bateman's in *American Psycho*: double-breasted, charcoal, with a pinstripe. In the rush of giving out so much money at once, he also bought a pair of Italian shoes that the sales assistant told him were "hand-tooled". If you stuck your nose inside, you could inhale the musty bovine scent of an Italian workshop.

He grinned on the Tube in the mornings as he pretended to be a commuter like other commuters. And he had a ragingly good time in Kitzbühel. A gang of new recruits snuck off to a nearby après-ski and jumped up and down to comical Austrian house music, its electronic beat layered with a brass oompah band. The recruits played truth-or-dare and snogged on the dancefloor. Roland went back with a chic and vampy Parisian-Lebanese girl who passed out drunk and fully clothed on his bed. In the morning, they went down for breakfast and told this anecdote to the others.

Whenever he had to look at the actual substance of his new job, he was catastrophically bored. But even that he quite enjoyed, since the boringness was so authentic, like going to New York and it being just like the movies. Being assigned to a project on Indian schools was a drag. Apparently, James had asked for him, which was mildly flattering. He didn't imagine it had any importance. Many quite random uni contemporaries remembered him more vividly than he did them.

When James called him into a meeting room, a tight little cubicle with a whiteboard and a flipchart, it was the first time they'd ever been alone together. James was nervous. Over the past months, he'd been asked many times where he'd got his idea from. No, he didn't have a background in education. No, he'd never been to India. He told the honchos at McKinsey and DFID, "Well, you're always reading and talking to people, and you get an overview of things." It was perfectly legitimate to misdirect the competition.

The reality, that it came from a chance conversation with Roland, was too haphazard to admit. It was the opposite of having an overview. Instead of observing humanity's colourful goings-on from above, and selecting an optimal endeavour, he'd just bumped into someone. For a moment he'd let his direction be set, like a snooker ball's, by collision. It was embarrassing and unrepresentative. An anomaly. It also made him look a bit weird and pathetic. It was too big a response to a forgettable chat. It hinted at obsession, confused feelings, stalking. He had to bring it up before Roland did.

Roland came into the cubicle and tried to connect, overdoing the greeting. He exclaimed, "Hey, man, isn't this so fun?" and went in for the hug, noticing too late that James was bringing up a hand to shake. They had to hug then, excruciatingly.

When they released, James was formal, professional. He said, "Yes, I'm sure it'll be very productive. Please take a seat."

"Thanks. How're you doing? Isn't it so crazy that we've ended up working together? The two of us sitting here having, like, an actual business meeting? Look at these shoes I'm wearing."

James leaned his head to the side of the table to see them and said, "They're very nice." He noticed that he'd subconsciously arranged his lever arch files into a low defensive dyke, and began disassembling it.

After McKinsey agreed to keep him on, James asked his sister Cleo for advice on how to talk to people. He acted as if this was a perfectly ordinary practical question, and she did the same. She said he shouldn't try to be super funny and charming right away; he could build up to that. If he just tried to frankly articulate what he was thinking, they would at least know what he meant. And since he meant well, that would come through. He hadn't quite mastered the technique, but he was persevering.

He said, "You're right: it's strange. And, related to that, I want to tell you something. I asked to have you on my team, on one level, because I thought your experience in India would be helpful."

Roland started talking. "Sure thing." Only as he spoke did he realise James meant to go on. But now James had paused. Roland made a clumsy after-you gesture, and James went on: "I was just saying, it'll be very useful to have you. We've only got a small budget for travelling to India, so there's a real risk of missing some contextual factors."

Roland said, "Sure. Great. I'd love to help. But surely there must be lots of actual Indians in McKinsey as well?"

James stiffened. He found this notion anti-intellectual, as if understanding a subject was about ethnic precedence rather than rational inquiry. "I don't think you need to be Indian to read a spreadsheet."

Roland could tell he'd made some incomprehensible error. "No, no, of course not. You know, I was actually meant to be studying Japanese. It's a funny story actually."

James said, "Yes. You told me."

Roland tried again to break through this bullshit corporate formality. "Maybe you were right to go straight into work rather than travelling first. But you've always been like that. Remember when we were in that boat together? It really is *weird*, isn't it, that we're doing this together now."

This gave James an extra jolt of stiffness. His face closed off and he began arranging his lever arch files. He gave Roland a little speech. "Roland. I am, um . . . *very happy* you're on the team." He glanced at Roland, who smiled and nodded encouragingly. James was much odder than he'd realised. "As you say, we've met several times before. But I'm – of course – your line manager for this project, and I can't give you any special treatment."

Suddenly Roland thought he understood: James was a newly elevated junior member of the boss class, and Roland was an outside-the-box hire with a 2:2. James didn't want some compromising friendship. It really was about the contextual knowledge. Oh God. And he'd been greasing up to James with this boat stuff. He cringed and lowered his eyes. "Of course. Of course."

James had now peeled back the outer layers of his subject and arrived at the core. "So, obviously, we spoke about Indian schools."

"I know. I know."

"And you had these ideas about scalability."

This was so painful. "I get it. No special treatment."

"But I want to be candid that we spoke about it."

All Roland could hear was humiliation. He said, "Yeah. I feel like, maybe we can make a fresh start from here? You know, it's not uni any more. Maybe let's just get on with the job."

"Oh. Okay. Is that what you'd prefer?"

"Yeah. Yeah, I really would."

Afterwards, Roland felt he'd been put in his place. It was totally fair enough. There was no denying he'd got a 2:2. This was grown-up life. He was an insignificant cog. He should be grateful to James. Even if James was a massive dweeb and the job was so boring he sometimes . . . No. It was a great job. Lots of people would be glad to have it.

Where they worked was genuinely incredible. They were on Whitehall. At one end of the street was Parliament, and at the other was Trafalgar Square. Power coursed out of Westminster and rushed down into the buildings where the business of governing was conducted. It poured into the Treasury first and ran on, dwindling, past departments like Health and Defence, past a statue to a forgotten general just labelled CLIVE, and there, almost at Trafalgar Square, across the road from McDonald's, was the Department for International Development.

Outside the door there was a real security guard, armed in the British manner with only a badge and a hi-vis waistcoat. In Egypt he'd have had a Kalashnikov. When Roland dodged around tourists in his pinstripe suit, or held up his pass for the guard, he felt like an insider: invited, admitted, a Londoner. In Cairo, he'd grown up knowing he was on the map's periphery, in a far-flung outpost of the mother country, connected to home by a long, thin red cord of Britishness. Now, in the centre of central London, among black cabs, red buses, and horse guards with swords and silver helmets, he felt like he, Roland Mackenzie, was balancing on the pivot point of the world.

They made their spreadsheets in a drab, modern conference room with triangular plastic speakers on the table for dialling into calls. James presided at the head like a stern father presiding over Christmas dinner. This whole hoo-ha of government millions and Indian development had been magicked from the recesses of James's brain. He'd come up with it in his spare time. Who does that? It was alienating.

The team took from James their cues on how to behave. And the cue was: work silently. In the mornings, as they unpacked their bags, there was no chit-chat to ease them into the harness. James was already there before them. Any conversations that started in the corridor died as they entered the room.

Roland found the quiet unbearable. It was so bizarre – it was so *inhumane* – to sit next to each other for hours without talking. Because expat kids didn't have menial summer jobs, his only previous work experience was smoking on the rooftop in Nagaur. He couldn't believe that this was what grown-ups had been doing in offices all day.

He sat as far away as he could from James's supervision, at the foot of the table. His smart new collar chafed his neck. The overhead lights glowed in their boxes. He would watch an entire hour tick down in the clock on his screen. To make himself look productive, he'd occasionally press a series of buttons to switch the clock face to a digital display, and back again. But once the hour had wound down to nothing, there might still be another six hours to go. Six! He'd never done anything for six hours.

The only interruption, part annoyance, part blessed relief, was people asking, "James, how do you want me to do this?" Which began to strike Roland as ironic, actually, given that he was the one who'd literally just spent two years in India. But the only questions he got weren't really questions: "Roland, could you make sure your datasets are laid out in order?"

The days were so long that by the end of them he'd forgotten what happened that morning. He barely had time to meet some pals and find a place for drinks and get some sleep before he was expected to turn up again. Five days out of every seven. Forever. It was like he was the only one who could see they were all trapped in the matrix.

Sometimes James would stride down one side of the long conference table, frowning and authoritative, to look over someone's shoulder at their laptop. Roland had to hurry to close his MSN Messenger chats with friends being similarly tortured elsewhere. It was insane that you had to pretend to be interested in your job and use these lame phrases like "pinging things over" "by close of play". Occasionally James came to look at Roland's screen, standing so close that Roland could feel the nearness of his body. And yet there was no human exchange. It was so surreal he wanted to nuzzle his head into James's midriff, just to make everyone break character.

Every now and then, James would summon their attention and give a weirdly over-enunciated speech: "I thought I should lay out some guard rails, or maybe handholds. To be frank, I'm not sure what the right metaphor is . . ." For the first time, Roland had an inkling that his twenties were not inexhaustible.

He could quit and go back to travelling. But in hostels in Mumbai and Goa he'd met sad, diminished characters who'd decided not to stick it out in normal life. Their conversation wasn't great tales of the road; it was gloating about discounted bus tickets and petulantly complaining about the Indians. They didn't seem to like the Indians very much, and never tipped. These supposed perma-travellers spent their days standing around bored as white extras in the background of Bollywood films. You got the equivalent of a tenner plus lunch. It didn't look like freedom.

The team, minus James, began having lunch together. They ate sandwiches and salads bundled up on the steps outside the National Gallery, looking down onto Trafalgar Square. Away from their laptops, the McKinsey–DFID joint team were eight quite similar young people. Most had left provincial towns and cities to go up to Oxford or Cambridge and then to London. The marks that came from their diverging career choices were still superficial, a few years in, and hadn't yet sunk into the marrow.

What loosened them up was laughing at Roland. He liked to lie full-length on one of the chilly steps, his head on the moss-smelling stone, and feel the winter sunlight on his eyelids. A weak memento of his afternoons in Nagaur. He loved to hear tourists' incomprehensible conversations, knowing that they were spending their money and time to visit this place where he, Roland Mackenzie, ate his lunch whenever he felt like it.

Twelve years he'd lived in Cairo, and he couldn't even exactly remember which pharaoh built which pyramid. Embarrassing. But there must be enough masterpieces in the National Gallery to teach himself the whole history of Western art. An hour in the gallery each lunchtime. He wouldn't even notice it. What an amazing thing to do.

Their group's only native Londoner, a girl called Sarah from Clapham Old Town, said, "Hey Roland. Don't you and James know each other from before?"

Roland opened his eyes and propped himself up on his elbows. "Yeah. We were in the same college. We even rowed in the same boat in first year."

"So, are you, like, his protégé or something?"

The others were watching.

"How do you mean?" Roland sat up fully. He didn't see where she was going with this, but it was clearly going somewhere. She was harder-edged than the rest; fast-walking, impatient, her opinions decided. They were once talking about a nightclub opposite Victoria Station and, when someone asked if she'd been there, she said, "Not since I was like fifteen. If you're happy to let some lechy old men grind up on you, you'll love it."

When Roland was fifteen, his big social event was the Katameya Heights ping-pong tournament.

Sarah was suppressing a grin that, needing a way out, tweaked the other angles of her face. "I just thought there must be some reason he let you get away with that today."

Roland had the familiar sensation of a trapdoor opening beneath him. "Get away with what?"

"Oh, you know, when he came over to ask you for the exam results in Gujarat."

Roland sank back onto the step and covered his eyes.

"You were just staring into space. And then, when you said, 'Sorry, what?' He said, 'Have you got the Gujarat exam results?' And you said, 'I never went to Gujarat.'"

The others yelled with laughter. But the laughter was friendly, the attention benign.

He flicked himself up off the chilly step and said, "Oh my God, that was terrible, wasn't it? I never went to Gujarat. Jesus."

"Not to be harsh, but you looked *so* gormless. Like you had zero gorm."

"Actually, it was even worse than it looked. I had like five chat tabs at the top of my browser. He must have seen them."

"I honestly thought he was just going to sack you straight away."

"Yeah."

"I mean, he probably should have."

"Yeah, yeah, he probably should have."

"Has he always been like this?"

"You mean this uptight? A million times yes."

There was a twinge of guilt. But the group was laughing and he was assuming his natural position as its focal point.

"When we were at uni, I remember, we were both at this end-of-year boatie party, playing spin the bottle. And James starts, like, calculating game theory." Roland did a robotic impersonation. "Please hold on with that shot. Must assess Never Have I Ever."

As the weeks went by, Roland became established as the butt of the jokes — and also as the one the others looked to. It was always like this. In school, he was the first boy to dance at every disco; that was power. It didn't matter that his dancing was ridiculous.

Some of the conventionally popular winner-types — prefects, first-team sportsmen — resented that so much attention was given to him. It offended their sense of the natural order: he wasn't good at anything they recognised. Some ended up hoping to break in him whatever it was the others wanted to get close to: some willingness to dance absurdly, a flourish of joy amid the conveyor-belt routines of school. But they couldn't pick on him because the girls liked him too much.

At work, just like back in school, he started to engineer mishaps with himself at the centre. He kept forgetting his laptop charger and had to go home to fetch it, which took hours. To James this was baffling, incomprehensible. He had no response. And then once, when James came back from the loo, thinking about GDP growth, he opened the door to find Roland demonstrating a Rajasthani wedding dance, clicking his fingers above his head and shoogling his hip.

Roland froze for an instant, as if playing musical statues, before dropping his hands, not entirely surprised to be caught. The team watched, rapt. They'd never had so much fun at the office. James silently went to his seat and began typing. Everyone on the team but him had been part of this. As Roland sat down, hot waves of shame broke over him. But at lunchtime, once the team escaped to the steps in front of the National Gallery, they howled and creased over and wiped their eyes as they did impressions of Roland being busted mid-shoogle. Roland thought of James eating his Pret sandwich alone in the abandoned conference room.

He said, "Let's have a drink. After work obviously. We could go to that pub where the MPs go to do their plotting."

Sarah said, "Are you going to invite James?"

Someone said, "Feels a bit mean not to."

But Roland cried out, "No way! Literally, no. I'd have to kill myself with a broken pint glass."

They went that evening, without asking James. They didn't see any MPs they recognised, but there was at least Nick Robinson, the BBC's politics correspondent. He looked like a newspaper cartoon, all bald head and rectangular glasses. Until then, Roland had only seen him on TV, standing outside Downing Street with a woolly microphone. Robinson was hunching forward over a small, circular pub table, listening intently to one of the many middle-aged men in suits.

Roland's group clustered numerously around their own little table in a jumble of stools and backpacks. They drank warm, sour pints of Carling and Foster's, sipping the tops off the brimming glasses, and pretended to lip-read the scandals that Robinson was hearing.

There was a point later on, after Robinson had left, when Roland was outside the pub, smoking with Sarah, the real Londoner. He was blabbering about how he'd been away when the smoking ban came in, so it was still really weird for him. She wasn't really listening, but her eyes were following every movement of his mouth. And when she leaned on the outside shelf, the back of her hand grazed his elbow.

A great bubble of happiness expanded in Roland's chest. He could see up Whitehall to Nelson's Column and the National Gallery. Empty buses were going past with lit-up insides. Policemen with sub-machine guns were standing outside the gate to Downing Street. He could see the cold white moon over Soho. And he was about to kiss this girl in front of him. He was living.

Before this evening, he hadn't thought about Sarah in that way. But she was a girl with eyes and hair and a figure. What did the details matter? He wished that this moment before the kiss, when everything was perfectly ripe and poised, could last for hours. But he'd already almost left it too long, and the mood was on the turn. He interrupted himself and awkwardly rushed out, "I don't know why I'm going on about the smoking ban. I really like you."

The next day in the conference room, the atmosphere was different: looser, easier, chattier. James noticed. Over the course of the day, he pieced together a hypothesis, and, mid-afternoon, he asked, "Did you guys go out last night?"

Painful silence. They looked at their laptops. For Roland, the non-speaking was too cruel, too ostracising, so he said, as if it were no big thing, "Yeah, we went to the pub. We actually saw Nick Robinson, you know, the BBC guy."

This was what James had thought, so his expression stayed set. He said, "Great. That will have been good for team bonding. Don't feel you should have asked me to come. To be frank, I would have liked to take part in the bonding. But I'll organise something another time."

Roland tried not to start thinking of jokes about James taking part in the bonding, and said, "Great. Yeah, I'd be so up for it."

"Great."

James resisted the urge to leave the room, to check on something back at the McKinsey office for the rest of the day, and not have anyone's eyes on him. Instead he stayed and did the tasks he would have done had this not happened, while the others sat quiet and ashamed in front of him.

Roland did not feel that this was what he was on this planet to do.

MARCH 2008

Far away in America, a bank called Bear Stearns, which thought of itself as the brash, scrappy underdog among the five investment banks of Wall Street, experienced what economists call a Minsky moment: the end of the boom; a sudden and catastrophic loss of confidence.

On the morning of Monday the tenth of March, Bear Stearns was flush with $18 billion in its electronic vaults. But, like any bank, it ran less on cash than on collective belief that it was sound. With an elaborate pattern of overlapping debts, Bear Stearns had lent out thirty-five times as much money as it actually had. This was normal and not a problem, as long as the people who'd given the bank their money didn't all ask for it back at the same time. Every night it borrowed tens of billions from other banks to keep the wheels turning.

That week, Bear Stearns suffered something like the Soviet Union did when the Poles and East Germans stopped believing in it: the riot police didn't lift their truncheons; the army didn't fire their rifles; and the tanks trundled meekly back to Moscow. Over the previous months, news about the credit crunch had made Wall Street's confidence ever more fragile. The worthless mortgages that the banks had built on were disintegrating. Banks were announcing losses of billions, tens of billions. Everyone in finance was trying to guess who was in more trouble than they were letting on.

That Monday, in a shift that none of the tens of thousands of individuals involved could have explained, like a flock of geese turning south, sentiment turned against Bear Stearns. Its stock price fell. When that falling was noticed, other traders started to sell, and it fell quicker. Rumours sprang up that it must be in trouble; then it *was* in trouble, and the rumours became true.

The Bear Stearns executives couldn't understand what was happening. In later years, many would believe they were victims of an enormous conspiracy. In that fateful week, they insisted on CNBC and in phone conversations and emails that there was no problem; they had $18 billion on hand. But that pile began to erode, faster and faster, as other banks and funds began to ask for their money back.

It turned out that the bank was like a floating soap bubble; once there was a rip in its skin, its marvellous shimmering shape resolved into a cold droplet plunging towards the floor.

On Thursday morning, the executives realised with astonishment that the bank was going to run out of cash. By Thursday afternoon, it was over. The other banks announced they would not lend any more to Bear because they feared it was too stricken to ever repay them. In this way, a bank that on Monday could have borrowed a hundred billion dollars over email simply went bust.

On the Friday of that week, at four a.m., the chairman of the Federal Reserve, Ben Bernanke, lay awake in the dark and waited for a phone call from New York. His wife Anna was sleeping with her back to him. On the bedside table, his BlackBerry screen kept flashing bluish light at the ceiling as messages came in. He was too hot and had pushed the duvet into the middle of the bed. His pillow was hot, too, radiating heat into the back of his neck, and he was sweating into his pyjamas. He'd tried to get some rest and had wavered in and out of consciousness for a few hours. But whether awake or not, his mind had toiled on, trying to evaluate the incomplete fragments of information he'd been able to gather. Was Bear too far gone to be saved? Just how many of the mortgages were rotten? Could Jamie Dimon be trusted?

Dimon was the chief executive of a far larger bank, JPMorgan, and had promised to help with a rescue. They'd called Dimon away from a Greek restaurant — his birthday dinner — on Thursday; that was only last night.

While he, Ben, was a professor gone into government service, Dimon was a banker born and bred. He was from a family of Greek traders who'd adopted a new surname in America. Tanned Mediterranean skin under grey-white hair. He could have been wearing a crumpled cream-linen suit and a Panama hat. Ben could imagine him on a busy quayside in Smyrna, with turquoise water slapping against the dock, and Dimon haggling up the price of the crates stacked behind him.

His voice was surprising in the boss of a bank. No Ivy League smoothness, rather the Noo Yoik drawl of a guy working in a bodega. He said *youz* when talking to two people and pronounced *probably* as *prawly*. A hustler's voice, that of someone who came out of every crisis richer.

There'd long been rumours that Dimon wanted to buy Bear Stearns. Now he was presenting himself as the indispensable friend, the responsible captain of industry, the public-spirited partner of government. Dimon wanted him, Ben, to lend some as yet unspecified number of the public's billions to Bear. That was at the very edge of legality, and so the money would have to be funnelled through another bank – Dimon's bank. Which was . . . fine.

But this was something that hadn't been done since the Great Depression. At that thought, Ben could feel heat collecting in the hollows of his palms. The newspapers and CNBC would freak out. Things were so brittle. He didn't know how badly hurt the other banks really were. Bear might be merely the first domino. Even if it wasn't, just the phrase "Great Depression", just the fact of him, the chairman of the Federal Reserve, saying it out loud, might be enough to tip the others over the edge, and call a new depression into being.

If that cascade began, if other banks began to fail as well, he didn't think that he, Ben Bernanke, aged fifty-four, an academic turned professor from Augusta, Georgia, just a man like other men, with hands and feet and a few pounds of gelatinous matter in his skull, would be able to stop the slide. A depression in twenty-first-century America. Evictions. Homeless camps. Hunger. The Dust Bowl. The best laid plans of mice and men go oft agley. Agley. Things were going agley.

As a student, he'd read the learned, contemptuous dissections of how Hoover blundered in 1929, when Wall Street collapsed and the dominos toppled outward across the country. Now it was he who had to decide. For him, hunger was generations away. His grandfather, who'd come over from Ukraine, he'd known hunger. Seen the pogroms. Was it Dimon's grandparents who'd come over? Maybe refugees from the Turks.

The abyss was supposed to have been left behind in crooked romantic Europe. But the abyss was right here. Bear was sinking and dragging them towards the edge. He had to get up. He had to get dressed. He was not going to have historians write that Ben Bernanke destroyed the US economy in his pyjamas.

So as not to wake Anna, he crept into their walk-in closet, took some clothes down on their hangers, and crept back out to the family bathroom. His eyes were tired and he could smell the sour fear sweat on himself. He was dehydrated, a headache coming on. He needed to take a shower and clear his thoughts. If he didn't bail out Bear Stearns, then Bear would go down and maybe pull everything else down with it. And if he did bail them out, maybe it would be like shouting *fire* in a crowded theatre, and everything would fall apart like that instead.

By the time he realised he'd forgotten to shower, he had his trousers on and couldn't go back. He ran the tap and splashed water under his armpits then onto his face. A Depression-era shower. In the past few years, the water companies had taken on a lot of debt. If they couldn't borrow what they needed for the usual refinancing, what would happen? What happened when the water company went bust? Could they be nationalised? *Nationalised*, in America.

Maybe he should shave. His neat beard clung to his cheeks and the area around his mouth. Its upper limit was an arbitrary line that he drew with a razor. In the mirror above the sink, he could see the stubble endlessly re-emerging high up on his cheekbones. There was a different kind of beard that kept trying to grow out, a beard from his grandfather's time, flowing, luxuriant, a shtetl beard. Yes, hunger. Poverty. Tuberculosis. The old world trying to climb back out of your pores. Could he trust Dimon? What if Ben lent him billions to save Bear and it collapsed anyway?

He went into the kitchen, which gleamed when he clicked on the lights.

The maid had been the day before. Empty surfaces. Order. Affluence. He hadn't lived like this as a child. He turned on the Nespresso machine. While he waited for it to heat up, he began trying to read his BlackBerry messages. But his mind was too full to absorb them.

Bailout or no bailout. There was more to it than that. There were nuances. Delicate paths through this apparently binary choice. But his brain was too alarmed to follow the threads. He realised he was on the verge of panic. The button on the Nespresso machine had lit up and was waiting for him. He pressed it, and thin brownish liquid ran into the cup. He'd forgotten to put in a new pod. He would do it again in a moment. First he had to take in some of these messages.

A few minutes later, Anna came into the kitchen. She'd put on a dressing gown and was squeezing her stiff shoulder. His mind flashed back to when Joel and Alyssa were babies, and he and Anna would be up together in the middle of the night. She said, "Can't sleep?"

"No. But go back to bed. Did I wake you?"

"You didn't." Of course he had. "Are you okay?"

"Yeah, I'm okay."

"Have they called yet?"

"No." He looked at his BlackBerry. "We said five. So eighteen minutes."

"Want me to make you a coffee?"

"It's okay. I was just making one. I'll make *you* one."

"No, no. You carry on with what you need to do."

She went over to the machine, and he, instead of reading his messages, watched her pull the handle to shuck out yesterday's defunct pod, and drop in another. The machine clanked and whirred. She tilted her head back and stretched her neck from side to side. He said, "Remember when the kids were babies and we'd be up like this?"

"I was remembering that, too." She put the coffee down on the counter beside him and patted his bald top. "You had more hair back then. Not a lot more, but some."

His panic had receded a little. He put his arm round her waist, then with his other hand lifted the hem of her robe and kissed it. "Thank you."

"What are you going to do for the next seventeen minutes?"

He sighed and rubbed his hands across his face. His eyes ached. "I've been trying to read these messages, but I can't take them in."

"Want to look at pictures of the kids?"

He smiled and, when he went to say yes, he found he couldn't speak.

She fetched one of the albums from her office and opened it on the gleaming counter. He saw photos of themselves twenty years younger, dishevelled and strangely dressed. His children in their original form: tiny, pink, mewling and almost sightless. Luke's Gospel: "From everyone to whom much has been given, much will be required; and from the one to whom much has been entrusted, even more will be demanded."

The panic receded a little further. The abyss was still there, but his courage was coming back to him. His eyes prickled, but he blinked the tears back. They looked at pictures of the children until the call came.

The fix jerry-rigged together overnight, like the contraption of duct tape and empty cartons that saved Apollo 13, was this: Ben Bernanke would use powers last invoked in the Great Depression to lend a still unspecified number of billions to Jamie Dimon at JPMorgan, who would immediately re-lend them to Bear Stearns.

On the conference call, Ben, Jamie and Hank Paulson, the Treasury Secretary, talked briefly about whether to just let the bank fail. Market forces. Schumpeterian economic theory. The creative destruction of American capitalism. But even as they said these phrases aloud, it was obvious they were too horrifying to contemplate in detail. Instead the billions were mobilised, gladdening the heart as they rushed into the fray in their serried ranks.

But over the course of that Friday, it became apparent that the fix could not hold. Rather than stabilising the bank, it convinced the last of the doubters that Bear Stearns was done for. Money gushed out the doors and windows as quickly as the Fed could pump it back in. By the afternoon, the question was whether the bank could survive until the end of the day. And at the close of business, there was only one escape route left: Bear Stearns would have to be sold outright to Jamie Dimon. Bear's employees pulled out their bottles of Scotch and said their goodbyes – a celebration like the last night before the fall of Saigon. When they looked out their windows, they saw the JPMorgan building right across the street.

The sale would have to be complete by the time the markets reopened on Monday, or Bear would have to declare bankruptcy when trading began. Since the first markets to open were in Asia, that meant Sunday afternoon, New York time. Hundreds of JPMorgan's bankers and lawyers trooped into Bear Stearns's offices like salvage crews. They rummaged through a growing chaos of paperwork, coffee cups and pizza boxes, searching for treasures and poisonous waste.

On Sunday morning, Dimon rang Ben and Hank Paulson directly, with no one else on the line. He'd started his career as a management consultant. Not at McKinsey – a lesser firm. He'd risen and risen until he now held the prospects for most of humanity in his hand. He said, "Ben, Hank, we've pored, combed through the books, and we just can't do it. My board is going crazy. The risks are just enormous. I wanna do what's right, but I can't do it if it's going to hurt the shareholders. I'm sorry I've gotta let youz down, but we just can't do it."

Paulson was a tall, rangy, Midwestern farm boy, who'd grown up in one of the new Christian sects that elevated work to a sacred duty. He'd been a star football player in college, then made it up to the top of Goldman Sachs before Bush asked him to be treasury secretary – Alexander Hamilton's old job. Even though Paulson was bald now and his voice croaked and rasped like an old cowhand's, his body still held the shape of the athlete he'd once been. His left pinkie finger, badly dislocated in his football days, had never been reset and dangled horribly. At Goldman he'd used it to intimidate people. Ben found him humourless.

Paulson seemed shocked by what Dimon was saying, but for Ben there was only the cold seep of realisation.

Dimon was still talking: "You said it yourself, Hank. They've got – they've just got too much. We don't even know how much. It's too big a risk for us. I've gotta fiduciary obligation. You know that better than anybody."

"Yes, yes, I do," said Paulson. Talk of obligations made sense to him. "A lot of this doesn't sit right. I've got Congressmen backed up on my other lines waiting to tell me they won't support a socialist bailout and that if they wanted to live in France they'd get on a plane to Paris. I'm taking a lot of pressure from that quarter. But Jamie, if you pull out of this thing, we're looking at . . . you know what we're looking at. It could easily drag you down anyway."

"I see that. I really do. And believe me, I wanna make this work. But you've seen the numbers. If we could get six months to go through the books and see what deathtraps, landmines they've got in there . . . But it would be suicidal to just haul this stuff on board and hope it's okay. It's just too big a risk."

Ben thought: This guy has nerves like steel hawsers. He's already got what he wants, we're practically begging him to buy Bear, and now he's going to sweat us for more. From a game-theory perspective, it's so simple: he has the cards, and we're in extremis. He can ask for anything. But how strong must his mind be to play the game with these stakes.

He asked the only meaningful question. "Hi, Jamie. I think I understand the situation. A lot of unquantifiable risk. What if it's even worse than it looks? Also Bear's board might vote against you. So might their shareholders. What could we do to mitigate those risks?"

"I, uh, I honestly don't know. I gotta tell you, my team's pretty set against this."

"But your team *are* in the business of pricing risk. So is there a price that would take these risks into account? Just hypothetically, what price were you looking at?"

Dimon said, "It's not just a question of price. Honestly, Ben."

"Sure, but what's this part of the equation?"

"Honestly, even to consider it, it's terrible. It almost brings tears to my eyes to say this, but we'd be talking something like three or four bucks a share."

"Four bucks!" exclaimed Paulson. "Dang it, Jamie. Just their building must be worth ten bucks a share."

"I know. It's shocking. But maybe the building would be a useful asset."

Now Paulson understood as well. "Oh. Oh, okay," he said. "Okay. I see. Four bucks, which includes the building?"

"I mean, that would help. But we couldn't finance something like this on our own. If it goes bad, it could sink us."

Paulson said, "Maybe in these exceptional circumstances, since the Fed is already extending a line of credit to Bear, maybe there's scope for a loan to help with the purchase. What do you think, Ben?"

Ben said, "Yes."

Dimon: "That's an idea. That would take us a long way. A long way. You know, we've found about thirty bill of bad mortgages, bad assets. Still got a sticker price of thirty billion. Maybe you could lend against that?"

Ben: "You mean, lend you thirty billion dollars of public money in exchange for a pile of worthless crap?"

Before Dimon could rise to this provocation, Paulson interjected. "Fair point, Ben. Very fair. None of us likes this. The public isn't going to like it, either. But maybe something like this is what's achievable. But Jamie, we'd need to lock you in. We underwrite this, you've got to stay the course, no matter what they've got in their books. Your guys find some horror show down there in their basement, too bad, you've got to eat it."

"That's fair. That's fair. And yeah, with that support, that does shift the balance. I could maybe get that over the line."

Paulson said, "Actually, one more thing, now I think about it. I don't want people saying we bailed them out with our tax dollars so they could go and buy more houses in the Hamptons. And I don't want the rest of the street thinking we'll ride to the rescue if they don't get things straight. This has got to hurt. You said three or four bucks a share? On second thought, that feels high to me."

Dimon said, "How about two bucks?"

Paulson said, "It's your call. Two?"

"Okay, two bucks. Wow. It's a tragedy. A great, reputable firm like that. Jimmy Cayne's going to lose a billion dollars in one weekend."

Paulson briefly lost his temper. "I don't give a goddamn what Jimmy Cayne loses. If he'd done his job, he could have kept his money."

And Ben thought: I don't know how we're going to explain this to people. But the alternative is the abyss.

James read about it on the thin pink sheets of the *FT*, over breakfast in his parents' kitchen. The table was a long trestle of rough wood, an urban fantasy of a farmhouse. At the other end was a wide shallow bowl stacked with artichokes, like a heap of scaly green hand grenades. Behind James's back was an ancient dresser his mum had salvaged and painted a very pale blue. On its shelves were Mason jars that his dad kept stocked with what he considered the superior varieties of rice and pasta: *casarecce* for pasta with sardines; *vialone nano* for risottos in the soupier Venetian style.

Sitting amid so much comfort and ease, the Bear Stearns article seemed quaint. A run on a bank. Even the phrase was a curiosity. It brought back GCSEs: the Wall Street Crash and the rise of the Nazis. Last summer he'd seen TV footage of the run on Northern Rock. Elderly Yorkshire ladies with thin scarves over their hair queuing along the pavement and clutching their pocketbooks. There was something nostalgic about it, like seeing Morris dancers; a funny corner of the world where these things still existed.

The *FT*'s headline didn't mention the word *abyss*. It said "JPMorgan to Buy Bear Stearns". The worst that had happened was that the authorities were forced to step in. The article blathered solemnly about the "ongoing credit crunch". Next to it was another, saying "Healthy profits at Goldman, Lehman ease fears that contagion could spread". James finished his bacon and egg sandwich, and went to the office.

Roland didn't hear about it. He didn't read the *FT*. And anyway, he was leaping, eyes closed, into a relationship with Sarah, the real Londoner from DFID. His mum had asked him whether it was really so clever to go out with someone at his new job. But to him it was just like *Friends* to have a tangle of affairs in a tiny group. He was encouraging some of the others to get together as well.

He spent Saturday mornings asleep at Sarah's house in Brixton while their livers worked away at the pints and ketamine they'd guzzled the night before. At some point, she'd need to pee too badly to stay asleep. She pulled on a long T-shirt and shuffled blearily through the molehills of clothes. After peeing and brushing her teeth, she'd make herself a cup of tea and get back into bed. She read *World of Interiors* and *Vogue* and, if she'd finished those, *Grazia*, while her boyfriend slumbered beside her. The house was quiet; she had the pleasure of Roland being uncharacteristically peaceful; all was well and everything in its place.

She found she could open the blinds or watch DVDs on her laptop without disturbing him. When his hangover started him snoring, she gave him a firm shove, and he settled back down. Unlike some of her friends, she liked boys, the way they were stinky and sweaty and noisy, like friendly farm animals, and how they blared around, rooting things up. Without them, it was easy for an all-female house to slide into a kind of intense, insular mind-meld, which started off fun but soon grew suffocating, the domestic order winding itself taut, and prone to snapping.

Even though she'd never thought she was the hottest of her friends, she'd always had boyfriends, one after another. Her looks were insufficient to pull boys in of their own accord. She didn't have the luxury of disliking how they behaved. It was reassuring to have one pre-caught and landed, lying ready beside her like a fish in a boat. And Roland had such capacity for happiness. Once he woke up, blinking and groaning, they'd have sex, which she looked forward to. Her teeth were brushed; his weren't. That was life.

She lived with two girls, Hannah and Clemmie, who she knew from growing up. The house was Clemmie's. Her dad had died in a motorbike accident while she was at university. Each summer, he went on a bike cruise with a couple of buddies to drink beer and complain about their families, their leathers looking increasingly incongruous against their specs and bald spots. Two years ago they were in France, swooshing around corners in the Alps, and then around one particular corner there'd been a family car coming the other way, heavy with two Parisian lawyers, their children and two weeks' worth of suitcases. He was dead before the ambulance got there.

The French dad sent Clemmie a handwritten letter over lots of pages, which she threw away unread. She didn't want to find out that it was her dad's fault.

Since her parents were already divorced and she was an only child, she got his money, which she used to buy a squashed, red-brick terraced house in ungentrified Brixton. Sarah and Hannah paid off an increment of her mortgage each month. At the back was a rectangle of scruffy grass with some unidentified plants around the edges. Gradually rusting in one corner were a couple of sunloungers and a pull-up bar left by a previous housemate. When they came back late at night and walked up the hill from the bus stop, they nodded to the black girls touting for business on the roadside. In the mornings, there were condoms stuck to the pavement.

The house had become a communal crash pad for an extended group of friends from South London private schools. There were Sunday lunches for a dozen and, in the cupboard under the stairs, cones, bibs and collapsible goals for a football team some of them belonged to. People's siblings and parents came by to drop things off. To Roland it was very different from the bare box his parents lived in. That spring, Clemmie even bought a dog, a tiger-striped whippet pup called Marge, which slept in a wicker basket and piddled on the kitchen floor.

Roland had his breakfast in his boxers and last night's T-shirt, then watched daytime TV with the girls and anyone else who'd stayed over or smoked on one of the sunloungers while Marge snuffled his ankles. He learned the names of schools like Dulwich and Alleyn's, and to refer to James Allen's Girls School as JAGS.

With the football boys, he went to the White Horse on Brixton Hill to watch the matches. They drank pints and crowded into the graffitied toilet cubicle to do bumps of coke off the corner of a debit card. Since most of the others were fans of Arsenal, which they insisted was actually a South London team, he was too.

Sometimes he had his arms around them, shoulder to shoulder, a bit high and with the beer buzz on the way up, singing, "One–nil to the Ar-se-nal, one–niiiil . . ." And sometimes he had his head in his hands, distraught, saying, "I just can't believe it." But that was no less enjoyable.

One of the football boys, Luke, his dad played double bass. On April Fool's, the dad and his pals played a gig in a Soho pub called the French House. In the throng around the bar, Roland saw the big gruff Scottish actor Robbie Coltrane, who played a Russian bad guy in one of the Bond movies, drinking a pint and chatting like anyone else.

The boys got Roland into gambling on the matches. He'd done enough maths to have an understanding of which odds looked exploitable, and – despite not really knowing much about the teams – regularly won little windfalls that he blew on pints and gear for everyone.

Another of the group, Alex, was working part-time for an Irish gambler while he finished his teacher training. The gambler had been barred from the local betting shops for winning too often. Alex's job was to go in and lay the bets for him, spreading them around as many shops as possible to postpone the inevitable day when he was barred as well. He carried a finger-thick wedge of banknotes in a security belt under his jeans. The gambler would ring him with a bet, and Alex would dash off on his bike to the nearest Coral or William Hill.

One Friday night, he took them to the dog track in Wimbledon. The girls came too, dressed up in leopard-print jackets, hoop earrings and bouffant hair for a night at the dogs. Roland was startled by how naturally Sarah's costume sat on her. No trace of the civil servant was visible under the blue eyeshadow and crimson lips. She looked entirely a mischievous South London hoyden. Maybe that was who she really was. Roland was never more attracted to her.

The track was so deep south that the streets were dark and the buildings low-rise. On the approach to the stadium, you could see the mineral-white floodlight glowing up out of the top. A grimy plastic banner sagged over the entrance: "Support London's last dog track". The stadium was cold, dirty concrete. There were black-and-white photos of when they had cheetah racing here in the 1930s.

Roland and the others swigged danger bottles of rum and ginger that they'd hidden in their jackets, and cheered on the greyhounds in their numbered bibs. Alex had told them on the Tube down that if you saw a dog taking a shit right before the race you should bet on it because it might have been dosed with speed. Before one race, Roland saw it happen. Number 4: Sailor Lad.

He grabbed Sarah's arm. "Oh my God. That dog just took a shit. I should bet on it."

Sarah said, "Haven't you already bet on this race?"

"Yes, but that's pointless now. That bet's gone. The shitting dog is going to win."

"Look who's an expert on the dogs."

"Do you think I should do it?"

"Yes! Go for it! Win me a big stack of cash, baby." She gave him an exaggerated pout and a boozy, gingery kiss. "Go on then. You'll miss it."

Roland was down to the last twenty quid of the hundred he'd taken out in cash to set a limit to his losses. At the counter, he used his card to bet another hundred. He was so sure of his win that he was fumbling to pay in time.

The dogs made their brief dash round the track, and Sailor Lad, high on life or methamphetamine, crossed the white line ahead of the rest. Had there been a good bar nearby, Roland would have taken everyone for cocktails and champagne. But they were in the far, dark reaches of Wimbledon. So, after the jumping up and down, he just kept betting until his winnings had dwindled back to nothing.

He was so happy he woke up the next day still grinning, some tension unwound, content just to doze the morning away, feeling the comfortable ache in his head and the scratchiness in his smoky throat.

The dogs, the house, the football, the friends who knew each other from Dulwich and JAGS awakened a greed in Roland, a feeling that he'd had just a taste and wanted much, much more. He wanted to work for the Irish gambler himself, to play in the band with his Grade 6 clarinet, to meet Sarah's parents, to get an Arsenal tattoo, maybe even to sleep with Clemmie, whose house it was and who was at the centre of it all.

*

At the office, whenever James glanced down the long conference table, he could see that Roland was bored. Roland seemed to think that because no one could see his screen it wasn't obvious he was browsing club nights on the internet or comparing football odds from different bookmakers. He only perked up when asking who wanted to go for lunch.

They invited James now, out of embarrassment. He ate his sandwich with them on Tuesdays, on the steps of the National Gallery. The team sat quietly, and James led a laborious conversation about how the project was going. By the second Tuesday, he'd have preferred to skip it. Maybe this was the solitary nature of command.

The problem of Roland's laziness he let drift. His McKinsey training recognised a classic management puzzle: how to motivate an underperforming employee. But his interest in professional puzzles was burned out for a while. It wasn't like the empty feeling after exams. When the HR administrator had to write again, superseding the paperwork for his sacking, to confirm instead that he was being promoted two rungs at once, there'd been something new: a sweet, airy morsel of something he hadn't tasted before – satisfaction.

He began leaving the office early enough to be home for dinner. His sister Cleo had moved back into their parents' house for a couple of months. It was the first time the whole family had lived together since James left for university, and would be the last. It felt like an Indian summer of childhood, a late month of unexpected warmth. His parents temporarily stopped seeing their friends, to be at home. Cleo was having deep chats with her dad in the afternoons. James left DFID early and then, when the sky didn't fall, even earlier.

They ate together three or four times a week, carrying on conversations from evening to evening. After dinner they watched a DVD, each in their own place in the darkened living room. His parents were rewatching the Italian neorealist movies of the 1940s and '50s: *Rome, Open City. La Strada. Bicycle Thieves*. Ordinary lives unspooling without direction.

Drab streets, bombed buildings, the shabby suits and empty bellies of old-fashioned hardship. Skinny Italians driven to acts of desperation. It was sometimes too raw after a day at the spreadsheets.

James's dad enjoyed being shattered by these movies, as if you had to suffer into truth. But there was only so much James and Cleo could sit through. With their minds still turning over the business of the day, they'd rather be entertained than shattered. Despite their dad's entreaties to give it just another half hour, that they were almost at the best bit, they went up to Cleo's bedroom, feeling like allied children.

Their mum had turned it from a teenager's pit into a pale, tasteful guest room. But the longer Cleo stayed, the more it regressed: hair straighteners on the desk. Clothes draped across the back of the chair. On the floor was a mosaic pavement of papers and books. She was applying to do a doctorate in environmental economics and had warned Agata the cleaning lady that moving a single sheet would mean disaster.

She picked her way across to sit on the bed, and James slid down onto the new carpet with his back against the cold radiator. Cleo said, "Bwoof. Poor Mum. And tomorrow it's *Germania Anno Zero*."

"But she loves that stuff, doesn't she?"

Cleo wobbled her head. She'd chopped the black, curling hair they both had into a practical bob. "Ye-es. You know she watches *The Wire* on her computer in her lunch break. She's got the DVDs in her filing cabinet, and she sits there in her office with her headphones on. If one of her students comes in, she pretends she's listening to, like, an analysis of Korean manufacturing techniques."

James yawned. "But Dad would love *The Wire*."

"Yeah. I think he's just having this Italian moment so she didn't want to interrupt. And then she got hooked, and now she's like three seasons deep and way too far ahead for him to catch up."

James had been learning that Cleo knew much more about their parents than he did. He was glad to be laying down the mantle of elder-brotherhood, which had never fitted that well. When she'd got together with her boyfriend, a smiley, wholesome Dutch physicist called Roger, James had felt he owed it to Cleo to be protective in some way. It was a relief to understand that that wasn't wanted.

He'd even started asking his younger sister for advice: on talking to people, on clothes. He needed some outfits that weren't suits or tracksuits. What were you meant to wear when not in the office or the gym? Not that he'd actually been to the gym this year.

Cleo had identified some shops on Oxford Street for him: H&M, Topman, Uniqlo and Zara. Clutching the list she'd given him like a warrant for entry, he'd made two categories of purchase. First, Silicon Valley mode: grey T-shirts, grey jeans, grey plimsolls. Second, well-dressed older man: shirts, slacks, a dark-blue jacket. When she told him to catwalk, he went into his own room and started with Silicon Valley, dressing himself like Mark Zuckerberg. He came back in, and Cleo grimaced.

"Oh," she said, "I've screwed that up. You look terrible. Sorry. My bad."

James refused to give in to embarrassment. Rather than sweep back out and pull the clothes off, he said, "Okay. I'll try the other stuff in a minute." He sat down with the faint chemical smell of box-fresh clothes around him. "How's the application going?"

"Oh, fine. Fine. I'm showing Gerald each section as I do it."

Gerald had supervised her undergrad and would take her on for the PhD as well.

"Have you decided about the subject?"

"Ugh. No."

James was sure it would be fine.

She said, "It's like, the good thing about doing a niche – like, are solar panels going to save the world – is I could end up the person who knows the most about that. Cool, I know."

"So cool."

"But I might actually prefer to do a big-picture thing."

"Like what's the ideal energy mix?"

"Like if you were the government, and you decided to stop climate change, what would you do first? Is it subsidies for solar panels, or tax breaks for electric cars, or something just totally arcane like more efficient cement-making?"

"What's the low-hanging fruit?"

"Exactly."

"That sounds more interesting to me. And you won't get stuck in the wrong niche if solar panels aren't the answer."

"True. Except the answer to the big-picture question is probably something unbelievably dull like giving people grants to insulate their houses properly. And there's more funding for the niches. If you want to do something about how maybe oil's got a great future after all – surprise, surprise – there's the BP bursary, the Shell innovators fund, etcetera. And I don't actually want to live with Mum and Dad till I'm old and crusty – no offence, bro."

"Good one. But aren't there just general scholarships?"

"Yeah, of course."

"Can't you just get one?"

"Well, maybe. But it's not guaranteed. I'm not Mr First Place in Every Exam I've Ever Sat."

"If that's what it's going to come down to, I can give you the money."

She looked at him strangely. "What?"

"I can classify it as a loan if you feel weird about it. You shouldn't have to choose your research direction based on who's going to give you a cheque."

"What, really? It's not cheap, you know."

"I know. But I've got my absolutely stonking corporate salary you all think is so evil, and I don't pay any rent. I don't really have any costs except buying lunch."

"So you've got absolute tons of cash?"

"Yeah, I really do. I was thinking of buying an investment flat just because it's kind of criminally negligent not to. I'm just waiting for the credit crunch to make the market dip."

"So, what, you'd actually just give it to me?"

"Maybe not all of it. But yeah, sure. I'm not using it for anything."

"Thanks, bro."

"Pleasure."

Cleo felt she should give him a hug, but they hadn't hugged since they were children. "Hopefully I'll get a scholarship anyway."

"Yeah, why wouldn't you?"

"Huh. Okay. Great. Maybe we need to start shopping higher up the food chain. Ooh, maybe we can get you some kind of amazing tailored suit. But okay, go put the other outfit on for now."

James went next door and peeled off the Silicon Valley costume. In its place he put on some grey slacks, a light-blue shirt and the dark-blue jacket. When he came back in, Cleo said, "Much better. Those T-shirts are quite unforgiving, aren't they?"

"What do you mean?"

To annoy him, and to show she wasn't beholden, she said, "It's been a while since you went for a run, eh, bro?"

He smiled, enjoying being teased.

"But this is really not bad. Looks good on you. And much better than showing up for dates in your work clothes."

James inspected himself in the mirror on the wardrobe door. The only clothes he'd ever worn were school uniform, office uniform, T-shirts, jeans and jumpers. He felt screamingly overdressed. "I don't know. It seems a bit over the top."

"It's grey trousers and a blue jacket."

"Yeah . . ."

"Look. You could go casual, like edgy T-shirts and cool trainers. But, like, is that really you? Won't they be a bit, like, *nonplussed* when you turn up like that and then start telling them about price elasticity or whatever your date chat is?"

He laughed and was slightly persuaded. He'd been arranging his dates on Guardian Soulmates; he was far more successful in that structured environment than in the university free-for-all. But he was surprised by how badly the girls he sat opposite in bars and restaurants reacted to McKinsey. More than one said, incredulously, "So you're like an *actual* management consultant?"

Instead of murmuring seductive repartee – which, in fairness, was probably above his level – he found that his competitive instinct for debate was turned on. The sharpening of intellect on another, like two knives rasping each other to a finer edge. Point, counterpoint. Argument made him feel awake, and he told an intense video artist from Milan, "Business is the biggest thing no one talks about. People don't even want to call it business. They want to call it economics because it sounds more abstract. Britain still has this very old-fashioned snobbish disdain for what used to be called *trade*.

"But where do they think aeroplanes come from? Or penicillin? Or the internet? This stuff doesn't just appear. And unless you live in the countryside, it's businesses that create the material reality we live in. The shoes you're wearing. This table. This salt shaker. The salt in the shaker." He picked it up and waggled it for emphasis. "Business and technology create the facts of our lives; culture is just the commentary on how people feel about it. Business is the last taboo."

Did he believe all this? To himself he sounded like Aaron in Kitzbühel, faithful that McKinsey was a force for human development. Maybe there was something to it. "Of course, you don't have to be interested in this stuff. But it's like saying your interest in the world around you only goes as far as chit-chat."

There wasn't much chat after that. James considered telling the video artist about Lenin and Taylorism and the Soviets' vision of planned progress, but thought he'd made his point.

The video artist, Brigida Rossetti, had only recently arrived in London and didn't know many people in the city. Her English wasn't yet good enough for this debate. Nor was arguing something she enjoyed. But there was something striking about this man's apparent passion for salt shakers. A strange people, the English. She'd heard they were a nation of hobbyists. They loved games and clubs and eccentric enthusiasms. In any case, she had nothing else to do that evening. With wordless intent, she got them both drunk, took him back to her room in a warehouse in Hackney Wick and fucked him.

James began to wonder if there was a dating site for people with more ambition. But Cleo said, "Can you imagine what utter dicks would sign up to that kind of thing? It's good for you to meet girls who stop you from going over completely to the dark side."

The distaste for his job, which was jokey with Cleo, was coming out in his parents as he spent more time with them. They'd been irritatingly relieved when DFID came into the picture, because, as they kept saying, he was "using his powers for good". Cleo mollifyingly interpreted: "I think part of it is they think you're quite clever and hard-working, so if you set your mind to, like, innovations in the landmine industry, you could really fuck some stuff up."

When everyone was in for dinner, his dad and Cleo cooked together. As part of the Italianophile phase Arthur was in, they made recipes from a stained, broken-spined copy of Ada Boni's fat compendium, the *Talismano della Felicità*. He'd paid far too much for an early edition, from the 1930s. It was traditionally bought in spring, the wedding season, as a gift for new brides. The previous owner had written some extra recipes on the blank leaves at the back. It almost made Arthur weep to see this pencil record of a long-vanished couple beginning their marriage.

He set it up on a wooden reading stand, also bought specially, and consulted the oracle by bending down to the counter and lifting his glasses above his eyes. Then, feeling he'd crawled close to the authentic core of Italian cuisine, he'd lament to his family about how hard it was these days to find good offal.

One afternoon, he and Cleo spent hours pre-salting aubergines, as Boni recommended, and comparing them with an unsalted control batch. Since the Thirties, aubergines had had the bitterness bred out of them. But it was interesting to check. While he and Cleo waited for the salt to permeate the bland vegetal flesh, they drank cups of tea at the kitchen table and had idle, meandering chats.

Arthur's music habits were independent of the *Italianismo*, so when James came home, they were usually listening to gliding, melancholy synth-pop. At the table, his dad fussed them about with wines from the same region as the dishes. He said it was traditional, even into the Fifties, to plant alternate rows of crops and vines so the same minerals would, as it were, season both food and wine from below.

Whenever the conversation turned to James, his dad began pressing him. He said, "If this project goes well, which I have no doubt it will, do you think there'd be a sort of opening for you to wriggle through if you wanted, with you being offered something permanent at DFID itself? Probably something pretty big, I'd imagine, given how much you've done for them already."

With Cleo there, James consented to speak more openly about himself. He loaded his fork with creamed spinach, and conceded, "Yep. It happens all the time. People switch to working directly for the clients. The clients like it because they get the same person for less money. But I wouldn't go to DFID. In the Civil Service, you can't really go anywhere except Number 10 or the Treasury."

James could see his dad wanting to get up in arms about why international development was less essential than totting up the nation's pennies. To head that off, James said, "It's like if you decided to become a chef, and instead of going to study under *nonna* whoever in Palermo, you got a job at the Dolmio sauce factory in Watford."

His dad was appeased, but he so wanted his children to be on the right path that he couldn't leave it alone. "So the idea is, just concentrate for now on really improving these schools, which I'm sure desperately need it, then see what comes next? I think that's very astute. Here's some fatherly wisdom for you: life's very unpredictable. You can't always plan what's going to happen."

James took another slice of the *polpettone* meat loaf, which, as his dad had said several times, was a bit dry. He could tell that his dad was already convincing himself that James had said it was possible he would stay at DFID. By next week it would be that he probably would stay.

Usually he didn't share unfinished thoughts about his trajectory; he only presented fixed and defensible positions. But he didn't want his dad to hold a false image of him, and so know him less. Reluctantly he said,

"Yeah, but I definitely don't want to get pigeonholed into DFID-type work. It's not the big leagues."

"Okay, okay." His dad nodded, turning that one over. "So what *do* you want to do?"

Right now, James wanted to eat his *polpettone*. But, tensing a little, he said, "One potential path is that, given the jump I've just made to Engagement Manager, if I maintained that pace of promotions, I might become the youngest-ever partner at McKinsey." Growing more determined as he resisted the gathering embarrassment, he pushed on: "It's surprisingly difficult to find out who the youngest partner was. There have definitely been some at twenty-nine, so for the record it would need to be twenty-eight. At this pace, I could maybe get there at twenty-seven."

His dad was aghast. "And this is what gets you going?"

"Not especially. To be honest, it feels a bit small. Like, by the time he was my age, Gauss had already finished his *Disquisitions* and never reached that standard of maths again." James ruefully shook his head.

"Maybe this partner business feels small because —"

His mum interrupted. "Alright. Enough, Arthur. You've made your point. Don't spoil this delicious dinner you've made. And don't say you've already spoiled it by making it too dry. With the sauce, it's not dry at all. And you know what? You spend your time writing about people twiddling about with flutes; I spend mine on how Japanese people put things in boxes. Neither of us is curing cancer or landing on the moon. So put your soapbox away, will you?"

James's dad looked at his plate and made a sad clown face. "You're right. *Sicuramente*, you're right. And very generous about the *polpettone*, which *is* too dry, even if I've covered that up with sauce. I'm sorry, James. I don't think you ought to drop everything because humanity needs more music scholars — although you would be a very good one. I just don't want you to —"

Mary interrupted again: "Yes, we all know in great detail what you don't want. So why don't you give it a rest and tell us what you're thinking for dinner tomorrow?"

Arthur sat there unspeaking while he relinquished the grip on his worry ball. Then, with an effort, he picked up another set of thoughts, and said, "Okay. Tomorrow's dinner. Interesting question. What Cleo and I have been considering – Cleo, do you want to explain?"

"No, no. You go for it. Just imagine I'm not here. Then you can carry on talking about James's job for the next hundred years."

"Alright, consider that criticism noted. And we spend just as much time talking about your PhD. Very gladly, as it happens. Even though both my children have inexplicably forsworn the arts in favour of their mother's love of spreadsheets. Should I feel slighted? Should I have been stricter about your music lessons? But anyway, dinner. At least there's that to keep your senses from atrophying. Cleo and I have been looking into chestnut-flour gnocchi. It's the wrong time of year really, but nevertheless."

And with that, they were off again, away from the deep structures of life with their questions of meaning and satisfaction, and back to the airier upper layers – to pleasure, curiosity, respite from the monotonous whirring of the self. How to grind their imported chestnuts into flour. And how the flour was said to make the gnocchi taste of autumn woods, high in the Apennines, where mist drifted between the tree trunks, and the bristly snouts of wild boar rooted through wet, orange leaves.

After a couple of months, Cleo moved out again. She and Roger went to walk the Camino de Santiago through northern Spain. They carried rucksacks and sticks, and slept in monasteries and *albergues*. For Cleo in later years, the memory of that time at home was occluded by the Basque country and Galicia.

She and Roger often didn't say anything for hours while they walked under the enormous sky, like mites crawling under a jar. The dried-out, brown-and-yellow fields and forests slowly parted before them, as if the trail were a zip opening up the land. They thought of being together not just for the next few years but for all their years to come.

Since they separated at night into male and female dorms, during the day they struck off from the path and had sex hidden in low expanses of grey-blonde wheat. Sometimes then, looking up through the sky, with wheat stalks scratching her neck, the chill ground against her back and Roger inside her, it was like he was plugging her into the living planet.

For James and his parents, there was the feeling of staying at the party after the fun had left. The Italian cooking petered out. Cleo emailed to say that her PhD proposal, on the economics of solar panels, had been accepted, with funding. Things settled sadly back to normal. This time together had been so little: family dinners, DVD nights, a closer than usual sense of each other, a last farewell to James and Cleo's childhoods. So little, but it loomed far larger in the heart than many months and years spent on weightier things.

After Cleo left, James's appetite for work sharpened again. His attention returned to Roland's laziness. He watched Roland lounging and sighing in his chair. Why was he here? If he didn't like being in this conference room, he could go anywhere else on Earth. The next time Roland sent over some data, James glanced at it long enough to check that it wasn't, by some fluke, different from the usual crap, plausible but unsound. Then said, "Roland. Can I talk to you for a minute?"

Roland had been told off enough times by enough teachers to know what was coming. Fixing a cheery expression on his face and trying to project honest good faith, he walked up the long table to where James sat. He said, "Hi, yes. Is there, um, a problem with the data?"

"In a sense." Then, "Actually, I think we should go outside. It's not fair to criticise your output in front of everyone else, even though I'm sure they know that's what I'm going to do."

"Okay, great. Great. After you."

They had no separate meeting room, so once they got out into the corridor, James said, "Let's go for a walk outside." They went along the corridor and through the security barrier in awkward silence as they waited for the conversation to officially begin.

James formulated: it was clear that Roland's work was bad because he didn't make any effort. He could either change that or eventually he'd lose his job. That was everything. It was a bright morning and they squinted as they walked down the few steps to the pavement. They tasted the metallic tang of fumes from traffic shuttling up and down Whitehall.

James said, "Let's go into the park." As they fell into step, he began. "So. It's clear —"

But Roland talked over him, holding up a hand in apology. He'd learned that the way to bring a bollocking to a swift end was to lead the denunciation himself. While they dodged around other pedestrians, he said, "Sorry. I just want to say I'm really glad you've pulled me up on this. I feel like my work, it just, like, hasn't been right. Really ever since I started here. Do you know what I mean?"

James was surprised. "Yeah. Yeah, I do."

They went under one span of Admiralty Arch and out onto the broad straight pinkish avenue of the Mall. Roland said, "I think I've been, like, *struggling*, ever since I started. I haven't quite found my feet, if you see what I mean."

"Right."

"I think it's maybe partly just adjusting to being in a new city and maybe, if I'm honest with myself, getting a bit too caught up in being here. Bit of immaturity, maybe. And then also not really internalising, like, what the expectations are at McKinsey. Which are a step up from uni, aren't they?"

"Yes."

"So actually, even though this is a bit . . ." — Roland rolled his eyes — "*embarrassing*, I am really grateful you've pulled me up. It's a great chance to, like, readjust. Take things from here . . ." — he held his palm out flat to mark a level — "to here" — and lifted his palm up a step.

"Okay. That's great. I thought you wouldn't want to admit there was a problem."

"Not at all. Not at all. It's good to get it off my chest. Thank you."

Roland carried on producing the right faces, making his expressions correspond to James's. But this was about as much bootlicking as he could manage. It was one thing to grovel for some woolly-bearded hermit of a professor who could barely remember his own name; quite another for a dweeb from his own year. If anything, Roland thought he was actually a couple of months older.

James said, "Obviously I can give you as much help as you need. It's my job, and I'd be very happy to."

All Roland could get out of his mouth was, "Mmm. Uh-huh."

James had said all he needed to. It was settled. They were on one of the loops through St James's Park and followed it around back towards Trafalgar Square. Two very young men taking a stroll in the park.

The sunshine had saturated James's jacket with heat. He took it off and draped it over one shoulder, while Roland walked along in his double-breasted pinstripe, getting hotter.

Groups of young civil servants were gathering on the grass for an early lunch. James thought that if Al-Qaeda were somehow to hire McKinsey for strategic advice, they'd stop blowing up random civilians on the Tube and instead conduct a lunchtime massacre of everyone who worked at the Treasury. If you could get two or three Kalashnikovs into the park, you could kill half the people who knew where the government's bank accounts were. Just as a mental puzzle, like doing the crossword, he started scenario planning how the Treasury would cope.

Roland interrupted by blurting out, "But don't you, like, I mean, just between us, don't you ever get bored of that stuff? Datasets, Indian schools, like, checking things against the census? Don't you sometimes just think, this is actually fucking dull?"

James was surprised again. His ability to read people really did need improvement. "I would say doing good work even while you hate it is actually *more* impressive than doing what you love."

"Yeah, okay. Whatever. And this is your brainchild and everything. But, like, you are a human too. Just between us."

"I wouldn't say anything to you that I wouldn't want getting back to the team. Because it definitely will. But yeah, I solved this problem months ago, before anyone else was even hired. I had the breakthrough then. Now it's just legwork. Which is fucking dull."

Roland was surprised, too. And surprise made them unexpectedly sympathetic to each other. "But what, you just have to slog it out because that's the job for now?"

"Exactly. And to be totally frank, it bores my tits off. But the question is how do we perform despite that. It's a test of character."

Roland wanted more of this, more connection. "Oh my God. Fucking hell. Those charts of exam results against prosperity. Jesus."

"Try how boring it is to correct those charts when they've been bungled."

"Ha. Yeah, sorry about that."

Roland searched for more points of contact but couldn't think of any. Their path met the Mall again and, as they approached Admiralty Arch, James said, "This has gone much better than I expected. But, you know, deeds not words. If the stuff you're submitting doesn't" – he mimicked Roland's step-change gesture – "then obviously you won't have much credibility."

"Oh, obviously," said Roland.

In the following months, Roland did reluctantly try slipping his wrists into the manacles called responsible behaviour. When he noticed a mistake in his spreadsheets, he didn't simply prepare to look innocent, but sighed and fixed it himself. A little more strain on the harness. A little more sense of self committed to his job.

James cajoled him onwards with ceaseless prodding and praising. Many times a day, he checked Roland's progress, encouraging or correcting him in front of Sarah and the others. He must have been reading some management textbook. There was so much of it that, after first finding it fucking annoying, Roland soon merely wanted it to stop. He began to feel he'd accomplished something if James just left him alone. It was obvious that this was what James wanted him to feel – and Roland was now actually herding himself, which was also fucking annoying – but he felt that unwanted flicker of accomplishment nonetheless.

Before, when he and Sarah went out in the evening, she'd always been the one to eventually say that they should probably head if they were going to catch the night bus. Roland insisted on living more expansively than that. He hated it when friends of his – people close to him! – used the phrase "a school night". School was over. He swept Sarah along into ordering more drinks or walking home for hours through the night-time city or having elaborate sex when they finally got in. For her, it was exhausting and wonderful to be the one swept – freed from the sensible choices she'd have made on her own.

But now Roland began to experience the sour, crabby ache of trying to concentrate with a hangover. He was bilious; mildly poisoned. His thoughts were slow to load. This part wasn't any fun. And just as even the most rambunctious bullock will eventually start to flinch away from the electric fence, Roland's thoughts on a night out began to turn to the next day's chores.

In the mornings, to get from Sarah's to the office, he took the Victoria line to Green Park then switched onto the Piccadilly line to Piccadilly. When he knew London better, he realised he should just walk from Green Park. But for now his geography of the city was the Tube map. And once he'd made this journey dozens of times, he could hardly not notice that there was an optimal place to stand on the platform, so that when he got off at Green Park he would be deposited at the entrance to the correct tunnel. For months he stood anywhere but in this most efficient spot. It was not for him to make himself fit more neatly into the vast machinery of London. Instead, he drifted around reading the billboards, or sat on one of the moulded plastic seats and daydreamed.

But now that he was exerting himself at the office, he began to savour the half hour of sleepy peace on the packed Tube. He closed his eyes and let the swaying carriage rock him around. Particularly at the end of the day, when he wanted to get home fast, he just stood in the right place already.

It was no secret that James was trying to train him, like his mum wiring an unruly plant to a trellis. And he knew he was susceptible to the massed example of millions of Londoners. He was in danger of becoming an ordinary weary commuter like any other. He should do something about this right away. Maybe he should just tell James to shove his job up his ass. He could go travelling again while he thought about what to do next. Not India again. Maybe Japan finally. He still somewhere had his *Kanji for Beginners*.

SEPTEMBER 2008

That September, Ben Bernanke and Hank Paulson, the imperfect men who happened to be occupying the jobs of Fed chairman and treasury secretary at the time, had to try and rescue another failing bank: Lehman Brothers.

By this point, America's finance industry was unravelling fast. The week before, Paulson had already had to nationalise the world's largest mortgage lender, and then the second largest. Because the banks were tied to one another by a tangle of reciprocal loans and investments, whenever one slipped down into the black vortex of bankruptcy, it dragged the others closer to the edge.

Lehman was going down the same way as Bear Stearns. It had developed the taint of calamity, the death smell of a doomed animal, and was abandoned by the herd. Other banks stopped lending to it.

On Friday evening, Paulson convened a meeting of the bosses of Wall Street in the cavernous halls of the New York Federal Reserve, a transplanted palazzo modelled on those of the Florentine bankers who'd paid for the Renaissance.

Ben flew down from Washington and arrived late. On the flight he couldn't shake the feeling that the other passengers were watching him. It wasn't unusual for him to be recognised. The passengers on the Friday night shuttle were mostly politicos heading to New York for the weekend, who would know who he was. But each time he looked down at his briefing notes, he felt sure that nearby eyes flicked up and stayed on him. They must know or suspect that everything was going wrong at once. America's financial system was ripping itself apart. All that held back the roaring chaos was him and Hank.

He'd never experienced imposter syndrome. As a boy, when his school didn't offer calculus, he taught himself. A formative experience. Usually he was *more* able than required. But for the first time he did not feel equal to the task. He had only a human mind, limited, fallible, trained on the flawed theories of the day. His only tools were a few flimsy degrees, some things he'd read, some hunches and convictions that over the years had solidified into fixed beliefs.

What was needed was a mind like the sun, that could stand outside the planetary economy and illuminate its complexities in a steady blaze of solar intellect. Maybe he could have made a decent attempt if he – and his staff, and the economics departments of the leading universities – had had a year to think. But Lehman would be bankrupt by Monday. And in the car to Dulles he'd been briefed that AIG, the world's largest insurance company, was sinking too.

In New York, it was a stickily hot and smelly summer evening. A group of skater kids outside the Federal Reserve building were obliviously eating gelato. If the meeting finished in time, he had plans to meet some friends from NYU for dinner.

As soon as he stepped out of the car, a group of waiting officials hurried him inside. The meeting had already begun without him. He passed into this cool, quiet citadel of finance, and relaxed. Just for a moment he thought perhaps there was no need to hurry after all. Perhaps the course of events had already accelerated beyond his ability to redirect it. The catastrophe was so close that maybe it had to happen. He could hear the busy clipping and echoing of his and the officials' footsteps, but he felt oddly as if he were floating. If he pushed against what was unfolding, he might simply glide backwards like an astronaut pushing against the wall of his ship.

He recognised fatalism, the enemy. He had to carry on working. There was still a chance that Hank could be persuaded. Ben had been on the phone to him a dozen times today. He'd travelled down every line of argument, and Hank kept saying, "I'm not going to be Mr Bailout, and neither is the president."

Ben was learning quite brutally that for all the institutional prestige and legal independence of the Federal Reserve, he was a high-class civil servant and Hank was in politics. The familiar decor of Ben's profession – the deference, the privileges – was being torn away to reveal the beams and joists of raw power. They were getting down to fundamentals. Somewhere several storeys beneath his feet were wire cages holding stacked bricks of shiny yellow metal. The largest extant gold reserve. Ultimately, that was why they were gathering here.

He arrived at a heavy, panelled door, as if the direction of the global economy was going to be decided in a members' club, and an official opened it for him. Inside, Hank was standing at the head of a polished wooden table, his rangy, athletic old body leaning forward as if supporting itself on his fingertips. He'd apparently been holding forth, but he stopped talking and turned.

In the high, windowless, wainscoted room, under a chandelier, two dozen heads swivelled to look at Ben. Jamie Dimon was there. Lloyd Blankfein, who'd succeeded Hank as head of Goldman. The Johns: John Mack from Morgan Stanley and John Thain from Merrill Lynch. It was like a meeting of the five families in the New York mob. A predators' convention. Lehman hadn't been invited.

Ben saw at once that Hank wasn't going to be persuaded of anything. He was glowing with righteous strength and power. This was what he must have been like as a quarterback, eager for half-time to end so he could get back to the fight.

Hank said, "Hi there, Ben. Come in and sit down. We've just started." And to everyone else, "As you can see, we've had Ben come down from DC. The federal government is committed to giving you every assistance to make this darn thing fly."

Ben sat down and said nothing. He let the discussion of Lehman heave back and forth. Hank related that he'd tried to sell Lehman to the Koreans, but they weren't buying. Then he pushed his plan to break up Lehman into toxic chunks and have the other Wall Street banks swallow one each. In effect, the banks would club together to bail out their stricken rival.

As it went on, Ben became aware that he didn't have anything to contribute. He'd offered Hank the Fed's chequebook and Hank had said no. The floating feeling came over him again. When he got to the hotel that night, he should write down for the historical record what he remembered about this evening. If in a couple of years he was eating cold beans in a shanty town beside the Washington Monument, he'd be able to tell his fellow hobos that he was there when the decision was made. He almost laughed aloud.

It was Lloyd Blankfein from Goldman who first noticed the catch in what Hank was proposing – perhaps because he knew him so well. Little Lloyd, very small, very clever, very affable. A Bronx boy who'd made it. Another smart Jewish kid who'd applied himself. In some ways he was unimportant: Goldman itself was probably too damaged to be much help. In his calm voice Lloyd said, "One second, Hank, can I just ask? I feel like we're missing something here. If we, if Goldman, all of us here, if we're each going to absorb a chunk of Lehman's debts, how much is the government going to underwrite? When Jamie took on Bear" – he opened his hand to indicate Dimon – "the government" – he nodded at Ben – "put up thirty billion dollars to mitigate the risks. You know better than anyone what our limitations are. If we're going to do this, I think we all need to know how much the government is going to help with."

Hank had known this question was coming, and attacked it. Even before Lloyd had really finished speaking, he said, "The government isn't going to be bailing out Lehman. I'm not going to be Mr Bailout any more, and neither is the president."

Uproar. Voices raised in anger and consternation. Someone was saying, "Fuck that, Hank. Fuck that." And someone else, "I'm not eating this for that asshole." Lloyd sat back in his chair to take it in. Not a word from Jamie Dimon, who looked uncharacteristically anxious. His great coup with Bear Stearns wouldn't be worth shit if all the banks went down.

Ben watched Wall Street's bosses argue like he was watching a shouty piece of theatre where, despite the drama, the ending had already been written. Dimon jolted into speech and started saying, "Hank. Hank. Can

I just say something here? Hank." Blankfein was doing sums in ink on the back of his briefing notes.

Hank was fighting his corner, relishing it, like a single ranger against a pack of bandits. He tore into them; they were wrong; they *could* afford it; they had an obligation to their industry. He told them, "Listen, goddamn it. If you own a hardware store in Columbus, Ohio, and you get in over your head, you don't ask the federal government to come and bail you out. No, you go bust and someone better takes your place. That's the American way. That's why we've got the most dynamic economy on Earth, and you all know it.

"Now, Ben here, I know his argument, and I respect his views, of course I do, that a bank like Lehman isn't a hardware store, it's just too big to be allowed to fail. But my God! My God!" Hank stared down at them like some fiery Midwestern preacher. His eyes were frighteningly pale. "That's even worse. Socialism, but only for the big boys. Government protection, but only for the rich. Heck no. Not on my watch. Not on my watch. We did it with Bear and if you ask me now, it was a mistake. We did it last week with Freddie Mac and Fannie Mae, and where does it end? At some point you've got to draw a line. If Lehman can't pay its way any more, it's gonna have to take its medicine like anybody else."

And that was that, really. Hank said the government wasn't going to bail out Lehman. Wall Street's bosses said they weren't going to do it either. There would be no rescue. This was the turning point. The consequences they could imagine for themselves. It felt like something grand and solemn should be said or done before each went his own way. But there was only shocked, speculative chit-chat, like the quiet ringing after a grenade goes off. Who was going to run the liquidation? Was there still a chance that Hank could sell Lehman to the Brits?

The bosses' thoughts turned to what this would inflict on their own banks, and the group broke up. Dimon came over to Ben to go through some details of the loan. While Dimon was talking, Ben kept trying to formulate the perfect put-down. Something like: *See if all your dollars are worth anything by next week*. But Dimon got what he wanted and left, shaking a hand, touching a shoulder, on the way out.

When the bankers had gone, Hank and Ben walked each other out through the high, vaulted, echoing corridors. Hank's mood seemed to have shifted. Now that it was just the two of them, he'd lost his bellicosity. He said, "I know you don't agree with this. And I hear what you're saying. Of course I do. But you see where I'm coming from on this, don't you?"

Ben looked up at Hank, whose bony sun-mottled head seemed to be bearing down on him. "I do. Yes. If you bail them out, there's no risk, and then they do even riskier things. Moral hazard. Econ 101."

"Exactly. Exactly." They walked a few steps without speaking. Then Hank said: "But." He grimaced. "It's going to be a bad day at the markets on Monday. A lot of people are going to lose a lot of money. Heck, *I'm* going to lose a lot of money. And I guess you are, too. I wish we could do something about it. But we'll ride it out, don't you think?"

"I hope so." And added, out of a simple impulse to reassure, "There's always the Brits. They might still go for it."

"Oh, they're not that dumb."

"No, I don't think so either."

"Have you looked at AIG? It looks like they're going down as well. The question is . . . Well." Hank let it go.

Then Hank's mood shifted again as his thoughts played out. With the slightest hint of a grin, he said, "And if the worst happens, and it's as big a shitstorm as you think, nobody'll have a darn thing to say about us bailing out the rest of them. Then we do whatever we need to. You and I'll be mighty busy boys."

Ben realised he didn't know or understand Hank at all. They went outside and stood on the sidewalk with Hank's blacked-out limo and Secret Service agents waiting at the kerb. The shadows were higher up the buildings than when he'd arrived. It was a relief to be back amid the traffic noise and striding pedestrians, with it all still turning and people still going about their business. Hank's strong hand gripped Ben's shoulder, and he stared into Ben's eyes. He said, "Don't lose heart. We'll get through this."

As Hank's car pulled away, Ben checked his watch. He still had time to meet his friends for dinner. But he realised he couldn't join them. He couldn't sit there, breaking bread, and omit to tell them that their pensions and their kids' college funds were about to get slaughtered. Thank God at least his own savings were going to get slaughtered too. But he could no more warn them than he could warn any of the millions of New Yorkers trying to make their way around him.

Over the weekend, the last hope – the Brits – indeed proved not quite dumb enough to buy Lehman Brothers. One of the five grand old investment banks of Wall Street went bust with more speed and less ceremony than a hardware store. There was no last-minute sale, and no bailout. The long-feared implosion of Wall Street finally occurred. When the markets opened, they crashed like they had on 9/11. Everyone tried to get their money out at once. The insurer AIG and another of the five investment banks, Merrill Lynch, tipped over into the tailspin of bankruptcy. Goldman and Morgan Stanley were going down as well.

The shock was so great, so swift and so indisputably catastrophic, that, just as Hank had predicted, the people who mattered changed their minds about bailouts. Now Hank did whatever he needed to. He yelled at the bosses of Bank of America that he would put each of them personally in prison unless they bought Merrill Lynch that very afternoon. They did it, and Ben sweetened the deal with billions of federal dollars inconspicuously routed via AIG.

That Tuesday, AIG itself was bailed out. But the general collapse wasn't halted. By the Friday, Wall Street was disintegrating so completely that Ben requested nearly a trillion dollars from Congress to bail out the entire financial system. He let the papers quote him as saying, "If we don't do this, we may not have an economy next week." And when Hank asked Congress to approve the Bill, he told them, "If it doesn't pass, then Heaven help us all."

The following week, Goldman and Morgan Stanley formally ceased to be investment banks, to qualify for more protection from the Fed. Lloyd

Blankfein kept Goldman alive by selling much of it to Warren Buffett at a knock-down price. Morgan Stanley did the same with the Japanese. Of Wall Street's five investment banks, Bear, Lehman and Merrill were gone or taken over, and Goldman and Morgan Stanley sold chunks of themselves for rescue.

In London, Lehman's staff were fired first thing Monday morning. The *Standard* had the story in its lunchtime edition. When Roland went to buy his sandwich, he saw the headline on the tall box that held the papers: "5,000 Jobs Go as Banks Crash". He didn't usually read news, but this sounded like a good tale. He peered at the front page on the top of the stack, under the gaze of a silent man huddled in a rainproof *Evening Standard* poncho.

When Roland saw the cover photo, he bought a copy and read it right there, with annoyed pedestrians bumping past him. The picture was of a girl he knew from uni, standing outside Lehman with a cardboard box. It was like coming home to find Tony Blair sitting on Clemmie's sofa. Worlds colliding; categories collapsing; the distant soap opera of news barging into his own circle.

No longer bothered about lunch, he hurried back to the office to show James, who must know her too. Someone had already spread several copies of the *Standard* across the conference table. The team was reading them standing up. Everyone was saying they should keep a copy as an artefact. This was meant to be the worst financial crisis since the Wall Street Crash.

The newspaper's columnists were dismayed and already training their cannons on the hubris of bankers alleged to call themselves "masters of the universe". But these were older people, with houses and children that depended upon stability. Among James and Roland's group, the mood was a kind of destructive elation: change, tumult, momentous days, a rupture from the usual steady flow of things. Down with the old and up with the new, whatever that turned out to be.

James was trying to glean some extra hidden insight from between the lines of the article. When things were in flux, when the social order's rigidity slackened, a bold individual could jink through the gaps to greatness.

Napoleon would never have made it from Corsica to Versailles without the revolution. It was when the established way of things went soft that an individual could press his own imprint into the times. You just had to be able to read the seeming chaos.

Roland said to him, "Have you seen who's on the front?"

James flipped the newspaper closed. The photo was of a good-looking girl he recognised from uni. She was standing on the street outside Lehman, glancing around like she didn't know where to go. "She was in our year, right?"

"Two years below us."

Her name was written onto the box with a sharpie: Masa Serdarevic.

James said, "Was she Croatian?"

"Not sure. I never really spoke to her. I think maybe Bosnian. Or Serbian. It's probably really bad to mix those up."

"And now she's on the front of the *Standard*." They were impressed.

They pored over the few meagre facts the newspaper had to offer. Masa was quoted saying, "I can't believe I did so many rounds of interviews to get this job. I've only been here two months."

It seemed that hundreds of now ex-Lehmanites were milling around outside the offices, talking to reporters and having their pictures taken. Roland said, "I bet we could get in there."

"Into their building?"

"Yeah. Like urban exploration."

"It would be something worth seeing."

With a rush of adventure, Roland said, "Why don't we do it, then?"

"What, just go there?"

"Yeah, we could just try it."

James thought this over. Somewhere there was a bigger stage than this DFID conference room. Perhaps today he could walk onto it. "Worst case scenario, it costs us a few hours' work, and we just get rebuffed and come back."

This was not at all what Roland expected. But he wanted to keep it moving forward, and said, "Yeah, exactly. That's exactly it."

"Okay then." James paused, but no objections occurred to him. "Okay, then, let's go. Anyone who wants to come, can."

Sarah looked at Roland. "You can't break into their building."

"Not break in. See if we can walk in."

"Yeah, I don't know. I don't think so."

James said, "I'm not going to spend time discussing it. We're going to lose half the day anyway. Those who don't want to come, there's plenty to get on with. Those who do, let's get going."

The team sized each other up. No one wanted to be first to decide. Gradually a feeling emerged, tentatively, deniably at first but finding reinforcement. Mouths grimaced. Heads shook sceptically. Shoulders shrugged as if to say it was a fun idea, but . . . When you got down to it, they were a group who'd got this far by following the rules. They had valuable jobs to lose.

James and Roland appraised each other. Neither would have been the other's first choice. James said, "Looks like it's you and me."

It was uncomfortable to be out of the office together, as if socialising. On the Tube, they stood, each holding a strap, and were relieved that the screeching of the train prohibited conversation. James tried to imagine where in a banking collapse the opportunities might be. Roland was live-texting the trip back to Sarah. There was no reception, but he'd queued up the messages: "On the Tube with J. No chat from the boss man." And "Made it. Still no chat from big J."

James, despite growing up in London, had never been to Canary Wharf. The Tube station was much higher, grander, cleaner and more industrial – more like a new airport – than the usual cramped Victorian passages. They went up an extra-long escalator to where a landscape of glass towers reached high above them. It was stranger than he'd imagined, a sort of miniature Singapore. The skyscrapers were so tightly packed that from above they must look like metal bristles on a hairbrush, a scratchy little island trying to float off down the Thames.

There were too many people on the streets, as in a revolution. The pocket park behind the Tube entrance was crowded with newly unemployed bankers. Some were drinking bottles of wine, some talking on the phone, some resting sadly on the sculptured benches. Other bankers still in their jobs, going to and from meetings, glanced in shock at this possible version of their immediate future, and stopped to speak to those they recognised.

Roland was delighted that something was finally happening. It was like a fire alarm at school, when lessons were interrupted and you could hurtle out to the car park, shouting and laughing. He gazed upward at a fifty-storey wall of glass, in which he could see a pale-yellow wodge of cloud being slowly shredded by the breeze. It was sick really that, at this time of day, he was usually cooped up inside.

At the Lehman building, most bankers had already dispersed. Some photographers with press cameras were loitering in case of action. Roland went over to one of the remaining groups of ex-bankers, men in their forties swigging rosé from bottles and smoking. "Hey guys. Do you know how we can get into the building?"

One who was talking angrily into his phone put it to his chest and said, "What for? It's all fucked in there."

"Just curious. Want to see what it's like."

"Here. Take my pass." Still holding his phone, he awkwardly pulled a pass off a clip on his belt, tearing at it when it wouldn't come. "See if you can set fire to something."

"Ha. Thanks. Has anyone got another one for my friend?"

Several took off their passes, and Roland reached for the nearest. The man who gave it to him said, "Knock yourself out," and smiled unhappily as he handed it over.

The passes had small headshots grainily printed on white plastic. Roland passed one to James with a grin. "Woop woop. If they look at the photos, we're screwed."

They put the passes on and walked side by side, performing self-assurance, towards the row of glass doors. Standing just inside the building was a straggly line of security guards: black guys in noticeably cheaper suits. One came out, and James said, "We were off-site this morning. Our things are still upstairs."

"You're working here?"

"Well, not any more. We just need to collect our things."

"No one is allowed inside."

"I know. We got the email. You have to leave once you've gathered your things. That's fine by me. But our things are still up there. I've got spare shirts, my hard drive, my running shoes, all kinds of stuff."

The guard looked at them: two assertive young white guys with posh voices, professional haircuts and expensive clothes, like the thousands of other posh young white guys at the bank. He said, "Okay. Okay. Come in."

They both said "thanks" as if this were expected and went in through the door he held open. As they were passing, he said, "But you must leave as soon as you are finished."

James said, "Nothing to stay for anyway."

Inside, the turnstiles were locked open and their passes weren't needed. They glanced at each other as they strode purposefully towards the lifts, but kept their faces straight. They got into a lift and faced the panel of numbered buttons. Roland said, "What do you reckon?"

"Just press one quickly."

Roland jabbed a button at random, and the gleaming brass door slid across. Once it was shut, Roland exclaimed, "Yes!" and held up his palm for a high five. They both wished he hadn't. But alone together in the polished cubicle, there was little choice. James patted his upraised hand and said, "Yes. Good stuff."

The door retracted again, and they ventured onto the scene before them. It was an ordinary office, with rows of desks much like their own, except abandoned. As they advanced, they saw many stories told in the limited semaphore of corporate furniture. Filing cabinets hung open and empty. An ergonomic chair was lying on its side in a corridor. Cables dangled where Lehmanites had stolen their work computers. They saw a woman pulling pairs of shoes out of the cabinet under her desk and forcing them into Sainsbury's bags, tearing the thin orange plastic. Further away, next to a window, two guys with their jackets off were lounging contemplatively in front of the view and smoking cigars.

As they walked around, Roland peeked into desk drawers and flicked excitedly through print-offs left lying around. There must be secrets everywhere. James didn't bother. He was searching for something bigger.

In a corner office, they found bales of shredded paperwork, neatly collected into white bin bags. Roland's gut told him this was major. The smoking gun. He said, "It's all here. Whatever they shredded. We could stick it back together."

"Like the Stasi documents in Berlin."

Roland didn't know about that but said, "Yeah, exactly," and ripped a hole in one of the bags.

James was getting the sense that the discovery here, the finding to be made, wasn't any individual object or document but the emptied building as a whole. He went over to the floor-to-ceiling windows and looked down at the square they'd just come from. Knots of bankers were drifting around the miniature park like tadpoles in a basin. A plane was taking off from City Airport, curving back round towards them. For a second he imagined it would keep curving until it smashed right into one of the banks. Concatenating disasters; the end of days. But it straightened up and headed away towards the Channel.

From behind him, Roland said in disgust, "It's all statements and spreadsheets. It'd take forever to figure out what the fuck it all is."

He came over, rested his forehead against the glass and looked down. The drop was an inch in front of his shoes. Although the wind was on the other side, he felt a wobble of vertigo and stepped back. A vague reflection of them standing beside each other hovered in the glass.

James said, "Not with a bang but with a whimper, eh?" He felt prophetic, as if present at the end of an era.

"Yeah, there's nothing here."

"Exactly. Exactly. There's nothing here. I bet if you went to, say, a tractor factory after the Soviet Union fell apart, you'd at least see machinery, I don't know, rolls of steel lying around. But here, now that it's stopped, there's nothing. It was all just . . . bullshit."

This was unexpected for Roland. He'd obviously had the wrong idea about James. He said, "Total absolute bullshit."

They watched the square.

James asked, "Do you think the other banks will go bust as well?"

"Me? What do *I* think? Um, I don't really know. But to be honest, I kind of hope they do. Like, fuck the lot of it."

"Me too. Me too. I know it's counterproductive. Maybe this is how the Mayans felt when their civilisation started collapsing."

"So, you reckon it's all fucked? We might have to live in the woods and eat squirrels to survive?"

"Ha, no. I don't actually think it's as bad as that. And we're on a government contract, remember, so our jobs are probably safe for a while."

"I don't really care if we lose our jobs."

"Me neither, in a way."

They carried on looking down. Roland said, "Nice work on the security guard by the way, at the entrance."

It was a long time since James had been complimented by someone his own age. His face opened up so fully it embarrassed him. "Oh, yeah. Thanks. And good job on getting the passes from those guys. I wouldn't have known how to do it."

Roland shrugged. "I just asked them."

"I wouldn't have known how." James wanted to say something more but didn't know what. So he said, "You know, I thought I'd told you before. But I'm not sure I really got it across. This India project was your idea."

"What?"

"Or rather, I got the idea from you. When you came back and I saw you at those drinks. You were talking about how education isn't scalable. That's what made me start thinking about it."

Roland was flattered. "What, really?"

James felt the release of confession. "Yes. I was working on something about oil before, predicting a crash. Actually, this might trigger it. Although this would be a demand shock rather than – but anyway, yeah, the thoughts I had from you turned out to be much more fruitful."

Roland raised his eyebrows and turned down his mouth, a mime of disbelief. "Wow. So like, you could say I'm the muse for this project?"

"Ha. Well, maybe your time in India. But yeah."

"Then you definitely can't sack me, can you?"

James laughed. "I suppose, now that your work isn't egregiously shit any more, I probably can't."

About two months later, they went to some leaving drinks for people from their cohort. The shock wave travelling outwards from Lehman had struck them. Because the banks were so paralysed, even the corporate empires on McKinsey's client list couldn't get a loan. They cancelled any spending they could.

As all kinds of companies did that, they removed item after item from one another's order books in a self-reinforcing cycle. Prospects were revised downwards, and downwards again. The Mini Cooper production lines outside Oxford went to reduced hours, then half hours, then were switched off. Woolworths went bankrupt after ninety-nine years trading; its sad remaining stock of CDs and novelty gifts was sold for whatever anyone would pay. The shops had white gunk smeared across their windows so people couldn't see the bare space inside. The newly unemployed stopped spending money, and the spiral kept turning down and down.

McKinsey couldn't be seen to make anyone redundant. One justification for its exorbitant fees was that you were buying strategic foresight. The Firm used this occasion to announce to its rivals and potential customers that it didn't need to let anyone go. So the three McKinseyites having their leaving drinks that evening, like the many who'd gone since the crash, hadn't officially been laid off. They were taking unpaid sabbaticals of indefinite duration. One had squeezed into a last-minute place at the INSEAD business school in Paris; the second was doing an apprenticeship at an artisanal bakery; and the third had been encouraged to pursue her ambition of writing a detective novel. The weekly alumni circular had taken on a different tone.

James led the McKinsey half of his team along the wide, noisy streets from Whitehall over to St James's. He went at the head of the little gaggle and found Roland next to him. Since their incursion into Lehman, they sometimes drifted towards each other. Around them, the restaurants were still busy, the brightly lit souvenir shops were still selling T-shirts and keyrings, the traffic was still noisy and hurrying. But it felt fragile, as if the big hidden motor powering the whole carousel might abruptly cut out, the wheels whirring on for a few seconds in the sudden quiet.

Roland said, "I asked Sarah if she wanted to come along, I hope that's okay. But she said no."

James didn't know what he was being asked, if anything. "Yeah, I'm sure that would have been fine. I think everyone's buying their own drinks anyway, so there wouldn't have been a numbers question."

"Yeah, great. She's not coming anyway."

"Okay."

"I'm sure you've noticed that, like, um, she hasn't been coming out at lunchtime."

James hadn't noticed. He said, "No, I hadn't noticed. Is she okay?"

"Yeah, she's fine, she's fine." Roland lowered his voice. "I think it might be, like, coming to an end maybe, our thing."

"Oh. Are you sad about it?"

"Definitely. Definitely. Well, no. Not really. I know that's bad. And she's amazing. She's really, *really* cool. But, like, nothing lasts forever, does it?"

"I suppose not. Is *she* sad about it?"

"Umm." This wasn't what Roland had been driving at. "Umm, yeah. She is. She definitely is. Yeah."

"So she's sad and you're not. What steps have you taken to . . . I don't know, to mitigate that?"

Roland was annoyed. James didn't get to supervise this part of his life. Had he ever even had a girlfriend? "Umm. I know I just brought it up, but actually I don't think it's fair to talk about her in detail. Especially since we work together."

"Okay." James checked over his shoulder that the others couldn't hear, and said, "Actually, even if you and Sarah do have an acrimonious break-up, it doesn't really matter from a work perspective. I got told yesterday: DFID are never going to spend this money we're planning for them. They're not going to fund any Indian schools. They can't afford it any more."

"Because of the credit crunch?"

"Yup."

"Sooo, does that mean you're not my boss any more?"

"Ha. Soon. They're still locked into the contract for this piece of work. So another few months."

"I won't miss it."

"Me neither."

"And then what? We get volunteered for an unpaid sabbatical?"

"Depends how deep the recession goes."

"You know they're pushing out all the Fs."

"What?"

"In the Myers–Briggs. The people who are Fs, feeling and intuiting, instead of Ts, thinking and reasoning. You must be a T, right?"

"Yeah."

"Okay, well, I'm an F. And the Fs are getting fired. So you'd better stop busting my balls or you'll feel incredibly guilty when I go."

"Wait, *what*?" James didn't know Roland could speak to him like that. "When do I bust your balls? And how do you know everybody's Myers–Briggs results?"

"I just hear things. If you spent more time chatting to people, you'd hear them, too."

James absorbed this. "You're probably right. I've never been good at tapping into those informal information networks."

"Informal information networks."

"Gossip. The rumour mill. I've never been able to locate the rumour mill."

"Do you want to know what else they're saying there?"

"Please."

"No team-bonding week in Ibiza this year. All we're getting is dinner in Pizza Express."

James was fine with that.

When they arrived at the Red Lion, it was jammed with McKinseyites and at shouting volume. Most were low-level analysts, but there were also a few partners who'd worked with those being pushed overboard. The leavers' speeches maintained the high-achieving, every-crisis-is-an-opportunity tone, straining to communicate that this was not a failure, that they had not failed.

But the mood in the pub was angry, mutinous, betrayed. For the first time at McKinsey, James heard people talking about how much they were paid. Some analysts were calculating how many analyst jobs you could save if each partner took a ten per cent pay cut. At the bar, a partner was trying to persuade a hostile circle drawn close in around him that this was just a blip and the good times would come again. Someone said, "But the difference is you've already had twenty years to fill up the old bank account."

James saw Eleni, who'd stayed in oil and gas and was beginning to be considered a star in the industry. Some of the rich-girl swishiness had gone. The waterfall of black Greek hair had been cut short. She'd become sharper-edged. He got the sense she was doing a lot of exercise.

She pushed through to him and yelled into his ear, "I guess this means you're not going to be the youngest-ever partner."

"Guess not."

"And no bonuses either."

Even without a bonus, the numbers printed on James's bank statements had grown large enough to buy a moderately nice London house while prices were depressed. If he bought now, then when prices swung back up, James would accrue far more than his bonus scheme was offering. But he hadn't done anything about it. Somehow it was too crude, too uninteresting. He said, "No, no bonus. Oil and gas must be brutal right now."

"Horrible. Everyone's being sacked."

"Are you going to go work for your cousins?"

"Absolutely not. Shipping is brutal, too. It's basically a function of GDP. The more things people buy in shops, the more stuff has to be shipped over from China. And no one's buying anything."

"So what, you're only going to make a few million this year?"

"Ha, yeah. If it carries on like this, my uncles are going to have to start flying commercial."

Nobody peeled off early from the drinks, except the partners, who escaped when they could, with relief, and went home to their Georgian townhouses and the Aston Martins they'd bought themselves as a one-off treat, to their families eating supper in clean, well-lit kitchens, the children in their private-school uniforms and the surfaces wiped by staff. By the time they were eating their healthy, pre-prepped halibut and gulping a restorative glass of crisp cold Montrachet, the younger generation were nailing sambuca shots and the leavers had admitted that everything was fucked.

On the last day of the DFID contract, James told what was left of the team to proofread their report for the final time. A couple of the DFID people had already been reassigned. Sarah, Roland's ex-girlfriend, had asked to be one of them. The McKinseyites were only still there so that the Firm could keep billing the government for their salaries. As of tomorrow, neither James nor Roland had a next assignment.

James had planned for the last tweaks to take the whole day, but they were done before lunchtime. Now he could email it to the list of senior DFID names he'd been given, by whom it would be ignored. They'd said there was no need for a presentation.

James clicked through to the end of the spellcheck's suggestions, sent the email, and said, "Okay, that's it. We're finished." The team nodded or sighed. No one said anything. Only Roland wasn't depressed. He'd never imagined that he was working towards something that mattered. He asked, "Are you going to send it to them or just put it straight in the bin?"

"I've just sent it. But by the time DFID's budget has recovered enough for anyone to look at it, it'll be years out of date."

Roland laughed. "Come on, James. Aren't you meant to, like, give us a well-done speech to make us feel better?"

"Okay, well, the way I think about it is, I suppose some of you believe this was a futile waste of time. Maybe it was. But each of us can know, for ourselves, what level of quality we were working at. And so you know how proud or disappointed you can be."

Roland laughed again. "Great speech. Shall we go out for lunch to celebrate? Do you have anything left on the expenses card?"

"Yeah, there's enough."

No one else seemed keen. They thought they might just go home.

James said, "Okay, that's it then. That's the end. Good luck in what you do next."

There were murmurs of thanks and goodbye. The team packed away their laptops. James said, "Oh, McKinsey people, don't forget to leave your passes at the lodge."

Roland said, "I'm still up for lunch if you are."

He and James went to a pub nearby and drank pints through the afternoon quiet. As of an hour ago, they were no longer manager and underling. Lounging on the banquette of a corner table, it felt peaceful and lordly to have nowhere to go and nothing to do. Good riddance to boring old DFID; good riddance to India. Let everything crash. And it didn't seem so strange that it was the two of them together.

IV

FEBRUARY 2009

James and Roland were sent up to the outer rim of Europe, to Aberdeen, to sack hundreds of people from an oil company called Subsea7. So many companies were sacking so many people that McKinsey was soon ringing up the discarded juniors on their unpaid sabbaticals and asking whether they'd like to get the next flight back to London.

Oil and gas, a gold-rush industry with disdain for financial planning, was defenceless against the downturn. Back in June, they could sell a barrel of oil pumped out of the North Sea for $140. Now it was February, and the price was $43. The big crash had come.

The Firm didn't like to consider itself expert in sacking people. It would rather sell "strategic foresight" than "restructuring". But when companies were failing, and it was time to get down to the pitiless red arithmetic of money in versus more money out, no one could do restructuring like McKinsey.

In the bland optimistic theory of business textbooks, the reason for hiring James and Roland was that they weren't entangled in Subsea7's loyalties or committed to its departmental fiefdoms. With rational detachment, they could identify and cull the lazy or superfluous. Like upholsterers hatcheting down through rotting fabric, they could hack every scrap of boom-time excess back to the naked frame. And they could do it while leaving the money-generating crux of Subsea7 cold, shivering and exposed, but intact.

The practical truth, however, was that Subsea7's bosses could have done this gory business far better on their own. They knew who and what was useless. But they shied away from choosing the victims on their own authority. So they paid McKinsey to send them a few hooded executioners who could be loaded up with hatred and sent away again. The common knowledge that the pushy young consultants up from London were getting paid the megabucks — while colleagues with children lost their jobs — simply contributed to the effect.

The office inadvertently booked James and Roland onto the same flight up. James was in the first row; Roland in the third. The Business section was now only three rows deep. The divider curtain had been moved forward; behind that, it was now all Economy. Once they landed, Roland darted up the aisle, queue-skipping, so they could disembark together.

They stepped through the door and into a braided current of wind running inland off the North Sea. It pushed their eyes into a squint and went through their London clothes as if they weren't there. Thick clouds dimmed the midday down to a greyscale murk. The airport's outside lamps were on. Beside the single-storey concrete terminal was an industrial airport with helicopters lifting off like wasps for the oil rigs. Behind that was a field where black-and-white cows huddled together in one corner. They felt a long way from Pret a Manger.

Inside the terminal, they wheeled their mini suitcases and felt the blood return to the capillaries in their faces. The destinations on the departures board were Stavanger, Bergen, Kirkwall, Reykjavik. Heavily built men in company fleeces, roughnecks with watery old tattoos creeping up from their collars, sat alone, drinking and texting. At WHSmith's there was a tall ziggurat of identical books: *Don't Tell My Mum I Work on the Rigs: She Thinks I'm a Piano Player in a Whorehouse*. The adverts on the illuminated billboards were for rigging equipment.

Roland said, "We should write down the names of these companies. These'll be our next clients."

"Ha. Yes. We'll need to hire lots more people to do all the sacking."

"You know they tried to persuade Julia to come back from literal Bali."

"Who's Julia?"

"In my intake. She's got this great story about her sister going out one night and – never mind. You don't know her."

"Is she coming back from Bali?"

"Yes, eventually, but not back to the Firm. She's going to do Teach First instead."

James said, "There's a kind of paradox, isn't there? That we're here to strike people off their ledger, and to do it we'll need to add more people onto ours. Makes you wonder if there's some way to just transfer them over to us."

"Like, instead of sacking them we just hire them all?"

"Yeah. Doesn't make much sense actually."

"No, sorry, mate. There's no clever way out. We're just going to ruin their lives, and they're going to hate us."

"They probably already do."

"They shouldn't though, should they, really? It's the bosses they should hate. We're just minions. I guess you're a mini boss. They can hate you a little bit."

"Tolstoy says this thing in *War and Peace* that the higher up an organisation you go, the less freedom you really have. At the bottom, you can do whatever you feel like because it doesn't make much difference, but at the top, if you're Napoleon or the Tsar, the responsibility is so big you just have to do what the logic of the situation dictates."

"That's such bollocks."

James laughed.

"You know my dad works in oil and gas?"

"Does he? No, I didn't – oh, that's why you didn't grow up in England."

"Expat oil brat."

"Is his job safe?"

"Don't worry. We're not going to have to go and sack my dad."

James didn't know what to say to that. It seemed too personal to comment on. He said, "I'm sorry, Roland. I know we're joking around. But I hope your dad's job . . . progresses in the way he wants."

Roland gazed at him with the beginnings of annoyance – the suggestion that his dad was vulnerable. James couldn't tell whether he'd said something wrong. He hesitated and said, "By the way, you might have noticed I'm still not always at the gold standard of reading other people.

So sometimes my communicating is a little bit off the mark. But I'm using this technique where I just try to say very clearly what I'm driving at."

Roland closed his eyes then started chuckling more and more as they walked along, leaning forward over himself to try and keep from yelling with amusement. James let him laugh himself out; he was used to this sort of thing. Eventually, Roland sighed with pleasure and wiped his eyes on the back of his sleeve. He said, "Ah, fuck me. Does this mean you'll tell me the exact truth about anything I ask you?"

James considered and said, "No."

Roland laughed again.

They collected their suitcases and discovered that the office had booked two cabs. Fares were now scarce and neither driver wanted to lose his. So James and Roland sat in one car while the other followed them, empty, to the Aberdeen Mercure.

On the way into town, Roland saw many types of greyness: the bulgy ceiling of cloud, gum-spattered concrete paving, pebble-dash walls in the cheap outer neighbourhoods, pale granite buildings in the centre, and everywhere ashen, unhealthy faces never touched by sunshine. In the murk, the yellow plastic bollards and the elongated arches at McDonalds glowed out as landmarks. Aberdeen looked remote, grim, weather-lashed, probably incestuous. A bit *Wicker Man*. His mum said that if Aberdeen broke off from the rest of Scotland and floated out into the North Sea, none of the Aberdonians would notice.

James, meanwhile, saw the differences from the last time he'd been here. Back then, he'd been told that Aberdeen, "the oil capital of Europe", had more millionaires than any British city outside London. Now the high-end restaurants had placards outside offering meal deals. On every street there were OFFICES TO LET. They drove down the shopping strip and, like a good consultant, he tallied the SALE banners in the plate windows. Signs of a boomtown going bust.

From the front, the taxi driver was saying, "The oil's still out there. It's not gone. And people still need tae have their heating on, don't they?" He gave them his card in case they needed a taxi while they were here.

*

Most of Subsea7's thousand or so employees worked in a business park just outside the city. Amid raw fields enclosed by drystone dykes, Aberdeen's oil bonanza had plonked down a roundabout, a car park and some glass office buildings rated to last twenty years. In the fields around it, the crops were shaved back to a sharp bristle of cold stalks.

But the McKinsey team weren't there. The guy running the study, Aaron Jumabhoy, whom James knew from Kitzbühel and Tesco, had chosen to set up in Subsea7's town office. It was only a couple of overheated upstairs rooms overlooking the port. Through the small windows, they could see floating arrays of industrial machinery. The decks of these ships, with no need of the streamlined casings and bonnets fitted on anything sold to consumers, were a heavy tangle of pipes and cranes. The hulls were high and steep, like walls. Most were floating idly, waiting for a job, while saltwater nibbled ceaselessly at the paint.

Aaron and James were the two Engagement Managers in charge. James had always assumed that Aaron wasn't a competitor. He was a few years older, i.e. behind James's curve. And it was said of Singaporeans that they were better seconds in command than leaders, as if the trained eagerness required to pull Singapore out of the Third World had cost some independence of spirit.

But as they prepped for Aberdeen, James noticed that Aaron had added *Dr* to his email signature: Dr Aaron Jumabhoy. He asked Roland, who told him that Aaron had finished a PhD in avionics in his spare time. Hard science, unlike James's entry-level bachelor's in bullshittable PPE. Of course James could have had a PhD as well. Eleni had one, in biochemistry. His little sister was doing one right now. He would be the only person in his family who *didn't* have one.

When he and Roland walked into the slanted upstairs room, Aaron grinned and said, "Hey dudes. Welcome to sunny Aberdeen. Glad you decided to join us."

They went through the ritual of welcome: handshakes – comparing opinions on Aberdeen – the Mercure was pretty basic – last time James was in a country house hotel – the Firm couldn't be seen to be extravagant in a crisis. And apropos of nothing, James said, "Is there a particular reason we're not in the main office? It just seems like, all things being equal, we should be in the middle of things. But I realise I've just arrived, and there might be something I'm missing."

Aaron went stiff. The team were listening. It was his first study as Engagement Manager. "No particular reason. I just thought this was a better location. And we're all set up now, and it's good."

"Got it. Are they quite hostile?"

"Yes." Dr Jumabhoy nodded. "Not really obstructive per se. But yes, they are hostile."

"Okay, but to me at least it really feels like we've got to be there. Isn't it McKinsey 101? I think Bower even talks about it in his book. How can we make contacts and pick up information if we're out here in a satellite office?"

Aaron tried to interrupt, but James spoke over him. "I know it's hard to be around that kind of animosity all day. But honestly I think it's good for us. If we're going to discontinue these people's jobs, we can at least look them in the eye. But like I say, I've just arrived, so I don't have all the facts."

Aaron's face kept smiling. He said, "Okay, yeah. I see what you're saying. This office obviously gives us more privacy for talking through sensitive decisions. Especially with how many people are going to get let go. But if it's really important to you . . ."

"I just think it's best practice."

"Okay, yeah, I don't mind. We can switch over."

James shrugged. "Great."

"Yes, that's fine by me. We'll lose half a day moving, but we can do it."

"Great."

In the little fleet of taxis that transferred them and their computers, James rode with Aaron to plan the sackings. Roland went with a couple of Aaron's team. They hadn't thought of themselves as *Aaron's* until just now. A swishy West London Indian called Priya, probably the niece of a maharajah, twisted in the front seat and said, "So Aaron was pretty cheesed off, wasn't he?"

She was looking at Roland, who muttered, "Yeah."

"He's a bit of a dick, isn't he? James."

"I don't know. Is he?"

"He's just pissed all over Aaron. Does he just want to be the big man?"

Roland blushed and shrugged at once. "Why are you asking me?" He'd thought this was going to be the fun car.

"Didn't you two come together?"

"The office booked us on the same flight." He shrugged again. Roland didn't want to be anyone's defender.

"He's not wrong though, is he?" said the other analyst in the taxi, who Roland hadn't met before. "It's 101. And we should at least, yeah, look them in the eye."

Priya said, "Oh yeah, that'll be fun," and turned back to watch the road unspooling in front of the windscreen.

James and Aaron agreed they would work separately. While Aaron slowly rotated Subsea7 like a doner kebab on a spit and sliced off the fat, James would search for divisions that could be erased in their entirety. The subsidised canteen employed twenty-four people. You could get a full Scottish breakfast for a pound. Lunchtime lasagne for a pound. On Fridays, fish and chips for a pound. Nobody was going to like getting rid of it. But nobody was going to like any of this.

James chose Roland to help him. Two neat and clean young men with English accents, they came in to people's offices and politely asked what they actually did all day.

James had assumed this would be a task of meticulous detection, of inefficiencies brilliantly uncovered, but there was blatant wastage everywhere. Half the employees barely lifted a finger. They spent days listlessly scheduling meetings or organising the holiday calendar. A company grown fat on oil. For James it was like finding ripe fields of wheat yearning for the scythe. Roland felt like a snitch.

They drove around in a fancy black Mercedes to which they'd been upgraded. The rental company didn't want its best cars seizing up through sitting around unused. The rear footwells were soon ankle-deep in litter. In what Roland called their *braggin' wagon*, they drove to the warehouse where leased machinery was kept, and took pictures with a digital camera. They counted the vans in the company fleet. James asked to see logs, accounts, inventories, lists of assets, the estimated resale value of the equipment; the salaries and notice periods of everyone in the room.

When they introduced themselves, some people were astonished, as if they'd never really believed that the credit crunch on TV had any connection with themselves. Certainly they knew that because the oil price was no good right now things were a bit different at work. But until James and Roland walked into their offices like oncologists striding in with test results, these people had never quite realised that the fractures crackling outwards from the banks in New York would penetrate into their very homes; into what they had for their tea; into their self-esteem and standing in the world; into the education and prospects of their children; that even what they considered most sacrosanct was not just at risk, it was already lost.

James thought this must be how the secret police felt during Stalin's Great Purge, thundering on someone's door in the middle of the night. You always made an entrance. They were the agents of destiny, the two horsemen of the recession. James saw you might start to enjoy it, and warded that off by becoming exquisitely scrupulous; so frank and fair it was impersonal.

Some they met wryly grinned and shook their heads, suddenly believing that on one level they'd always known. Some said, "Are you going to do to us what you did to Enron?" and felt they'd scored a point. Some just left, walking out of the room or the warehouse to do who knew what. Many others told them they were wasting their effort: when the oil price went back up, they'd all be hired back on; this was just a needless sham the bosses wanted them to go through.

The employees James and Roland's own age were often outraged.

They'd got their degrees in geology or marine engineering from Aberdeen or Dundee; they'd taken out mortgages on five-bedroom houses and bought their Mercs and BMWs on finance. Some were married. They'd kept up their end of the social contract.

One was pregnant. Not distant in age from them, already huge and bewildered, shocked out of the gathering animal calm of approaching birth. She had to manoeuvre herself between the arms of the office chair to hear how she was getting sacked. She was too surprised to cry. Through the low-level mental static of many nights' shallow sleep, she said, "You can't sack a pregnant woman. Can you?"

Roland couldn't handle it. He said, "It'll be okay. Don't worry. It'll be fine."

"What do you mean?"

James took over. "You're right that being pregnant entitles you to some special protections in employment law. I have a leaflet on them here. I'm sorry to say you can still be made redundant. But you'll be entitled to statutory maternity pay."

"What's that, a hundred quid a week?"

"After the first six weeks, yes, roughly. A hundred and seventeen."

"What am I going to do? My mortgage. Seriously, what am I supposed to do?"

They looked at her across the grey desk, with nothing to offer. Afterwards, Roland said to James: "I mean, there's nothing we *can* do."

And James said, "Isn't there?"

There were many more people to fire. They went once into a staff kitchen on the second floor, a bright, narrow galley with a kettle, fridge and microwave, to find it crammed with Subsea7 employees sombrely holding cans of beer and white plastic cups of prosecco in the middle of the afternoon. A farewell drink. Goodbye and good luck. Maybe some of us will meet again. When James and Roland blundered in, the small crowd just stared at them as they reversed back out. Roland couldn't stop himself saying, "Sorry."

The middle managers, the heads of department, usually tried to get back on side. They welcomed James and Roland with discreet commiserations about the difficult job they had to do. They talked exasperatedly about sub-prime mortgages and Wall Street, and handed over cost-cutting plans they'd drawn up for eliminating everyone except themselves.

The head of the R&D unit came to plead with them directly. Alan was one of the small, dark Scots, a Pict, stocky and swarthy, in his forties, dressed in a fisherman's jumper below a black beard with twists of white, like fusilli. He gave them the visitor tour of his workshop on an industrial estate by the docks. The double-high room held two boats, necklaces of pink buoys, a dozen white iMacs, racks of thermal clothing, crates of cables and tools.

His team had their computers hooked up to an underwater maintenance robot and to something that he — joking but not really joking — called the future of the company: a model of a floating turbine for generating electricity from the tide "when the oil runs out". The workshop must have cost as much as a hundred canteens.

James sincerely admired the equipment and had a long, interested chat with Alan about it. But the chat became sad towards the end. James said, "You must know yourself that all of this is going to go."

"This is valuable stuff here. I'm sure you'll do what you can."

"Actually, this might sound harsh, but I won't. It's not my personal decision, to bend the process for the things I like. There's a logic to what gets cut. It's not preference."

Alan screwed up his mouth and nodded a few times. "Fair enough."

A small number of those they met, with no pattern of age or status, seemed relieved that fate had drawn their number. It was as if they could now put down the burden of getting on with life. They could stop waking up early, stop putting on office clothes and stop pretending to give a fuck about any of this. There was one woman in particular, Janey, who did contracts in the leasing office. Early fifties, probably less than a decade to retirement. A bit overweight in the normal way; sandy hair in the practical Scottish woman's style — shortish around the sides and puffy on top, like a muffin. She was the only one who spontaneously smiled when James said they were from McKinsey.

While James was telling her candidly that she should prepare to be made redundant, she became happier and happier, elated even, as if a great freedom was revealing itself to her. Roland thought she was about to cast off her clothes and stride naked and euphoric into the hills. He wanted to strip and go with her. He felt like a malevolent corporate robot was wearing his face, using its cold pincers to waggle his arms and work his mouth.

The employees often asked, with varying degrees of distrust, "This'll be your first time in Scotland?" And Roland was off on one about how his mum was from Inverness and his dad was at Schlumberger. Pushing their civility as far as it would go, he told them he'd grown up in the industry, so he knew what it was like. After their first day there, he stopped wearing his pinstripe suit.

But although Roland put forth all his charm, the Aberdonians didn't come to him. When they'd recovered from the initial jangling shock and realised they had questions, they asked to speak to James. Word had got around that he would give it to them straight. It was Roland who remembered all their names and brought up details of what they'd spoken about. But they looked past him at James.

A rumour began that James had given the pregnant girl ten grand of his own money to cover her mortgage. No one dared ask James about it because doing so might somehow break the protective spell. Roland had three meals and fourteen hours with James every day and would have known if it was true. It irritated him that James's prestige among the Aberdonians rose higher.

Eventually, in trying to get Subsea7's employees to forgive him, Roland pushed too far. It was with a thick-handed former roughneck who, when too old for the rigs, had made the difficult step to an indoor job. His face was mottled grey, and he smelled of stale smoke. He probably wasn't going to get hired again after this. Roland was explaining how his mum was from Inverness and how he understood the industry so well, and this man said, "So, what does your dad think about you doing this?"

Roland was thrown. "Oh. Umm."

"Coming up to Scotland to sack people out of the industry."

Roland sat back in his seat. His attention went diffuse. Frosted glass on the door. Tiny knobbles on the table's surface. Suddenly he'd had too much of corporate surroundings. It was like eating masses of bland food; at some point the body said no. The former roughneck was still looking at him. Roland threw up his hands. "I don't know. You're right. You're absolutely right."

James intervened before this could get further out of hand. "So, just to come back to where we were. There's a legally defined redundancy process, which you can read about in this leaflet. This is us formally letting you know that you're at risk of redundancy. From now, we're in the consultation phase. Any actual decisions will be taken by Subsea7."

"I'm getting canned, amn't I?"

"My personal opinion is yes."

That evening, they were sitting on tall stools at a high-up square table in the gloomy bar at the Mercure. It was a Monday and there were only a couple of other travelling businessmen sipping chilly pints and checking their BlackBerrys.

The two black-shirted barmen were leaning their bums against the fridge cabinets while the news played on mute above them. The BBC correspondent Nick Robinson, with his bald head, square glasses and fluffy microphone, was standing outside Number 10. It was still evening in London, though it was already dark up here.

James had a plate of fish and chips on the stool beside him. After each bite he wiped the grease off his fingers with a maroon paper napkin, and tapped the keys on his laptop. Roland wasn't eating. He had a pint he was glumly staring at. James was delicately filleting the information from Alan in the R&D workshop.

As in most departments, Alan made supposedly innocent mistakes about how much money they'd spent. He forgot expensive equipment; he misplaced tranches of receipts; his list of costs omitted about half his team, whose details were on a separate sheet, which had also been lost. A kind of desperate, last-resort guerrilla defence, trying to hide at least a few survivors from the inevitable.

James quite enjoyed that they tried to fight their corner. Sorting it out was like a sudoku of cross-referenced salaries and bills for arc welders. Alan was wilier than most, but if James didn't blunder, he had enough information to win this game sooner or later. Alan had misplaced the salary records from 2005–2007; James reconstructed the figures from submissions to HMRC, and experienced a little release of contentment when the numbers matched up.

He didn't mind that Roland wasn't contributing. It was companionable to have him sitting there. After a while, he took pity and asked, "You alright?"

"Might go back to London this weekend."

"Oh yeah?"

"Yeah."

James articulated carefully. "From an outsider's perspective, it seems like you're – like you've got a suboptimal reading on the daily happiness scale."

Roland laughed through his misery. "A suboptimal reading on the happiness scale?"

"Fine. I was just checking you're okay. You know I am technically your line manager. There's a duty of care."

"No, no. Don't get all – fuck off, okay? *I'm* totally fine. *I'm* not getting sacked."

James could tell he'd done the right thing by broaching the topic. He was supporting Roland. But what to say next? He tried, "I see. Hmm. At least that's something, isn't it? Unless you *want* to be sacked?"

"Maybe I do. It's not like this is fun."

"I don't think you should quit."

"Why don't *you* quit? You enjoying this? Or are you that desperate to be the big boss?"

"Ha. No. Well, maybe it's useful at the margins to have this experience. A little taste of forensic accounting. But really I think of it more like in school when the teacher's off sick and the substitute just gets you to watch a video. The recession's an enforced pause. Nobody can do anything. Competition suspended. It's quite relaxing in a way."

"Not for the people we're sacking."

"No. Not for them. Though of course there's a big-picture argument that we're doing them a favour."

Roland scoffed.

"Seriously. It's like: the recession can only end when companies start growing again. To grow, they need to weed away the excess costs that are choking them, i.e. the people whose jobs don't make sense now that things have changed. The faster those people are fired, the faster companies can adapt and start growing and hiring again."

"Do you believe that?"

James thought. "I'm not sure yet. That's the theory. But there's a question about who gets sacked and who doesn't."

"The bosses."

"Yeah."

"And it's not like you need to be a genius to be the boss of an oil company. It's just a big pump, and you literally just pump money out of the ground. And Aberdeen fucking sucks as well." Roland put his face down on a stack of files.

James looked at the whorl in his sandy hair. He did not want Roland to go to London for the weekend while he stayed in the Mercure. "How about this? Why don't we find the things that Aberdeen is good at?"

Roland didn't lift his head.

"It's close to beautiful countryside. So let's do that."

"It's dark. It's always dark here."

"Not now. This weekend. Don't go to London and spend the weekend complaining, which'll only make you feel worse. Let's find out what the best mountain is and go up it."

"Me and you?"

"Yeah. We can invite Aaron and his team as well, but I don't think they like me very much."

The prospect of something entirely unexpected cut through Roland's mood. He brightened up. "Like some weird little weekend mini-break for me and you? To turn my frown upside down?"

James went awkward. "It's just an idea. It's not a work thing. It's not obligatory."

"No, no!" Roland smiled. "I'd love to go on a weird weekend."

"It's not a weekend, necessarily. There are plenty of mountains we could get to on a day trip."

Early on Saturday morning, James stood with the hotel receptionist in the stuffy corridor outside Roland's room. After knocking for a while, he'd gone down and asked her to bring her key. She unlocked the door and he went inside.

The room was warm and had the thick cosy reek of a teenage boy's. Roland was sleeping curled up on his side with the thin duvet wrapped around him. James switched on the light and said, "Roland. Roland!"

Nothing happened. James didn't want to touch him in his sleep. He pushed up the window to let in a stream of cold air, yanked the duvet away and shouted, "Roland! Wake up!"

Roland squirmed. His hand groped around for the missing duvet, and he mumbled, "What time is it?"

"Ten past seven."

"Oh, later. Later, okay?"

"We've got to get on the road now, or we'll lose the light this afternoon."

"It's okay. You go without me. It's okay." Roland pushed his face into the pillow.

James thought. He went into the bathroom, filled the complimentary plastic cup with water and came back. "I've got a cup of water here that I'm going to throw on you."

"Oh fuck off, James."

"Three. Two."

Roland mumbled, "Okay. Okay. I'll be down in a minute."

"One."

Roland didn't move. James splashed the water on his face. As it hit him, Roland's limbs convulsed. Then he jerked upright and said, "Okay, you're right, you're right." His eyes blinked open and shut, and he rubbed his hands over his pale, skinny body. "I'm up, I'm up. We're going. Great. Amazing. Let's go." He yawned, closing his eyes again, then by an effort of will sprang to his feet. "Let's go climb a mountain. But wait, do I have to dress like that, too?"

James, after detailed online research, had procured top-of-the-range technical clothing. Purple Norwegian trousers with reflective patches. A fluorescent-yellow survival jacket. Spotless hiking boots. He was sweating into his merino-blend base layer, which was wicking it away. He said, "This is the best outdoor gear on the market."

"Looking at you is hurting my eyes. Are you colour-blind or something?"

James strove for a comeback but didn't get there in time. "Can you just get dressed already? I've got something downstairs you're going to like."

Roland rolled his eyes and said, "Yes, boss." He hunted around for clothes while James sat on the desk chair. The stiff, bulky jacket stood up off him. Roland picked up a pair of jeans and put them on. While James waited, he put on a hoodie, the black leather loafers he wore to the office and a single-breasted grey coat.

James said, "Are you being serious?"

"I packed badly, okay? I packed like a complete idiot, okay? I was late and I just put some stuff in my bag, and I know I should have looked at it properly, but I didn't, and now this is all I've got."

"No other shoes?"

"No, I'll wear these. They'll get ruined and I'll probably fall over every five minutes, and it'll be a life lesson to me to get better at packing. Okay?"

"Okay. Then let's go. I've got lunches, maps and breakfast for you in a bag. We're going to a mountain called Lochnagar. There's a Byron poem, which you can google if you haven't read it."

Outside it was dawning and the air was fresh off the North Sea. The old-fashioned iron streetlamps were still on. The Mercure was on a once-grand street. Opposite the hotel was an ornate granite balustrade overlooking a little park. Last night's chip boxes were scattered around.

Right outside the hotel was a boy racer's jerk fantasy of a car, a flashy low-slung purple Lamborghini, its wing mirrors tucked in like the ears of a sleeping puppy. James said, "Ta-daa!"

Roland laughed incredulously. "Oh my *GOD*. What . . . ?"

"Thought it might cheer you up."

"You bought me a *car*?"

"Oh no. No. I rented it. There's a hire place near the beach. They've got dozens of these things, going cheap."

Roland laughed again and shook his head. "Amazing. Amazing."

"Do you want to drive first?"

"It's your thing. You paid for it. You go ahead. Honestly."

"No, no. I —"

"Honestly. I still need to wake up a bit. You drive. I'll drive back."

It took James until they were out of town to get the hang of the car, which twitched under him like an untamed pony. But once he had, he hurtled along, letting the spluttering, crackling engine noise rip through the early-morning quiet.

At first, Roland inconspicuously clung to the door and the side of his seat. But they didn't crash and gradually Roland's trust in authoritative confidence took over. He relaxed and ate the bacon roll James had brought him, carefully trying to let the crumbs fall back into the paper bag.

After a while, he said, "Umm. Aren't we, like, *way* over the limit?"

James's concentration loosened, and the car slowed down. "Oh yeah. But I think I'm staying safe. Or do you not?"

"I don't know. I mean, yeah, it doesn't feel like we're sliding around or anything."

"I can drive slower if you prefer."

"Um, I guess it's fine."

"It's a shame not to drive this thing like it can be driven."

"Yeah, true."

"Otherwise we could just close the Lamborghini factory and all drive Ford Mondeos 'til the end of time."

Roland raised both eyebrows. "Right. Okay. Then, well, drive on, James."

For a long time they didn't talk. The Lamborghini swayed from side to side across the flickering white centre line, eating up the miles. It began to seem almost weightless, flowing unstoppably past the few other slow-lumbering cars.

The road ran along the side of a shallow valley and, as the turbulent dawn broke through the clouds, they could see the stretched shadow of their car flitting at eerie speed over fields and walls down below.

A feeling in Roland was rising to the surface. They reached the edge of a village; a housing development of ugly peach-coloured new-builds. As James throttled back sharply, Roland heaved a big breath and said, "Can I say something?"

James's eyes flicked over to him. "Yeah."

"You were a bit of a prick to Aaron when we arrived."

"The thing about the office?"

"Yeah. You made him look like a gutless wonder."

"Yeah, you're right. I realised afterwards. I've apologised to him. I think he's okay about it."

"Oh, right."

"Yeah."

"Why'd you do it? He's a decent guy."

"Hmm. I suppose misplaced competitiveness. Competitiveness coming out in the wrong form. I'm a bit sensitive about not having a science degree. It's not an excuse."

Roland thought it was wonderful that James was getting in touch with his emotions. He hurried to share: "I'm a bit sensitive about getting a 2:2."

"I'm not surprised."

"I guess it shows that everyone's in the same boat, feeling insecure about themselves."

"I wouldn't say that. How'd you manage to get a 2:2?"

Roland looked out the window. "Just being lazy. Just pure laziness and complacency and being an ungrateful idiot."

"You were so bad I nearly had to sack you from the India project."

"Fucking hell. Aren't you supposed to be cheering me up?"

"Okay. Sorry."

The sides of the valley steepened and closed in on them. The fields and woods gave way to Christmas tree forests. They turned off onto a single-track lane, where the car's low metal belly clunked on loose stones and branches.

Finally, the landscape opened up into what looked to them like bona fide wilderness. A long lake with hills all around, its dull grey surface shining in spots where sunlight had poked through the clouds. A few tiny birds coasting far off. The land the scruffy brown of dormant heather. Dense stands of pine trees in its groins and armpits. They could see a broad path leading upwards like a ribbon over the hills. The clouds were so low it was like a lid had been fastened across the landscape, and the path ran up against it.

James said, "We might not have much visibility."

"Are you a mountaineering expert now?"

"I just mean we won't be able to see anything."

"I guess we could go to a pub instead. There was one in that village we went through."

"Nice try."

They pulled into the car park, and clambered out. They stretched themselves, shivering as they lost the cabin warmth and letting their eyes adjust to the directionless light. There were a few other cars. A slim old woman with loose grey hair and a tweed poncho was shaking out a red tartan rug to put in her boot. Some kind of well-trained gun dog waited proudly by her knees. She reflexively said, "Good morning," and concealed her deprecation of these two young idiots who'd brought a flashy purple sports car to Loch Muick.

One was taller with curling black hair, his brooding head big and heavy, handsome but over-large, like an Easter Island statue or the minotaur. His face was too old for him, the features grave and serious. He was dressed like a fluorescing clown. The other was much slighter, boyish, Tintin-like, with the Scottish complexion evolved over generations in the rain: hair the colour of sand, skin white and pink. His expression was open, friendly, looking around for things to see. He was wearing unsuitable black loafers, a hoodie and a thin grey coat. The cigarette he was lighting made him seem like a rebellious sixth-former.

The woman nearly let a comment escape: if they were foolish enough to get themselves lost, the risk to the men of the mountain rescue would be on their consciences. But she suppressed it and instead spoke to her dog: "Nell. Hup." The gun dog sprang lightly onto the tartan rug and settled itself.

James swung his ultra-lightweight bag across his shoulders, and they crunched out of the gravel car park. Once they were alone, Roland said, "That woman thought we were such massive dicks."

James was happy to be outdoors, and said, "Maybe we are massive dicks. How would we know?"

"I know. I know. It's just, well –"

"I'm surprised you didn't tell her your mum's from Inverness."

"Oh God." Roland stopped and put his face in his hands. "I can't believe I've been doing that."

"Yup. Yup. Alright, but keep walking. We'll lose the light."

Roland resumed trudging.

"What I don't get though: isn't your dad Scottish as well? Mackenzie?"

"Scottish name only. His granddad or something. He's from Peterborough."

They leaned forwards into the hill, their breathing first growing raspy and then calming as they settled into a rhythm. Their feet rose and fell in time. The air around them was still and empty, any sounds absorbed by the fog. The other walkers coming down the path looked at them strangely. It became a shared, unspoken joke. Look how people look at us.

As James walked, he worried about the recession being an enforced pause. Shouldn't he be using this opportunity, when everyone else was pausing, to gain some ground? Roland interrupted: "You're from London, right?"

"Canonbury."

"You should go to Egypt some time. You'd like it."

"Okay."

"It's kind of amazing. And quite a weird place to grow up. The kids club used to be, like, a club for British officers. They had these games you don't get in Britain any more, like carambole. It's like snooker, but there's only three balls and no pockets. And on the walls they still had oil paintings of soldiers with mutton chops and those white pith helmets."

"Wow."

"Yeah."

They kept slogging up the hill. James tried to estimate how many calories he was burning. Sweat was running down his torso. The survival jacket was, if anything, too warm. Roland said, "I'd hardly ever been to England before I started uni. And everything in Cairo, like at our school, was kind of more British than Britain. Like the blazers and calling the teachers *masters* and all that stuff."

James didn't see the relevance of this to climbing Lochnagar. But Roland seemed to be unburdening himself, which was good. Roland said, "I always wanted to live in London. But the weird thing is, once you get to know it a bit, I don't know, I actually find it quite boring. It's very, like, tidy, and everyone goes to bed super early. And in Cairo, you've got the desert, and the city of the dead, and –"

"The tomb of Alexander."

"Yeah, somewhere. But in London, it's just like, do you want to be a banker in the City, a lawyer in Holborn or a civil servant in Westminster. But really it's just like, do you want to drink Coke or Pepsi? Like, can you even tell the difference?"

"Well, we're none of those things."

"You think what we're doing is any better?"

James didn't want to get into it again. They stopped and looked back the way they'd come. They could see the broad path rolling down to the car park, where they could make out their tiny Lambo, a purple speck on the retina. From here, they could see the shape of the air in the valley, like the space inside a bowl.

Roland said, "So, Jim. Do people call you Jim?"

"No. I have to say I don't like it."

"It's quite *Star Trek*."

"Life, but not as we know it?"

"Exactly." Roland appraised the path above them. He was getting cold and his nose was running. "I guess you're pretty committed to going to the top of this hill, aren't you?"

James sighed. His new boots were pinching and he must have burned at least some number of calories. "There's not much point stumbling around in the clouds. The objective was actually to cheer you up. Are you cheered up?"

"Oh, yes. I'm so cheery. Actually, I am cheered up. Thank you. It's really thoughtful of you."

James went awkward. "No, no. Not at all. I value you as a colleague."

Roland laughed. "Great. I value you too. Shall we, like, go to the pub?"

They drove back and settled in for lunch. The pub, being close to Balmoral and the royal tourist route, was comfier and friendlier – a bit more English – than the rough drinking sheds they'd been to in Aberdeen. Their legs ached slightly from the walk, which had unwound them a little. They found they were in no hurry.

After each pint, James roughly calculated how long – if they metabolised one unit per hour – before they were safe to drive. The departure time retreated ever deeper into the afternoon. They talked about the same subjects again, except looser and more enthusiastically: Egypt, *Star Trek* and a seam of space books they'd both read as teenagers, in the years when everything sticks: *Dune*, Asimov, *The Hitchhiker's Guide*. Roland read them because they were what was on his dad's shelves; James because he read everything. From their memories they pulled out and compared, like Top Trumps, the images still tinged with teenagerhood: the spice planet Arrakis; the restaurant at the end of the universe, with galaxies exploding outside the windows.

James had never spoken to anyone who wasn't in his family, or a teacher, about books he'd read for fun. He talked about *Star Trek*'s assumption that all countries would coalesce into a global superstate and then explore the galaxies, just as the pocket kingdoms of Mercia and Northumbria had coalesced into England, and set out on the oceans. And then about the supercomputers that ran Earth's government in *I, Robot*. The paradox was that, in order to do what was best for humans, the computers surreptitiously took all power away from them.

Roland hung his head too low over the table and said, "Ugh."

"What?"

"I know you think you're the supercomputer. You're the humans, James. We're all the humans."

James was unexpectedly embarrassed. Maybe his teenage self *had* thought that. He said, "No. I just mean, theoretically —"

Roland waved this away. "Oh, it doesn't matter. It doesn't matter. You don't really get off on deciding who to sack, do you?"

"No. I mean, there are some aspects that are quite satisfying. Like I was doing this thing with Alan's accounts —"

"Fucking hell, mate."

Roland explained for a long time, forgetting why he'd started, how well you could live in Goa. You could sleep in a beach hut for a pound a day. Then food. That was a bargain too. The only real expense was booze. But you could definitely live well for like five hundred quid a month.

James said, "So, with my savings, we could both live there for . . . seventy-five months. So that's, what . . ." His brain wasn't finding the numbers. "Four, no, six years. A bit more than six years."

Roland remembered why he'd brought this up: "We should quit and move there. We could go right now."

It would be simple: back to Aberdeen to pick up their passports. Fly to Heathrow and connect to Mumbai. Then the beautiful leisurely all-day train journey down the sparkling coast into the tropics. They could be dragging their wheely suitcases over sand, with the warm soft ocean rustling beside them in the dark, by dinnertime tomorrow.

Roland's heart was full of India again, more so than when he'd lived there. A year or two earlier, he really might have gone.

James said, "And what do we do there?"

"Whatever we want. Swim in the sea. Have breakfast. You could do some yoga. Might chill you out. Or actually, you'd get way too into it and become, like, the chief yogi."

"Is that what you did when you were there?"

"No. Just smoked and watched DVDs. Wasted my time, really."

The tremulous possibility of Goa slipped back over the border into fantasy.

They carried on drinking and talking until Roland discovered he'd run out of cigarettes. To try and coerce himself into quitting, he'd begun smoking cheap, disgusting Lambert & Butlers. He hadn't quit, but he enjoyed it less and smelled worse.

They went out to buy some, roaming across night-time village streets with the drizzle cool on their hot faces. They couldn't find a shop and, after some time, went back to the pub. Somehow, the lights were already up, the music off, and the chairs upside down on the tables. James explained several times that they wanted to take a room, but the door was shut and bolted, with them outside it.

They decided to sleep in the car but discovered that the Lambo's racing seats didn't recline. James pulled his survival hood over his head and tried to curl up. Roland fidgeted for a while until he found his cigarettes in his pocket after all. He smoked while James grunted and coughed beside him.

The booze pushed them just below the surface of consciousness and held them there for a while. They kept shifting position, trying to evade the aches that pursued them from joint to joint. Sleep's blanket shrank ever smaller.

Finally, Roland heard or sensed someone outside. Opening one eye, he saw that it was morning. An elderly female head, with curled grey hair and a plastic bonnet above, and the stiff collar of a beige overcoat pressed into the jowls, floated angrily in the windscreen.

He blinked in shock, sat up coughing, rubbed his face and opened his other eye. The face was still there, attached to a person standing on the pavement and bending down to peer into their car. The person looked obscurely furious. When Roland steadied his gaze and met hers, she gave a rageful shake of her head and marched off.

James had woken up too but closed his eyes and tried to pass out again. Roland cuffed him and said, "Wake up. Wake up. We've got to get out of here. The natives have turned against us. They don't understand we've come on holiday by mistake."

"What?"

"Just drive."

James nodded blearily. With a weight settling in his forehead, he turned the key to fire up the painfully loud engine. They drove like careful citizens back to Aberdeen.

After that weekend, they were like two gears adjusted into the right alignment. Their spinning sets of metal teeth, instead of grating, clicked over and over, running in elaborate quickstep with each other.

They noticed that so much about their jobs was funny. The hostile Aberdonians. The ridiculous mismanagement. Aaron told them he'd just caught the COO trying to buy a discounted helicopter. Gallows humour. Jokes among the hangmen.

The car rental place charged James the extra cleaning fee for smoking in the Lamborghini. Roland offered to pay, but James said, "Ultimately, the whole thing was my idea. And I am technically your line manager."

Roland opened his wallet, took out the notes inside and threw them at James. They jumped out of his hand then curled and slipped down through the air until they landed near his feet. He said, "You're not technically the line manager of my life, okay? You pompous ass."

James felt very cosy. Without realising it, he was becoming happier.

For his part, Roland was starting to think that James was the strangest person he'd ever met. He was like an alien. More and more often, when they were working silently, James would interrupt to say, "Wow. This spreadsheet's just thrown up something really interesting." No irony at all. He wasn't cool. He didn't know how to have a good time. But still. He had something. And whatever it was, he had plenty of it.

They got into the habit of driving up and down the coast to anything that could be classed as an attraction. They were the only people at Neolithic stone circles, on distillery tours, at a Michelin-starred restaurant in a pretty village, where the chef came out and sat at their table for a melancholy chat. They seemed to be the only tourists in Scotland.

One weekend, Roland was going down to London for a friend's party. After their trips, it would have felt harsh not to include James. He said, "It's not a big deal. But if you're around in London, and you feel like it, then it should be fun. It's fancy dress. And, like, just to warn you, people really will dress up. You'll need a proper costume. If that sounds like a total nightmare, don't worry about not coming."

James booked a flight, finding a pretext to put himself on a different plane to Roland. He didn't want to seem to be constantly hanging around. He took his debit card to a costume shop in Covent Garden and asked for the best outfit they had. He came away as a formal eighteenth-century pirate captain: three-quarter-length coat in red and gold, a floppy black hat with feathers, a sash, a cutlass, an eyepatch.

The party was in a warehouse in Hackney Wick. He arrived too early, at the stated time, and had to go to a pub to wait. He sat at the bar with a pint and with his body language communicated as hard as he could that his clothes were not in any way noteworthy.

Finally Roland arrived with a big group who'd all been together at someone's house beforehand, and took him inside. The costumes were unlike any he'd ever seen. One guy was dressed as a BDSM Margaret Thatcher in a wig and mask, wearing a strap-on over a skirt suit and pulling a dirty coal miner on a bondage lead. There was a girl who'd come as a lamp. She was wearing an entire chandelier on top of her head, with the DJ's green lasers catching in the cut glass that dangled around her. Another had come as the figurehead of a ship. The cardboard prow protruded from her back as if she were still stuck to it, with the rest of the ship implied. She was painted white and wearing a toga over one shoulder. On the other side of her torso, a white-painted breast stood naked and imperious.

Roland's costume had been made by one of the girls he'd arrived with, a fashion student at St Martin's: a suit made of innumerable differently coloured cloth butterflies stitched together. As he moved, it was as if a bright swarm were constantly settling on him and rising off again.

He'd thought about warning his friends what James was like. But he didn't want to prejudice them against him, nor to spend his night babysitting. After some hellos, he left James to sink or swim. At first, whenever he glanced across, it seemed to be going as he'd feared it might. James going alone to the bar, for something to do. Or talking emphatically to someone who was glancing around. But he clung on.

As everyone got drunker, it got easier. Someone had some pills. James took one with an unexpected absence of fuss. And after that, they were in the bright blur of music and dancing and delightful gabbled conversations that were forgotten even as they were happening. Everyone was beautiful and beloved, the music was coming out of their bodies, and the world spilled over with joy.

Hours and hours later, they shuffled out into the chilly bright morning. Their ears rung, their jaws were stiff and they were in a bleak industrial park. Some of Roland's butterflies had fallen off, and they could see patches of pink skin. But they were still up, still coasting. James went home in a minicab. He was surprised to find he still had his cutlass. He was very comfortable in the back seat. It seemed unbelievably quiet.

He let himself into his house and went down to the kitchen for a glass of water. His parents were sitting at the long farmhouse table, having breakfast in their dressing gowns. When he walked gingerly down the stairs, experiencing every step, they shared a look of amazement. His dad said, "Have you just come in?"

"Umm. Yeah. Morning."

"Well! Well, that's ... wonderful. Good for you. Do you want some coffee? I could make you some breakfast and you could tell us about it?"

"Umm." James considered for a while. His thoughts were sluggish. "Umm, no. Thanks. I'm just going to get some water and go to bed."

His mum said, "I'll get it for you, darling." While she ran the tap, the feathers on his hat kept bobbing down into his vision, and he kept brushing them away.

His dad said, "Who were you with last night? Was it that new friend you work with?"

"Don't interrogate him," said his mum. She passed him the water. "Here you go, sweetie. Make sure you drink it. You'll feel better when you wake up."

"Okay. Thanks. Yes. I was with Roland and some of his friends. There was someone there dressed as a chandelier."

"How wonderful," said his dad. "You know, if you ever want to bring Roland or any of the others here for dinner – or just to watch a film – we'd love to meet them."

James nodded heavily a few times. "Thanks for the water."

Slowly he climbed up the endless stairs. The sun was so loud in his room. His waistcoat had so many buttons to undo. But then he was naked, with the sweat evaporating from his shivery skin. He was so tired, but strangely not sleepy. What a feeling he'd had. If every head of state took ecstasy once a week, it would be the end of war.

He would have loved to put his hand on the figurehead's alabaster breast. He dimly remembered talking to her about their shared interest in ships. Were the pyramids originally clad in white alabaster? What *was* alabaster? Maybe Roland would know. He should close the curtains, but they were so far away. His thoughts turned in an ever tighter spiral – breast, pyramids, Roland, curtains – until – poof! – he was out.

Downstairs his parents were euphoric. Everything they said came out with laughter. They talked about the parties in the squat they'd lived in as students, a seven-bedroom Georgian townhouse on Regent's Park, with mould under the carpets.

Arthur lightly held his wife's hand across the kitchen table. It was so odd to think that they and the others they'd lived with had become so plausible as grown-ups. Matthew, who'd broken off his PhD and been the first to move out, owned a Spanish restaurant. Soraya, who'd irritated everyone by never doing her share of the chores, was an undersecretary of state. Wild, tireless Johnny had married rich and been knighted. Michael was under a slab in Highgate Cemetery, his novel never finished. And once, still visible through a clear pane of time, it was they who'd been luminous with youth and light of heart.

Arthur said, "I'm so happy for him." His eyes went watery. "Don't tell me off for blubbing."

"Oh, Arthur," said Mary. "You've become a soppy old fool, you know that? What's that line of Larkin's about being soppy-stern?"

"I don't remember."

"You've become soppy and I've become stern. I can feel it. Ugh, I don't know how I got so serious. I hope I haven't given that to Cleo along with my ankles."

Arthur reflexively said, "You've got lovely ankles."

"That costume." She shook her head. "Could you smell it?"

Arthur nodded. "Suited him though, didn't it? Went well with his black locks. I still think he should grow them out."

"It did suit him. Maybe he'll find a girlfriend. But tell me now, do you think I'm still too young and beautiful to be a grandmother?"

"*Far* too young and beautiful."

"It would be nice though, wouldn't it? I could happily forget everything I ever learned about industrial policy – just like *that*." She snapped her fingers. "Maybe I've had enough of being a distinguished professor and it's time to become a sweet little golden-hearted granny."

"You sound like you want to become an apple."

She gave him a cross look, and said, "I could spend all day dressing my little pumpkin in the sweetest outfits and listing all the things my daughter-in-law is doing wrong. I'd retire the day after the three-month scan."

"I think Cleo will be first though, don't you? She and Roger seem pretty set."

"Yes. Although James is so handsome."

"But women don't just care about handsome."

"Lucky for you."

177

"Lucky for me."

They both smiled.

Then Arthur said, "Thank God for Roland, whoever he is." And they clinked their coffee cups together.

V

2010

James, Roland and Aaron's team laid off so many people from Subsea7 that the top floor of the office building was abandoned, like the forgotten upper rooms in a sprawling Sicilian palace.

But after they were finished, things didn't go back to normal. Instead of being brought home to London, they were kept in Aberdeen to restructure another oil and gas company, and then another. They had the misfortune of becoming experts. Their experience became unassailable, a trap.

They really did develop an eye for it. On the introductory walk around a company campus, James and Roland would clock the fleet of cars, the subsidised canteen, the comfortable atmosphere of employees who weren't being hurried, and think, This is all going to go for a start.

Meanwhile the recession was biting deeper into Aberdeen's townscape. The Michelin-starred restaurants shut down and their chefs moved back to France. The supercar rental place went bust. The nightclubs stood empty in the evenings, dance music escaping sadly from the open doors and the bouncers guarding a queue rail with no one behind it.

When they were down in London, the financial crisis could feel like a blip. Or like something happening to the poor and provincial. But up here in the north of Britain, the once-gaudy town was sinking back into drabness. The sparkle of money faded and went out. Bookies and charity shops advanced like mould across the high street.

Roland quit without telling anyone. His body still transported itself to the office, but he was gone. When he and James sat across a table from someone, with James giving it to them straight, he hung his head and stared at the scuffs on his shoes. He should really polish them before sacking someone.

Soon, quite soon, in a few months, he'd be in Serbia. He'd booked his ticket for Exit Festival, in a ruined castle in a town called Novi Sad. Some of his friends were talking about getting there by rail. It took more than twenty-four hours on a party train crammed with Brits. Total carnage. But good carnage or bad carnage? And would someone, like maybe him, have to keep a packet of pills up their butt that entire time?

While James recited the spiel about a consultation period, it occurred to Roland, with a flutter of the heart, that it was completely possible he would miss the flight back from Belgrade. Have a spicy Balkan breakfast in his own time, then head off, head out and away into the expanses. What came next after Serbia? Bulgaria maybe? And then Turkey. Istanbul. Tiny coffees so thick and bitter they were like shots of Brent Crude. No. No more thoughts of Brent Crude. Veils. Scimitars. Those funny little red hats that Abu the monkey wears in *Aladdin*. And then after that, Central Asia and the 'Stans.

While his mind was roaming off onto the steppe, on horseback, his physical form was still there in the oil and gas firm Baker Hughes. His senses, much as he tried to ignore them, carried on faithfully making sketches of the external world and bringing them to him, like cats dropping off headless birds. A man's hands trembling with unarticulated feeling; yet another father asking how he was supposed to pay his mortgage. No matter how vividly Roland imagined the scratchy pain of stuffing a stiff plastic baggy up his sphincter, he couldn't stop this from reaching him.

James worried about him. Roland seemed trapped in a miserable loop: sacking people, hating it, and unable to stop. He didn't seem to be moving in any direction, just performing the grim daily cycle of redundancy notices, and switching himself off in front of reality TV each evening. It seeped into James, too, this cumulative sadness of the people he told that they would lose things dear to them: their careers, their houses, their self-esteem. In the abstract, economic theory held: swift redundancies would lead to quicker recovery and hence new, better jobs. But he stopped believing in it.

Or rather, he gradually became convinced that the axe wasn't falling in the places that theory called for. The bosses weren't losing their jobs or homes. They weren't leading from the front and sacrificing themselves for the greater good. How many ordinary jobs could you save with the CEO's salary? It was simple arithmetic. McKinsey, too, was making a healthy surplus that could have kept most of these people employed, at least for another year. There had to be a better way to fit this puzzle together.

He found that, once or twice, and then every morning, he involuntarily paused before opening the door of his hotel room and striding off to meet Roland at the car. In that momentary pause, he had to rally himself, like a general calling his wavering troops back into order. As one restructuring led to another, and the career pause enforced by the recession began to stretch into years, a slow panic gathered in him. The thing about time, unlike money, was that you couldn't not spend it.

He'd be twenty-seven in a few months. His young person's railcard would run out. The state no longer classified him as young. He'd also soon be above the age limit for joining the army as an officer. Ever since 9/11, the army had been there as a back-up. If all else failed, you could go have experiences in Iraq and Afghanistan. It was at least something in exchange for these irreplaceable years.

He wasn't that far off the age at which Zátopek won three golds in Helsinki, the zenith of his career. Of course it wasn't athletics James was doing. But what was it?

He binge-read the weekly alumni circular, which had changed since the Lehman collapse. Ever more of the younger cohorts, instead of ascending up the ladder to banks, corporations and branches of government, were opting out. They were doing Teach First, set up by another McKinsey alum, or launching their own brightly optimistic start-ups to better the world, or helping UN agencies with the Haiti earthquake. It occurred to James that each person doing this removed one competitor from the corporate race, themselves.

Meanwhile he had to endure tedious, lengthy dreams about losing his boarding card and having to check the infinite pockets of his yellow hiking coat. There were so many pockets, and zips within zips, and the departure lounge monitors showed that his flight was already boarding. The dream wasn't hard to interpret.

In his quarterly performance reviews, the partners told him he was "paying his dues up there". Everyone could see he was "putting in the hard yards". It was no bad thing to show you could take care of unpleasant, lucrative business for the Firm. This would be taken into account. The day would come when rewards were paid out. Advancement. In the meantime they gave him some more cash. Sometimes a fear came to him: that the Firm was secretly a ladder to nowhere. That at the top there was just more of the same. Yes, it functioned well and employed intelligent people. But what was it *for*?

One weekend, back in London, James slept with the alabaster-breasted girl from the costume party. She was a legal adviser to the Labour leadership, called Thirza. James got her number from Roland, who said, "Thirza, eh? She *is* an utter babe. Ooh, she's big time though. So big time. Are you sure you can handle it?"

James didn't see why not. He took her to a seedy, smelly Soho pub, The Blue Posts, where he'd been with someone from Guardian Soulmates. The food options were crisps or peanuts, and the murky carpet exhaled sour fumes of beer. Thirza asked for a pint and, perching on a stool, a gangle of long limbs folded across each other, said, "I'm surprised you picked this place. I thought management consultants preferred the slick and shiny."

She was very grand and seemed to hear unintended meanings in the things he said. He felt like an exotic stranger, unable to know what about himself was interesting. She told him, "You're very unusual, aren't you?"

Later on, he said, "You're very good-looking. I found your naked breast fascinating." And she laughed from her belly.

When they were deciding whose place to go back to, he said they could go to his, but she should know he lived with his parents. She was amused again, said "*very* unusual" and kissed him, lightly holding his face between cool, pale hands.

At her flat, which was decorated like an adult's, with paintings and wooden furniture, he felt like a mortal who'd climbed Mount Olympus and with one outstretched, trembling hand, touched the breast of a god.

It became one of his favourite memories, making him smile whenever he thought of it. But it never occurred to him to ask her out again. In later years, he couldn't understand why. He suspected that this was a chance of happiness blithely overlooked.

To pass the spare time he had in Aberdeen, he sometimes went to see the experimental machines in Subsea7's R&D department. The unit hadn't been sold off in the end — one of many McKinsey recommendations that hadn't been followed through. Instead everyone but Alan, the swarthy, stocky, bearded engineer who ran it, was made redundant. The machines were jumbled into a chilly pre-fab in the car park. Alan didn't have the budget or staff to do much more than keep them oiled, listen to the radio and fill in the crossword.

He sat there like a fisherman waiting for a boat, in a thick roll-necked woollen jumper tight over his solid midriff. A space heater sat loyally at his feet. He drank his tea, pulled his fingers through his black beard and waited for the good times to come again. The oil price was already recovering. Doubtless the money would soon flow once more.

It was a surprise when James first visited. Alan had assumed he was at heart a big-shot corporate bell-end. But he seemed to have a sincere interest in marine engineering. Alan left some gaps in their chat for James to say he regretted raining destruction on Subsea7. But James didn't try to take it back, and Alan liked that about him.

On the second visit, Alan made them both tea with the kettle he kept on his desk. Because there was no plumbing in the pre-fab, he poured in water from a thermos. They sat beside each other on orange plastic school chairs, drank their tea, ate Hobnobs and with words dismantled and reconstructed the machines.

Most often, they talked about the "future of the company" tidal generator. It looked like a thin yellow canoe, less than a metre long, and was floating in a clear IKEA storage box. It had two arms sticking out to the sides, each holding a turbine that could be raised to the surface or lowered underwater. Alan's thinking was that, because water was so much thicker than air, a turbine in the sea could produce far more power than the flimsy wind-driven ones they were now putting everywhere.

Accidents of geography had given Britain some of the strongest tidal currents in the world. Every time the tide went out in the North Sea, all that extra seawater, trillions of gallons, unimaginable quantities, had to rush around Britain and into the Atlantic, and then back again. This briny juggernaut had to squeeze itself through narrow gaps: to the south, the English Channel; in the north, the Pentland Firth. There was also a thin channel running dead straight through the Orkney archipelago, off the north coast of Scotland. Alan reckoned that if you stuck some turbines in there, you could keep Britain's lights on when the oil ran out.

For James, the scale of these thoughts, looking down as if from orbit at the island of Britain, at the motion of one sea draining into another, was a respite from himself. He said, "Actually my sister's doing her PhD in renewables. In solar panels."

Alan said, "Uh-huh." He wasn't interested in solar panels. Building on land was basically cheating, without the wet cold and the Atlantic wind and the saltwater that was death to moving parts, and the sea always bucking up and down or losing its temper. No one had ever seen a memorial for guys killed installing solar panels.

James was still enjoying the dreaminess of zooming his perspective so far out. "My sister says that as much solar energy hits the Earth every forty minutes as human civilisation needs in a year."

Alan made a sceptical face. "If you can capture it. And tidal energy actually comes from the solar system as well. The moon."

This struck James as an idea of great beauty. He said, "I get it. The movement of the moon, dragging the water along behind it, creates the tide."

"It's not just —"

And James said at the same time: "Yes it's —"

They both stopped. James said, "After you."

"No. On you go."

"The sun's gravity must pull the seawater as well. Can you see it in practice?"

"Oh, yeah. Oh, absolutely. When the sun and moon are in a straight line with the Earth, you get the strongest tide. And when they're at right angles, like this" — he put the heels of his hands together and made the angle with his palms — "you get the weakest. The planets have an effect and all, but it's tiny really."

"So you must be able to predict the tide strength and the power output for practically forever in advance?"

"Well, the shape of the land might change after a few hundred years. But yeah, there's no bollocks about if it's a sunny day or not."

As James dipped his Hobnob into his mug, the wet stain of tea at its lower edge suddenly looked like a crescent moon. In his head, Alan's machine was like the old mills where a donkey in a harness walked in circles to drive the millstones. Except instead of a donkey, it was the moon itself being placed in harness, a vast cold white sphere turning eternal circles around the Earth. Imagine using the motion of heavenly bodies to boil a kettle. Such guile. Such Promethean audacity. Mastery of the universe.

He tried to share this feeling with Roland. Once, he managed to cajole him into coming to the pre-fab. But Roland moped and didn't drink his tea. James tried to enthuse him by talking about orbits, glancing at Alan all the while. It was unfamiliar, trying to make a social situation coalesce, and he couldn't do it.

One late morning in March, their BlackBerrys and those of the other McKinseyites all went bananas at once. The unceasing hail of pings heralded an article in the *Wall Street Journal*. The former managing director of McKinsey, Rajat Gupta, had been charged with insider trading. He'd passed confidential information to an old buddy who ran a hedge fund, Raj Rajaratnam. Another McKinsey partner, Anil Kumar, was involved as well.

The Feds had Gupta on tape in September 2008, when America's banks were sliding towards the abyss and Gupta was on the board of Goldman Sachs. The CEO, affable little Lloyd Blankfein, rang to say that they'd found a way to save the bank: they were going to sell a chunk to Warren Buffett.

On the tape, you could hear Gupta put the phone down on Blankfein, pick it up again and ring his friend. Raj bought a tranche of Goldman shares for pennies on the dollar, because Goldman appeared to be sinking. Once the Buffett deal was announced, and Goldman's shares leapt back up, the number in Raj's bank account went up by tens of millions. It was that easy when you and your friends were at the top.

Roland took this news with uncharacteristic cynicism. While the other consultant made exclamations of excitement and shock, Roland just shrugged, said, "Cunts," and carried on tapping desultorily at his spreadsheet of staff costs.

James wasn't shocked either. It was naive of the others, embarrassingly deferential, to imagine that the head of McKinsey should be better than anyone else. *Someone* had to have that job. All Gupta had beaten to get it was other people. But Roland should be up in arms, yelling about crooked fat cats and bringing the bastards to justice.

At lunch, eating jacket potatoes and beans out of polystyrene boxes in the soon-to-be-closed employee canteen, James said, "Hey man, are you okay?"

"About what?"

"This Gupta thing."

"Oh. Yeah. So we're part of a criminal enterprise now. Big whoop."

James, with a rush of adrenalin, said, "Maybe you *should* quit. Go to Goa and live cheaply while you figure out what you want to do next."

"What's the point? I'd just lie around watching DVDs anyway." Roland gazed at James with such pure unhappiness that James had to look down, to where his baked beans flowed like lava between dusty white cliffs of potato.

Although it made James gasp inside, like starting to swim in cold water, he could see clearly and certainly that Roland had to leave McKinsey. There had to be a way to get him out.

That evening, he rang Eleni. In the years since he was almost kicked out of the firm, he'd learned to read the politics of careers. So he wasn't surprised when she picked up and right away said, "It's not great for you that they're Indians."

"No. It's not terrible. It's not a real black mark. None of these Indian guys ever knew anything about my entry-level little school project. Gupta wasn't even in charge any more."

"No, but, you know."

"Yeah, I see it. Young guy gets big double promotion by working on Indian stuff, shortly after HR says he should be let go. There's enough to raise a question. Or rather, enough that it would unpleasantly remind people of Gupta if I did become the youngest-ever partner, which I'm now really not going to."

"I mean, if you can pull off something like that school contract again, then . . . *maybe*."

"If I even want to any more."

"Do you not?"

"I slightly think, what's the point? There are bigger things going on in the world."

"Very true."

"Speaking of which, how are things in Greece?"

"Bad. Really bad. The Germans are fucking us. Every summer it's, 'Oh, *kalispera*, Greece is paradise, which direction is the *tavernaki*?' And now things have gone to shit, it's like, 'You're a bunch of corrupt Mediterranean layabouts, you've got to shape up and make Athens more like Hamburg.'"

James was surprised by her vehemence. She'd always been detached and analytical. He said, "Ha. Yes."

"Don't get me wrong, Hamburg does a good job. It's a good port. Good for them. But they're degenerates. They've got a red-light district there a mile long, where these serious-face German lawyers and economists go and stuff their cocks up poor skinny girls from Eastern Europe. You don't have that in Greece."

James thought: Really? But from his interviews with the prospective unemployed he'd learned to steer away from irrelevant arguments. He said, "Have you been recently?"

"Not for a while. You should come and see it. I invite you. Come in the summer. You'll see that Greece is a penniless little Balkan democracy with no real economy and fantastic people. But the banks blow everything up, and who suffers? Not the fucking bankers. Not Wall Street. Okay, Gupta might get a few years, and I wish him many more. But you don't see the sub-prime guys doing a perp walk in handcuffs. Instead it's the poor Greeks who suffer. It's some poor old Yianni who goes out on his dinghy to catch squid who's got to take it on the chin because his pension is gone.

"You can imagine what Greek mothers are like with their sons. Typical Mediterranean sexism. And they're giving them up. They're so desperate they're giving up their sons for adoption because they can't feed them properly. I can't talk about this any more."

A few weeks later, and quite unexpectedly, James made the decision that defined the rest of his life. He was in the near-empty bar at the Mercure, where he and Roland had been on and off for more than two years. He was eating fish without chips in an attempt at weight reduction, and his non-greasy hand was totting up the costs of various people's salaries.

An email popped up in the top right-hand corner of his screen, from one of the partners: "Looks like there's another restructuring job coming down the pipe. Welltec. Heard of them? Robots mainly. Not confirmed yet but should happen. You guys must have restructured practically every company in Scotland by now! The partners do see and appreciate it. There's a gold star next to your name."

James certainly had heard of Welltec. He and Eleni had been sent there for a few months after Tesco. They were one of many, many oil and gas companies in Scotland that remained unrestructured.

He went back to his spreadsheet and his fish. But after a few minutes he found he couldn't concentrate. Instead he was ever more awake, alert, his systems switching on, even though it would soon be time to read a chapter of *The Years of Lyndon Johnson* and go to sleep.

He drank a pint of fizzy yellow Scottish lager to tranquillise himself, but it didn't make him tired. He went up to his room and, in the shower, felt as if he'd just been for a jog: adrenalin flowing, his torso radiating heat as the water fell on it, his mind heightened but empty. He lay on his narrow bed, the towel wrapped like a skirt around his waist, and tried to read *Johnson*. As soon as he found his page, other words came to him: more restructuring; another six months at least; gold stars next to my name, like in primary school.

There were bigger things going on in the world. How old was Napoleon when the revolution broke out? Phone; Wikipedia. Twenty! And at twenty-six he invaded Italy.

James thought of the evening he got his finals results, in another drab business hotel, in Milton Keynes. At what point were drab business hotels not temporary accommodation but your chosen surroundings? Big Eddie had sent him some emotional email. When James found it in his inbox, its language had sounded foreign. Flowery. Maybe it was that he had coarsened since then. Corporatised. "Exams are only a measure of the thing; they are not the thing itself." Hard to argue that the thing itself was restructuring, or gold stars.

What was Eddie doing now? Google. He'd married James's old philosophy tutor, Margot, in the college chapel.

Nothing and no one stayed as you'd left them. James remembered how he'd felt on the day his dad drove him from Oxford back to London, how new, how shining, a bright new blade fresh from the forge.

He lay there imagining that light was blazing out of his eyes and projecting turbulent shapes onto the ceiling.

After some hours, his body started to tire and, still somewhere between waking and sleeping, he became entangled in another episode of his dream about the lost boarding card. He knew he was dreaming and struggled to get out, his feet twitching under the duvet. But instead of escaping, he kept burrowing down through the lower strata of sleep, down through the layers of the unconscious mind until he fell as if falling out the bottom of a mine – and dropped into the black lake of oblivion. His thoughts went out, and he rested.

A little later, still before dawn, he clicked awake, his mind on full, with the answer sitting crisp and hard-edged before him like a birthday present: he was going to buy Alan's prototype, set up a company and convert Britain to running on tidal power. It was that simple.

A great energising relief ran through him. It was as if he'd been struggling to hold too many elements together and, relaxing, found they resolved into an unexpected shape. From cacophonous jangle, a strong clean chord.

It would be hard. It would be so hard. Perhaps impossible. Like the story of Jacob trying to wrestle with an angel. He felt fresh again.

Walking down the corridor to Roland's room, it seemed fitting that the motion sensors turned on the lamps to light his way. He didn't mind right now that his midriff bulged over the waistband of his boxers.

He had an access card for Roland's room, from needing to wake him at weekends. James went inside, switched on the light, pulled the duvet away and sat on the edge of Roland's bed, whispering, "Roland! Roland!"

Roland flinched and squirmed, his eyes still closed, and muttered, "It can't be the weekend. I haven't agreed to anything."

"Wake up. I've found a way to get you out of McKinsey."

Roland went rigid. He relaxed again, opened his eyes, rubbed his nose and sat up. "What time is it?"

"I think it's about five."

"Are you having a breakdown?"

"No. I've figured out what we're going to do. We're going to found an energy company and turn Alan's tidal generator into a real business."

Roland was still waking up. "Can I have my duvet back?"

James tossed it onto him.

"And there's a dressing gown on the back of the door if you want it."
James put it on.
Roland said, "Okay, five a.m. Tidal energy. Okay. Okay. Cool."
"We're going to save the world from climate change. We're going to alter the course of history by ending the need for oil and gas. We're going to take our place in the pantheon of great men and cover ourselves in glory."
Roland smiled. "Sounds ace. Do we get extremely rich and famous as well?"
"Yes, presumably."
"And we have our own company and can run it however we want?"
"Yes. However we decide."
"Amazing." He yawned. "And you've, like, done the maths? Like, the unit economics and where the money's going to come from, and all that?"
"No. To be frank, I'm pretty sure the maths won't add up, until we make them add up."
"Ah." Roland's smile broadened. "I *knew* you wanted out as well."
"We'll be getting into something much bigger."
"Yeah, fuck McKinsey, let's do it. Where do I sign? Let's shake on it."
They stood up in the dingy, messy hotel room, the harsh overhead light above them, Roland skinny in his boxers, James in the dressing gown, and shook.
Roland said, "To freedom."
James said, "To freedom and glory," thinking as he said so that those were actually opposites.
"Fantastic. And to us."
"To us."
They were too elated to go back to bed. Instead they went for a long walk around the city while the sky lightened and the sun came up. A profusion of plans babbled happily out of them. They spoke and spoke, James about getting the rights to the prototype, Roland about how nobody in their company would ever have to wear a suit again.
When places started to open, they had a slap-up breakfast in a greasy spoon and made toasts to each other with mugs of sugary tea.

VI

SPRING 2011

They now had what James had always wanted: one great cause, sacred and imperative. As he saw it, the company was for glory, achievement and the good of the planet, so what was for the good of the company was good, and what was not for the good of the company was irrelevant.

Having the company made all of life simple and joyous. It cleared away the unsatisfying clutter of normal existence. Previously ambiguous questions such as whether to move out of his parents' house or what to do at the weekend resolved themselves into: What is best for the company? And a company was not just a legal construct; it was a group, a fellowship, a band of companions, a party of willing souls, an expedition, Shackleton's company of explorers setting out in their fragile vessel.

He thought of young Bolshevik cadres before the revolution, giving up their comfortable bourgeois existences, going willingly to the Tsar's prisons in Siberia, annihilating themselves in perfect service of their cause. He thought of Jesus telling his disciples, "If you would be perfect, sell everything you have and follow me."

James was twenty-seven and never had a boss again. Until that moment, he and Roland had lived as employees, as if in the warm, dark, cosy-fetid hold of a ship. What happened up at the helm was not their concern. Their preoccupations were how to get a better position, and the whims and characters of their superiors and colleagues. Even James had never cared about what was best for McKinsey. Now, however, they were up and exposed. The wind blew away the comfy indoor reek; the horizon was a wide blue empty circle around them, as if the ship were the fluttering needle on a gigantic compass. And they had to choose the direction.

They no longer had the pleasure of being praised, nor of complaining, nor of appealing to authority for fairer treatment. They could not be judged but by themselves. As the company grew, they gained powers: to summon other people and send them away; to instruct and reward; to punish. Everyone they worked with brought them requests, concealed small things from them and might one day have to be made redundant by them. They spoke first, and last; their opinion was decisive; and if they were wrong, all would suffer.

Since what we think about is who we are, their outside world transposed itself into their inside one – the external becoming internal, the internal slowly becoming permanent – and they became different men.

To start this company, they needed Subsea7 to sell them the rights to Alan's prototype, which it had no reason to do. No amount of money they could scrape together would mean anything to a corporation that size. And since neither of them was a marine engineer, they would have to persuade Alan to leave his safe and generous salary to follow them.

Before speaking to him, James checked the perhaps apocryphal wording of Shackleton's recruitment ad for the *Endurance* expedition: "Men wanted for hazardous journey. Small wages, bitter cold, long months of complete darkness. Constant danger. Safe return doubtful. Honour and recognition in event of success." Thousands applied.

By the time they walked across the car park and pulled open the lightweight door to Alan's pre-fab, James was flying. He speechified at Alan, who sat on his orange plastic school chair and pulled his fingers through his beard.

James tried to stay sitting down as well, but was too full of feeling. He got up and declared, "You'll get paid less. There'll be constant uncertainty. If it doesn't pan out, we'll lose everything. But if we *do* make it work, we can save the planet from climate change and power our civilisation by slinging a yoke around the moon. Instead of drinking tea and listening to the radio, you can make your mark. You can earn a place in history. Alan Forbes, inventor of the tidal turbine."

Alan raised his eyebrows, and said, "I thought this might be what you were wanting to speak about."

"Yes."

"By the way, I quite like drinking tea and listening to the radio. I built this device listening to the radio."

"We'll get you ten radios."

"Hmm." Alan didn't like that. He said, "I've been thinking about it and all. I hope this doesn't sound harsh, but I've been thinking . . . I built the device. So, em, what do I need you pair for?" He smiled.

James was off balance but quickly said, "Um, well, for a —"

Alan talked over him. "What I mean is, I'm an engineer, not a business guy. And you two are young, but you do actually want to take care of the business side, right?"

"Right."

"And I'd be in charge of the device."

"Right. Head of engineering."

"And what happens with Richard and Kirsten?"

"Who are Richard and Kirsten?"

"My kids."

Roland cringed. James said, "Oh, sorry. I didn't know that. How do you mean? Are they looking for jobs?"

"No, they're children. They're at school. They're at Robert Gordon's at the minute. Was your plan to ask me to work for buttons and take them out of there? Because that's not going to happen."

"No. Not at all. Like I said, I didn't know about that parameter. But I'm sure we can figure it out. This undertaking shouldn't not happen because of school fees."

"And if we build a prototype — leave alone a full-scale machine — somebody'll need to move to Orkney to test it. So were you thinking that would be the head of engineering? Because I'd either need to move the family up there, and Catriona, that's my wife by the way" — Roland cringed again — "would have to quit her job, which would be more lost income, *or* I'd need to live apart from them for months at a time. Which I don't want to do."

James was floundering. "We'll do whatever's needed. With the school fees, if you need to be paid more, we can be paid less. I can be paid zero if need be. And with Orkney, isn't it a half-hour flight from here? You could commute. Or do a weekly commute for the testing phases and be here the rest of the time. I'm sure there's a way."

Alan shifted forward and braced his hands on his knees, turning his elbows outward. "See, though, my point is, I'm not an unattached young guy like you two. What are you, about thirty?"

James nodded non-committally, and said, "I understand. I hadn't thought enough about the family element. That's obvious. But if you tell me what we need to factor in, we'll factor it in. You're an engineer. It's problem-solving. These problems can be solved. We will do anything – *anything* – that's needed to make this work."

Roland thought: We don't even have a company yet, and already we'll do *anything* for it?

They talked more about practicalities – time frames, expenses – with Alan sticking to hypotheticals: I *could* come; we *would* need. Then James had to go for a call with a copyright lawyer. Roland, on a hunch, said he wasn't going to join. Instead he just hung around in the pre-fab, kneeling to inspect the yellow model bobbing in its IKEA storage box.

Alan said, "Tea?"

"Yes, please. Or, actually, no. Thanks. I hate tea."

Alan was amused.

"I grew up in the Middle East, where it's sweet tea or coffee."

"Oil brat?"

"Yeah. My dad works for Schlumberger."

They chatted for a while, loosening up. After a while, Alan said, "If your pal's got any sense, he'll be thinking about if he can replace me with someone else."

"Oh, definitely. He loves contingency plans. You should try organising a weekend with him. He'll be thinking, what if he needs to replace you, or what if we can't get the rights and need to design a new machine, or what if he could replace me with someone better."

"Replace *you*? I thought you two were, like . . . I don't know. I thought it was you two together."

Roland shrugged. "All I mean is, I wouldn't be surprised if he's thinking about what if he needs to replace himself."

"I don't believe that."

"He literally might be. Doesn't mean he doesn't want it to be you though."

Alan said, "Hmm" and went quiet again. Roland carried on pretending to examine the machine and waited. Eventually Alan said, "Is he for real, like, your pal?"

"For real how?"

"He's got a lot of big chat, doesn't he? Invent the tidal turbine. Do something with the rest of your life. Also, I suppose, make a pretty hefty stack of cash if it comes off. And he says he'll do anything, he doesn't need to get paid. I mean, is he for real? You've known him for years, have you?"

"Oh, yeah. Ages. Since uni. We rowed together in our first term."

"You *rowed*?"

"It was an Oxford thing."

Alan said, "What a pair of twats."

And they both laughed.

Then Alan said, "So, what *do* you think of him?"

Roland felt the weight of what might hinge on his answer and twisted out from under it. "Well, at the end of the day, you've got to make up your own mind about this kind of stuff, don't you? With your kids and everything."

Alan was surprised. "Huh. Okay. Yeah, obviously I will."

Roland could feel him retreating into himself, like a plant's exploratory tendrils recoiling after touching something wrong. A few seconds later, Alan heaved himself up and went over to his desk. He started typing, little flurries at the keyboard. Emails. He still had his job to get on with. Roland felt something passing him by: the gap for a delicious through-ball closing as the defenders scrambled back into position.

Out of sudden fear, he spoke. "What I *would* say about him, though, is that he's totally . . . like, on his gravestone it would say 'He actually did it.' As in, loads of people say, 'Oh, wouldn't it be cool to start an energy company?' But his thing is that he really does it. The reason he's a manager and I'm not, even though I'm actually a month older than him, is that he had this idea about how to improve schools in India. Anyone could have had that idea. It was actually kind of my idea. But he's the one who turned it into a real thing, with, like, the government and loads of people working on it."

Roland felt like he and James were getting married, and this was the wedding speech. He said, "On the downside, he doesn't see himself sometimes. When something he does is shit – you know, he does sometimes actually just make a mistake – he can't see it and thinks it's gone wrong for some complicated reason to do with him being so brilliant.

"And it's always got to be his way. Like, if you ... get involved, it's not going to be that you call the shots because you invented the machine and James just does the paperwork. Like, no. Not at all. And, oh God, he can be so weird. Sometimes, you think you're just having a drink with a normal person, and then he starts going on about one of his ideas, and you're just like, please, can we just talk about the Premier League or something, just for like five minutes.

"But he loves having the piss taken out of him. If you ever want to soften him up, just take the piss – the more schoolboy the better. Say he's got a tiny knob, that kind of stuff. He can't get enough of that.

"And it is true he's not interested in getting paid. He honestly wouldn't know what to do with the money. He'd probably just spend it on, fucking, I don't know, upgrading his laptop."

Alan was satisfied. He wriggled his shoulders deeper into his ergonomic chair, tilting it back. "Did he really give that pregnant lassie fifty grand?"

Roland rolled his whole head in irritation. "It wasn't fifty grand, it was ten. And he let me tell everyone it was bullshit, but it turns out he did do it."

"He's not got some kind of hero complex, does he? Because fuck that."

"No, it's more like he just assumes there's an answer for everything. She needs money, he has money. In his mind, it just fits together. And he likes making things fit. I actually don't think he cares about her as a person at all. And it was fucking weird of him not to tell me about it."

Alan was amused again. He took Roland in, and scratched his neck where the beard chafed it. "He *is* quite weird, isn't he?"

Roland felt the familiar guilt-prickle of having got carried away. Maybe he'd gone a bit far. James wasn't *actually* an emotionless psychopath. To even it out, he said, "But because he's got this thing about being bad at reading people, he just tells them exactly what he thinks. So he's like *extremely* trustworthy. He's probably the most trustworthy person you've ever met." As he said this aloud, he realised it was accurate. Oddbod James, such a solid bloke. Who knew?

Alan's smile was intensifying into serenity. He said, "I'm taking the family to Morocco for our holidays in a few weeks. Poor wee numpties. They're not going to like it when all their holidays after this are on the west coast." He laughed. "I got fucking sick of Arran when I was a kid. And no new car for a long time. But the Audi's only a couple of years old, and Catriona's Merc will run forever. I think I probably won't sell my boat."

"You've got a boat!"

A deep, delighted laugh. "I fucken do as well."

Roland said, "What a twat."

Alan said, "Kids at Robert Gordon's, got my own boat. I'm practically the Queen of Sheba. My secret is, see how I've been in oil and gas since 1989? Well, I haven't pissed it up the wall on hoors and motorbikes like some folk I know. As long as I don't drop the ball on school fees, I'm golden."

Roland said, "Sounds like you're going to do this thing."

"Oh, sounds like I am, doesn't it?"

"If Subsea7 let us buy the rights."

"Oh, they'll let us have them. For one single pound."

"How do you know?"

"Because the guy who's going to decide is Catriona's cousin, and I already asked him."

*

When Roland left, Alan locked the door to the pre-fab and took some golf clothes out of a filing cabinet. Plaid trousers, polo shirt, argyle jumper, spiked shoes. One of his pals wore a ridiculous white-leather golf glove. Alan and the others tried to put him off by doing the Michael Jackson "Thriller" dance.

He stripped down to his boxers and socks, and smoothed the black hairs on his hard round belly. The polo shirt was tight on it. He sometimes regretted that he'd never be slim again. He'd been slender, swivel-hipped even, as a football-playing student in Dundee. But he'd stopped playing in his thirties because the twisted ankles and pulled ligaments went from occasional to frequent and then constant. Since then, the pints and fish suppers and barbecues had accreted like silt in a river. But day-to-day he didn't mind. He liked feeling immovable, planted, thick-trunked. He didn't want to be one of these quite pathetic young guys you saw now who went to the gym and watched their waists, then shaved their armpits and hit the sunbed before a night out.

When he sat at the stern of his Wayfarer, his weight on its fulcrum, his hand on the long smooth wooden tiller, he felt as strong as an Orkney whaler in an Atlantic gale. Catriona was on at him sometimes to eat more healthily, but he was much fitter than her despite her skinniness and her salads. He'd spent so much of his childhood going up the hills with his dad, marking routes for the Grampian Club, that he'd have it in his legs for life. And she'd said before that she liked the weight on top of her. He'd start worrying when she stopped saying that this or that friend of hers just needed a good shag to get her head straight.

This evening, he could play golf because Catriona was picking up the kids from their activities. That wouldn't have happened even a year ago. They'd been in a long phase where the kid-care fell to him. But the pendulum swung back and forth. When the kids were little, Catriona took six years off unpaid to look after them. That was when they'd been most distant, their lives so different that they virtually ran in parallel, not touching. There'd been a night with someone else, at a conference in Bergen. He told himself he was sorry about it though he wasn't really. He'd blanked the woman's name and face from his memory but kept a faint, well-worn image of her bending over in front of him.

His golf clothes on, he thought about adding a jacket to disguise his outfit for the walk to the car. It wasn't even five o'clock. But there wasn't much anyone could do to him. He was the only one left who knew how to extract any value from these machines. Without him, they were just fragile assemblages of steel and rubber bands. And it seemed like he was going to be fucking off anyhow.

He flicked the lights, locked the door and walked across the car park to his Audi. An A4 saloon, about 30,000 on the clock. No new car for a good while, unless Catriona paid for it. When she went back to work full-time, once the kids were under way, her career became the family priority. She stayed late in the office; she went to the drinks. If both her client and her child needed something, well, the kids had a father. If a kid was sick and someone had to take them to the doctor, being late for work, it was him. He picked them up from their after-school clubs, gave them their tea and put them to bed.

The kids were calmer when it was just him, not distracted by contrasting energies. For tea, he made them the kind of healthy veggie stuff that Catriona wanted him to eat himself. They ate with their plates on their knees, watching *The Simpsons*, and the family idiom was embellished with its catchphrases. When Catriona came back, it sometimes felt like she was intruding.

With her, his role had been straightforward. He was the trainer in the corner of the ring, holding the water bottle, wiping the brow, always saying: You can do it, champ.

But Catriona had been the family's priority for quite a few years now, and it was beginning to be his turn again. There was a bit more space in his marriage for him to do what he felt like. Today she was leaving the office on the dot of five so he could play golf. A few years ago, she would make a pained grimace whenever he mentioned a little weekend project the guys had going. Now she told him to fill his boots or asked if she and the kids could come help.

There were times – like when he was standing in wellies in a coppery-red, peat-tinctured burn in a birchwood outside Nairn, him and his pals putting up the mink traps he'd designed, to kill the bastard minks and let the water voles recover, and he glanced up and saw their wives blethering away in their earrings and North Face jackets, and their kids looking for vole tracks or surreptitiously throwing bits of picnic at each other – there were times when he thought, I've absolutely nailed it, this thing called life.

His pals were like him: the first generation in prosperity. His parents were teachers at Peterhead Academy, and he didn't leave Scotland for the first time until he was in his twenties. Now his children went to private school and knew their way through the purple flight-connections corridors at Heathrow.

One of his pals had moved out of town and built a massive Scandinavian-style house next to another little burn. Just because why not, they'd set up a miniature hydro to power his lightbulbs. His mum always said he must save an awful lot on his electricity, and when Alan said it definitely came out more expensive than just plugging into the mains, she was utterly baffled as to why they'd done it.

They played golf; they went on Alan's boat; and they certainly did believe their luck because it wasn't luck at all: it was education and work and pragmatism and the opportunity that came from the oil. When Alan's parents were growing up, the kids on the poorer farms didn't have shoes. Even when Alan was a kid, his older relatives had never been as far south as Edinburgh. It was the oil that changed that. Lanzarote for everyone. And now it was goodbye to oil and gas. Twenty-two years was maybe long enough. He could always go back.

The implicit deal with Catriona, unspoken because totally understood, was that he could pursue this new project, so much larger than vole traps and mini hydros, as long as it didn't touch the fundamentals of their life, whatever those were. Certainly it didn't include fancy holidays, which the kids could do without. And a few savings here and there were definitely worth the chance of making the step up from an engineer's pay packet to company-owner-type money.

He knew she was thinking: why not just wait till the oil price recovers and do this with Subsea7? What she didn't understand was that Subsea7 was never really going to get behind something that wasn't oil. And Jesus Christ, he'd earned a bit of a flutter. He might not get the chance to build something this big ever again.

He was looking forward to the piss-taking when he told the others. He'd be hearing variations on "Ring me if you need a job when you go under. I could do with a dog-walker." And on the way back to the clubhouse, "Good on you, Alan. Let me know if I can help."

A few days later, Eleni was on one of Shell's little shuttle planes that ferried the senior team back and forth between the offices in London and headquarters in The Hague. Life had got much cushier since she left McKinsey. Instead of working for a company that traded on its employees' brains and exertions, and sweated them accordingly, she was now at one that, even in a recession, pumped money out of the ground.

She'd put herself in the plane's back corner seat, twisting her shoulders into the padded cream leather so she could scroll Rightmove on her phone. To everyone at Shell, Eleni pretended to be simply another striving individualist. True, there was a certain indefinable glossiness she couldn't rub off. But with the meticulous care of someone leading a double life, she disguised any sign that the listings she was skimming weren't for two-bed flats in the outer zones but townhouses in Chelsea.

Her parents were pressuring her to buy while the market was still depressed. Her dad kept sending her links to places within a street or two of them on Cadogan Square. She knew how it would be: her mum would be coming round twice a day to drop off some flowers she thought would be perfect for the drawing room, or have a quick chat about the summer, or about Christmas, or Easter, or her dad's birthday, and, while she was there, passing on a few tips on how to run a household properly.

Eleni was already in trouble with them because she was only going to Greece for a week this summer. They didn't seem able to accept that she only got a certain holiday allowance from work. They thought surely it must be negotiable, and therefore that she was choosing to spend what was left of her youth in a sad office instead of on the island. They were proud of her having such a real job but not when she let it interfere with what was truly important.

Really, she'd prefer a chic little flat in a cooler part of town. North of the park maybe. But ultimately, it was their money. And her dad was right: it would be crazy not to buy right now. And the bigger the place, the greater the uplift in value when the market recovered. Even though her mum would soon be saying there was no point having all these bedrooms if you weren't going to fill them with grandchildren. And even though none of her colleagues would ever be able to visit. But hey ho, if she didn't want her parents to have a say in what she did, she could just live off her salary.

James rang, and she was pleased to think about something else. With him she'd never felt any need to disguise herself. Her being loaded didn't affect him. He sounded happy, and within a few seconds he asked her to become a co-founder of a start-up he was launching. Clearly, she wasn't going to do that. But she felt the responsibility of helping James think this through, suspecting she might be the only person he ever asked for advice. She said, "Okay, so. Marine energy?"

"Tides, not waves."

"There are a few of these companies now, aren't there?"

"The number one's called Pelamis. But they do waves. Their device is like a giant articulated snake with lots of sections. It's a very interesting design. They're already supplying electricity to the grid."

"But it's practically nothing, isn't it? Less power than you'd get from a diesel generator in a shed."

"Yup. It's still early-stage."

Eleni sighed. James did everything the hard way. It was like he actually didn't believe in working smarter. He'd rather push a boulder up a hill than just put it on a trailer and drive it up. "And you're doing this with that guy Roland?"

"Yes, and Alan Forbes, the engineer who invented it."

Roland was feckless, a good-time Charlie whom James had unfortunately glommed onto for lack of better options. She said, "Okay. Do you want my opinion?"

"Just a sec. Let me make my pitch."

For James, it was like being in one of the films he and Roland watched through long evenings in the Mercure, *Armageddon* or the *Dirty Dozen*, pulling together a cast of misfits for the mission of a lifetime.

Eleni said, "I suppose your machine has a USP."

"I was going to come on to this, but, essentially, tidal energy isn't that complicated. It's just turbines in water. The main barrier is cost. Because the turbines are attached to the seabed, whenever you have to do maintenance, you have to do it underwater, and it's super expensive. So . . . our device floats."

"Clever."

"Yep. And once marine energy starts getting deployed into deeper waters, the machines will *have to* float."

"If you can make it work."

"If *we* can make it work."

"Ha."

"Alright, here's my pitch. You're –"

"Hold on. Do you mind if I say something first?"

"Go for it."

She clicked her tongue. "Maybe I'm seeing a false causality here, but I look at how last time we spoke I said you'd have to come up with something big. And now you've suddenly got this grand scheme for which nothing is costed, nothing is planned out. And my concern is that to find something big you've grasped at something that doesn't really have legs."

James's enthusiasm briefly sobered up. "Well," he said, "I don't remember you saying that. And to be honest, I would obviously listen to what you said, but I wouldn't start a company just because you told me to."

"Sure. Of course. It's just . . . I know it sounds fun, and I'm sure you'll be able to make it go as far as it can go. But, friend to friend, my gut is that this is the wrong vehicle for you. You're going to spend years killing yourself to build one rattly machine that'll probably only kind of half work."

"I don't –"

"Why don't you choose something that already has some real momentum? You like being rude about Shell, but you could climb the ladder fast here. And then you're not struggling along with one engineer. You could grow a hundred companies like this instead of exhausting yourself on something that might turn out to be impossible."

At the word "impossible", James's enthusiasm caught again. He felt like Christopher Columbus being laughed at for saying the world was round. Even if that was a myth. He said, "So, it sounds like you're not going to join up?"

"Ha. No. It would be fun to do something together." She shrugged, still holding the phone. "But yeah, maybe leave yourself a way out. After two years, ask yourself: 'Knowing what I know now, would I still get into this?' Your enemy here is the sunk cost fallacy. Path dependence. Don't let yourself think 'I've put so much into this, I just need to put in a little bit more.'"

James was feeling so much like Christopher Columbus that he didn't mind having sunk costs explained to him. He said, "When we overtake Shell, you'll have to take me out for lunch."

"I'd love that. And I'll take you out for lunch if you go bust. But listen, we're landing — I've got to go. Good luck. Call me if you want to talk."

When Roland and James emailed in their resignations together, pressing *send* after three in the gloomy bar at the Mercure, Roland felt like an acrobat at the high point of the leap from one trapeze to another. One swing left behind, the other still rushing towards him; at the top of the arc, not yet falling but drifting. Soon the next swing's wooden handle would smack into his palms. Soon he'd have to plunge into a new set of stunts and routines. But not yet.

His new partner suddenly irritated him. James kept asking if he should order some champagne. They could see a few never-touched bottles of Veuve Clicquot on a shelf behind the bar. Roland found it annoyingly formulaic – too obvious, too trained a response, as if they had to buy the appropriate object to know that they were happy. The ant-like contentment of feeling everything in the same way as everyone else. He wished James would fuck off for a while.

In the following weeks, it seemed like everyone at McKinsey sought them out. Just as many Londoners perennially wondered whether they should move to the country, the consultants asked themselves, Should I stay in the elite Jesuitical seclusion of the Firm, always at one remove from victory and defeat, or enter the hurly-burly of business on my own account? The grand vizier's nagging question: Would I be a better king than the king? They interrogated Roland and James as if to find an answer for themselves. How much cash on hand? Market sizing. Who were the competitors? James treated the critiques as free consulting and used them to sharpen his thoughts.

One of the oldest partners, a bit of a genial buffer by this stage, told Roland, "All your generation want to start these do-gooder companies now. When I was coming up . . . a business to save the climate . . ." – he shook his head with nostalgic pleasure – "you'd have been considered a complete muesli-muncher. And there weren't any 'angel investors' back then. A ludicrous term, really. People with money to throw away. Back then, you had to go to one of those prudent, penny-pinching branch managers and get a loan. If you'd shown up with an untested machine and no hope of turning a profit any time soon, they'd have rung the funny farm. Of course, Silicon Valley's changed all that — for the better, oh almost certainly for the better."

Roland enjoyed being part of the future. Finally, he was the same person in the office as he was at the pub. Over drinks, attention just came to him. Ever since school it had been like that. Sometimes it was as if he were a bonfire, and the diligent, rule-abiding squares were standing around him silently in the dark, reflecting him. But they turned away when it came to business. Now, however, they were asking him, "Roland, what's your prediction for climate change?" "Are you worried about double-dip recession?" And while James got into the detail of the energy market, Roland told people, "We're basically doing it because we hate living in Aberdeen." And "We'll probably go bust by Christmas. I'll have to move in with James's parents."

For years, the person he pretended to be in the office had been slowly asphyxiating him. But now it had turned out for the opposite. He could behave however he wanted. The partners smiled as he talked. Being older, they registered the jeopardy that he and James were so casually taking on. And they said they knew someone — an investor, a lawyer, a grant-giver — who might be worth a chat.

As he collected these tokens of help, Roland felt he was coming back to life. His pinstripe suit and expensive Italian shoes he carried in a black binbag to the nearest charity shop. He was going to be something of liberating simplicity: himself. Instead of the suit, he tried out dressing like a hipster lumberjack: skinny jeans, black-and-red plaid shirt, beanie. It was a shame he couldn't grow a beard.

Of course he also wanted to save the world. He almost read the idealistic management literature that James passed on. The titles told him all he needed to know — *The Double Bottom Line: Doing Well by Doing*

Good. He let his friends and parents know that this was the future of capitalism. It didn't occur to him or James to be afraid. They had no debts, having started university when tuition fees were minimal and easily paid off. James lived at home. Roland could stay at a flat in Maida Vale that his parents bought while prices were slumped. Neither had been taught to worry about putting money by for children, sickness or old age. Day-to-day, they needed almost nothing.

They were keyed up at times, as before giving a speech. Perhaps the machine would fail. Surely there would be picturesque disappointment for them to weather. But there didn't seem to be any danger they personally might lose anything that couldn't be replaced.

Once they handed in their access cards and left the McKinsey building, everything went quiet. No partners gave them instructions; no clients sent requests. The daily email traffic ceased. The only messages in their new company inboxes said "Thanks for choosing G-suite". To show themselves that they were busy, they wrote to-do lists. The more items that needed doing, the calmer they felt.

A name for the company was difficult. "Moon Power" was too menstrual. "British Sea Power", it turned out, was the name of an indie band. For now they stuck with the placeholder they'd registered at Companies House: Drayton–Mackenzie Ltd.

Because James didn't want to waste money on an office, they met every weekday morning in his parents' kitchen. Roland didn't think it would be so extravagant to have just a little room somewhere. It needn't be fancy. Maybe just with their names on the door in those golden letters and a landline on his desk to make calls from. But James said they couldn't afford it, and the cash in the company account was James's savings.

James said they should start at nine, but, as a co-founder, Roland exercised his right to arrive whenever the fuck he felt like it. Before going to James's, he often went to a coffee shop nearby, where he got over-caffeinated and watched TED talks on his MacBook. Half the baristas were now Spaniards and Italians his age who'd moved to London because of the recession at home. Sometimes, looking out through the window as people in office clothes streamed to their jobs, Roland was overcome with a feeling of gratitude and specialness. Praise be to Allah, the compassionate and merciful.

James was very glad that Roland seemed enthused. This was how he imagined life in a start-up: him and Roland at the kitchen table, sketching out the borders of their future empire. It was like being Larry Page and Sergey Brin in a rented garage near Stanford, puzzling out the rudiments of the company they were still calling Googol.

In this moment of hunger for ideas, James was deeply affected by a manifesto that said "We wanted flying cars; instead we got 140 characters", by the Californian billionaire Peter Thiel. He said that the boom in computer science since the 1980s had sucked in all the inventors, and all the money, at the expense of the hard sciences. The iPhone had put a personal computer in everyone's pocket, but it was slower to fly across the Atlantic today than when Concorde launched in 1976. No human had walked on the moon since 1972. The really cool stuff, the sci-fi dream of human advancement, wasn't apps but steel, power, engineering in extreme conditions. Like, say, a tidal turbine in the North Atlantic.

They kept being interrupted by James's parents, who coddled Roland like a charming new son-in-law who was really a bit out of James's league. They made him cups of coffee while James was trying to get the day started, and asked about places he'd lived. They believed unshakeably that James's India project – the one time before this he'd used his powers for good – was due to Roland's influence.

Arthur asked Roland, "Do you know that in the period he was studying India, he never once went there?"

Roland, playing the role they wanted, said ruefully, "He's more interested in his spreadsheets."

"Yes, more interested in mathematical abstraction than in colour, sound, flavour, the embodied experience."

Roland, who could tell that James was trying to catch his eye, ignored him and said, "It's a real shame."

"You were there for . . . ?"

"A couple of years in the end."

"Wonderful. Wonderful."

"You see it in a different way when you're not a traveller, you know, when you're involved in people's lives."

When James finally couldn't take it any more and said, "Dad, sorry, we've got to get on with it," Arthur and Roland raised their eyebrows at each other, as if acknowledging their shared opinion of this person they were bound to.

At lunchtime, Arthur would come back in and interrupt again by saying, "Just pretend I'm not here." Roland's presence inspired him to take down his disintegrating copy of Ada Boni and attempt some new dishes: ravioli stuffed with zucchini flowers, *torta salata* with home-made pastry. He clanged about with pots, piling up ingredients and muttering to himself until he induced Roland to say, "Oh sorry, is there anything I can help with?"

James carried on typing as they moved place mats around him, chatting merrily about food or music or how James had always been difficult. When Mary came in, she said, "Really? The pasta machine? Roland, please don't feel you have to participate in this." But she too couldn't resist falling into conversation. She told Roland an anecdote James had never heard: she'd accidentally knocked the wing off a swan ice sculpture at an economics conference in Cairo. And she'd love to know whether Roland thought the Arab monarchies would collapse when the world moved off oil. Roland looked for an opening to tell his hapless tale about trying to study Japanese and ending up in provincial India. But it seemed less glamorous than it used to, and he let it drop.

James went on working. In those months, his sheer capacity for work slowly astonished Roland. There was something uncanny about it. He didn't fidget. He didn't get distracted by his phone. He didn't obstruct himself with the minor weaknesses that would have made Roland feel closer to him. His ability to withstand boredom was like a superpower. He could sit on the hard wooden chair at the kitchen table from before

Roland arrived until after he left, immobile apart from his typing hands, and concentrate. It was as if his body were an electric wheelchair that he parked and turned off. Roland thought he must be getting piles.

Sometimes James would suck in a great lungful of air, as if he'd been holding his breath, sit back and say, "Okay that's done" and get up, jiggling on his toes, hurrying to take the piss he'd been bottling in.

Towards the end of the day, they'd agree some task for tomorrow — like making a list of energy companies with investment funds. This grand endeavour of theirs still bored Roland in the detail. But he'd arrive the next morning and find the task complete. He tried to tell James they should divide the tasks equally. But they both knew that was bollocks. Roland said, "It's like the fairy story of the little elves and the shoemaker. You're my house elf."

"And you're the shoemaker? That's such cobblers."

Roland shook his head while James grinned. Dreadful.

Seeing James alone at the kitchen table, typing intently while he and Arthur amused themselves, Roland began to think there was something touching about him. Touching and deluded.

Since James hadn't done physics in his degree, he seemed not to know that he, everything, the universe, was lent its light and motion by the bang it started with, and was winding down. One day the stars would wink off. The sun would burn the last of its fuel and go out. The Earth's molten core would set solid. The oceans would freeze. Life would die off the surface. The Earth would go silent and, released from the sun's orbit, drift off into the infinite dark.

That was the direction of time, from the bang towards dissipation, entropy, disorder. Life itself was just an unexpected flourishing along the way. And yet here was James, stitching things together, connecting one thought to another thought, laboriously hoisting up mental linkages and cross-linkages until his fragile idea became something fragile but solid. It was like trying to halt the tide of undoing. Poor sweet numpty.

As for James himself, he was discovering the joy of stress. Now that his efforts weren't defined by an employer's requirements, they became boundless. This cause could suck up all his intellect and exertion and still need far, far more. When he woke at night and found that his sleeping mind had unknotted some problem, he was exhilarated: he'd managed to harness even his subconscious. McKinsey idiom warned about "drinking from the firehose". Don't try to take in more than the mind can absorb: "Let's not try and drink from the firehose." But he *was* drinking from it. Simultaneous crash courses in marine engineering, in energy markets, in investment models. The more he poured into his mind, the more it grew.

He tasted fulfilment. This was no longer some arbitrary test. Nor was he just an economic function, an information processor that McKinsey paid for the same way it paid for pencils. He was engaged in humanity's great struggle upwards.

Every day, he thought of Clausewitz's wry maxim: "In war everything is very simple, but the simplest thing is difficult." Put simply: his savings were enough to keep Alan paid and his kids at Robert Gordon's for one year and four months. By then, James and Roland had to bring in more investment or the company would fold. Every day that passed was one day less. James had never experienced such clarity.

Alan's part was to take his floating yellow model and rebuild it in steel, twenty times the size. It would be a functioning prototype, able to ride the rough winter seas, harvest the tide and send electricity ashore. Once that was up and running, they'd build a full-scale device, five times larger still, the size of a plane. But even the prototype would take years.

Unlike the immaterial business of designing an app, their machine required crude matter: heavy, inert, resistant to manipulation. Iron ore had to be hacked out of the ground. Anchor chains had to hold against the tide. Special paint to resist the hungry salt; cables, bolts, electronics that wouldn't fritz out when doused by a freezing wave. More and yet more: a wave pool for testing, a warehouse, at least two boats. And as soon as the machine was out there, the sea would try to destroy it.

The money they were spending on Alan, which was all their money, didn't cover any of this. Far from it. What they could afford was for Alan to make models on his iMac and write out wish lists of equipment. Since

Alan was practically their entire cost base, they should extract all they could from him. That was Start-up 101.

But, for reasons James couldn't understand, Roland had appointed himself Alan's protector and barrack-room lawyer. Anything Alan said he might like, Roland argued for so insistently that James could only acquiesce or turn it into a question of who was really in charge. So he acquiesced. Alan wanted a week's holiday in Ullapool during half-term. That didn't tally with James's idea of Bolshevik zeal. But Alan wanted it, and off he went.

One afternoon, they were at the kitchen table, making a list of skills they needed to buy in, which unfortunately came not on reliable hard drives but written into the flawed organic matter of human beings. James was snacking on translucent sheets of prosciutto. He was in a black silk dressing gown embroidered with a swirling green and gold dragon, which his mum had brought back from a conference in Seoul. Roland thought he could do with a shower.

Since Roland had watched his TED talks and founder inspo YouTube videos about how to start a company, a bothersome thought had kept pulling at his sleeve. Once he'd had enough of their meeting, he said, "So, Jimmy."

"Yes, Rolly?"

"'Rolly'?"

"Okay, whatever. What's the question?"

"'Rolly' is terrible."

"Yes. Fine. What's the question?"

"I've been thinking about, I guess, how the company's set up. Like, Alan literally invented the machine, and he owns twenty per cent of the shares."

"Honestly, Roland, I really don't think he should have more than that. He's getting paid, remember? That's the trade-off. More cash, less equity. I really don't think you need to lobby for him to get more."

"No, no. That's not what I mean. But it's like, forty per cent for you, forty per cent for me, and twenty per cent for Alan. Right?"

"Right."

"Okay, so, to just put it bluntly, how am I worth twice as much as Alan?"

James had a slice of prosciutto in his hand. He put it in his mouth and chewed, gaining time. He made the "I'm hurrying" gesture with his hand. Finally, he swallowed and said, "It's a great question. Isn't the best thing we could do for the mission to upgrade *ourselves*? Why don't we find someone who knows energy, has founded start-ups before and literally give them the company?"

"Yeah, okay. But like, in practice, why me? What skillset am I bringing?"

James felt like he had when Will Cambourne accosted him on the quad years ago: he wanted to run. But he said, "If Eleni had signed up, she'd have got an equal share as well."

"What, seriously?"

"Obviously we'd have had to discuss it."

"That makes literally no sense. There'd be no one in charge and no one would invest in a company like that."

James shrugged. "Actually, Eleni is the only one who does make sense. Being rich is a real asset."

"Okay, but still, why me?" Roland was now pretty sure he knew the answer, but he was going to make James say it.

"That's what I'm saying: why either of us?"

"If you don't want to tell me, that's up to you. I don't think it's a very sound basis for a company. But hey, yeah, up to you."

They went back to their laptops. James tried to concentrate but couldn't. A sound basis was what this stage was all about. He knew Roland was trying to get under his skin, and yet Roland had managed it. Maybe he could go upstairs and email Roland from there. Better just to push through: "Like I was saying, it's an interesting theoretical question. Also, it could seem to an outsider that you and I have been, to some degree, starting to become not just colleagues but friendly."

"What are you talking about? We've been friends for like three years."

"That's great. Glad to hear it."

"I haven't been going on weird weekends in Scotland with anyone else, have I?"

"I don't know. That's up to you."

"Well, I haven't."

"Okay. So, yes. As you say, we've been friends for a while, and starting a company solo is very different."

Roland nodded as if thinking, and said, "Can we just be honest, please?"

James tensed. "Okay."

"Is it that you want to bum me?"

James yelled with relief.

Roland gave him more of the schoolboy stuff that James hadn't had in school: "Honestly, mate, if this is a gay thing, you don't need to invent a whole company. You just be who you need to be."

"Those weekends *were* quite romantic."

"*So* romantic. I thought you were going to propose."

James laughed and said, "But what, are you in love with Alan now? Everything he says, you're just like, *yes, Alan*."

"It's just we've got to look after him. He's the only one who understands any of this. No need to get jealous."

"Fine. Just remember you own forty per cent of the company and should be interested in it prospering."

"Forty per cent of fuck all is still fuck all."

"I didn't know your maths was that good. That must be how you got such a good degree."

"Ouch. Okay. I see. You've got me there. But whatever, I own just as much of the company as you do."

"Probably a mistake on my part."

"Probably."

"Great."

"Great."

James's internal monologue began to babble out of him like spring water out of a carved stone face. He let go of being careful with his words. At the end of one lunch, when his parents had gone back upstairs, he said, "Isn't it funny we were literally in the same boat, what, eight years ago, but didn't really know each other?"

Roland wasn't particularly keen for the lunch break to end. He considered the topic. "I don't think we'd have been friends then."

"Oh no? Why not?"

Roland pantomimed a big eye roll. "Oh, I don't know. I remember you being a kind of a full-on psycho keen bean back then. Big difference from now . . ."

James laughed comfortably. "And what were you? Heading for a 2:2?" His attempt to use this for banter again didn't quite land.

Roland said, "Yeah, you're right, I was dicking about. I had a good time though. When I was on *Cherwell* – did you ever meet a girl called Danni Marquez?"

"No."

"She was the deputy editor, and I was the star reporter, and we shagged in the office under the desk."

"Amazing."

"Why don't I do that any more?"

"My parents might walk in."

They both laughed, and James was pleased that he'd got them there. He said, "I didn't really have a good time at uni."

"No?"

"No."

Roland came up with a cover story for him. "Maybe because your parents are academics, it was a bit less, like, novel for you."

"Maybe that was a factor."

"Must have been."

"I was quite unhappy though."

"Really?"

"Yeah."

That was enough for the time being. This piece of personal history was now an established fact between them.

They soon discovered that in business everything was simple, but the simplest thing took forever. To get investment, they were approaching oil and gas giants like Shell and BP, who were by definition interested in the energy business. They were also going after venture capital funds, the American-inspired investors with the billions and the audacity that for a small company were like rocket fuel.

To ask Shell or anyone else for investment, they had to get themselves introduced. And an introducer – some tenuous friend of a friend who knew the team at Shell – had to be identified and persuaded to do it. These potential introducers would say "Let's have a coffee," in three or four weeks. After the coffee, during which they pitched themselves, practically begging, an introductory email would be sent. But the team at Shell didn't reply. They had to be delicately harassed without breaking the fragile, spun-sugar links of personal connection. Finally, Shell agreed to schedule a meeting for six weeks in the future. But then it was Christmas, and the meetings were postponed to the new year.

Their standing was nil; their leverage was nil; they had nothing to offer but promises and aspirations. They had to thank people for talking to them.

Meanwhile, Alan would sooner or later reach the point at which he could go no further without spending money on a warehouse, a boat, a steel hull, none of which they could afford. Then they would be paying him to play golf. James calculated that, at their present burn rate, they would go bust on 24 February 2013. But then Alan bought some modelling software, and the bankruptcy date came forward to 18 December 2012.

Even Roland caught himself worrying about component suppliers at the weekend. But he found that if he had a raging bender on the Friday night, it wiped his thoughts as blank as if shaking an Etch A Sketch.

One evening before Christmas, a year from bankruptcy, Roland persuaded James to come to a party in an office block in Shoreditch. One entire floor had been turned into an enormous flat/gallery. Through the floor-to-ceiling windows you could see the financial district at night. There were a few sofas, a DJ, a trestle table with ranks of prosecco flutes, and a concertinaed room divider displaying arty photographs of the tent city at Occupy Wall Street. In one, a tanned babe in sunglasses, pink bikini and cowboy boots held up a cardboard sign that read "We are the 99%". Roland thought: If only. He hoped he wasn't becoming laddish.

It was a dispersed kind of party. Some people were dancing. Others were sitting on sofas and drinking tea. Someone was leaning over the kitchen counter, watching videos on a laptop.

Roland and James drank prosecco and looked out at the city. Its towers loomed big and empty, vacated for the weekend. Roland said, "You should neck like ten more of these and get on the dancefloor. There's some MDMA going around. Watch the sun come up through these windows."

"I'm actually going to head quite soon. I want to get up early tomorrow and make some progress on the profiles of the Statoil team."

"You don't have to lie: you're going to do it tonight, aren't you?"

"Yeah."

"It's up to you, obviously, but I don't think it's good for you. Like, you're not just a machine. You are actually a human being."

"Yeah. Maybe. At the moment, I just find the more I do, the more I *can* do. It feels good."

They looked out at the towers. Roland said, "Do you ever worry it's, like, not going to pan out? We'll just run out of money and have to get our old jobs back at McKinsey?"

James smiled. "No. I never really worry about it."

"Me neither. I'm never going back there."

"So you're glad we decided to do it?"

"Oh, yeah. I'm glad I've experienced it – starting a company. And I definitely can't think of anything better."

"So you're enjoying it?"

"I think so. But . . . I don't want to be a downer, mate, but there is part of me that still thinks: there used to be all these different things – Japan, India, London, Aberdeen. Now it's just this one thing. And yeah, by the standards of having a job, it's miles better than the bullshit most people are stuck with. But it's not exactly wild and free, is it?"

James hadn't realised that "wild and free" was required.

"But, like, I guess, we win this money, and then we'll be away."

"Well, then we'll actually have to build the machine."

"How long do you reckon that's going to take? Like, years, right?"

"The whole thing?" James beamed. "Maybe decades."

"Decades. Wow. Yeah. And are we, like, a hundred per cent sure this is what we want to be doing for decades?"

James was startled. But he told himself that Roland had always needed cajoling; he was still recovering from his unhappiness at the Firm. Like with a hot bath, he just needed to ease himself deeper into it.

2012

The day before the start of the London Olympics, an Italian man in his sixties had breakfast in a red-brick Gothic palace redone as an upmarket business hotel. On the side tables, beside the buffet, were photos and short bios of British athletes. He read a couple while choosing his pastry. Last night, at a dinner organised in his honour by Mervyn King, the governor of the Bank of England, there'd been much gossip about the prime minister trying to shoehorn himself into the opening ceremony.

But he wasn't here for athletics. He was Mario Draghi, president of the European Central Bank, doing the job for Europe that his old classmate Ben Bernanke was doing for America. He controlled the presses that printed the euro. And Europe was still very fragile. The shocks from the Lehman collapse simply wouldn't end. Europe's presidents and chancellors had just held their nineteenth crisis summit.

Mario spoke as little as he could in public. If he said some awkward phrase, he could trigger a stampede of investors rushing to get their money out of Europe. In the worst case, that would bankrupt, as a minimum, the governments of Italy and Spain, and so destroy the euro. Every sentence that he planned to say on the record, his staff checked for unintended consequences.

But this afternoon he was going to go off script.

He could feel himself growing tense. His forehead was trying to frown, his shoulders to rise up and protect his neck. There was an urge to ring his staff and find fault with them. They'd been able to sense that something was going on.

But no. None of that. He was going to enjoy his coffee and his *pain au chocolat* and his boiled egg. With a paradoxical will to relax, he forced his forehead and shoulders and fingers to unclench.

As if touching an amulet, he rubbed his thumb over a memory of summer 1964, when he was sixteen. He and his younger brother and sister came back from their holiday on the coast. While the younger two went upstairs to retake possession of their bedrooms, Mario sat down at the kitchen table with a stack of letters. Bills, notices from schools, reminders to make medical appointments for his siblings. His father had died. His mother would die soon. Now, he, Mario, opened the envelopes.

Another amulet: at MIT in Boston, in the 1970s. The elite of economics. Half a dozen Nobel prizes among the professors. Of the students, Ben was now head of the Federal Reserve, Mario head of the ECB; Paul had won the Nobel. Before arriving at MIT, Mario had not known anyone could work that hard.

His scholarship covered less than half his costs, so he taught on the side until his daughter was born. After that, needing more money, he took a job at an IT firm forty miles from Boston. He would start at six a.m. and drive home after midnight. His daughter didn't even see him. But he saw her, asleep in her cot. He learned about himself that he could withstand this intensity, like clay that in the kiln doesn't crack but sets harder.

In the breakfast room in London, he consciously appreciated the elegance of the tiny white eggshell-thin espresso cup restraining the oily black liquid within. He sipped. He ate his egg. It was marginally overcooked.

That afternoon, as Mervyn introduced him to the crowd, the nerves came on again. A tremor in the thorax. An irrational stab of hatred for pink, overweight, complacent old Mervyn, whose commiserations about the euro's troubles contained too noticeable a drop of schadenfreude: that Britain had not joined, that sterling was not mixed up with these unsound Italians. Fuck Mervyn, that old maid. He looked out from his chair at two hundred faces. There was Christine Lagarde of the IMF, who'd come over from Paris, one of his few allies here. There was Jim O'Neill whom he knew from Goldman. Crispin Odey, the hedge funder, a big, brawny man – in another life he would have been a farmer – sitting with his arms folded over his paunch, betting heavily that Mario would fail.

They were in some supposedly grand room, maybe nineteenth-century, built with the profits that the London counting houses derived from the trade ships plying across their empire. The neoclassical pillars were a little clunky, the red marble too dark, the overall effect too heavy. When he was teaching monetary policy in Florence, he often lectured in the Palazzo Medici, under Giordano's extraordinary pale celestial blue and gold fresco of Olympus. Florence's bankers had paid for the Renaissance; London's for . . . Turner? He didn't know.

In any case, the Medici bank had been bust these five centuries, and the Anglo-Saxons had the money now. He had to come to them. These two hundred bankers thought his euro was a monstrosity, an ugly experiment doomed to collapse. They called the southern Europeans the PIGS – Portugal, Italy, Greece and Spain. They were betting that Italy would go down like Greece: it would not be able to pay its debts. And when the Italians finally capitulated to financial gravity, the rest of Europe would decline to bail them out. Italy was too big to scourge and resurrect, like Greece had been. It would drag the euro under. The single currency would disintegrate. They would be back to the lira, the guilder, the drachma and all the Balkanised diversity of European coinage.

The Anglo-Saxons' bets against Italy were themselves pushing the Italians towards the edge. These bets made it more expensive for Italy to borrow the money required to keep the government functioning. If Mario, out of some destructive impulse, said he didn't have faith in the Italian finances, the bets would grow colossal. He could bankrupt the state of Italy with two sentences.

Mervyn had finished talking. There was the customary applause. Mario stood, went to the lectern and thanked him. He looked down at the two hundred faces, pink against their dark suits. They saw a man in functional glasses. A former professor with black-and-grey hair imperfectly combed from its parting. For "within" and "finance" he said "witheen" and "feenance". There were round American vowels in there too, when he thanked Mervyn for this *honor*.

The nerves were still on him, and he began with a spontaneous detour.

He told them that, years ago, when the single currency was being planned, it was often said the euro was like a bumblebee – a creature that shouldn't exist. He didn't want to use the word *Frankenstein*. And now he'd come to tell them the euro was turning into a real bee. But they, not being involved in the euro, hadn't heard the bumblebee analogy before. And he forgot to explain that the bumblebee was supposedly too heavy to fly and yet it flew. He lost them.

Nonetheless, as he looked down at these faces, some blank, many sceptical, as he had looked down at thousands of audiences before, he stepped out of the tight circle of fear. He was beyond calculation. What he had decided to do he would not alter now. While he talked, he unconsciously put his hand in his pocket.

He gave them the three McKinsey-style points he'd written with his staff:

1. The euro is stronger than it seems.
2. In the past six months, we've made it stronger still.
3. Those from outside the euro area – i.e. you – often overlook how politically committed we are to the single currency.

He spoke easily, humorously, anticipating their objections: "Of course, while I was glorifying the merits of the euro, you were thinking 'But that's an average, and in fact countries diverge so much witheen the euro area that averages are not representative.'" They listened to him. He was not some foreign bureaucrat haranguing them incomprehensibly. He was easy to like.

And then he departed from his notes. There was another, fourth, point. He felt a great peace and levity, an urge to laugh. He paused. He folded his hands. He said, "Witheen our mandate, witheen our mandate, the ECB is ready to do *whatever it takes* to preserve the euro."

He paused again, to make sure they'd absorbed his meaning. He turned left, he turned right, letting them see him. Odey had uncrossed his arms, and his brawny form was sitting up on the edge of his chair. Christine looked moved. He went on, "And believe me, it will be enough."

Yes, he, Mario, would do anything. He would bail the Italians out himself. He would print money and give it to them. He would print trillions if he had to. And if the hedge funds tried to resist him, he would just keep printing more and more until they were forced to concede. Whatever it takes. Italy was not going bust. The euro was not going to disintegrate. They might as well stop betting on it.

There was muted uproar in the room. Jim O'Neill was on his feet, warbling about this "extraordinarily important intervention". The message had been received.

On the way out, Mervyn touched his elbow, almost obsequiously, and said, "Is this on the level? The Germans are on board?"

More or less. He'd have to call Jens at the Bundesbank right away. Jens would hate it, but Mario had left him no choice. Last year, many people, including Jens, had assumed that Jens would get the job as head of the ECB. But Mario had got it.

He said, "Yes, we are creating a way of lending to distressed countries. But I hope we will not have to use it." He would have to tell his staff to start creating. He could see them at the room's edge, beaming at him.

By the time, close to midnight, that he arrived back to the hotel after yet another dinner – at which there was no athletics talk, just twenty people at a long table taking turns to ask him what he meant by "whatever it takes"; he'd barely been able to eat anything before the waiters tried to take it away – the acute, life-threatening phase of Europe's financial crisis was finally over. The aftershocks would keep rolling for a while, but the source had been soothed.

Over the course of that afternoon, the Anglo-Saxons, believing their opportunity gone, rushed to unwind their bets against Italy. The rates at which Italy could borrow fell back to normal. As of tomorrow morning, the Italian government could again afford to make decisions, and – if they had any sense, which was not guaranteed – they could steer away from the whirlpool.

He hadn't printed a single banknote. But by saying that the euro was safe, he had made it safe. The power of speech.

As he undressed alone in the impersonally luxurious hotel room, he remembered his time at the Jesuit school, as a teenager. He was known as someone who, despite being easy to get on with, was always diligent. He'd seen very young how close beneath the pleasant surface of things was the black pit. That was nearly half a century ago. And now: another stumble into the pit narrowly avoided. He'd been at this a long time. He'd lost very early the luxury of being irresponsible.

It was at that age, as an adolescent, that he decided to go into economics like his father. Back in the '20s, his father had a job at the Bank of Italy. When Mario became the bank's governor, he had them find his father's name in the archives. Carlo Draghi had worked on the financing of hydroelectric dams in Germany and Hungary, and always felt himself to be a European.

The day after the speech, Mario was sitting in the crowd at the Olympic opening ceremony with his wife, who'd flown over that morning. Christine Lagarde, who was in the crowd, too, could see them from her seat. Mario and Maria. It was like a joke. Everyone called her Serenella. She was a professor of English, a clever, funny woman from some historic Italian dynasty. Mario was pointing at something down in the arena. Their heads were together. How was it possible for him to be so at ease? An extraordinary man. And yet, no more than that. Just a man, with his wife, waiting for the show to begin.

VII

SEPTEMBER 2012

Just under two months from bankruptcy, James and Roland finally met the investment team at Statoil, Norway's state oil firm. Eleni introduced them. Since Roland had given his suit to the charity shop, he had to buy another – this time from Zara, the cheapest they had.

The meeting was in a high-rise office building next to Paddington. The windows overlooked the railway lines, running away towards Heathrow like giant zips laid side by side. James was twitching with adrenalin, but to Roland it all somehow felt flat and anticlimactic. He watched James stand in front of a whiteboard faintly stained with red and green lettering and give their spiel: the elemental power of the seas, a harness around the moon, climate change, the cleverness of having their turbine float.

James was not good. He argued rather than persuading, like a barrister appealing to some all-seeing judge who would rule that James was right: Statoil *had to* give them some money. Roland tried not to wince, and wriggled. Unable to keep watching, he looked out the window and saw a Heathrow Express slide along the tracks and away to the west, the carriages shifting in alignment against each other. He'd have to teach James how to give a talk. He'd make it a joke. A gay joke. Like teaching golf: it's all in the hips.

Roland had expected the Statoil team to be Norwegians. But the boss was another Scot, a very small, wizened, raisin-like older woman called Melanie, who was wearing a shirt under a sleeveless company fleece. She looked like a tiny ancient child. Melanie queried some points, but it was to clarify rather than rebut. And she went on, "Look, I don't think the level of support you mentioned is going to happen. But we are big believers in predictable renewables. When the sun's not shining, the electricity's going to have to come from *somewhere*. You might know we're already invested in Pelamis." Somehow it seemed that, despite James's delivery, what they had was enough. The numbers they'd sent over in advance, the objective characteristics of Alan's machine, were enough. Everyone stood up, and there was much smiling and shaking of hands.

In years to come, all Roland clearly remembered was how bad James had been. James felt it was the first time he'd scratched a mark into the smooth indifferent surface of the world.

The £500,000 Statoil allocated was their minimum investment. After James haggled them to exhaustion, they agreed to take only an outrageously small six per cent for their money. Since six per cent equalled £500,000, that implied the company was worth £8.3 million. On the share certificates they typed up in Microsoft Word and printed off on the screeching machine in James's dad's study, they each now had a stake worth around three million pounds. Alan's stake was about one and a half.

Even though they high-fived, and Roland said, "Congrats on getting rich quick," there was no joy in it. Instead it was a kind of emptiness. It was as if their bodies hadn't kept up with the good news. Whatever gland produced the feeling of satisfaction hadn't yet squeezed it into the bloodstream. The stress was gone, for now, and they had what they wanted. But it almost felt like despair.

As he stapled the sheets of paper, James said, "I've got a drawer for important documents. I can put yours in there if you don't have a safe place."

"I think, on balance, I probably won't lose my bit of paper worth three million pounds."

"Alright, don't get cranky."

Roland stopped initialling his pages and said, "Did you really have to haggle so much? If our machine fucking sinks, we'll have to tell them we've lost half a million of their quids." They went on with their stapling and initialling in angry silence.

One evening, on impulse, James walked Roland to the Tube. The air was mild and London felt full of promise. It was as if the streets and traffic were a movie set, and everyone else an extra in their story. As they arrived at the Tube, James said, "Well," and they both grinned. They shook hands and Roland waggled his eyebrows, subverting the too-sincere emotion. James said, "We're on the way."

"We're on the way."

Over lunch a few days later, James's dad opened a bottle of *franciacorta*, which he said was the Italian champagne, sweetened in the bottle, unlike the sickly vat-sugared prosecco that was so inexplicably popular. He shouted up the stairs for Mary to come down.

As they toasted one another, Arthur said, "It's lovely that when everything else seems to be going to rack and ruin, and everything's being cut, and they're closing the libraries – my God! They're closing the libraries; I still can't really believe it – it makes you want to weep. But you two young people are erecting something new and splendid from amid the rubble."

That thought was deposited in some deep-lying substratum of their minds, like gold in an abandoned mineshaft. They'd used up some of their potential and, for better or worse, this was what they'd got in return.

After Statoil, meetings with other oil and gas firms racked up fast. No pitch deck was as persuasive to investors as knowing that someone else had put in real money. With each financial endorsement they collected, the herd impulse grew stronger: £500,000 from BP; £750,000 from Shell. More from others. James was contemptuous of these managers who couldn't think for themselves.

They took the company card to a cash point outside a Sainsbury's, and Roland snapped a picture of all the digits in their on-screen balance: £1,742,836.04. Already the huge pile had eroded a little. Roland said, "Obviously you're not going to want to, but like, why *don't* we just take out, like, half a million each, fuck off to India and live like kings?"

"You've got a card. Knock yourself out."

Gradually they realised they weren't getting the really big money, the venture-capital money. Because the oil giants' investment teams were engineers or accountants by training, they doled out sober packets of cash, enough to keep building and no more. In practice, it was enough for James and Roland to start buying equipment.

But what they wanted were the VC guys, American-inspired hotshots anxious to get in early on the next Facebook. Instead of consistently growing their stack by the benchmark 1.07 per cent a year, their job was to multiply it a hundredfold. And in the strange, skewed financial conditions that followed the Lehman crisis – as Ben Bernanke, Mario Draghi and others kept the injured economy on a drip of cheap credit – the VCs amassed billions in what they called dry powder, just waiting to be deployed.

Instead of handing out carefully measured aid parcels, these guys could roll in like the US Army with music blaring, choppers whumping overhead and heavy howitzers blasting cash in every direction. That was what James said they needed – to hire more engineers and build faster, and avoid having to sell off their company piece by piece over the years before the machine was ready. But the VCs were no more interested now than they'd been at the beginning.

They spent a few hundred of their pounds on flying up to Orkney, to look at the strait through which the North Sea emptied itself into the Atlantic. Neither of them had actually seen it yet.

At Heathrow, for the first leg up to Aberdeen, they were no longer allowed in the BA lounge. Their Executive Club Silver memberships had expired. For the first time since their first year with McKinsey, they had to sit in the noisy shopping mall of an airport concourse.

They found a seat near a huge muted flatscreen TV, like a video installation endlessly recycling the news. Blocks of subtitles stuttered across the bottom in yellow or blue text, lagging jerkily behind the pictures. A new far-right movement in Greece was beating up foreigners. It called itself the Golden Dawn and ran soup kitchens for the destitute. Commentators were arguing about whether it was or was not like the 1930s.

Roland said, "You spoken to Eleni recently?"

"A few weeks ago. She wanted to know who we're talking to at Shell."

"Is her family, like . . ." – Roland nodded at the screen – "okay?"

"They're shipping magnates. I'm sure they'll be fine."

"Oh, okay. Well, that's great."

James paused writing notes to himself and looked at the screen. "I don't really get why they're still protesting. It's actually been resolved, the fiscal problem. But I suppose – well, evidently they don't understand that."

"They're evidently still hungry."

James rolled his eyes, a gesture he'd adopted from his friend.

They watched the soundless screen for a moment. The Greek names kept being autocorrected into gibberish: Mr Tea Practice, Mr Carotid.

The Orkney archipelago, when they got there, puttering in low under tattered clouds, looked like the edge of the world. It was as if the Eurasian land mass, stretching all the way from Vladivostok like a stone glacier, had calved some islands into the Atlantic, starting with big chunks called Britain and Ireland. And here, at the furthermost extremity before it was all water, the islands were ever tinier, the land and sea jumbled together on a finer scale, pixellating down into an intricate mishmash of earth and ocean. Thick beams of sunshine angling from the clouds spotlit patches on treeless hills, on thin fields, on the shiny metallic surface of a loch. They could see a sturdy fishing boat with a red hull and white cabin chugging motionlessly in the sunlight between two islands.

Alan met them in the terminal, which was just a room with a cafe counter and a shop selling puffin-themed tourist merch. Alan seemed thrilled, jovial, chattier than they'd ever seen him. Months of working alone at home, mainly on his computer, had tested his capacity for solitude. There was a flurry of talk – how was the flight – first trip to Orkney – a Stone Age village you should go see – you know the Orcadians call this island the mainland.

But once they were in the rental car, heading down a single-track road towards the main town, Kirkwall, the conversation ran out. Despite their hundreds of phone calls, it suddenly seemed they hardly knew each other. How tenuous it was to be starting a business together.

Alan fell back on admin. "I've got the boat booked for 3.30, so we can just drop your bags and go, if that's fine for you."

"Great."

"Great."

There was a pause, and Roland said, "How's *your* boat? Been out in it much recently?"

"Ehm, a bit. A wee bit. I took the kids out in the holidays. But I've been quite busy."

"Of course. Of course."

There was another pause. Alan said, "Oh but, see, for the hull, I've been speaking to Harland & Wolff, the guys in Belfast that built the *Titanic*. They can knock it together, and we can tow it up round the west coast to here."

Roland could feel there was a joke to be struck but couldn't line it up fast enough. James said, "Thanks for doing that, Alan. We'll take a look at what they're offering."

Alan glanced at his much younger boss in the passenger seat. "They know what they're doing, like. And they're not exactly overflowing with business, so it'll be a good price."

"Let's look at it together."

"Okay."

The practicalities began crowding in on Alan. "And actually, we need to make the call on two blades or three."

This was a decision without any safe middle ground. If you had three blades, then when you lifted the turbine up to the surface for maintenance, at least one blade would still be underwater. Which negated the whole elegance of having the machine float in the first place and pared back the cost savings of their design. But with two blades, Alan now said, you risked a strange effect called gyroscopic precession. This meant the rotor would wobble slightly, its nose moving in a tiny circle, like that of a spinning top. And if the wobble was too strong, it would rip the turbine to pieces.

Three blades would be safer. But if their design didn't create major cost savings, the VC funds wouldn't get excited enough to back them. So: three blades and risk their endeavour slowly starving for want of cash, or two blades and risk sinking their machine. Neither option seemed good.

But this kind of dilemma was James's comfort zone. On the most abstract level, running a company was just a series of interesting decisions. To not just guess a number – two or three – but to choose correctly meant weighing up engineering, hydrodynamics, investor psychology, and being right about them. The only field of human action that rivalled this complexity was warfare.

There was a human element, too: Alan. Alan was the human element. James could feel the stiltedness in the car. He said, "You're the head of engineering, and –"

"Ha. I'm the whole of engineering."

"Exactly. And yeah, we should decide on this trip."

"Exactly."

They drove without speaking. Because the untiring breeze meant there were no woods, everywhere they looked they could see into the distance, as if looking at the bones of the land.

Alan felt the awkwardness, too. "Ehm . . . I've got to say, well done, you pair, for getting the money in. Now we can really get started. So, ehm, good job."

"Thanks," said James. "But we still haven't got the VC money."

"Right," said Alan. "Right. But still, you two are getting your job done. Now I've got to do mine and get this thing built."

James said, "We have complete confidence in your abilities."

"Hmm."

Roland leaned his head forward between them and said, "Yeah, Alan, don't fuck it up."

Alan grinned with relief, turning to shoot back a grateful glance. Roland went on. "To be honest, getting the *Titanic* guys involved isn't a great sign. It's going to be hard to interest the VCs if the machine's at the bottom of the Irish Sea."

The boat was strangely unromantic, like a floating staffroom. Everything inside the cabin was made of MDF. At the front was an MDF instrument panel fitted with an incongruous steering wheel, where Roland stood chatting to the driver. He was older, in his sixties maybe, his face cured brown by the weather, short like Alan, with pure white hair straggling out from under a beanie.

Even though sunshine was bringing out the island's contours in brightness and shadow, there was no warmth on the boat. The sea cold seeped up through the thin floor. James and Alan were fine – James in his luminescent hiking gear and Alan in his well-worn sailing kit. Roland had got carried away with nautical attire: a woollen roll neck, a navy peacoat and a knitted black watch cap that sat above his ears. But he was still wearing his trainers, and the cold soaked up into his feet.

Kirkwall was at the bottom of a long, deep bay, like a cul-de-sac. As the boat motored away from it, they still had land on both sides. Precarious fields, sheep. Pale grass. A concrete bunker from one of the world wars. Through the back windows, the shrinking town was just a scruffy line above the water. The only mark was the Viking cathedral, its spire facing down the bay.

Roland told the driver, "We're probably going to need to buy a couple of these boats because we'll have people coming and going all the time."

The driver said, unreadably, "Oh, yes."

"Yeah, the plan is to build a whole array of tidal machines up here. Orkney could end up being the Silicon Valley of marine energy."

"Oh, very good."

"Seems like a really interesting place for it."

Roland was about to let slip that his mum was from Inverness, but the driver said, "Oh aye, oh aye. Lot of history in Orkney. Lot of raping and murdering." He chuckled.

James glanced up but went back to the diagram of the current that he and Alan were studying. In their tidal strait was an islet called Muckle Green Holm, around which the hurtling waters swerved and eddied, jumbling themselves into turbulent flux. No good for a spinning rotor.

They chugged out the mouth of the bay and through a dense scatter of small islands. One was just large enough for a single field and half a dozen black-and-white cows. The cows must go on and off by boat.

The driver told Roland, "There's a little island just by St Margaret's Hope where the farmer died a couple of years ago. His pigs got so hungry they broke down the door and ate him." The driver looked at Roland. "Nobody wants that bacon. So they've fair taken over the island. Must be cannibals by now. Inbred, too. Oh no, I wouldnae eat that."

Roland started to suspect he was being teased. But before he could ask anything, the driver said, "Alright now. Take a look at this."

They were coming out from under the lee of a largish island, and the view was opening up. Ahead was a low wall of drab coast belonging to yet another island. But to the left and right, there were gaps leading out to open ocean. As they moved forward, the islands shifted into alignment. The driver pointed out the gap to the right. "That's the North Sea through there." And to the left. "That's the Atlantic."

They could see it: a straight highway of galloping grey-green water, the wave-caps curling close behind one another. Millions of liquid tons moving unstoppably, interrupted only by the rocky protuberance, the size of a tennis court, of Muckle Green Holm. The driver said, "Now watch this."

They stood and peered out the forward windows. For a moment, nothing happened. But then the prow shivered as if struck. It had crossed an invisible border into the current. As it pushed on, it swung around, the force of the water sending the boat downstream. Within a few metres, the boat had turned and was heading rapidly out to open ocean. The Atlantic gap was dead ahead.

The driver raised his wiry grey eyebrows. "Nae bad, eh? Awfy lot of power going through here."

James said, "Enough for every house in Britain."

"Aye, that's what they say. Why you'd want to . . . Anyhow, you'll be wanting to look at the other machines."

Already they could see several surreal contraptions sticking out of the waves, industrial experiments years ahead of their own. Odd shapes in raw, rusted metal, standing in this marine desolation. Roland thought of *Mad Max*.

The boat zipped past these contraptions, running with the tide, then turned a foaming semicircle to face directly into the current. It slipped backwards, losing ground. The driver grinned at them and pushed the throttle forward. Quarter power. Half power. The engines' top note rose to a sharp whine and then above the level of human hearing. A steady bass roar came from underneath them. The walls rattled. At three-quarter power, the boat began to make headway. The driver wiped his brow and raised his voice to say, "Phew! No need to call the coastguard just yet."

The closest machine was a pair of parallel steel columns that reached up out of the waves. Fixed between them was a turbine, like a dismounted jet engine, that could be lowered into the current. As the boat bounced on the chop, they saw that the turbine's angled blades were dented and in some places ripped like the sharp edges of a torn tin can. The driver said,

"Shame really. Nice guys. They put the turbine too far down, too close to the bottom. But down there, you've got boulders, awful big things, getting dragged along like cars. They send it down, the sensors and what have you go haywire, then they bring it back up, and that's what it looks like. Another hour, and it would have been smashed to bits."

James thought: Not an issue for us.

Over on the shore was a cluster of grey sheds, like a farm's outbuildings. That must be the hydrogen plant. Some companies here were harvesting electricity in the tidal strait, moving it onshore by cable and using it to generate hydrogen.

Next was a single steel column with a walkway built like a T-bar across it. Somewhere in the water beneath them was a steel kite the size of a horse, flying figures of eight in front of the current. Alan thought: That's never going to work. James thought: What heterogeneity of design, like the early days of the motor car. Roland thought: It must be the world's loneliest kite, flying down there in the dark.

The driver said, "Seen enough of this one?"

They nodded, and he steered over to a grid of flashing red buoys. Somewhere below was something like a wind turbine but fixed to the ocean floor. He said, "To get it in, you need a special ship, from Holland, to drill into the seabed, like. It's got these legs that it puts down." He demonstrated with his fingers. "They used it for those other ones, too. For this one down here, they brought the boat and put the legs down, but the tide was stronger than they thought. Then the weather comes in, the wind's going against the tide, and this special ship starts yawing fit to keel over. The Dutch boys had to abandon ship." He laughed. "The ship got dragged out through that gap and halfway to Reykjavik. Snapped one of the legs off. It'll still be down there somewhere."

James and Alan gave each other a look of satisfaction: hence why their machine would float – no need to drill it in. James said to the driver, "It sounds like you're not very optimistic about tidal energy."

"Oh, no, no. I wouldnae say that. If you're needing lots of boats, that's lots of work for me. And you'd be surprised what all's going on up here.

It's not just fish and sheep any more. Not by a long shot. They're going to build a spaceport in Sutherland."

James glanced sceptically at Alan, who said, "I mean, let's see if it ever happens. But yes. I think the plan is for smaller satellites. It's not meant to be fucking Cape Canaveral."

The driver caught Alan's eye, and they acknowledged each other as men who knew what they were talking about. The driver said, "There's no big cities up here for the rockets to crash into if they go wrong. Kirkwall's so small that if a rocket hits us, with any luck we'll be dead before we know it."

Roland enjoyed the boat ride, but he said no when James suggested a second boat trip, to see the Pelamis machine, the hydraulic sea snake that undulated on the waves. He'd had enough machines for one day. From the window of the twin hotel room, he watched James and Alan clamber into the car. As soon as it pulled away, his heart lifted. He was at liberty, like a sailor on shore leave in a foreign town.

His conscience reminded him about the Stone Age village. There was a pamphlet about it on the desk. He picked it up and lay down on his single bed to read. It did look kind of amazing. There were pictures of one-room houses, sunken into the ground, with short stone beds and dressers and fireplaces. Built before the pyramids at Giza. As he looked at the photos, their colours slightly off – they'd probably been taken back in the nineties – there seemed less and less need to actually go there. Wasn't the ultimate luxury to say no to things?

He pulled off his shoes and took out his phone. On YouTube, there were all these videos of people doing a dance called the Harlem Shake. It would be cool to do one on a boat. First it would be him dancing alone, then cut to, like, the boat totally crammed with dancing fishermen. Maybe in Viking costumes or those yellow raincoats. Not worth trying to explain it to James and Alan though. They'd just start talking to him about cables again.

As he scrolled, some quiet part of his mind thought how strange it was that, of everyone he'd known at uni, James was now the one he saw every day. There was James's wheely suitcase parked at the end of the other bed.

It was all amazing stuff, of course it was. The moon. Boats. Vikings. Much better than what most people were stuck doing. At least no one could tell him what to do. And he wasn't in an office. He had, though, sort of thought that when they got the investment, that would be it, somehow, like on *Dragons' Den*, when the contestants had pitched their ideas and the podgy old investors with their melted faces and shiny suits said, "You win. Here's a big cheque." Then there was some fun music, everyone smiled and hugged, and that was the end of the show.

But actually, since they got the money, everything was kind of the same. Now they were trying to get some other money and having meetings about numbers of blades and so on. He just wasn't sure all this was really *him*.

He caught himself, with a hot wash of shame. He couldn't bail on James. Roland's self-critical mode clicked on: even thinking about quitting was such shithead behaviour, like being here in Orkney, maybe for the only time in his life, and not even being assed to get out of bed and see the Stone Age village. Really, he'd got no better since Tokyo, when he flew all the way there and then just drank cheap shots in tourist bars instead of visiting the National Museum. He'd still never learned a single *kanji*. And he'd fucked up his degree.

He stayed in bed, wincing, grimacing, still watching videos of the Harlem Shake but not enjoying it any more.

They had dinner that evening in the hotel restaurant. Fish and chips in a high cold wood-panelled room. James imagined scruffy Victorian merchants bundled up in scarves and coats, recruiting Orkney men to crew the whalers. Hunting for whale oil. Another form of energy from the sea.

Roland felt like James and Alan were talking past him, as if they were the adults at dinner. They found it easy to chat once given a practical subject: the Pelamis machine. Apparently it was very impressive. It wouldn't be easy to catch up. As soon as possible someone was going to have to visit the potential suppliers – turbine-makers, keel-riveters, cable-rollers – scattered around northern Europe.

Roland interrupted. "I'll do it. I'll do all of them." He sensed a thought pass between James and Alan, and said, "You can give me the technical specs. Alan needs to get on with the machine. James needs to bring in more money. I'll go. I won't fuck it up. I do actually have a science degree, you know, unlike you, James. I'll do a hundred per cent of it. Like, full on."

James and Alan agreed. The talk moved on to the Sutherland spaceport. It would be cool if it actually happened. James knew he should take Alan to the hotel bar and buy some drinks. The human element. Caesar was idolised by his troops. How to become idolised by Alan? He had so much to read about gyroscopic precession.

It was a boon when Roland said to Alan, "Do you want to have a pint and talk about suppliers? I want to get into it as soon as I can."

Late that night, when Roland blundered into their room, whisky-blind and stinking, James heaved him onto his bed. He took off Roland's shoes, smelling his nasty cigarettes and the sour booze sweat, while Roland muttered and moaned. Would Roland piss the bed? Maybe. But James wasn't going to carry him to the dingy bathroom and hold his dick for him. So he put him in the recovery position and tucked him in, very grateful that Roland had got so drunk, and that he hadn't had to.

After the trip to Orkney, it was as if time accelerated. Or, rather, as if their sense of what constituted a single event was stretched. When he was a student, Roland often had a whole adventure in an afternoon. Now, getting just one thing done, like visiting the suppliers, took months. A year skipped by in two or three beats. Time began to happen less in events than in periods.

Roland travelled everywhere he might conceivably be needed: the Belfast shipyards, where water lapped idly in the wharves; neat, warm Dutch technology parks, like the campuses of a technical university, where tall blond Dutch people wore fashionable trainers and design-forward glasses.

A small port town in Denmark, Esbjerg, where invisible giants assembled Europe's wind turbines as if they were Meccano. Each blade was as long as an aeroplane, and they were laid out in rows of a hundred at a time. To go once around the rack of turbine blades would take hours on foot – you had to be driven in an electric jeep. Each section of the turbines' columns, lying on its side, framed a circular view of docklands and sky big enough to drive a lorry through. Gazing through one such pipe, with the spotty Danish drizzle in his face and the rotting sea tang in his nostrils, Roland reassured himself, "I am definitely living enough. Almost no one sees this."

He didn't just look. He bought parts, tools, a special flexible cable that could sway as their machine bobbed on the surface. It came from a three-generation family of cable-rollers in Hamburg. They celebrated his astonishingly expensive purchase in a pine-clad seaman's canteen, with schnapps and fish burgers.

At the end of his meetings, he didn't rush back to the airport. He hung around, chatted, asked his suppliers what else they were up to. Some made their apologies and moved on to the next appointment. But most were inventors and engineers, enthusiasts. They weren't in it for sales meetings. They were pleased to take him into their workshops. In Copenhagen, where he bought software that adjusted the angle of turbine blades to match the strength of the current, the boss, Lars, took him home for a back-garden barbecue with his husband Thomas.

After dark in the tree-filled suburbs, it was much colder than Roland had expected. Lars and Thomas lent him a heavy old sheepskin coat that ponged of sheep, and a matching hat with earflaps. As Roland sat there, wrapped up on a bench between the two Danes, cutting chunks of pork chop and feeling the blast of the barbecue's heat on the right side of his face, smoking cigarettes and drinking tins of freezing beer while his fingertips went numb, with Lars and Thomas lapsing more and more into Danish as they got drunker, he thought: There's no way this isn't really living. I'm so deep beneath the surface of Denmark. No outsiders ever see this. If Lars and Thomas ask me for a threesome, I'll do it.

He slept on a leather sofa whose surface adhered to his face. In the morning, before his flight, he hurried to the shop that sold the sheepskin coats. It was back in the centre of town, small and overheated, its airspace clogged with wool. Roland was hungover and under-slept, with sweat at his hairline.

As he tried on the coats that the shop lady brought him, growing ever more overheated and claustrophobic, the night before began to feel suspect. Was it really that amazing to get drunk in a back garden? He bought the coat anyway and wore it amid the garish orange and blaring announcements of the EasyJet flight back to Gatwick, his toxin-rich sweat soaking into its pelt.

After Roland's visits, it often turned out there was something more the suppliers could do to help. They suddenly realised they'd given Alan the price they charged BP. For a start-up, for Roland, they could do better. Or, since the order was so small, they could move it up the queue, so their special cable wouldn't take an outrageous eight months to arrive but would be with them by summer. James called it "the Roland dividend", as in the peace dividend at the end of the Cold War.

Whenever Roland was back in London, he was restless. But he came to accompany James to meetings with venture capital funds. James had worn the VC guys down until they agreed to listen to his pitch.

These meetings were not like those with the engineers and accountants at Statoil or Shell. They were not in corporate office blocks near Paddington or Waterloo but in discreetly luxurious outposts of California. In the corners of the conference rooms, boxes of contending products were piled up like a rich kid's Christmas toys: glasses with screens on the lenses, a bike that connected to the internet, a headset that could read brainwaves. The VC guys wore Fitbits and heart-rate trackers. Their bosses, rich understated men, far richer than the salaried employees of the oil firms, wore beautiful fabrics exquisitely cut into suits, jackets and Loro Piana turtlenecks.

The meetings went badly. James recited his hectoring spiel, putting in clever new arguments he'd dreamed up, while the VC guys lounged in their chairs with their listening faces on. When he finished, they politely asked obvious questions: Who are your competitors? How long till your device is in the water?

But there was no excitement, no willing suspension of doubt, no sniff of gold rush. Everything remained intelligently sceptical. These funds hadn't even invested in Pelamis. Very soon, they moved the conversation on to "So, how do you know Eleni?" The business part of the meeting had been concluded.

After one such meeting, Roland and James sat together on James's parents' sofa, with little to say. Roland hadn't taken off his backpack. James asked, "How was Hamburg?"

"They say it'll only be another couple of months."

"Great."

They watched whatever was on TV: *Neighbours*. *The News at Six*. Football if there was any. A documentary about Detroit going bankrupt – rolling footage, shot from a moving car, of abandoned city blocks. Houses falling in; the underlying grassland reasserting itself. James said, "Remember when we were in the Lehman building?"

"Mmm-hmm."

"Didn't it feel like civilisation was collapsing?"

"I thought the recession was over."

"It is."

"Then why won't they give us any money?"

James, for all his cognitive horsepower, couldn't figure it out.

He searched for the answer in his spreadsheets. With a trepidatious sense of sexing up a dossier, he twisted his business models to produce ever more ambitious forecasts. He went up to Aberdeen to see the warehouse Alan had rented. Boxes had begun to arrive from Roland's shopping. Alan laid out their contents by category: turbine parts, sensors, hull. Around each set, he marked a border in black duct tape on the smooth concrete floor. He'd also hired two engineers: a woman called Maren, about

James's age; and a slightly younger part-time post-doc from Aberdeen University, called Chun Ho, or Charlie.

James had tried to connect with them by remembering details of their CVs. But by next year he would run out of the money to pay their salaries. If no more cash came in, they would have to be told, "Sorry that you followed where we led; our promises came to nought; you're now worse off than when you quit your job to join us." Nor did he have enough cash on hand to buy the rest of the expensive equipment still needed for the machine. Without it, Alan's carefully organised categories were just a million pounds' worth of spare parts.

That was the nature of a start-up. But the frustration was swelling in James like a river behind a blockage.

Alan was explaining how he was going to put these pieces together when, impulsively, like a cloudy solution abruptly crystallising around a speck of dust, James made a decision. He interrupted: "Oh, by the way, sorry to interrupt. But I've got an answer to the question about the number of blades. We're going to have two blades. But I've realised we can actually have two sets of two."

"Two sets?"

"Yeah. So the answer's not two or three, it's four. We'll have a set of two at the front of the turbines and two at the back. That way, we can justifiably say we're launching the most powerful tidal machine in existence. And if we can't say that, why would any VCs invest in us?"

Alan couldn't hide his irritation completely. He scratched an ear, as if in thought, and resisted flicking his gaze to his assistants. James thought: Shit. This was a mistake. I should have brought Roland.

He said, "But of course you're the engineer, and this is a big change. So please do, um . . . I want to give you an opportunity to voice your opinion."

"Two sets of two? I mean . . . where'd you get this from?" With horror, Alan imagined James talking to other engineers.

"I've just been looking at the problem."

The rug shifted under Alan's feet, and he smiled bitterly. "Having two sets doesn't make any difference to the wobble. It just means you have two wobbles. The money's not going to do us much good if the machine rips itself to bits."

"We'll just have to mitigate that risk. And a machine won't do us any good if we've got no money to finish it."

"Hmm." Alan scratched the neck skin under his beard. The oil price was back up above a hundred dollars a barrel. Had been for a while. Subsea7 were hiring again. No doubt, he could get his old job back, probably with more money than before.

But he'd not quite given this a fair go. And it wouldn't be fair to Maren and Charlie either, to walk out so soon after hiring them on. He'd been trying to be fatherly and encouraging with them. They were still overly private, reticent – contracted labour rather than part of the team. They must be freaking them out. There would be questions for him after James left.

How the fuck had James come up with this? Alan needed time to think it through. He said, "So, ehm, the most powerful tidal turbine in existence . . ."

James smiled.

Alan said, "But this is *your* decision. If it sinks . . ."

"Yes. On my head be it."

Alan persuaded himself. Two sets of two. Why hadn't he thought of that? And who was to say it wasn't doable? For generations, Scots had been getting the officer class out of their self-created predicaments. He'd just have to build it. "I hope you're not telling these investment guys it's in existence." He gestured at the parts.

"Ha. Of course not. But if we get the VC money, that'll make it easier."

"Right."

"After all, we're not just trying to build another machine here. We want to build a machine that alters the course of history."

"Absolutely."

They had scraped through this moment. But that evening, when Alan and Catriona went round to some friends' for dinner, and Alan's glass of Chardonnay kept going down like water, he found himself saying, "The guy's honestly a freak. I honestly think he might be a virgin. He's got this podgy wee belly like –"

"Speak for yourself," said Catriona. "Did he give you in trouble or something?"

"No, but he's just got this fucken stupid voice." Alan put on a smug, plummy, English wanker's accent. "'Umm, Alan, can I talk to you for a moment?' Fuck *off*, you bell-end."

James went happily back to London and wrote "the most powerful tidal machine in existence" into his PowerPoint. He became so impatient for the next VC meeting that, as he and Roland waited in the comfortably unobtrusive lobby, he almost lost his self-control. He kept checking the time on his iPhone, goaded further by the unchanging digits. His heart jumped in its bony cage. At one minute past the appointed time, he stood up off the sofa and said, "I think we should go in."

"What?"

"I just want to make sure they haven't rescheduled. The secretary might have forgotten to email us. We should just go in, check, and if they need more time, that's fine."

He moved towards the frosted-glass door, and Roland put up both hands. "No, no. Stop. Don't do that." James had finally gone fully mad. "Don't touch that door."

"Why not? If they need more time, we can —"

The door opened, and behind it was an elegant man in his fifties, his shoulder-length hair threaded with grey. Blue suit, gold watch, no tie, crisp white collar standing up around his jaw — evidently the boss, courteously greeting them himself. He smiled and said, "Marine energy?"

James said, "Tides not waves."

"Lovely. Come on in."

The meeting was as flat and inconsequential as the others. James's new wonder-weapon was a squib. He repeated it to make sure they'd heard: "The most powerful tidal generator in existence." The analysts ranged along both sides of the gleaming walnut table nodded, and the boss said, "Lovely."

Before long, they were being moved on again. The boss asked, just curious, whether there was good sailing in Orkney. "I've been round the Hebrides a couple of times. I've always wondered whether Orkney is worth it. Strong tides, I suppose." He said this like a friendly little joke. They didn't know about the sailing.

On the way out, James was bewildered. He'd never experienced something like this before. He couldn't see even where to begin working.

Roland said he'd meet him back at the house. Enough with these pointless meetings. He'd noticed which office the boss went into and knocked on the frosted glass. He heard, "Come in," and tentatively went inside.

The boss, despite his shield of good-humoured sophistication, looked annoyed to see him again. But he cleared his face and said, "What can I do for you?"

Roland put up his hands as if apologising. "I'm really sorry to bother you. I'm not asking for anything. I know you don't want to invest. But I just wanted to ask . . . it would be amazing, if you don't mind, just to tell me, like, completely straight, no filter, why this thing doesn't appeal."

The boss assessed him from behind his desk.

Roland said, "Honestly, it would be so helpful to know. Totally off the record. It might just save us spending years going down the wrong track. Any pointer you have would be appreciated so much."

The boss smiled. "Okay," he said. "Honestly?"

"That would be so great."

"Honestly, it's too small-fry. Our job here is to look for the next Google. What you're pitching – yes, it's interesting on a technical level – but basically it's a complex and expensive way of producing electricity. I can already buy electricity everywhere. It literally comes out of the walls. Even if your machine works, are you going to get enough power out of it, cheaply and reliably enough, to convince British Gas or EDF to buy from you rather than from the hundreds of coal and gas plants they've been buying from for decades? Personally, I doubt it."

Roland wanted more but could feel that this person had reached his fill of him. He just said, "Thank you so much. Really appreciate your insights."

"Any time."

Roland let himself out.

In the Draytons' kitchen, it was already night outside, and the windows were black. James said, "They think it's what, *not big enough*?"

"'Too small-fry' is what he said."

"That's fucking ridiculous."

"Don't take it out on me."

"I'm not taking it out on you. What did he say about —"

They were interrupted by James's dad clumping down the narrow stairs. "Evening, boys. Pens down, I think, don't you?" And to Roland, "Are you staying for supper?"

"Umm, I don't think I can actually."

Arthur picked up the mood. "Oh, sorry, have I interrupted a high-powered business meeting? Hammer-and-tongs debate, creative destruction?"

"No, no," said Roland. "We just —"

James spoke over him. "We just had a frustrating meeting with a fund. It's not a big deal."

"From what I hear, the business life is full of frustrations. I see the puce-faced old money-bagses once they get rich enough to start going to Covent Garden. Do they seem happy? Do they really enjoy *Die Zauberflöte*? I can't help but notice they get *very* annoyed if the champagne is slow at the interval. Is that a sign of inner contentment?"

Arthur hadn't spoken to anyone since breakfast.

"And if they love the opera so much, why not skip decades of frustration in the temples of Mammon and just sit in the cheap seats. It reminds me of when Alexander —"

James interrupted. "When Alexander met Diogenes on the way to conquer India. And Diogenes said, 'What are you going to do after you conquer the whole world?' And Alexander said, 'Lie in my hammock in the sun.' And Diogenes got into his hammock and closed his eyes. Yes, yes, very good."

Arthur raised his eyebrows. "I'm glad you know that story, m'lad. I told it to you, as I recall. I'm not sure these banker types have heard it."

"So what do you suggest? We jack it in and become academics? I'm not sure they're handing out London townhouses to music scholars any more."

"If this house offends your sensibilities, might I suggest that you're old enough —"

Roland jumped in. "Sorry, Arthur. It's a tough moment. This fund we met today, they said our business is too small-fry."

"Too small-fry? That's absurd. It's not even grammatical. And what you're doing is huge." Arthur sent a mollifying glance towards James. "Harnessing the power of the moon. Who is this cretin? Clearly someone who's going to lose his clients unconscionable sums. I presume he'll soon be knighted."

James said, "No, they're a successful fund. That's why we went to them."

"Maybe so. But he's clearly got this one dead wrong."

"Well, actually, he's got a point. Ultimately, we are just selling electricity."

"But yours will be the finest, most desirable electricity. I'll buy it. Maybe the faculty could. They've got an awful lot of light bulbs and such."

James wanted to say, "We're not a fucking utility, Dad." But instead, very deliberately, he said, "I can see you're trying to make me feel better. I appreciate it. I'm sorry I was short just now. But if we talk more, we're going to have an argument. So why don't you cook something with Roland? You enjoy that. I'm going to go upstairs for a while."

His father's end-of-day mood had spoiled and was spoiling further. He said, "Alright. Off you go then. Get it out of your system."

James tensed again. "I'm not going to say anything else." His dad was standing between him and the stairs. "May I get through, please?"

Arthur stepped aside and exaggeratedly held out a palm, even, when James's back was turned, executing a discreet bow. Roland knew them well enough not to feel particularly awkward. He slung his backpack over his shoulder, but Arthur said, "I think I'm going to have a large glass of the Meursault my sister brought. You'll have one, won't you?"

Roland glumly sat back down.

*

He managed to escape while Arthur was chopping garlic. A little buzzed from the wine, he climbed the stairs to James's bedroom. James was in bed with the lights on, still in his suit and curled up like a foetus.

Roland dropped himself into the armchair. James's mum had redone this room while he was at uni and, inside its calm soft-pastel orderliness, his mess of clothes and files seemed like a hasty encampment. Giving James the opportunity to disagree, he said, "It's not your fault."

James didn't reply.

Roland thought: Fuck you then.

After a while, James said, "We could move into one of those abandoned houses in Detroit. For food, we could grow crops in the garden, and we'd make hard cash by salvaging scrap. Alan and his assistants can have the rest of the company's cash as their redundancy. They'll actually do quite well out of it."

For Roland, it was like that bit in *The Wizard of Oz* when the curtain's pulled back, and you see that the man behind the grandiose booming is just a sad, delusional swindler, a cheat, a self-deceiver, a persuasive maniac who talked innocent people into his hallucinations. He was too angry to speak.

He waited, and after a while it became apparent that James had nothing for him. He stood up and said, "I guess I'll see you then."

"See you."

Roland waited a little longer, then said, "Okay, see you." And went.

James stayed in bed. "Too small-fry." It *was* ungrammatical. A fry was a young fish. Too small a fry, it should be. Just a tiddler, this endeavour of his, when looked at with the objectivity of self-interest. He'd thought he was moving pieces on a godlike scale: the North Sea goes here; the moon goes there. But the whole time he'd been in a niche, an unpromising niche, and couldn't see it. To think they'd given each other share certificates supposedly worth millions. Like Saddam's tinpot generals awarding each other lavish decorations until a real army arrived and wiped them out.

*

Some time later, his dad came in. He leaned his head past the door as if expecting something to be thrown. "Truce?"

James sighed. "Truce."

"Do you want some supper? It's pea and ham risotto with my famous chicken stock."

"Can I eat it in bed?"

His dad hesitated, then said, "I'll bring it up. Do you want a glass of wine?"

"Yes, please."

James ate the starchy rice in its ambiguous neither-solid-nor-liquid state. He drank the sour, refreshing wine – an inverted pale-yellow dome suspended in mid-air. His mood lifted out of the wallow. In his humbled frame of mind, it struck him as profound that his thoughts could be changed by mere food and drink.

There were excuses available. As Peter Thiel said, investors at the moment were interested in software, not the crude materiality of physical objects. But really he should be grateful to this fund manager. His comments were like an irritating, awkward experiment that refused to fit your theory – and that eventually forced you to tear that theory down and replace it with another, one degree closer to the truth. The experimental method. Textbook history of science.

Really, this was a lesson in humility. You couldn't blame the outside world for not conforming to your ideas. It wasn't the world that was wrong, it was you. Either you could be humiliated and angry and hurt, or you could let that go and start building a better model. He began to search where he always had: within himself. In some ways, it wasn't complicated: if tidal energy wasn't going to beat gas and coal on price, and you still needed tidal to win, you had to assume that gas and coal were finished. Some people believed that; or rather, some people believed that fossil fuels would have to be switched off quickly rather than in some hazy future. Or rather, again, some people were willing to take that bet because they'd make out like bandits if they were right.

Did James believe it? He could, if he had to. But he needed something spectacular to appeal to the jaded futurologists of venture capital, something that could not be mistaken for small fry. Not just an expensive way of making electricity.

They'd have to attach it to something bigger, connect it to something. In those grey outbuildings on the island of Eday, they were converting electricity into hydrogen. That was a fuel you could put into anything, with zero carbon emissions. Its only waste product was water. Theoretically, you could run the whole world on hydrogen. A clean new fuel for human civilisation.

It was a stretch. Certainly it was a stretch. There was a reason no one used hydrogen: it was too expensive. Those projects on Eday didn't even know what to do with the dribble they managed to produce. But it wasn't about choices any more; it wasn't about having an overview and selecting the optimal project. He had to grasp at whatever he could reach.

The following morning, when Roland arrived, James had pulled off his clothes but was still in bed, straining to think of a way that hydrogen made sense.

Roland was shocked that James hadn't got up. He should be making amends, and instead he was lolling around. In defeat, you saw who people really were. With scorn in his voice, he said, "You alright there?"

"Just thinking about what to do next." His hydrogen idea was still too fragile and ungainly to be exposed to others.

"I'm meant to be going to Rotterdam this afternoon. Should I still go?"

"Yes, yes, of course. Absolutely."

"Okay. I guess I'll do some prep in the kitchen then."

"Okay."

Roland got up. James said, "Umm."

"Yeah?"

"Is there any chance you could grab me some toast? I haven't had any breakfast."

"That's the laziest, most outrageous shit I've ever heard."

James was surprised. "Alright. Don't worry then. No need to go off at me."

Roland had almost ceded his righteousness. But he recovered. "Fine. I'll get it. What do you want on it?"

"Nutella? And maybe a coffee?"

While Roland fetched the toast, James lay in bed imagining every detail of a hydrogen company, like a blind man running his fingers over an unknown object. The costs would be extreme. They'd need an entire team of hydrogen experts. They could do it if they had the VC money.

From his McKinsey training, he recognised the error of trying to solve a problem by complicating it further. It was said to be as with paranoid schizophrenics: if they discovered that it wasn't the CIA rummaging through their laundry, just their mum, then their mum must be in the CIA. Each contradicting fact just entangled you further. The self-disciplining question – the freeing question – was: If you knew then what you know now, would you still have founded this company? Just as Eleni had said.

But none of the textbooks mattered if you pulled it off. And there was something glorious about being at the furthest extremity of the possible, like a test pilot pushing a rattling plane to the very edge of disaster. He was in the fight now, and he intended to win it.

When Roland came back up to say he was heading to the airport, James got out of bed and hugged him. Roland said, "Mate, you could do with a shower." But he was touched.

James said, "Don't worry about yesterday. I think we'll look back on it as a very positive step."

Roland felt sorry for him.

For the rest of the day, James pottered around his room, reading a few pages of Terry Pratchett and playing a custom battle on *Total War: Shogun 2*.

A hydrogen business. Okay. The problem was that there were no customers. Toyota and Volkswagen didn't make hydrogen cars. The answer came to him like a smile: rockets. The vehicles that already ran on hydrogen weren't Toyotas but space rockets. He and Roland could sell their hydrogen to NASA. They would be the Shell of space travel.

In his mind's eye, he saw the connections light up like lines drawn between stars. From the infinite twinkling scatter, the shape of a bear; from the random trajectories of galactic matter, a meaning.

The starting point was the moon. As it moved, its gravity dragged the North Sea through that strait in Orkney. He and Roland would, like electric fishermen, pull a current from that current. It would flow along a cable to shore, and there, via electrolysers, generate hydrogen, a clean fuel whose only emission was water. The hydrogen would fuel the rockets that NASA fired back up towards the moon. What could be lovelier?

Surely *that* was a fish worth frying. What did JFK say about the Apollo programme? *We do these things not because they are easy, but because they are hard.* And something about talent. James pulled out his iPhone and googled . . . "because that goal will serve to organize and measure the best of our energies and skills." Yes.

He was so happy his eyes itched with tears. He should write to the fund manager and thank him. He couldn't wait to tell Roland.

When Roland came back from Rotterdam, having bought a socket that would connect their flexing power cable to the device's hull, he wasn't surprised that James had a new plan to take over the world. But he could see it from the outside now. Hydrogen. Moon energy. Empires in the sky. James's notions had got him out of McKinsey; he'd always be grateful for that. He said, "Have you spoken to Alan about this?"

This wasn't the reaction James had been imagining. He said, "No, not yet. Because it's you and me running the company, not me and Alan."

"Yeah. And you know, like, he left a real job to come work with us."

"What do you mean, a real job?"

"You know what I mean."

James's left eye twitched. A thread of muscle had begun spasming. He had to keep clenching that eye shut. "What is it with you and Alan? It's like you're his lawyer."

"I just think we have a responsibility. You know, mate, he *trusted* us. Like the Norwegians trusted us with their money. We can't just fuck it all up."

"Who said anything about fucking it all up?" James began explaining again how hydrogen-powered moon rockets were the best thing for the company.

Roland looked at him with something like pity. Some mist of glamour had cleared. Soon to turn thirty, standing in his parents' kitchen in his Korean dragon dressing gown, a bit overweight, keeping one eye shut to keep it from jumping, and babbling about the moon.

Alan would sort this out. He'd understand the engineering. And when he refused to go along, that might well, after a period of pain, turn out to be a blessing. Alan could go back to Subsea7; Alan's kids could do their GCSEs in peace; they could give back what remained of the burdensome money; and he – and James, too – would be free to do anything at all.

Humouring him, Roland said, "Remember they want to build a spaceport near Inverness. Maybe the hydrogen could be sold to them."

"Yes, exactly!" He knew Roland would get behind him. James might just have to cajole him into place.

Because their machine's steel hull hadn't been cast yet, Alan had mocked it up in plywood. It was as long as a swimming pool and looked as if some Renaissance inventor had tried to build a submarine. Inside the plywood case was a painstakingly labelled array of components and wiring, like an exploded diagram. Alan took photos of it every night in case vandals broke in and moved the parts.

At the side of the warehouse stood a small indoor cabin that was Alan's office. They took him in there to talk, leaving Maren and Charlie to unpack a crate of waterproof electronics from Lars in Copenhagen. They were going to plug in the circuit boards then dunk them in the sink.

Alan's office didn't have the extreme order of his build. Everywhere were stacks of black box files labelled "Invoices" or "Custom Parts I". There was only one chair – his – so James stood and Roland squatted precariously on a large pink buoy.

On the wall was a framed piece of paper with a typewritten quote: *Adventure is just bad planning* — Roald Amundsen. English people thought that Captain Scott was romantic: the doomed expedition, the injured comrade going out into the blizzard to die, the sentimental letters found on their bodies. But Alan knew those men were fools, killed by typical nonchalant posh-boy incompetence. While Scott was starving, Amundsen was tossing surplus food to his dogs. Amundsen knew his business.

Roland watched Alan's face as James pitched his plans. Already the spiel had grown more assertive. Instead of ragged overnight thoughts, it had the high-handed confidence of a McKinsey presentation: we have scried the squiggly figures in the spreadsheets, and the answer is this. Alan didn't interrupt but, as he listened, he grew restless. He slumped in his seat then sat back up; he combed his fingers through his beard; and he shook his head. Finally, when James paused during a *tour d'horizon* of the global hydrogen market, Alan said, "Can I say something here?"

"Of course."

"Where . . . em . . . where's this coming from? Because to me it makes no fucking sense at all."

Then the argument began in furious detail: costs, build times, how much electricity was needed to generate a useable amount of hydrogen. Roland couldn't follow. Maybe it *would* be better if James and Alan ran the company together. But Roland understood that everything James said, Alan resisted.

Eventually, Alan cut James off: "Look. At the end of the day, I'm the only engineer in this room, and, not being rude, you don't understand what you're talking about. To be honest, your two blades thing might have sunk us already. But with this, we're fucking dead. We're done. And I've got to say, it's you that's killed us. I mean, I've got to tell Maren and Charlie to start looking for other jobs."

"But hydrogen has —"

Alan was getting angry. He closed his eyes and interrupted. "See how there's five of us. And you two aren't even engineers. So that's three. There is absolutely no way three of us can build a tidal device *and* a hydrogen electrolyser. If we were Subsea7, *maybe*. But we're not. And neither you nor me knows fuck all about hydrogen."

That pinged in Roland's mind: Alan wasn't a hydrogen expert. As long as they were a tidal company, he was central, the inventor of the device. If they expanded beyond that, he might become just one of James's employees. James should reassure him, tell him that with a hydrogen team underneath him he would become bigger not smaller. But James didn't understand that others would worry about being diminished – and Roland didn't say anything. James just grinned and said, "With the VC money we can hire more engineers."

"Look. We've got a solid tidal project, which is hard enough. Why don't we get that done, and then you can start dreaming up what you want to do with the electricity."

"Or how about this? We phase it. We don't spend any time or money on hydrogen until we've got the tidal device running."

"Running? It's not even got a hull."

"But it will. Roland and I have total confidence in you."

"It's not about you having confidence in me. I said I could build a tidal machine, and I can. But things go wrong. And if it rips itself to pieces, then..." He shrugged.

James kept arguing but couldn't bring Alan to say that he agreed. Eventually, they realised they might as well stop. James said he would walk down to the burger van and pick up lunch for everyone. Alan watched him all the way out the warehouse's metal door, then stood up and said, "Fuck. *Me*. What's he been smoking?" He looked at Roland. "Can't you have a word with him?"

Roland glanced out through the internal window at Maren and Charlie, who were still unpacking Lars's electronics, like children given a pointless task to keep them away. He wished he were in Copenhagen eating pork chops. He said, "I don't know. I'm not an engineer."

"Nor's he. But he listens to you."

"I don't want to get in the middle of it."

"In the middle of it?"

Roland shrugged. He couldn't look at Alan and kept his gaze on the floor. Alan opened the door and, before leaving, said, "That's fucking pathetic."

Maren and Charlie looked at Alan curiously, but he didn't trust himself to speak to them. He kneeled by his long plywood machine, his knee hurting on the concrete floor, and pretended to examine the shape of the bow. Look how far he'd managed to get already. He just needed the hull, a few more parts, a little more time.

James came back from the burger van with a clutch of greasy paper bags and a suggestion. He handed out the bags and then, putting his own aside, told Alan, "What I'm proposing is very testable. If I can't attract VC investment within six months, I'll admit I was wrong, and we'll give up hydrogen as a bad plan. Deal?"

"You don't have to make a deal. You're the CEO."

"Yes, but if you don't believe in it, nothing will work."

Alan wished he had more time to think. Within six months he could have almost everything but the hull. After a few seconds he said, "No hydrogen until we've got the device working?"

"We might have to do a little exploration, just for proof of concept."

"Six months?"

"Six months." James extended his hand. "If it doesn't come off, I'll be accountable."

Alan shook his hand. "Fair dos."

He accepted but, from then on, his tentative friendliness towards James, the sincere willingness to at least try and meld their thinking, was gone. They were not friends. He and Roland were just head office, like a thousand corporate pricks before them.

Roland, beneath his shame, felt a certain relief: only six more months.

MAY 2014

Six months and three weeks later, James and Roland were sitting, shoulders almost touching, on a flight to San Francisco. Roland had hoped, and indeed begun to believe, that the seat next to them would be taken by an absolute babe. There was something sexy about planes. The confinement, the sensory deprivation, made the body yearn for stimulus. Maybe a bit of reciprocal wanking under a single-use blanket. But their neighbour turned out to be a fiftyish man in a black jacket and black polo neck, probably a gallerist travelling on business. Roland huffed and sulked.

James was wary of Roland's mood. Over the past few months, he'd refused to visit any suppliers and become crotchety whenever James tried to get him to actually do something. James felt like he was Roland's mum. So he stayed at the benign, non-confrontational distance he remembered his own mum adopting when Cleo was in her difficult years.

No one in the company was really speaking to James. Alan now openly treated him like a hindrance to work on the machine: concealing, disputing, defending his work from James's interference. Maren and Charlie didn't know or trust him. The VC funds had barely responded to his emails about hydrogen.

It was all a lesson in humility, and in patience. A positive step. Normally he could at least have talked to Roland about it.

The only time without tension was on Tuesday or Wednesday evenings, when Roland stayed to watch Champions League on the big TV that Arthur had bought for neorealist movies. There had never been football in the house before, but it became a habit: Arthur cooked dinner, and they ate from plates balanced on their knees in the living room. Arthur chose which team to support based on whose home city he preferred, and spent the first minutes of each game weighing up the relative attractions of Manchester versus Amsterdam. Lowry versus Van Gogh. Eccles cake vs *stroopwafel*. Mary, with surprising tribalism, always supported the English. James couldn't but notice that Wayne Rooney, a grizzled veteran of innumerable campaigns, with probably only a couple more seasons at the highest level, was younger than him and Roland.

On the plane to California, Roland seemed hyped up again. He blabbered and ordered drinks, scrolled through the movies and wanted to chat. James kept his distance. About six or seven hours in, with the cabin droning and the moving pictures on his screen making ever less sense, Roland fell asleep. James didn't sleep. Nor did he watch a movie or read a book. He looked unseeing into the grey plastic underside of the tray table folded up in front of him. A low dose of adrenalin ran continuously through his bloodstream. His mind turned short loops, wearing itself thin.

They were flying to meet Peter Thiel. James had spent these past months on the phone, harassing his contacts and his contacts' contacts, pestering people beyond what they could bear, to get a fifteen-minute slot with Thiel. James thought of him as living in the tiniest, brightest circle at the very top of humanity. His friends didn't work in tech; they ran tech giants. Everyone he knew was the head of something. For James, it was like gazing in the window at a ballroom, with archdukes and princesses waltzing in swords and diamonds. He was outside in the dark, shivering with the nameless multitudes, as they watched those brilliant figures dancing. And now one of them was coming to the door, giving him a chance to speak and, perhaps, the slimmest of chances to talk his way inside.

James didn't register Thiel's budding notoriety. He wasn't interested in it. To build out of thin air, to turn your thoughts into walls, computers, desks, factories, thousands of employees, was itself a kind of miracle. Thiel had done it again and again. First with PayPal, in the early days of the internet. Then Palantir, the data company said to have helped catch Bin Laden. Thiel was Mark Zuckerberg's mentor and the first investor in Facebook, which now included Instagram and WhatsApp. After PayPal, those involved in it, with Thiel's help, started Tesla, YouTube, LinkedIn . . . For maybe half the human species, the daily experience of being online owed something to him.

He wasn't even a technologist. Like James, he was a non-engineer for whom engineering was merely one of many dimensions. He built his machines out of people and money. Those machines were companies, which, once started, could power themselves, achieving what engineers thought impossible: perpetual motion. Thiel's chosen task was to find the points at which technology and human behaviour met, and fuse them together into a single glowing node, each node a company and each company altering the nature of what it touched.

And, like a clarion voice coming over the sea from the far west, was Thiel's creed that there were greater adversaries to be wrestled with than computer science. Space flight. Supersonic travel. Limitless energy. This was it. To be occupied with the prospects of the species.

That night, in their twin beds in a business hotel near the airport, their confused bodies, believing in their internal blindness that morning must have come, kept trying to wake them up. James and Roland were rarely more than half asleep, shifting positions, aching, eyes streaming, distracted by the foreign noises outside. It was James's first time in America. When they eventually reached seven a.m., they went downstairs and waited, stupefied, for the coffee machine to be turned on.

Thiel's assistant had booked them a cab to the former army base where his office was. They lolled drowsily on the back seat. It was so bright and quiet, the air so mild, the roadside gardens so lush and tropical. Broad, prosperous American streets; everything so open and expansive; the road signs funny like near-miss translations: yield! When they stopped at a signal, they heard seagulls. And then, on the left of the road, the Pacific: a grey-blue landscape shifting and murmuring, the ocean on the other side of the world.

James noticed that the driver, instead of using a satnav, was navigating with an iPhone stuck to his windscreen. This must be coming to Britain soon. You could probably make a few million by shorting the company that sold TomToms.

The army base wasn't how they'd imagined. There were elegant white modernist buildings set among lawns and shade-giving trees. The leaves were ruffled by the onshore breeze. It was peaceful and vast, a marriage of Silicon Valley with the US Department of Defense. They waited in an airy lobby, feeling very British, their own accents sounding stilted as they spoke to the receptionist. Both drank more coffee, and James tried to feel alert. His eye was spasming even though he'd had very little screen time on the plane.

Each time a door opened, they half rose, thinking it was him. Eventually, the receptionist stood up from behind her desk and said, "If you'll come this way for me."

Thiel was in another light airy room, with stacks of documents on a conference table. Through the wall of white-framed windows, they could see the ocean again, the jagged shadows of palm trees on the lawn. Thiel was in his forties, dressed as if for a country club: tan chinos, blue blazer, striped tie. He was slightly hunched, his face narrow, with his sandy hair cropped close. He looked like the nerdy kids at uni, dressed for the debating society.

He shook their hands, and James felt a thrill at touching him. Thiel said, "Good to meet you. Thanks for making the trip." He must have said this thousands of times before. But when they began to chat, he seemed in an unhappy, critical mood, as if he hadn't eaten.

Roland gushed, "I just wanted to say we're both *really* big admirers of your essay about the hard sciences. I actually grew up in the energy industry, and, um, I suppose all I'm saying is, um, it really made sense to me."

James was amazed: Roland was putting on some kind of bumbling Hugh Grant English voice.

Thiel said, "I think that essay served its purpose as a statement of intent. There are several elements I would update now, particularly on biotech and drug development, where the situation has grown more positive despite the egregious regulatory obstructionism." Roland had nothing to say to that. Thiel went on, addressing himself to James, "It always seems a little intrusive, but my team put together some background information on you and your company. They mentioned you've done some work on increasing the cost-efficiency of education. It's a subject I'm very interested in."

James thought: A godsend. Unconsciously, he began imitating Thiel's formal, abstract way of speaking. "Yes. It was about improving outcomes for a population rather than a single school. It was actually Roland's idea."

Thiel said, "Oh, really?" and glanced at Roland, who shrugged awkwardly. Thiel went back to talking to James. "If I understand correctly, the aim was to prioritise funding for cities where improved education would have the greatest economic effect?"

"That's right."

"It's an interesting approach. But my contention is that your approach – though I applaud the effort – is an attempt to achieve greater results within the parameters of the existing system, when the real issue is that the system is unfit for purpose."

This was not like any investment meeting Roland had ever been in. Usually it was all about whether their plans were realistic and how much money they could make. Now Thiel was saying that education was "the most perfectly anti-technological sector of the economy: prices are going up, but output stays the same. A degree from Harvard or Yale is actually an insurance product: a guarantee that the children of the elite will receive preferential treatment in the labour market. The actual learning could be provided with a few thousand dollars and an iPad." Was Thiel saying he wanted to replace Harvard with an iPad? Was this a spiel? A Thiel-spiel?

Beside him, James was trying to keep up. So many thoughts were branching outwards at once. He tried to find something to add. "So, in a system where students learn on their own, those who succeed would be those with the most talent and initiative rather than those who can afford the best teachers?"

"That's precisely it. The history of science and technology is clear that autodidacts have the most interesting minds. Faraday, Galileo, Da Vinci. They were all dropouts."

Roland was freezing into silence. He remembered something about

Thiel giving scholarships to students who dropped out of uni to start businesses. Was that a good idea?

But Thiel and James were already onto how the concentration of tech in Silicon Valley was leading to groupthink; then Thiel's plans to build floating island-cities for a hand-picked population. James was overwhelmed with ideas.

Finally, Thiel said, "I'm glad you and I understand each other on some of these issues. I wish we had time to discuss some of them in detail." To their astonishment, James and Roland saw a shy smile briefly appear on his otherwise grimly serious face. James recognised something in him, and his heart went out to this odd, brilliant man.

Thiel said, "I'm sorry to say I now only have about ten minutes left to talk about your company. Please do give me your pitch, if that's convenient."

James tried to speak convincingly. He talked about climate change, but Thiel didn't seem interested. Nothing sparked. Roland thought he was making an effort not to look at his watch. But when James mentioned throwing a harness around the moon, Thiel said, "Very cool." And when James pointed out that seawater was a thousand times denser than air, meaning there was more power to be harvested from the tide than from wind, Thiel nodded, nodded faster, and interrupted. "Yes," he said. "The factor here that's been widely overlooked is that the West has been in an energy crisis ever since 1973."

James hadn't even talked about the implications of hydrogen. But Thiel was away: "Real oil prices have never recovered from the Arab embargo. Meanwhile, thanks to ignorant eco-freakery, we have less nuclear capacity today than we did when Jimmy Carter was president. These high energy prices are, I believe, a major explanation for why the pace of technological advance has become so sluggish and hence why living standards for ordinary people have stagnated." The ideas again began setting each other off: the importance of fracking in the Permian Basin – the low input costs of coal-fired factories in China – the West's reliance on tech to stay ahead of the Chinese – the way that, until the

Industrial Revolution, the size of a country's economy was just a function of how many people lived in it.

When he came back to James and Roland's endeavour, he said, "I appreciate there are engineering challenges that don't obtain on land. But it's ludicrous to assume these challenges can't be overcome. With all due respect, it's a rotor turning in water; it's not fusion. How many engineers do you have?"

James said, "Three."

Thiel looked shocked, then annoyed. "You need to be thinking more like three thousand."

James was seized by a sudden fear that he'd thrown it away. "There's a good supply of marine engineers from the oil and gas industry in Aberdeen."

"That's a positive." Thiel nodded. "You may know the venture-capital consensus is that clean tech is a money pit. A lot of funds were burned investing in solar companies that either weren't ready or ended up being undercut by the Chinese. The space is considered dead. That's probably why you haven't gotten much traction." For the first time, he seemed to be enjoying himself.

"In my view, it's a clear example of how almost all asset managers are blinded by groupthink. The most meaningful opportunities are often in those blind spots. And I see your next steps as eminently achievable: increase your engineering capacity a thousandfold and then see if it's so difficult to make a turbine turn in water."

Roland thought Thiel liked impressing them. Or impressing James.

"As for the hydrogen part of the business – do you know Elon Musk? He has an electric-car company that's practically the only survivor from that first wave of clean tech. His space company doesn't run on hydrogen, but I can make an introduction."

Now Thiel did look at his watch, standing up as he did so. James and Roland stood up, too. "I'm sorry we're out of time for today. I see a huge amount of promise in this company. I believe in your ability to lead it." He seemed to be checking off a list of criteria. "I think you need to radically upscale your ambitions. I'd be delighted to be part of that process, as an investor and also with some advice and connections."

On the plane journey home, they were still reeling.

The stewardesses made their rounds. "What can I offer you to drink, sir?" Square paper napkin on the tray table. Plastic glass on top. Mini bottle of Californian red. The wine cold and velvety.

Roland said, "Quite a weird guy, wasn't he?"

James felt protective. "Very intense."

"He liked you, though."

James shrugged.

"Do you really think unis are stagnant backwaters of received ideas?"

James was too tired to think it through. His brain tried to start, turning over but not igniting. "Maybe it's different in postgrad. I don't know. My degree was pretty basic. I didn't do sciences though."

"To be fair, I have a science degree, and I barely did any."

James reflexively said, "You barely did anything."

"Yeah, Thiel definitely won't let me into his floating country."

"You're an entrepreneur. You're first on the list."

Roland watched a movie while James tried to strategise. Thiel's money was enough to get their prototype finished, but not to build the full-scale machine nor to hire three thousand engineers. Complex questions arose, like how to use Thiel's money to bring in more; how to stop Thiel growing too dominant; how to time the exchange rate. But his brain only acknowledged these tasks; it did nothing to complete them. The big sponge was dry.

As Roland watched, his mind drifted. Millions of dollars. Silicon Valley. It was strangely un-strange. Maybe, once they were home, they'd be amazed in retrospect. Or maybe it didn't feel strange because it already fitted them. Maybe without noticing, he and James had become high-powered entrepreneurs criss-crossing the Atlantic to pull the levers of capital and technology. Or maybe James had.

He swivelled his head. James was leaning against the cabin wall, trying to fall asleep. His skin was grey. He looked exhausted. Was it possible that dweeby old *James*, of all people, was secretly a person of great consequence? It was like a big reveal on *X Factor*, when some dowdy homespun mum contained a voice like Whitney Houston's.

Certainly, James was better at being an adult than a young person. His adolescent awkwardness had somehow become courtesy. The harsh raw opinions had become a kind of frankness, honesty, plain-dealing. Even Alan would take criticism from him because it wasn't personal. Back at uni, and afterwards, James had been a bit of a steamroller, smashing into obstacles and getting stuck. Now he was like water, patient and relentless, always flowing forward.

Roland was his passenger — though he didn't treat Roland as one. If anything, the opposite: he was always nagging Roland to vote his share and not just agree with him. Maybe he didn't want to realise what a passenger Roland really was. Roland suddenly felt very fond of him. It was insane and touching of him to give Roland the same share in the company as himself. He really would have shared with Eleni, too. The truth was that James didn't really need him. A sense of melancholy affection settled on Roland. It had somehow turned out that James was a massive baller. He'd be fine on his own.

Roland cuffed him on the shoulder. James opened his eyes and said, "What?"

"You're not asleep, are you?"

"Next time I'm going to get us some sleeping pills."

"Hold on." Roland pressed the overhead button for the stewardess and, when she came, asked for two more bottles of wine.

James spoke past him. "I'm alright actually."

The stewardess hesitated, and Roland said, "Don't worry. He wants one. He just hasn't realised it yet. You know, he's a rising star in the business world."

The stewardess broke from the mechanical dialogues of her shift. "Oh, yeah? What do you do?"

"He makes rocket fuel out of water."

The stewardess, who was probably only their age, though it was hard to tell under the make-up, said, "Rockets? Very cool." She seemed genuinely impressed and gave them an extra bag of crisps each.

While Roland poured, James said, "I really don't want it."

Roland picked one glass up for himself and put the other in James's reluctant hand. "Look at you, having air stewardesses think you're cool. Pretty soon you'll be in the mile-high club."

James laughed through his tiredness. "Oh Jesus, what are you on about?"

"Were you thinking about work stuff just now?"

"Yeah, how to make sure we —"

"No, no. Listen to me." Roland raised his plastic cup, and they twisted towards each other in the tight space. "Okay. So. I know you always say we've done everything together."

"We have."

"Shut up for a second, will you, please? Now, okay. I'm going to be honest. I thought this hydrogen rocket thing was complete bollocks that was going to kill the company, and so did Alan."

"I got the feeling you weren't enthused."

"Well, we all thought you were wrong. But you were right. You're like, fucking, I don't know . . ."

"Christopher Columbus."

"Alright, you're like Christopher Columbus. And you've got the last laugh now. You got this guy to back us, even though — just a sidenote — I do think maybe he's a bit . . . whatever." Roland gathered himself. "I know you're going to say this is just one item on the to-do list. But it's a big one. And *you* did it. Not us, you. So, well done, mate. You're in the big league now. Congratulations. Enjoy it for once. You've earned it."

James sighed. For the rest of the flight, he relaxed more deeply than he maybe ever had done. But first, he pressed his plastic glass against Roland's and said, "Thank you, old friend."

VIII

AUGUST 2014

It was Cleo's wedding. She and Roger were married in the upstairs room of a pub near her parents' house. They hired a humanist minister called Agnes, whom Arthur called "the humourless minister". He kept telling people that even her name, meaning lamb, i.e. of God, was screaming out that she secretly wanted to be a real vicar instead. For weeks before the wedding, he kept jabbering in this mode, filling the air with commentary so that there couldn't be silence. He had to be kept away from Cleo.

Roger's family came over from the Netherlands. In their honour, Cleo extracted some supposed Dutch wedding customs from Roger: herring to be served at the reception, a flower crown instead of a bouquet. Roger's dad, also a physicist, told James confidentially, "This Dutch stuff is very friendly but I have to say it means nothing to me. Heleen and I were married at the town hall, in our lunch break."

Almost all the guests were young people, Cleo and Roger's friends. They were in their twenties, unmarried themselves, no kids yet, not yet used to weddings, and giddy with the big day. When Cleo came in from the stairwell in her dress, there was a great bellow of approval.

James's parents insisted that Cleo invite Roland, on the grounds that he was practically family. He showed up in a three-piece orange suit, for the glory of Holland. When James's mum saw it, she said, "Jesus. You look like a bottle of Sunny Delight."

Roland blushed and went tongue-tied. "Oh, um, I thought, the Dutch thing."

Mary recovered herself. "Of course, sweetheart. Of course. I'm sorry. I didn't mean that. Roger's parents will love it."

The suit attracted attention, as he'd intended. He was soon embellishing a story to everyone he met. "I honestly thought it was a Dutch thing. But actually I think I look like a bottle of Sunny Delight." By the end of the canapés, he was the most popular guest.

James found that anything at all made him laugh or turn sentimental. He remembered ordinary stuff: him and Cleo dressing up in their mum's clothes. Sneaking out together when still very small on a family holiday in the Pyrenees. They walked the quarter mile into the village while their mum and dad were still asleep and came back proudly bearing a baguette and *pains au chocolat* to their panicking parents. It was unsettling to be able to say "more than twenty years ago" about your own life. He couldn't think how they'd paid at the bakery. Even this oft-told anecdote was blurred by time.

He wanted to do something for Cleo, to render her some profound service. His happiest moment of the wedding was the few hours he spent, the day before, cutting crudités. His mum would not countenance any under-catering but had to help Cleo with the flowers. It fell to James to chop carrots, celery and peppers into perfectly regular stacks. With each slice and spin and slice, he thought: For Cleo. A journalist from *The Times* was emailing him. They wanted to write a short article on the unknown British start-up that had caught the eye of Peter Thiel. James replied that it would have to be next week. And when the journalist tried to insist that it would be great to get it into tomorrow's edition, James simply didn't reply.

During the speeches, they learned that Roger's real name was Rogier, pronounced *Row-chear*. Cleo said that in her head she was an economist like her mum but in her heart she had music from her dad. She cried and said sorry for being such a nightmare for a few years. Her mum looked like she wanted to go up there and grab her, but limited herself to cheering and banging the table.

When Arthur stood up, Mary grew nervous, pressing her palms together in front of her mouth. The night before, she'd said to James, "He's so worked up. I just hope he doesn't embarrass her." But Arthur put himself aside and turned in the performance the occasion required: urbane, warm, funny, keeping the camera on Cleo. And even though he said, "I've been thinking about this speech for the past twenty-eight and a half years, since you were the size of a bag of flour," his voice didn't crack. Afterwards, James saw his mum put her hand on his cheek.

With the speeches done, the seating plan broke up. Empty chairs appeared. People roamed around laughing and yelling. Roland came to sit next to James. He patted James's thigh and said, "Hey bud."

"Hey."

They drank their drinks and looked at the crowd. After a while, Roland said, "You been to a wedding before?"

"Not really. My uncle's, when I was a kid."

"I guess this is the beginning. Like *Four Weddings and a Funeral*. In a year or two, we'll have a wedding every weekend."

"Yeah, Eleni's got a kid already."

"Shit! I forgot that. Why didn't they get married?"

"She said she doesn't have time to organise a big Greek wedding. And her parents don't mind as long as she and Damien are engaged."

"How old is she?"

"A few years above us. Thirty-five, thirty-six."

A waitress gave them coffee. They found space for their cups on the table, amid flowers, place cards and cake-smeared plates.

"Well," said Roland, "I don't want to be crass, but there's a ton of single girls at this party."

"Are you looking for a wife now?"

"No, mate, you're my wife. But you're the bride's eligible older brother. Hotshot entrepreneur. Stopping climate change. It's wall-to-wall fanny in here for you."

"Oh, that *Times* journalist asked if we could do Tuesday afternoon."

"Fuck them. Don't reply today. It'll just make them keener."

Later, one of Rogier's friends was DJing cheesy hits. Cleo was singing in a circle with her girlfriends – "I *AM* the one and only". James found himself unoccupied. He milled around by the table of drinks. He drank a glass of water and let the sweat cool at his temples. To his relief, Roland slapped him on the back. He'd been snogging one of Cleo's schoolmates on the dancefloor, both tottering and clutching each other with their eyes closed.

Roland said, "Let's go downstairs."

"What about that girl?"

"I need to sober up a bit. I'm not sure I could offer, like, the most amazing shag of all time right now."

They went down to the pub. On a banquette, they found James's parents, both with their glasses on, peering at their phones. His mum said, "Of course we're alright, sweetie. We oldies just need a bit of a breather. You two go to the bar."

James ordered two espressos. Roland said, "No, no. Cancel that. We need two Jäger bombs."

The barman glanced at James, who said, "Fine." And to Roland, "I thought you wanted to sober up."

"Oh, come on. The Red Bull will keep us awake."

They watched as the barman poured a can of Red Bull into two tumblers. Then he poured two shots of Jägermeister and floated one in each glass of Red Bull. Roland said, "Cheers mate. Congratulations." They downed the astringent chemical broth. Roland shook his head and ordered two more. "Right," he said. "There's an army of girls up there dying to meet a future captain of industry. Especially ethical industry. Rich guy but good guy. Girls love that."

"Looks like it's working for you."

"Oh, no. For me, it's just the orange suit. It's you *The Times* wants to talk to."

"Can you fuck off with this? I told them they've got to speak to you and Alan as well."

"No, no. Mate, mate. I don't mean it like that. I mean, like, you're a legend for taking me on this amazing ride with you."

"Okay."

The barman made another two Jäger bombs in front of them.

"Like, a real legend."

"Okay. What are you trying to say?"

Roland put his face in his hands. "I'm sorry. I'm sorry. I didn't want to talk about this today."

"Seems like we're talking about it."

"Mate, I love you. You know that. But the company's taken off. You don't need me any more."

"What do you mean?"

"I mean, it's you. You're Neo in *The Matrix*. You're the One. I'm just the other guy. And, like, thanks, it's been amazing."

"Are you being serious?"

Roland shrugged.

"I can't believe how selfish you are."

"I didn't want to talk about it. I said I didn't —"

"Whatever. And no, I refuse. I don't accept your resignation. And you can fuck off, too."

"Fine. Fine."

They downed their Jäger bombs in angry silence and then stayed for a pint. They had a drunken hug before they went back upstairs.

The following week, they were given a tour of the building site for a new WeWork. Thick plastic curtains hung down where internal walls were going to be. White dust lay on the floor like flour, and the windows had a thin protective sheet stuck over them like on a box-fresh iPhone. The salesman showing them around, an eager American sent over to get the Brits moving, tried to talk smoothly over the screech of drilling.

James had thought the Thiel money would simplify things. Instead, the problems grew larger and more complex: find offices, hire engineers, bring in VCs to dilute Thiel's importance, talk to space companies about selling them hydrogen and, most of all, get the machine finished.

It was not the time for Roland to start playing up. But James was realising that this was the nature of adult life. There were no breakthroughs into clear open space. Every time you were just getting into your stride, something tripped you. It was like trying to construct a functioning car out of pasta shapes: every time you, with supreme care and delicacy, got this improbable object moving forward, something snapped again.

Roland was behaving no better than he had years ago at DFID. He couldn't be arsed, and so he started breaking things. Contradicting him would just give this whim more substance. The answer was to delay him. Roland changed his mind every few months. James would just keep him here until the next whim came along. Roland kept giving him meaningful looks, mooning at him, trying to broach a conversation. James just ignored him.

The salesman was saying, "Over here we're going to have the kitchen area. Free coffees, filtered water and beer." He grinned performatively. "For those late-night brainstorm sessions!"

Roland thought this was maybe why Americans were so good at business: they could pitch filtered-water taps without finding it funny. Roland felt himself to be in the calm light limbo of a criminal who has confessed and is waiting to be sentenced.

The salesman said, "How many desks are you going to need? You mentioned four initially, but you might want to expand, and I can give bigger discounts on the bigger units."

James turned to glare at Roland. And with such spleen that the salesman became uncomfortable, he said, "What do you think? How many are we going to be?"

His bad mood was made worse by the little *Times* article. James had been nervous before the interview, preparing lines of defence for imagined critiques of their shareholding structure or the price of hydrogen. But nothing he prepped made it into the piece. Instead, it made much of him living with his parents. The picture it gave was of a stereotypical millennial dreaming up grand plans from his childhood bedroom.

The journalist had got a supposedly unbiased outside opinion from Javier Ferrer, the CEO and chief engineer at Pelamis. Ferrer said that James and Roland had evidently managed to attract some hype but didn't even have a machine in the water. "Many companies find the ocean conditions much more challenging than they expect." The article said their claim to be building the "world's most powerful tidal turbine" depended on two sets of twin-bladed rotors, an untested idea that risked destroying the turbine itself.

The article annoyed Alan too, by not mentioning him. On the phone, James said, "I literally gave him your number and told him to call. I was clear that you invented the device. I've learned the lesson: next time I'll make it a condition for giving the interview at all."

When he hung up, he said, "Do I have to man-manage Alan now? Can't he just get on with it?" He suddenly understood why the East India Company and the Jesuits preferred to recruit children, so they could be moulded before they became annoying.

Roland shrugged. No one seemed to think it noteworthy that he hadn't been mentioned either. "I think Alan sometimes feels like he's up there doing all the work, and we're down here taking all the credit."

"This article was supposed to be a good thing, and . . . We need a PR firm. Someone's got to find out which the good ones are. Can you hurry up on hiring the assistant."

In a replica ocean in a floodlit hangar in Southampton, Alan, James and the other two engineers performed the final tests on their turbines. The testing pool was so long it dipped to mimic the curvature of the Earth. Its tiled sides and floor were studded with video cameras. On the ceiling above it was a railway track on which crouched a robot train, with a cable running from it down to the turbine. The train could drag the turbine through the water to simulate a current.

They'd made the twin blades out of anodised aluminium, which didn't corrode in saltwater. It was expensive but shone like polished gold. On the first few runs, the golden blades didn't shake themselves to pieces, and James and Alan relaxed a little.

But Alan realised the turbine was trying to generate far too much power. A cubic metre of water weighed as much as a car. When the turbine was doing ten knots, it was the equivalent of being hit by a hundred cars every second. The rotor blades couldn't take it for long. The sheer force of water would bend them back on themselves. Alan had built them much stronger than blades used for wind turbines, but they'd need to be stronger still.

There was no time to re-manufacture them now. It would have to wait until they built the full-size machine. They were already keeping a list of necessary changes. He and James reassured themselves that this was exactly why you made prototypes.

For now, they'd have to angle the blades so that, when the torrent was in full flow, they slipped off some of the force rather than catching it all. At the beginning of each cycle, every six hours, when the tide was picking up, the blades would have to be dead on, to catch all the force they could. As the tide grew stronger, they would tilt in continuous minuscule increments to slip off ever-larger amounts of force. The beautiful part was that the angle of the blades was a function of tide strength, ergo determined by the positions of the moon and sun relative to the Earth.

Once Alan and his assistants had done what they could, they drove the turbines and the machine's delicate internals up to Orkney. The only part still missing was the hull. On the journey, Alan sat next to the lorry driver to stop him going above fifty. Maren and Charlie stayed in the back for the 700-mile journey, to watch the boxes.

When James and Roland flew up, Alan took them out on the workboat he'd bought. It was simple, solid, like a lifeboat, with twin Volvo engines that shook the cabin at a low pitch. Roland insisted the boat be ceremonially renamed. He bought a bottle of Moët from the Kirkwall Sainsbury's and smashed it on the sturdy prow. James wanted to call her *Nike*, as in the Greek for victory. Roland suggested *California*, since Peter Thiel had paid for it. Alan liked the idea of a boat called *California* slugging her way through cold northern seas, and painted the letters himself with a draughtsman's steady hand.

Alan drove them out in the *California* to the western edge of the archipelago, where the wave machines were. There was something he wanted them to see. They chugged placidly through the sound until they approached the final headland separating them from the Atlantic. Then Alan said, "Alright, guys, Life jackets on." Inflated tubes of tough red plastic, bent into a keyhole shape around their necks and down their chests.

As they came around the corner, the boat began to pitch and buck. The dark cliff on their left pulled back like a curtain, and in the afternoon sunshine they saw ceaseless ranks of high jade-green rollers bearing down on them. They came in off the open ocean like dunes of seawater, the height of a cottage and as wide as a town. Their tops were webbed over with skeins of white, and their foaming crests threw up so much spray that pocket rainbows hung between their peaks. Over slow centuries they were pounding the dark cliffs into rubble.

The *California* climbed a slow diagonal up the face of each roller, the view through the windshield filling with water, then reached a crest from which they could briefly see thousands more sunlit waves marching towards them, and slid down into the shady trough behind. Climbing, sliding. Climbing, sliding. James and Roland's stomachs began to feel loose.

Alan steered south until they could see a machine called the Oyster — a two-hundred-ton flap of steel bolted into a rocky beach under the cliffs. Each time a wave came in, the flap lifted. When it crashed back down, it squeezed two hydraulic pumps at its sides, as if pushing down a bicycle pump. Up and down, squeeze, squeeze. That was how it generated power. But as they looked, they saw that something was wrong. The pumps, each thicker than a human body, had been torn from their sockets. Each time the heavy flap came down, it was beating them into an unsalvageable tangle of steel and machinery.

Alan said, "Storm came in last week. Everyone's saying they're completely shucked."

James got the hint. Yes, yes, the twin-bladed rotor. That could be us. He looked with irritation at Alan's black beard, with its twists of white, at his solid belly, which always made him think of a pot-bellied stove, his swarthy Pictish skin and his short Pictish stature. The Picts had been practically exterminated from the historical record. Alan was not irreplaceable.

But James's task here as CEO was to let Alan vent off his excess emotion. He said, "Yes. I see. Do you know, are they going to try again?"

"Nah. They can't even afford to take it away."

"So they're going bust?"

Alan laughed. "You're the expert, like, but I don't think they're going to be getting a lot of investment in that thing."

"Maybe we could hire their engineers, if they'd be useful."

"Mm-hm. Our machine's practically finished, though, isn't it? All we need is the hull."

James almost despaired. They'd never do something historic with that mindset. He said, "But we'll be onto the full-size version soon enough. And if we need more money for hiring, we can raise more. Do you want me to talk to their engineers?"

"No, no. I'll do it." Alan had been getting to know the guys from other companies also stationed up here in Orkney. They drank together in the fisherman's pubs of Kirkwall and Stromness, alternating between camaraderie and suspicion.

On the way back, they swung past the Pelamis machine. The sections of the mechanical sea snake were painted alternately red and yellow. Each jinked up and down in the waves, squeezing hydraulic pumps inside the hulls. Rumour was that Pelamis were planning a major test. Each time those red and yellow sections jinked up and down, they sent electricity to the national grid. Pelamis were still years ahead.

Once the *California* rounded the headland back into calmer seas, Roland went out of the cabin. He sat on a moulded plastic bench at the back of the boat. Lukewarm sunshine fell on him. In the boat's wake, the water was being churned glassy-smooth.

They were close enough to land for his phone to have signal. He'd begun learning Japanese again, this time on Duolingo. Now that he was leaving the company, the whole inexhaustible multiplicity of human existence stood open to him. He could go anywhere, live in any country, do whatever his heart desired. But as he confronted this limitless blank infinitude of choice, nothing leapt out at him. His heart didn't have a burning desire for anything. So . . . Japanese again? Maybe.

He was doing a few of these gamified exercises every day. Just while he thought of something new. *Eki* – station. *Tamago* – egg. He had a suspicion that learning Japanese shouldn't be this easy.

Once he'd collected his daily trophies from the app, he switched to Tinder. There were girls even up here. Lauren, 26, wearing a beanie and smoking what looked like a spliff. Her face was at a sharp angle, and her body wasn't in the shot. Chubby? Roland swiped no. Next was Aurora, 23. Photo taken on holiday somewhere, maybe Thailand. Aurora was waving a jug of some pink cocktail beside a pool. Pretty good body. Her self-description was "South Ronaldsay 4 Life".

Why did they use Tinder here? The Orcadians must all know each other already. Maybe it was just a way of letting everyone know you wanted to get laid. It would be tragically romantic if he fell in love with a fair Orcadian maiden just before he said goodbye to the islands forever. With her Norse blonde hair and ice-blue eyes, she'd be pacing the lonely shore and waiting for him to come back to her. Maybe it would be Aurora, 23. He swiped yes. He carried on swiping until he reached a screen that said *There are no more matches in your area.*

Soon after, James came out of the cabin and sat down beside him. "What you doing?"

"Bit of Tinder."

"Maybe I should get it too. It's kind of fascinating."

"Oh, yeah?"

"I just think, instead of people trying to pick a marriage out of the ... let's say, twenty people that an average person meets at work or through friends or whatever, you have the choice of thousands. You increase supply. Better choices, better marriages. An uptick in the sum of human happiness. They should give those guys the Nobel."

"Sounds like you should download it."

"It's similar in athletics. There's far more supply of talent these days, and so the records get broken. Poor old Emil Zátopek wouldn't stand a chance against the East Africans."

"You should tell your Tinder dates about this."

"I will."

They sat unspeaking as the *California* motored slowly along the sound. Then Roland said, "Are we going to talk about me leaving?"

"If we have to."

Roland sighed. "I was assuming you'd have some way you wanted to arrange it."

"You thought I'd figure out your exit plan for you?"

Yes, Roland had. "I just think, at the end of the day, it's obvious you don't need me any more."

"Bullshit. Of course the company needs you. Just look at Alan." They glanced in through the cabin's back windows to where he was standing at the wheel. "He's getting more and more hostile to me."

"He's not hostile. He just can't see where it's all going. Like, he thought he was going to come and invent a tidal machine. Now there's this hydrogen angle he's not an expert in, and VC money comes into it, which he doesn't really understand either, and actually you, not him, had this big idea about the two sets of two blades. He thought he was going to be the inventor, but he's got to follow you, and he doesn't know how to feel good about it."

"You see. I could never read him that well."

"You've just got to talk to him."

"Okay, well, if we're talking about it, my opinion is: this is the best job you're ever going to get. Here you're part of something meaningful. If you quit what we're doing, you're just someone with a bad degree and a few years at McKinsey."

"Easy, mate, easy."

"I just think, if you leave, you'll spend two years figuring out that you don't actually want to be a ramen chef or whatever you're thinking. You'll ask me for your old job back and I might not even be able to give it to you any more. So then you'll have to have some random mediocre career."

Roland nodded a few times, restraining himself from giving James some truth bombs of his own. Eventually, he said, "I know you believe this company is the answer to everything. But I happen to know you just pulled it out of your arse."

James shook his head. "Fine. But can we postpone this until the machine's in the water? If it does sink, I'll need you to deal with Alan."

Roland looked at rocky islets drifting past in this northern sea. It would be sad never to see this again. And he didn't have a vivid picture of what came after departure. He could take some time to think about it. "Okay. I'll go once it's in the water."

"Thank you."

"It's fine."

They shook on it.

James began to allocate twenty minutes per day to Tinder. He met women immediately after they finished work because if it went on too late the drinks just made him sleepy. After about nine o'clock, his mind would be invaded by calculations of how many hours were left before he had to get up. A few times recently, he'd sat down in his morning shower, his back to the wet cubicle wall, and fallen asleep.

With the women, he had the same problem as he'd had on Guardian Soulmates: they didn't seem to grasp that running a tidal energy company was incredibly cool.

When he explained about putting a yoke on the moon, and rockets that emitted only water, they treated him like an eccentric. Because he mentioned climate change, they construed him as a harmless do-gooder. He could have mentioned Thiel's millions but wouldn't stoop to invoking the legitimacy of cash.

He had to put in unexpected efforts to keep them interested. Living with his parents didn't go over well. And of course he'd let himself get visibly overweight. He tried to tell them that there was nothing complicated about moving out or slimming down. Both just required time and mental energy that he preferred to spend on the mission.

Sometimes they slept with him. But even then he couldn't turn off his brain. He was once going down on a stylish, skinny, very-alien-to-him woman who wrote for *World of Interiors* when he noticed that he'd been thinking for some time already about the oil price. He'd read as a teenager that it was crucial to vary the pattern of tongue strokes and so avoid monotony. The lad's-mag advice was to draw the letters of the alphabet around the clitoris. Instead of the alphabet, he'd been drawing B-R-E-N-T—C-R-U-D-E.

He tried to saturate his mind with sensation. The mercifully soft carpet under his naked knees. His chest leaning against the end of the bed. Fuzzy tiredness between his temples. Shoulders touching the warm undersides of her thighs. His spasm-prone eyelid resting closed. The musky, blood-temperature body part under his tongue. She was making encouraging sounds and grazing his head with her fingers.

This was the moment he was in. This. This. But Brent had been over a hundred dollars a barrel in the summer, and now it was collapsing like it had in 2008. Sure, prices were inflated before, because Russia had invaded Crimea in the spring. But still, the collapse was essentially because of what he'd predicted when still a trainee at McKinsey: shale fracking in Texas. Instead of two major oil suppliers, Russia and Saudi, the world now had a third. The glut of oversupply made prices crash.

He felt the satisfaction of completing the world's hardest crossword. Things made sense; reality was essentially comprehensible. And an oil crash meant Alan was losing the fallback option of getting a job at Subsea7. Maybe that would make him five per cent less hostile to James ... ten per cent?

The interiors journalist began jerking through her abdomen. Muscle spasms arrived closer and closer together until she came, holding the squeeze for a few seconds and then relaxing all the way out. James relaxed too. Another task complete. Ye gods, he was tired. It couldn't be much later than eleven. If he got away in the next twenty minutes, he might be in his own bed by midnight.

Roland soon noticed that James, despite their agreement, carried on trying to bind him in.

Thiel had said it made a company look unserious if the CEO and executive chairman were practically unpaid. So James assigned them each a salary of a hundred grand, and encouraged Roland to enjoy it. The money felt superabundant, unspendable. He was in the top two per cent of earners. But no crazy purchases – he should save for his travels. So he just restricted himself a little less and let some more of his personhood emerge from under the limitations of cash. He liked cabs, so he travelled by cab. Instead of finding out which restaurants were cheap, he just went where looked tasty. When he was in a shop, he just bought what he liked. It was much simpler.

James also manoeuvred him into being the one who hired the new people – an assistant and two more engineers – so that Roland would feel responsible for them, which he did. After the interviews, Roland slightly lost his temper and told James, "You agreed that I'm going to leave. So . . . just . . . fuck off, will you?"

James smirked and put up his hands in faux innocence.

Roland's parents told him he needed to move out of the flat in Maida Vale. His dad had retired, and they planned to be in the city more often. His mum came to rearrange the flat and announced herself by calling out, "Knock, knock, the bailiffs are here." She gave him a big kiss on the cheek. "Hello, sweetheart. If you aren't packed, I'm throwing your stuff out the window." Roland wasn't packed. She pretended to box his ears, and they got on with it together.

While they were putting his clothes in suitcases, his mum asking about Cleo's wedding, he said, "By the way, I've decided to leave the company."

"Oh, for God's sake. Why? I thought you were just getting settled."

He talked as they packed and, as he explained, his mum understood, as she always did. The big decision of her life was to get out of Inverness. To pursue only one job, to live always in only one country, seemed parochial.

As they spoke, he began to miss Egypt: the noisy, dirty freedom from the orderliness of northern Europe; the expansive heat; the feeling of living among the ancient dead; and beyond the city's edges, the romance of the desert. She said, "Well, if you're going to quit, maybe it's not a bad time. Before you have a family to think about."

"Exactly. But the tricky thing is, I don't want to sign, like, a year-long lease on some new flat when I'm just about to leave."

"Roland."

"Can't I just stay here for a month or two until it's organised? It's such a waste of money to pay for a whole year somewhere. I can sleep on the sofa bed when you guys are here."

"No. Absolutely not. Your father would go spare. You've done very well out of this place. Now it's time for us to enjoy ourselves a bit without you under our feet."

"I won't be under your feet. I'll keep my stuff in the cupboard in the sitting room so you can have the wardrobes. And I get up earlier than you guys now, so I can put the sofa bed away before you even see it."

"What did I just say?"

"I just think it's so wasteful. The company has only just started paying me properly. James says we're in the top two per cent of earners now."

That made her think.

"And now I'm going to give most of that cash to some landlord for a flat I'm not even going to be in for very long."

"Well, where are you going today? Can't you stay there for longer?"

"I actually don't have anywhere lined up." He shrugged helplessly.

"For God's sake, Roland. Where were you planning to take these suitcases?"

"I don't know. Maybe I could stay with James's parents for a few nights while I get myself organised."

"You are absolutely not going to impose on them any more than you already have."

"I don't think they'd mind. I could probably sleep in Cleo's old room. But can't I just stay here a bit longer? It's been four years. What difference does it make if I'm here a few more nights?"

Lorna wavered. She would not have him go like a refugee to James's parents. Roland saw her wavering and said, "I literally won't even go in the bedroom. That's yours and dad's, totally."

"It's *all* mine, you rat! Why didn't you organise anywhere? I told you *months* ago. You've done this on purpose."

"No, I haven't." Roland looked offended. "You don't know how busy we've been trying to get the machine launched."

"You're spoiled is what you are. It's because I've been a soft touch all your life."

"That's not true. Everyone used to think you were *so* strict. Dad was the one who used to sneak me out of homework to play tennis with him."

Lorna smiled. "He loved that." Then she made an *argghh* noise and said, "I must have done something terrible in a past life to be lumbered with you."

He looked as humble as he could.

"You sleep on the sofa bed. Your things go in the living-room cupboard. And I don't want your wet clothes hanging up everywhere. You can send them to a laundry service."

"Thanks, Mum. Honestly, I think it makes sense."

"I'm going to make random inspections, and if this place isn't spotless – and I mean *immaculate* – then you're out on your ear, Sonny Jim."

"Totally, totally."

"And if you so much as chip one of my new plates, then woe betide you."

"I won't even use them. I'll use paper plates."

"Don't be ridiculous."

"Okay."

"And shut up for a minute, will you? I need to think about how I'm going to break this to your father."

APRIL 2015

Once the winter storm season abated, they towed their machine's steel hull out of the *Titanic* dockyards in Belfast, motoring quietly out along avenues of high dormant cranes and tall grasses overgrowing the outlying quays. The hull was industrial yellow, canoe-shaped and as long as two buses end to end. Without its turbine arms, it looked like a yellow submarine silently following in their widening pale-blue wake.

At first, they watched it nervously, tensing each time a cold wave broke over its prow. But the boatbuilders had sealed it properly. It didn't sink. Instead, it obediently stayed always a cable-length behind them, riding low enough in the water that the waves ran over it. They gradually relaxed, but sometimes stood up abruptly to check it was still there.

The tug was crowded. As well as the three drivers, James and Roland had decided to bring everyone they had. James said that in years to come, when the company had swelled to thousands, people would brag about having been on this boat. It would be like saying you were with Mao on the Long March. Alan was up to six engineers and an assistant: Maren, Charlie and five new faces. They were mostly dads with beards, fleeces and Iron Maiden T-shirts. James and Roland also had an assistant, a young woman fresh from Oxford and Imperial.

Everywhere you turned, there were people bundled up in puffer jackets and beanie hats, drinking tea and chatting. Their eyes were shining with the heightened feelings of being on an expedition. They slept on board. In a stowage locker they had a dozen sleeping bags neatly packed and stacked like colourful artillery shells. On the first evening, James unfurled them and laid them out in two rows. But some animal instinct for shelter asserted itself over this tidy militarism, and each of the team crawled into a corner or under a table. They slept with the boat rocking and the engines' deep throb beneath their heads.

The tug had a kitchenette with an electric hot plate on which every evening they very slowly heated a large pot of pasta water. Penne with tuna and tomato. Penne with Bolognese that Alan had pre-made and frozen.

The young assistants made jokes about so many carbs. James's favourite, his own assistant, who was bolshy, argumentative and clever, and whose parents had burdened her with the name Mary-Rose – a bad omen on a ship – turned out to be a vegetarian. On the Bolognese night, she ate penne with cheese and, to James and Roland's slight bafflement, said, "You're lucky I'm not vegan."

Before getting into their bags, they went outside to smoke and look at the stars. Roland bundled himself up in his pongy Danish sheepskin coat. They drank harsh red wine from tumblers, switched off the onboard lights so they were running dark, and gazed upwards till their necks ached.

There were two nights when the sky was so icy-clear that the blackness above and around them was like a dome-shaped star map. Out here on the sea, far away from the cities, they could see the milky smudge of the galaxy, a stain of light from billions of suns. James, Roland and the engineers, every one of them a childhood space enthusiast, pointed out to each other that the Earth was actually *inside* the Milky Way. It was all around them. They were just looking inwards towards its thicker centre.

James raised his tumbler and said, "A quick toast, everyone. I want you to remember, when you're getting frustrated with suppliers or" – he smiled at Alan – "getting frustrated with me, this is the endeavour we're engaged in. We're making rocket fuel."

Roland gave the cue the team needed: "To rocket fuel."

They repeated it, nudging their tumblers against one another, each quiet and full up with a great truth that only these few of them knew.

When their necks got tired, they looked at the moonlight on the waves, a ceaseless shifting of black and sparkling silver. Above the waterline, they saw humped black gaps in the starscape, island hills silhouetted against the sky. They saw the orange glow from lone houses on the shore.

As James and Roland leaned on the rail, their mental surroundings opened up from the smallness of rooms to the islands, the sea and the universe. James in his exhilaration muttered so the others couldn't hear, "How can you think anything is going to be better than this?"

Roland had no answer.

In the mornings, Roland went outside to check that the yellow hull was still following them. He drank his coffee in his cosy sheepskin coat and let the breeze clear away his hangover. It troubled him that "rocket fuel" had been the wrong toast. It would inflame Alan's fear of being sidelined.

The engineers covered the tug's main table with diagrams and laptops. They were modelling how to add a small tip to the end of each turbine blade, like the wing tips on an aeroplane. Without them, the water slipping off the blade spun itself into an eddy, causing turbulence. Charlie was checking the readings from inside the hull. Alan was writing out contingency plans for if the machine sank.

James was always up first. He wasn't sleeping well. He went back and forth between steering the engineers and organising the next, far larger, funding round. This would raise the tens of millions required to test the prototype, hire a group of hydrogen specialists and build the full-scale machine. The negotiations were the sort of complex, high-stakes mental sport that James usually enjoyed. He was having arguments with a dozen VC analysts at the same time – about whether the money VCs had lost on solar was a special case; the likelihood of the Chinese getting into tidal as well; the probable outcome of the Paris climate summit in autumn and how far they were behind Pelamis, who were also organising a funding round.

But he wasn't enjoying it. He imagined pressing a button to just auto-resolve the negotiations. He would take an average result. No need for an optimal or even merely excellent conclusion. Just okay would be enough. His eye twitch was bothering him. Several times a day he tried to remember whether it had always been in his right eye or if it had started in his left. Early one morning, the breeze stirred the seawater up into a wobbly chop, and he suddenly felt dizzy.

Roland saw him go pale. He stepped closer and said, "You okay, mate?"

James said, "Oof," and staggered. Roland grabbed his elbow and guided him down onto one of the side benches. James rubbed his face, trying to snap out of it. His fingers were trembling. Sweat burst from his body and, for a moment, the boat's sounds seemed far away.

Roland put James's feet up on the bench and asked Mary-Rose to fetch a Coke. The team kept glancing across. As James opened the can and drank, pouring the reviving sugar into his system, he came back to normal. Roland said, "You okay?"

"Yup. Just felt a bit weird for a second there. Probably seasick."

"Maybe once the machine is in the water we should all take a holiday."

"All you ever want to do is go away."

"Woah. Okay. Easy."

"You're right. You're right. Sorry. That was unfair. Holidays for everyone. Once it's in the water. Okay, now, let's get back to it."

As well as the engineering and the VCs, James was applying for a million-euro grant from the EU. The programme, for futuristic technology, was called Horizon 2020. He'd assigned the paperwork to Mary-Rose, which really was too much of the company's welfare to put in the hands of someone so green. But he wanted to give her the chance to outstrip what could be reasonably expected, to shoulder an unfair burden and, through an extreme and no doubt personally costly internal effort, earn the rank that James thought she was capable of.

As he saw it, the point about Mary-Rose wasn't where she was but her trajectory. Because her mum and granny had both got pregnant underage, the granny was only thirty-one when Mary-Rose was born. Neither Mary-Rose's mum nor stepdad had a job. It sounded like the kind of family that the tabloids told horror stories about. Mary-Rose was the first in her family to sit A-levels, let alone go to uni, and then she'd got a first in history and economics from Oxford. James recognised the will to ascent.

Because her life experience was of propelling herself upwards out of her surroundings, she was used to not accepting what her elders – like James – told her. She didn't have the easy willingness to obey that James saw in graduates who came off the middle-class conveyor belt. In some ways, she was totally opaque to him and in others distressingly transparent: he saw a raging need to learn, and the obstructive pride of chafing at being taught.

When they talked, she was prickly, touchy, reflexively contrary. Instead of carrying out his instructions, she questioned his decisions, which he enjoyed. Finally he had someone to speak to about these things. James, trying to give her a way out of her ridiculous name, told her that actually his mum was called Mary. She said, "That's a nice name. My name's Mary-Rose."

Another contradiction: she gave more of herself to the company than anyone except James but appeared in deliberately unacceptable clothes: short skirts, ripped tops, black PVC bondage boots. On the boat, she wore a huge, oversized inflatable black jacket from which her fishnet-clad legs stuck out like two pipe cleaners. The older engineers, with daughters nearly her age, hated it. After getting the job, she'd shaved an undercut into her hair and dyed it crimson. She seemed to be communicating: *I am not one of you, and yet you will accept me because I am undeniable*. James thought she was fantastic.

He believed, as he did of Roland, that eventually she would stop getting in her own way. If she could be held on course, she would gradually let go of what obstructed her. She would see sense. When the time was right, he would explain that he didn't easily belong in this milieu either – or in any. Then she could get a haircut, and he'd start bringing her to investment meetings. She was the only person he thought could take over the company one day.

Getting the million euros from the EU required such specialised knowledge of grant-giving that they had to hire a professional applier. This was a former official in Brussels who would fill in the three-hundred-page form, no-win, no-fee. If they won, he took fifteen per cent: €150,000. How many applications did he write each year? Mary-Rose did her best to prevent James from hiring him. She said, "It's completely unethical to let €150,000 of public money go into some guy's pocket."

James smiled. "He might be corrupt as well. Maybe that's why he has such a good success rate. He might be giving kickbacks."

"I mean, literally. And a hundred and fifty grand is six times the median income. That money's supposed to help stop climate change."

James, teaching her now, said: "So, what do you think we should do?"

"*I* could do the form. It doesn't look that complicated. And you could increase my salary by ten grand. Then the company would save a hundred and forty grand overall, which we could spend on the relay Charlie wants for sending the signals from the device directly to the *California*."

James smiled again. "Okay, first of all, you're not asking for enough money. You should have asked for half the fee, and I'd have negotiated you down to thirty. And to make it more palatable to me, you should have asked for it as a bonus rather than a recurring salary obligation. Okay?"

Mary-Rose did not like being reminded she was an apprentice. But she was hungry to know what apprentices were taught. "Okay."

"Secondly, we're not going to do that. Your proven success rate is zero. We want that grant more than we want a cheap deal on getting the grant. Having the Horizon 2020 stamp gives us legitimacy with governments so we can get other kinds of help. And you don't have time; you have your own job to do. Do you see?"

"I thought you said there was an opportunity, in the way we run this company, to show how capitalism can be better."

"Yes, that's true. We are showing that."

"But isn't this exactly that kind of decision? Ethics versus material advantage. And you're saying we should take material advantage."

James felt wry and looked out over the waves. Why couldn't Roland engage like this? He said, "I appreciate this good-faith dissent, I really do. It's the kind of thing they used to dream about at McKinsey. But I said I'd give one of the VCs an answer to some pricing questions. Can we talk about it this evening?"

That evening, they took their already habitual places around the tug's cabin and ate penne with sausages and cheese. Mary-Rose ate penne with cheese.

Charlie wound Alan up by saying that next time someone else should do the cooking. "There's a reason you've got the Hong Kong Kitchen in Aberdeen, but it's not like there's an Aberdeen Kitchen in Hong Kong."

Alan was chuckling and saying, "Nice one, Charlie, you can empty the septic tank tonight," when his phone vibrated against his thigh. He read the messages and said, "Hold on a minute. Hold on." He caught James's eye. "See this big test Pelamis have been running? Well, it's failed. Like, completely. Apparently it nearly sank. And the power's off. Doesn't sound good for them."

Some of the team cheered. Amid the sudden volley of chatter, James noticed that only Mary-Rose asked the right question: "Is that a good thing or a bad thing for us?"

Alan went into his mood of gallows gaiety. "First the Oyster. Now Pelamis. Maybe we'll be at the bottom of the sea soon enough." He caught James's eye again, and James stared back at him.

Later, as James unfurled his sleeping bag, Mary-Rose asked if they were still going to talk. So he spoke to her for half an hour, squeezing one eye shut against the twitch, about ethics and pragmatism, ends and means, how you could only alter the world if you treated it as it really existed and what degree of imperfection was justified in service of their cause.

While the engineers up in Orkney fitted the bare hull with turbines and electronics, James and Roland met the first VC firm in their funding round.

It went strangely. This fund was supposed to be a sure thing. Their analysts had haggled out even such far-ahead items as preferential terms for more investments in future. This deal was supposed to build momentum with the others. But in the room, it was oddly tensionless. There was no sense that something was approaching consummation.

In the cab back to the office, they were both quiet. They sat in opposite corners of the back seat and looked out of opposite windows. After a while, Roland said, "I almost feel like they wanted to cancel on us, but it was too late to cancel so they thought, we'll just meet them and sit through it for an hour."

"Mm. And did you notice what they said about Pelamis?"

"It was weird, wasn't it?"

"Yeah. If Pelamis is maybe less far ahead than we thought . . . You tell me: it didn't sound like a positive, did it?"

"No."

"Alan says Pelamis's round has collapsed. Every investor they have has pulled out."

"Maybe everyone else will fall apart, and we'll be number one."

"Maybe."

They lapsed back into quiet as the cab moved through the end-of-day traffic.

When they reached the office, Roland paid. He and James disagreed about the cost of cabs, so Roland paid with his own money. The first time he did it, James smiled with pleasure, and Roland said, "I know what you're thinking."

"Getting used to the hundred-grand-a-year lifestyle?"

"Yeah, yeah."

"It's going to be difficult to go back to sleeping in a hostel for fifty rupees a night."

"Have you ever been to a hostel?"

"How much money have you saved up?"

Roland had saved zero.

But James didn't understand that he, Roland, didn't need money. He could set off for wherever with nothing, and figure it out as he went. James had no idea. Roland hadn't really had a chance yet to figure out exactly what he would do, which he knew was bad, but it wouldn't be hostels.

They took the lift up to their floor of the WeWork. Most of the other companies had gone home for the day. The empty communal space was like a hipster cafe designed by management consultants. It could have been in almost any city of the world. Alongside the white tiles and bare industrial ceiling, there were pod-shaped chairs, tall ferns and enthusiastically pro-work slogans sprayed graffiti-style on the walls.

Roland pulled two pints of free craft beer under a giant *Thank God It's Monday*. It made him feel like he was being brainwashed in some dystopian penal colony. James didn't care; maybe it would increase the team's enthusiasm by five per cent.

Their own office was a glass cube on a corridor of other glass cubes. James had refused to pay the premium to be next to a window. The light reached them through so much glass it was tinted slightly blue, as if they were underwater.

When they sat down on their swivel chairs, James was still trying to understand what had happened in the meeting. Roland's plastic cup squidged between his fingers. "Want to see something lols?"

"Okay."

It was fun when it was just them, as if everyone else had gone to bed and they were still up. For James, the obligation to always be everyone's guide – patient, interested and supportive, in possession of the answers they sought – could be put away.

With an air of showmanship, Roland pulled off his jacket and tie. He went over to the bank of locked filing cabinets he'd insisted on buying and from his pocket produced a key. He opened the first drawer with a flourish – inside were neatly folded jumpers. In the next were T-shirts. Above them pants and socks. James was laughing. Every drawer was packed with Roland's clothes.

Roland pulled on a pale-pink hoodie while James said, "You are such an idiot."

"Alan got me into it. The filing cabinets in his pre-fab were full of golf gear."

James laughed.

"My mum said I'm not allowed any clothes in the bedroom wardrobes. And the living-room cupboard is pretty small."

"Wouldn't it be easier just to rent a flat of your own? I'm sure you could get a good deal on a two-year contract."

"Yes, yes, very good. Why don't you get a flat?"

"Yeah, yeah."

"What do you do with your cash? I mean, you don't pay rent, and your parents buy the food. Are you, like, secretly addicted to online poker?"

James looked shifty, and Roland said, "It's not really poker, is it? It would actually be quite you, in a way."

"I save it up in case the company needs it."

"Oh, mate. Oh, no. It's a sickness, you know that? It's like you've managed to Stockholm-syndrome yourself. Why don't you try living a little?"

"Thanks. I'll put it on the list."

They drank their beer and thought their thoughts. Roland checked the Champions League schedule on his phone. James feared they'd missed the moment of maximum prestige attached to Peter Thiel. A couple of years ago, he'd been purely a contrarian genius. Now he was vocally supporting a reality-TV huckster, Donald Trump, for president. It made Thiel look like a wacko. The ideal time for the funding round might have been two years ago.

Roland interrupted. "Once I'm gone, don't have an office romance with Mary-Rose."

"What?"

"She's much younger, and you're her boss. I know she wears those short skirts, but just don't do it."

"Mate. No."

"But you might fall into it." He put on a silly, infatuated voice. "*Oh, Mary-Rose really understands the company. Oh, Mary-Rose is so talented. Oh, Mary-Rose, let's go for a drink and talk about the funding round.* And then – oops."

James shook his head. "You sound pretty jealous. Am I not giving you enough attention, you poor sausage? Do you want to go back to being my number one monkey?"

Roland turned melancholy. "You know, mate, you're quite weird, but I will miss you. I really will."

"Don't quit then."

Roland rolled his eyes. He wished James wouldn't call it *quitting*. "Mate, you'll be fine. You'll be so fine."

The launch date crawled painfully, incrementally, closer. They began to count down in weeks, and then in days.

Alan passed on rumours that Pelamis was in deep financial trouble. It seemed that their investors had waited to see the results of the big test before committing the next tranche of funding. Pelamis had spent their reserves in reaching that point. They couldn't afford to try again. Alan reported from the Kirkwall pubs that Pelamis's employees had been told to take other jobs if they could get them.

As Pelamis plunged towards unexpected bankruptcy, the VC meetings James had scheduled were called off. The emails came separately, but all within the same week. Expressions of regret – very promising technology – difficult environment – not the right time – would love to stay in touch. The flock had changed course.

James cut his prices to levels he would not have told the team. He offered terms that were little better than vassalage. He made promises at the outer edge of credibility. But his hooks and levers slid off an implacable politeness. One of the most sympathetic asset managers, who really believed that they were like the first discoverers of oil, sent a long WhatsApp: "I still 100% think you can make it happen. But everyone got badly stung on solar/green tech before and now Oyster + Pelamis seem to show that marine is NOT an exception. The feeling in the industry is that marine energy isn't ready. The tech is just not there yet. Will definitely be huge but could be 5 years, could be 50. V hard to invest in those circs."

James kept this to himself.

Their own test was approaching. The team were exerting themselves hard and happily, like rowers pulling in unison, like the best mornings on the Isis, years ago. The team could do it. The twin blades hadn't wobbled in the pool. Every hour that passed, the launch into Kirkwall harbour came closer. Every evening, he rang Alan and asked, how many days.

He could feel the stress in his body. It was as if a mild electrical current were continuously running through him. Every muscle was pulled into an almost imperceptible tension. His arms and lower back ached even though he did no exercise. The tinier fibres, little more than gristle, like those that operated one corner of an eyelid, fluttered in the current. His eyelid twitched open and shut like the doomed Oyster. He began waking up early, tired but sleepless. He lay in the dark until it was six o'clock and the rise-and-shine hormones began clearing the fog from his brain.

His only way to relax was to drink. Not great volumes, but something strong, which would hit his system fast and stun it into unclenching. Alcohol was miraculous in its speed. He slugged back a whisky, and, within seconds, the adrenalin dropped, his grateful muscles relinquished their grip, and his mind floated free for a while. He stopped at a pub on the walk home from the WeWork. After some trial and error, he'd settled on a double whisky and a red-wine chaser. There was some mellowing chemical in the wine. Roland called it mong juice. There was a cost in the mornings, and in reduced sleep quality, but he was willing to pay it. He knew this was short-termist, but they were almost there.

Once, in the pub, a young barman said, "Are you playing catch-up?"

"Sorry?"

"Are you playing catch-up? You going out?"

James realised it was Friday. The others in the pub were noisily beginning their weekends. That whole way of life, going out on a Friday night, felt very far away from what was really going on.

For the last few days before the launch, everyone moved to Orkney. Roland declared that anyone could bring their family, and the company would pay to put them up. He expected more resistance from James, who just irritatedly waved it through.

The Kirkwall Hotel filled up with toddlers, teenagers, wives and boyfriends. Nearly thirty people in all. Gaggles of them could be seen getting to know each other over a long breakfast or heading off to "explore the town". They were occupying nearly half the hotel's rooms. James calculated that it would soon be cheaper to build a company dorm next to the warehouse.

The hotel staff were swept up in their endeavour. Every evening, when the engineers trooped into the lobby like miners returning from a shift, the receptionists asked, "How'd you get on? Launch tomorrow?"

James pronounced the correct phrases of welcome to the families, but they vanished from his thoughts even as he turned away. Roland felt like the manager of a holiday camp. All he needed was a red coat and a clipboard. Did he know where Maren's boyfriend could get some Clarityn? Was there space for everyone in the cars? What time was dinner? He organised excursions: the Neolithic village. The whaling museum. A scuba guide for Maren's boyfriend, who wanted to see the German fleet scuttled in Scapa Flow. He sometimes felt like Maren's boyfriend's personal assistant.

This was his final service to James and Alan. In two days, in one day, the machine would be in the water, and he would have kept his promise. His parting gift was to coax the collective mood into the ideal composition: laughter, togetherness, friendship, a belief that they belonged to something meaningful. He wanted the plus-ones, before they turned out the light in their hotel bedrooms, to be telling the engineers how proud they were.

He became an unwilling receptacle for the group's feelings. Maren's boyfriend, a coder from Nottingham called Steve, told him that Maren worried James didn't like her. One of the wives let slip, as if by accident, that they'd really needed this job. There was even something from Alan's wife Catriona, who was far quicker, sharper, more stylish than he'd imagined, a kind of smiling corporate velociraptor. Surrounded by fleeces and waterproofs, she wore a luxy cashmere jumper and knockout earrings. She said to him, "It does Alan good, you know, to do something he believes in. The poor guy was getting quite bored at Subsea7, clocking off early to go play golf at honestly a very low standard."

In his state of valedictory benevolence, Roland let this happen. And then he snuck upstairs alone. He sat at his room's shallow, inadequate desk, intended more for decoration than for use. Framed in the single window was a northern European scene: the small stone-built Kirkwall harbour, cold clear water, a fishing boat with an orange hull.

Flat on his desk was a window into Japan. He'd bought again the textbooks he'd failed to study in Nagaur. Every day he studied one exercise and learned ten words. *Watashi wa Roland desu.* My name is Roland.

There were innumerable lives he could have once he'd left. The limitless variety of human experience, so multitudinous that a single human span was only enough to miss out on practically all of it. But he'd quietly, happily, begun to like the idea that, for the first time he could remember, he was going to finish something he'd started. No more half-assed notions.

Ejiputo kara kimashita. I am from Egypt.

Back downstairs, he saw Catriona play up to the role of colonel's wife and speak about Alan in faux complaint. She told the team, "I love it when you're testing up here because it gets Alan out of the house for a week. There's only so much golf I can get him to play." Alan's subordinates were delighted by this wind-up. Mary-Rose was dazzled by her.

Roland found Alan and Catriona's son, Richard, smoking outside after dinner, leaning against the hotel's stone wall and watching the quiet harbour on the other side of the road. He didn't need his school fees paid any more: he was a skinny, awkward student, taller than his dad, doing maths in Edinburgh. He blushed whenever he was asked a question.

Roland smoked beside him and didn't ask him how his course was going or whether he wanted to be an engineer as well. It was still light even though dinner was over and the babies had long ago gone to bed. The colour of the light had shifted up the spectrum – the yellow had faded out of it and now it was almost white. They smoked and watched this pale calm light fall on the pale calm seawater.

Four years Roland had given to this company. And all that time this beauty had just been sitting here. What an egotistical irrelevance all this effortful striving really was. Before he went back inside, he clapped Richard on the shoulder and confused him by saying, "You're a good kid."

*

One evening, the machine was ready. There was nothing left to be checked. The list of improvements would have to wait. They would launch first thing. At the nervous dinner that night in the hotel restaurant, everyone drank too much. The hotel had put them on one very long table, like a gala banquet. The talk was about tomorrow and about Pelamis – it was said they now didn't even have enough fuel money to take their boat out and do maintenance.

Roland gave a speech in which he lost his ear for the correct tone. He said, "It's been more than four years since me, Alan and James started this company with a little model floating in an IKEA storage box." And, "Whatever happens tomorrow, it's been the great pleasure of my life so far to be involved."

He could see James not looking at him. He lifted his wine glass and said, "I salute you." It was a bit weird. But Alan said, "Alright, pal. Maybe you've had enough," and everyone loved him again.

The hotel's kitchen staff came in early to make them a packed breakfast: white Styrofoam boxes leaking baked-bean sauce. Sausage and egg rolls. Thermos flasks of coffee. As they left the hotel, the kitchen staff applauded and wished them luck.

The company and their families ate at the end of the industrial pier, a broad, dead-straight concrete road that led out from the shore and stopped in mid-water. Someone's toddler kept trying to fall off the unprotected edges.

Their long yellow machine lay a few feet from the drop. It was jacked up on scissor-lifts so the turbines wouldn't have to rest on the ground. It still looked like a submarine, but now the turbine arms and their golden blades – wrapped up in heavy bags like Formula One tyres before a race – extended out from each side. From the machine's flat top sprouted a colony of antennae. Under the hull was a huge, vaguely sinister metal coil, like some thick blind worm: the flexible power cable from Hamburg, which would carry electricity from the floating machine down to the fixed socket on the seabed.

A crane on caterpillar tracks clattered up the road towards them, the racket of its engine too loud to speak over. The engineers fastened chains from its hook to rings on the machine. The driver raised a thumb at Alan, asking a question. Alan raised his thumb in reply. The driver fired up the engine again.

Before the driver could begin, Alan changed his mind and ran over to him. By the time he reached the cab, he managed to make it look like a casual jog. For weeks he'd been visualising catastrophes: the hooks ripping off, the machine dropping, the turbine arms cracking as they hit the concrete. He told the driver not to lift yet, just to raise the hook enough to put tension on the chains.

A motor whined. The chains went taut with a singing metal sound. Nothing broke. Alan had the engineers check the fastenings again.

While Maren brought the *California* around and parked a little way offshore, Alan lowered pink fenders over the end of the pier until its hard surface was entirely shielded. Just in case a freak wave ground the machine against it.

James munched automatically through his cooked breakfast and said nothing. This was Alan's show.

Eventually, Alan nodded to the crane driver. The engine clattered, and they heard it begin to strain. The long heavy yellow machine rose a foot off the dock. The crane drove towards the edge at minimum speed, the ridges on its caterpillar tracks clicking forward, the machine swaying slightly despite the driver's care. Alan saw a vision of the crane driving straight over into the sea. Or the counterweight on the crane's rear proving too light; machine and crane tipping forward.

The driver lowered the hook, and the machine descended slowly into the lapping wavelets. They saw the chains lose tension as the water took its weight. Two engineers on the back of the *California* hauled in their guide ropes, drawing thick hawsers through hooks on the machine. The engineers were sweating and uncomfortable in bulky drysuits, hoods and gloves. Once the hawsers were fast, they climbed down the *California*'s ladder into the sea and swam awkward front-crawl over to the machine. They kneeled on its flat top, and the families standing on the dock looked down onto their heads as they detached the chains.

Then the chains were off, and they looked up grinning and squinting.

More checks. Then Alan personally took the helm of the *California* and towed the machine, side-on, a few metres into the relative safety of open water. For the first time that day, he breathed out. "Thank fuck for that. She's in."

They waved and called goodbye to the families on shore and towed the machine out to the tidal strait. They'd taken on board an industrial diver called Stuart. A former marine, now in his forties, his usual job was to look after wellheads on the bed of the North Sea. He was small, with thick arms, hollow cheeks and hair shorn down to a blonde-grey stubble. He lived for weeks at a time in a pressurised metal chamber attached to the leg of an oil rig. For the other six months of the year, he spaffed his danger money surfing in Morocco or motorbiking to Vegas. He'd come off a Harley in New Mexico, and he had steel pins in his leg and shoulder that he didn't tell Alan or James about.

Today he was going down on a safety line to attach the power cable. They'd have to do it quickly, at slack water, between the tides. Otherwise Stuart would be swept out into the Atlantic, far below the surface. He sat outside, at the back, and smoked.

The mood on board was jokey now. Alan permitted himself to say, "Thank fuck we didn't sink in Kirkwall harbour. I could just see that happening."

Mary-Rose and some of the others had not yet seen the tidal strait. James found that if he kept pointing things out to them, kept opening his mouth, it dissipated the bubbles that were forming in his chest.

They chugged closer and, as they came out from under the lee of Shapinsay, the archipelago shifted into alignment around them. They saw the islands line up. Before them lay the straight channel. From the boat, the water looked homogenous, a cold grey-blue mass hurrying from the

Atlantic into the North Sea. But inside were fantastical shapes, invisible whorls and corkscrews. James pointed out the island of Muckle Green Holm, the patch of land the size of a tennis court, which the hurtling waters swerved around, eddying into spirals and vortices.

They waited out of the current for the tide to settle. It was already long past lunchtime, and they ate sandwiches the hotel had given them. A blue haze gathered over the sea and islands to the west. As it spread towards them, it resolved into a refreshing drizzle. Near-infinite pinpricks punctured the sea's shifting surface. Near-infinite tiny circles expanded from each puncture. The boat drifted.

Roland did his daily words on his phone: *Wakarimashita* – I understand. *Wakarimasen* – I don't understand.

James asked Alan, "How are you getting on?"

"Not sunk yet."

"Not sunk yet."

They watched the drizzle on the waves. James asked a question he knew Alan would hate. "Do you reckon we'll be able to fire it up today?"

Alan grimaced. "Maybe today. Maybe tomorrow. Depends how quickly we can get everything secure."

Finally the tide settled. Slack water. They had less than an hour before it started running back the other way. Alan towed the machine into position, lining up its GPS tracker with the mark on his display. The previous week, they'd installed a power socket the size of a manhole cover on the seabed. It was lying down there waiting for the machine's cable to be plugged in.

In the so-called Eday power station, really a freezing, corrugated-iron cubicle, they'd rigged up a single light bulb with a camera pointing at it. When electricity flowed from the machine, the light should come on.

Two engineers in insulated survival suits and life jackets kneeled on top of the machine. They were waiting by the release catches on the anchor chains. Alan stood at the back of the tug, the breeze tousling his black hair, and said into his walkie-talkie, "Ready?"

"Ready."

Alan looked at James, who nodded. Alan said into the radio, "Drop anchors."

The engineers released the catches. From the boat, they could see no difference. After a moment, the radio said, "Anchors down."

Stuart had his frogman suit on, the heavy cylinder on his back, the mask perched on his forehead, the respirator dangling below his chin.

They could see one of the engineers clamber across to another release. He raised a thumb to Alan, who gave the command, "Drop cable." Alan didn't wait to hear anything back, just turned to Stuart and said, "You're up."

Stuart checked his watch. Roughly forty-six minutes before the tide began to move. He stepped off the back of the *California*, and the familiar cold rushed into his neoprene hood and gloves. The trapped water would warm up soon. His chest and vital organs were snug in the drysuit. He kicked over to the machine, face down. The Darth Vader noise of the respirator. *Oosh-choo, oosh-choo*. He had a resting heart rate of 46 bpm.

Visibility was as bad as usual: with his arms out straight, he couldn't see his hands. He brought his wrist close to check the instrument readings on his watch. The circular screen glowed: forty-four minutes and counting down. Air tank ninety-nine per cent full. A big company like Shell would have paid for a second diver.

The engineers standing on the machine passed down the end of the safety line, which he clipped into his belt. He turned back to the tug and gave the okay symbol: his arm a circle, his fingers touching the dome of his head. In his ear, Alan said, "Good luck." With no ceremony or response, Stuart pressed the valve to release air from his buoyancy vest, and sank.

Below the surface, he found the thick cable hanging down into the depths. Not swaying too much. The cone of light from his head torch showed him the section near his hand. He released more air from his buoyancy vest and, lightly touching the cable so as not to lose it, began the descent. The muted brightness overhead faded and went out. When he turned his head, the torch found only the drifting silt in front of his mask. The *oosh-choo* of his breathing. His gloved fingertips running down the cable. The depth gauge on his wrist ticking over steadily.

This was what he lived for. The constriction, the black, the sensory deprivation. It must be like this inside a gimp suit. Every time he went down, he smiled around his respirator and had the same thought: Maybe I'm a secret deviant.

Soon he knew he must be almost at the bottom. He slowed and pointed his toes downward so his fins would touch first. Nothing. He sank lower. Still nothing. Where he expected solidity, only more descent. A tingle of vertigo. Being lost in a void. And then his fin scraped rock. It had only been an extra couple of inches.

They'd attached a red light to the socket that he was supposed to plug the cable into, but he couldn't see it. He took a line from his belt and tied it loosely around the cable so as to find his way back. He began the protocol for finding objects in minimal visibility. Three kicks forward. Right turn. One kick. He'd once searched for a colleague's body like this. Found him after about half an hour of being with him in the dark. Stuart pushed that thought away. The *oosh-choo* of his respirator.

Nothing. Right turn. Three kicks. And there: a glimmer of red, surprisingly close. He swam over. He ran the torchlight across the socket's cover. All fine. He'd installed it himself.

He checked his watch: twenty-seven minutes. On the slow side. He began to hurry, and his breathing speeded up. The air gauge would go down faster. He followed his line back to the cable. He started to drag the end of the heavy, dangling cable towards the socket. It was like having a tranquillised boa on his shoulder. Three decades of weight-training paid another dividend.

Back to the socket. Nineteen minutes. Breathing heavily. He sank down and rested his knees on the bottom. It was hard and pebbly. The mud must be ripped away by the current. There would be boulders charging around here before long. He plunged his head down almost into the socket and pulled off its protective cover. He held the lip of the socket with his one hand to pull the cable close.

Suddenly Alan was in his ear: "How you getting on? Everything okay?"

Stuart thought: Let me work, and pressed the okay button on his wrist. He had the end of the cable in the socket and – alone, his torch the only light in that black landscape – crouched on the bed of the ocean to see what he was doing. The locking mechanism he'd practised in Alan's warehouse. Click, turn, click.

With a shock, he realised he could feel the water moving, very gently. He checked his watch: four minutes until their arbitrary mark. Fuck. But it was done. With a rush, he went for the surface. Air into his buoyancy vest. Hand running up the cable. He didn't use his instruments. He judged his speed the old-fashioned way, watching the bubbles he breathed out rising in front of his mask.

The current was growing more insistent, tugging at his legs. He was having to hold on to the cable. Alan was in his ear, sounding worried. "Stuart. If you're not already on the way up, let's get going." Stuart didn't press his okay button, just savoured the feeling of effortless ascent.

From the *California*, they saw his black head abruptly pop up. A few seconds later, the engineers said over the radio, "It's all done."

Alan restrained himself from celebrating. "Great job, Stuart. Fucking great job. Thank you."

The tide was picking up, and the *California* was having to move her engines up through the revs to stay in place. Alan freed the hawsers to the machine. It floated backwards a few feet, shivered, and stayed in place. The anchor chains were holding.

James said to Alan, "Stuart's done well."

"Rather him than me."

"Think we'll be able to fire it up today?"

Professional pride held Alan back. The habit of caution. Not putting himself at the mercy of promises. "Mm. Six hours to let this tide go through. If we get the checks done, and everything's okay, we can maybe catch it coming back the other way."

Nine p.m. The team were tired. The northern summer evening painted the sea in shimmering tones of pink and yellow. The grass on Eday was going silvery. The checks were done. Far off and unseen, the moon flew around its track, pulling at the ocean beneath them.

A new tide began to run. They saw the water begin to move, almost imperceptibly and then with gathering force. The twin golden blades on each turbine began to turn. On one of Alan's screens, a chart of power generation flicked up off the zero line and rose steadily. They were pulling electricity from the sea. Another screen showed the angle of the blades already adjusting infinitesimally to match the current. And on the monitor showing the bulb sitting on a table on Eday, the light clicked on.

Alan said, "Oh my God."

A spontaneous, self-forgetful roar from the team. Hugging. Exhaustion and relief. Mary-Rose cried and said, "I don't know why I'm crying."

Alan wasn't celebrating. Amid the ruckus, he was bent over the screens, watching, but he was filled up with delight. James was beyond all strategy and striving, as if he were just a bubble borne on the tide. Roland thought: Goodbye. Goodbye, my lovelies.

But then the long yellow machine bucked painfully in the water, like a tethered beast speared in the heart. The power chart dropped to zero. The readings from the turbine sensors cut out. And, after a flicker, every screen went dead.

IX

It wasn't the twin blades. Nor the eddies coming off Muckle Green Holm. It was the cable.

Another strange underwater effect. As the tide ran past it, the cable began to whip around in circles, like a vertical skipping rope, with one end fixed to the seabed and the other attached to the machine on the surface. The cable whipped around, faster and faster, until it shattered.

The long metal eel actually burst. There was practically nothing to salvage. The fragments Stuart found were no larger than a fist. James kept a jagged lump on his desk as a paperweight, as a reminder that he should have known better than to think, for those few seconds, that he'd made it. Another lesson in humility, in patience. He asked himself how many more there were going to be.

The problem could be handled. Alan insisted it wasn't even that complex. It would just take time – months – for the cable-rollers in Hamburg to make a replacement. Roland lost his temper with them on the phone, which didn't help.

Roland texted ahead from the *California* to make sure the families in Kirkwall didn't greet them with celebrations. As they motored unspeaking back to the dock, it occurred to him that there were thirteen people on board. Maybe that was it. When they reached the hotel, the boyfriends and wives and children who'd been making fast friendships were now awkward with one another.

James and Roland avoided speaking alone in the days it took Alan to figure out exactly what had happened. Finally, James came to Roland's room as Roland was packing to go back to London. The wheelie suitcase was lying open like a book on the unmade bed. Roland was rolling up his shirts and pants to wedge them in.

James sat on the chair while Roland kept packing. After a while, he noticed, on the desk beside him, Roland's *Genki* book of elementary Japanese. He sighed and said, "So."

"So."

"How do you think they are?"

"Mary-Rose is totally fine. The others will be fine in a while."

"She's tough."

Neither wanted to start talking about what came next. James considered lines of argument until eventually he just said, "Don't go yet."

Roland shook his head. "Be fair. You asked me to stay, and I've given you a year already."

"True. True." James leaned forward and rested his forearms on his thighs. He stared at the stitching on his hiking boots. For a moment, he wondered how they were made. How did they preserve the internal shape of the boot when they stitched the upper layers to the sole?

Roland said, "I really don't want to kick you when you're down. I'm gutted, too. But you'll be okay. Alan says it's not that difficult to fix."

James nodded. "Do it for me? Just a few more months."

"Come *on*. How would you feel if I said 'Okay, now it's my turn. You've got to quit the company and come live in Japan with me for four years'?"

"True. Completely true. I just think if you leave right now, you'll break some of the team. They really love you. And if you quit just when we're in this trough, I think some of them won't come back from it."

Roland shook his head. Then shook it again, his anger gathering. "Honestly, mate. Can you let me pack?"

But on Monday, after James had waited abjectly for nearly three hours, not working but merely staring at his desk, Roland arrived at the office. James shot him looks of gratitude, which Roland ignored. After his relief had passed, James began to think Roland was laying it on a bit thick — he still hadn't understood that he'd never find anything better than this.

James had to let him sulk, and thank him for doing what was in his own best interest, while Roland played the martyr. Sometimes the patience you needed was unimaginable.

In the one big room of Kirkwall Airport, as they waited near a display of cuddly-toy puffins and Highland Park whisky, Alan asked James, "How's the funding round looking?" When he said "round", he felt he was using the jargon.

The stress on James's body, which he'd expected to abate after the launch, and which did abate for those carefree seconds when the machine was working, had tightened his muscles to a higher pitch. It hurt.

He held Alan's gaze and said, "All of them have pulled out."

"Fuck. Already?"

"Before the test. I decided not to tell anyone."

Alan took that in.

"After the Oyster and Pelamis, and now us, the funding is going to dry up for every marine energy company, if it hasn't already."

"It's already started, from what I've been hearing."

"Yup. We're in a comparatively strong position. We're lucky to have got the Thiel money quite recently. We've still got a good amount of cash on hand."

"So, you didn't let Roland spend it all on cabs and fancy offices?"

James smiled. "Exactly. If there's going to be a winter for marine energy, I think we have a good chance of surviving it."

Roland began studying Japanese in the office. An hour a day after lunch. Headphones plugged into his laptop, muttering under his breath, "*Arizona daigaku no gakusei desu* – I am a student at the University of Arizona."

When Mary-Rose asked why, he told her to ask James. She asked him. "Why is Roland learning Japanese? Are we opening a Japan office?" James told her it was a personal matter between him and Roland.

James didn't dare talk to Roland about anything that pointed more than a few hours into the future. And Roland didn't mention that, more than a decade after giving up on it, he was again applying to the JET Programme.

It bothered him to think that his only plan for life after the company was to rehash something from when he was younger. When he was young, the list of possible plans had seemed inexhaustible. But there could be no doubt that Japan would be a colourful and adventurous change from turbines and spreadsheets. And he'd had enough of drifting wherever he was carried. He was going to complete something hard. Really hard. Funny, actually: it was quite James of him.

Maybe he could get a Japanese girlfriend. Everyone said that was the best way to learn a language. Maybe they'd get married, and he'd stay in Japan and have cute little black-haired half-Japanese kids.

He quickly learned the phonetic scripts, *hiragana* and *katakana*, that he'd last skimmed over in the breeze-block annexe in Nagaur. Two vertical squiggles, like dangling eels: *ee*. An oval on its side, like a pig's nose: *noh*. He reread *The Chrysanthemum and the Sword*. The Japanese culture it described seemed less alien and seductive than it did back then. He found he had criticisms. Perhaps his ability to embrace the world was fading with his youth. He became impatient to leave.

While James waited for the new cable to be rolled, he withdrew into a cocoon of thought, as when McKinsey tried to sack him or the VC called his endeavour small-fry. And, as then, he re-emerged with something larger.

He and Roland flew up to Aberdeen. In the warehouse-workshop, the engineers were noodling around with a hydrogen electrolyser. Once the new cable was plugged in, and electricity was running ashore, they could start generating hydrogen. It would be a trickle. Even one heavy steel cylinder would take weeks to fill. They might be better off just filling a balloon – an elegant, airborne proof of concept. Roland said, "Yeah. Like the *Hindenburg*."

James sat on the pink buoy in Alan's messy cabin of an office and, while Alan and Roland listened, said, "Okay, my thinking is:

1. Every marine energy company but us is running out of cash.
2. Through sheer dumb luck, we have cash in the bank because our Thiel investment was quite recent.
3. This is our opportunity to buy every other marine energy company for a pittance and become the undisputed leader in the field."

Alan looked aghast.

James went on. "We let them go bankrupt so we're not liable for redundancy payments. Then we buy their designs and any useful kit. We hire their best engineers. Javier Ferrer at Pelamis for example."

Alan said, "And what happens to their other engineers?"

Just for a moment, James was profoundly bored of having his decisions resisted. If Alan was as good an engineer as James was a CEO, they wouldn't be waiting months for a new cable. But he just said, mollifyingly, "We can't afford to hire everybody. Those we take are going to be on survival salaries as it is."

"What if *we* go bankrupt because we've spent all our money?"

The stress-induced muscle clench had been spreading through James's body, tightening by degrees, like a guitar string. The ache had spread from his lower back into his right butt cheek and down his right thigh. It was painful to sleep on his side.

He wanted to tell Alan, *Then you can fuck off back to Subsea7*. But he nodded as if thoughtfully and said, "It will certainly bring us closer to bankruptcy. A lot closer. But it's when everybody's weak that you can seize the advantage. We absorb the others, and we'll have all the technology, all the know-how and all the talent. If we survive, we'll be unstoppable."

Alan sometimes felt like James lived in a megalomaniacal dreamworld. Very neutrally, he said, "Right now, though, right, we don't even actually have something that works."

James nodded and said, "Yes. Yes, I know."

When James took the keys to Pelamis's warehouse from Javier Ferrer, he felt like Caesar receiving the surrender of Vercingetorix. The gallant

Gaul, last to resist Caesar's army, threw down his weapons at Caesar's feet. Caesar had him taken to Rome and strangled for the crowd. James merely remembered what Javier had told *The Times*: "Many companies find the ocean conditions much more challenging than they expect", and, taking his keys, said, "Thanks."

Javier, a small, slight, red-bearded, canny Catalan in his fifties, catalogued the items of value in his warehouse and named which of his team were worth keeping. James realised that he liked him. Admired him even. Already Javier had suggestions for how to market their hydrogen. He was not, like Alan, an engineer to the bone. He'd captained his own ship. In googling him, James had discovered that *Ferrer* was Catalan for *smith*. As in ferrous. A good omen.

Javier told him that he'd been called to marine energy by a near-religious experience. He was swimming near the city of Vigo, in Galicia, when a rip current dragged him out of reach of land. The waves were so big that each one threw him forward, tirelessly, unendingly. As he waited to drown, his thoughts became detached. He began to understand that the ocean had inexhaustible strength. Each wave was like Poseidon's bicep, and another, and another. When he was rescued, he swore he would put that strength to use.

He took James down to Stromness harbour to see what had become of his machine. He hadn't had the money to tow the mechanical sea snake back to land. The Scottish government threatened to sue him for not disposing of it – for egregious pollution. So the Stromness port authority did him a favour and used it as scrap metal for their breakwater. The alternating yellow and red segments, which once had jinked up and down in the waves, were crumpled into the raw heap of rubble and boulders on the outer edge of the sea wall. Where boulders had been dropped on top, to prevent the mechanical carcase sliding into the sea, the steel had burst. Saltwater was inside the shell, gradually transforming the expensive hydraulic rams into rust.

They looked down on it from the sea wall, and James said, "I'm sorry."

"No, no." Javier shook his head. "Really . . . really . . ." An unexpected smile of great amusement opened up his face. "We were never going to get enough electricity out of it. This was the wrong path. Wave energy . . . it's too difficult. The motion kills machinery. Everything gets worn out or smashed. Tidal power is the future."

James thought: With people like this, and Mary-Rose, I can move the world. Javier might make a better head of engineering than Alan. Maybe. It was premature. James needed to watch him for a while. Javier was not a follower; he would try to impose himself on the company. That would cost stress and effort to restrain. But better a strong beast you had to fight to keep in harness than an obstinate little mule with no imagination who only ever said that it couldn't be done.

As they bought up the bankrupt remnants of the Oyster and two other companies, James and Roland began to see themselves as a rescue vessel, pulling engineers and blueprints from the wrecks. But even though they saved only the most talented, it soon meant there wasn't enough money to go around. At the end of each month, James saw the payroll accountants cut off an ever-larger chunk of the cash they'd salted away.

The muscle clench in his right side was still getting worse. In the mornings, his right Achilles was so stiff that his foot couldn't bend and he had to walk sideways down the stairs. He'd been inured to some degree against the imminence of bankruptcy. But now there were twice as many people to support, and the machine had only worked for eighty-four seconds.

One lunchtime, Roland was eating a banh mi in the communal area under the faux-graffitied slogan *Do What You Love*. Mary-Rose came over with her Tupperware and, determined not to be shy, said bluntly, "Can I sit with you?"

"Sure. I'd love that. Of course." Roland stood up and ushered her to the pod-shaped chair next to his. "What have you got for lunch?"

"Umm." The question felt personal to her. "Just some rice, leeks, spring onion, some soy and sesame sauce."

"Looks delicious."

"So, um, what do you have?"

"A kind of Vietnamese baguette. There's a place just by the Tube. Want a taste?"

"I'm good."

They ate, and Roland tried unsuccessfully to start a conversation. She didn't follow any of his leads. After a while, he just let her eat, her asymmetric wave of dyed red hair dangling down towards her lunchbox. A silence emerged, and stretched and stretched, until she said, "Can I, like, ask you something? Off the record."

Roland hastily swallowed a mouthful of bread and pâté. "Go for it."

"Am I, like, going to lose my job? Because I need to start registering with tutoring and waitressing agencies if I am. I would ask James but he's so, like, *Onward, Christian soldiers*."

Roland laughed. "You're so right. That's exactly what he's like. He *wants* to have a long, uncomfortable journey to the Middle East and then, when he gets there, the more Saracens waiting to kill him the better." He shook his head. "The man's deeply disturbed. But happy I guess. Anyway, no, you're not going to lose your job."

Roland didn't know whether she would or not. But waffling about something else should help her worry diminish. Mary-Rose warily said, "Okay. Well, that's good. But are you sure? Because we're spending all our money on hiring these new people. And it's not that I don't think we have a responsibility to hire as many as we can. But I do the payments, so I know how much we have in our bank account. And we don't have anything coming in, do we?" Mary-Rose had since childhood been able to read the signs of financial mismanagement: the sense of dwindling, the assurances it would be fine and the sudden stop.

Roland smiled generously. "Am I sure? It's literally my company. People always forget that. After you've been here a bit longer, you'll see that these crises come around every year. That's what it's like in a start-up. But . . ." – he raised his palms in resignation – "what can you do?"

"Okay."

"Do you want me to add a month to your notice period? So you'd get paid for longer if you got made redundant?"

"Er, yeah. Sure. That would be great."

"How about two months?" He smiled.

Now she smiled too. "Ha. Okay. But that also means I have to stick around for ages if I quit, right?"

Roland shrugged. "It's up to you. If you want the extra months, just let me know, and I'll get the lawyers to change it."

"Okay. Thank you."

He could see he'd managed to reassure her. Her oppressive anxiety had lifted somewhat. But it had been transferred to him instead. What if Mary-Rose *did* lose her job?

One evening soon after, when it was just them, James told Roland, "We're going to have to cut the team's salaries. It'll give us an extra two or three months." Roland froze, and James went on. "I haven't been taking mine anyway and can put that saving back in the pot. But I'll cut mine back to zero officially as well so that the team sees and we save on PAYE. You should keep yours because you need it to save up for travelling."

Roland said, "Mate, don't drag me into this stuff. If you can't afford me any more, I can go today."

"Okay."

"You should know I've applied for the JET Programme."

"The Japanese teaching thing?"

"Yup."

"Okay."

They sat unspeaking in their glass cubicle. James said, "I know you've stayed longer than you wanted to, for me."

"Not just for you. For the others as well."

"Right."

Roland softened. "I'm sorry. I really am. But I kind of think you've got to ask yourself is it worth it, living like this? Always stressed out of your mind."

"I do see what you mean. But it's only for a few months. I heard we're going to get the EU money: half a million up front and the other half million once we demonstrate some things we can definitely demonstrate. But they're so fucking slow at actually handing it over."

"Hm."

"You're right, of course you're right. It's always just a few more months."

Roland said, "I feel like you're going to ask me to do something."

"One last thing while you wait to hear from JET."

Roland tried to speak, and James spoke over him. "I know. I'm sorry. It's always one last thing."

"Before you start, I don't want you to cut Mary-Rose's salary. She can't afford it. You can take it out of mine."

"So you'll stay till you hear from JET?"

Roland was in a groove of learning vocab and saving up. Unlike the previous extensions, this one was good for him. "Yeah, I will. Ask me your thing."

"Can you please talk to Alan and persuade him to accept a pay cut? If he accepts it, the others will too."

"The deal with Alan has always been that giving up his job at Subsea7 doesn't have an impact on his lifestyle."

"I know. But his son isn't in school any more. No tuition fees at uni in Scotland. And the oil price is in the shitter again so he can't just go back to Subsea7."

Roland didn't say anything, and James watched him. Roland said, "If you try to bully him about the oil price and his son, he'll fight you or quit. The reality is that he's put too much of himself into this now to not do whatever he can to get it finished. If you just, like, ask him for help, he'll help."

"You see. You're so much better at this stuff than me. And Alan finds me annoying."

"You *are* annoying."

James knew he would do it.

To steer Alan's emotions, Roland had to let them mesh with his own. He felt like Robert De Niro at the end of *Heat*, turning his car away from escape and re-entering the human tangle.

He talked to Alan about his family, listening and sympathising, mirroring Alan's feelings back at him. Alan said his kids hadn't missed out on much because of his decision to work in a start-up. Some foreign holidays. Some more expensive crap they didn't need. Catriona didn't believe in spoiling them either. And it would be something for them, too, wouldn't it, to be able to say that their dad invented the tidal turbine.

Richard, once he'd finished his maths degree, wanted to go into finance. Alan laughed with his mouth shut and it came out his nose. "I mean, who do I think I even am, too good for finance? But it's not exactly what you'd choose for your kids, is it? I was kind of hoping he might do a couple of years of maths – solid subject – and then transfer to engineering. But if hedge funds are what he really wants to do . . ."

"You could talk to James about it. He really, like, believes in that stuff. Efficient capital allocation, more prosperity and whatever."

Alan waved that away and spoke about his granddad, who'd been a crofter. "He was still farming when I was a kid, just near Peterculter. He had these big swollen hands from working in the cold. He couldn't hold a knife and fork properly, or a pen. And I mean . . . that must have been it, like, for practically everybody in my family for thousands of years, ever since they invented agriculture. Maybe a couple of guys pulled onto the boats or into the army. And then, for my dad's generation, there was university. The first step up away from the land. There's that thing they say about teachers: if you can do something . . ."

Roland couldn't quite remember it either. "If you can do something, do it, and if you can't . . . be a teacher?"

"Something like that. But he could have done anything if he'd been born in a fancy family in London. But apart from farming, school was all he knew much about. And then after him, me. Lots of doors open. Engineering. Being here for the oil. Even with what I've saved and what I earn with you guys, me and Catriona have got more money than our parents really understand. If they knew what Catriona's clothes cost . . ." He laughed. "And then after me a fucking hedge fund. Well." He sighed. "Maybe I just don't understand it." He was trying not to dislike it. "At least he'll earn way more than I have."

Out of consideration for Roland, he interrupted himself and said, "Except if the company takes off in a big way, obviously."

Roland didn't care. He didn't want to know Alan's dad's story, or Richard's. But he asked, "What about Kirsten?"

"Oh, she's on a good track; she wants to be a doctor. She literally wants to be a cardiac surgeon and do transplants." Alan began to smile, and made a joke he'd clearly made before: "Maybe she can do mine if I don't slow down the chips a bit. But they're grafters, both of them. Good Scots kids." He grinned at Roland. "A few less pennies in their dad's bank account won't hurt them."

James could not, in asking Alan to take a pay cut, have made him feel strong, magnanimous and proud of his children. Roland did it with concealed distaste, like kissing someone he'd already decided to break up with.

Alan said he would let the rest of the team know and even, as Roland was leaving, gave him a manly side-by-side shoulder-hug. "Dinnae fash. The cable's nearly done."

Then finally, finally, the new cable was ready. James and Roland watched the wavelets from the crowded and swaying rear deck of the *California* as Stuart, somewhere down below, plugged it in.

There were now so many engineers that the tug rode low in the water. James had studied headshots to make sure he could identify them; beneath each photo he wrote down the ideas this engineer had brought.

When the turbines began to turn, and the light bulb in their corrugated-iron cubicle of a power station came on, there was no jubilation. Instead, a learned wariness. One problem solved; onto the next one, like a computer game with levels stretching to infinity.

Alan shook hands with the team. The new engineers' handshakes were awkward, undeserved, like unused substitutes collecting a cup winner's medal. Javier Ferrer mimed doffing his hat to James and Roland. "Congratulations. If it doesn't destroy itself into pieces, you now have the world's number one marine energy machine."

James said, "By default."

Javier's accent blended the Ys and Js at the beginning of words, landing on an imaginary phoneme somewhere between the two. He said, "Not yust by default. Jou have built a machine where there was no machine before."

"*We* have, Javier. It belongs to all of us."

Javier nodded deeply, not wanting to argue with a fellow leader's necessary fictions.

Down inside the massive heaving grey-green seas, where the sunlight from the surface couldn't reach, the golden blades turned in the dark. When the tide ran from the Atlantic to the North Sea, they spun clockwise. At slack water, the rotors drifted idly for an hour. When the tide ran back into the Atlantic, the rotors spun the other way. Gyroscopic precession did not wrench them free of the machine. The tumbling, swerving flux coming from Muckle Green Holm didn't knock them off their cadence. The angles of the blades adjusted themselves continuously, incrementally, to match the rising and falling power of each tide — and beyond that, to match the positions of the moon and sun. The little light bulb on the table blazed for the length of each tide. At slack water, it grew dim and went off.

Many more things broke, but none were existential. The tiny motors controlling the angle of the blades fritzed out. It was too much for them to be in constant slow motion. They had to adjust once per second rather than continuously.

The stress on James lessened. His body relaxed a little. And it was at this point, as the extremes of tension retreated, that the electro-organic machine he inhabited went haywire. The first sign was that he woke up at night uncomfortable with thirst. His tongue was leathery. He stumbled down the flights of stairs to the night-time kitchen, starting to hurry as he came awake and the thirst grew sharper. By the time he was at the sink, he was rushing, fumbling with the glass. It was like pouring water into sand; the first few glasses made no difference. He drank and drank until his belly distended, and soon he was pissing pints of clear liquid.

Standing over the sink in the solitary and magical hours, he thought about the girl who drowned after taking ecstasy. Leah Betts. Every year at school they heard about her, in between chlamydia and stranger danger. She took a pill and, believing herself thirsty, drank so much water it killed her. He tried to remember how many litres it was. The amount he was sucking down did feel unhealthy.

During the day, these late-night worries seemed unimportant. He was exhausted, maybe more than usual. He could barely climb the stairs at WeWork. But tiredness was normal. And he was losing weight for once, which was positive. Quite quickly in fact.

He was now planning Roland's departure. He would buy him out, and Roland would head to Japan with James's savings. Finding the advantage even in this, James would then have near-total control of the company. He would no longer need Roland's agreement to overrule Alan.

One evening, after dinner with his parents, with his dad telling exasperated anecdotes about faculty politics, he went upstairs to read about hydrogen electrolysers in bed. As the hours went by, he realised he didn't feel well. A kind of lethargic wooziness was gathering in his limbs and behind his eyes. The printed text on the catalyser prospectus was going fuzzy.

He must be getting a flu. Influenza – not unlike tidal energy – the influence of the planets. Maybe a thought for his next pitch: we are the good version of flu. Maybe not. He'd get some Day Nurse on the way in tomorrow. He lay back on his pillow, feeling even woozier and heavier. He became uncomfortably aware of his heart beating, and soon after that he passed out.

When he flicked back into consciousness a couple of hours later, he knew he was going to die. The overhead light was still burning, but the room was blurry. He tried to sit up, and his head flopped over to one side, as if he were tranquillised. The dark blob of his phone was on the bedside table. He groped for it with his left hand and managed to pull it onto his chest. He couldn't make out the screen. He closed one eye and then the other to try and focus. It remained a fuzz. His eyes opening and closing in turn, he tried to call the house's landline. His parents were downstairs. But his fingers were clumsy and growing slower. He didn't know what buttons he'd already pressed.

With gathering panic, he gave up on the phone. He tried to shout, but only a groan came out. His parents were two storeys away. He tried again, and his body coughed, even that an effort. He managed to whisper, "Help. Help."

Adrenalin helped him move. He rolled out of bed, hitting his face against the edge of the table on the way down. The pain could be attended to later. He began crawling on his elbows across the soft carpet, sinking into it. The light burned steadily, and the familiar room was quiet. The door was only a few feet in front of him. But he couldn't get there. As his arms and legs shut down, his purpling face came to a stop on the carpet.

His inner alarms were ringing freely now. He experienced terror. The last of his self-control gave way. He tried to scream. But like a paraplegic all he could do was blink at the brushed cream fibres in the carpet. His exhausted eyelid blinked, and blinked, and stopped.

X

The first thing he saw when he came to, six days later, in the Royal Free in Belsize Park, was Roland talking on his phone. He was in a room where everything was wipe-clean. Beige plastic. Lino floor. Moulded handles for the infirm to cling to. Tubes of various thicknesses dangled out of a wall. James was so grateful not to be dead that salt water trickled out of the corners of his eyes and ran down his temples to the pillow.

He saw Roland notice that he was awake and flinch into action. He pressed a button on the wall, put down his phone and hurried over to take James's hand. Roland's boyish face loomed over him. They'd never held hands before.

Roland said, "Hey, buddy. Can you hear me? Are you okay?"

James hadn't used his voice in nearly a week. He rasped, "I can hear you. Am I okay?"

Roland went into exaggerated stiff-upper-lip mode. "Oh, yeah, you're absolutely fine. Never better. Fit as a fiddle." The manner slipped. "Actually, you *are* fine. Ish. You've got diabetes. You've been in a coma. And you've also got two black eyes from where you hit your face on the bedside table. But you're not, like, going to die."

James was starting to get readings from his body's innumerable sensors. "My face doesn't hurt."

"It looks like you've lost a fight."

"Okay."

"You're meant to say 'You should see the other guy.'"

James raised a smile.

Roland wanted to say something extraordinary, to name what he'd felt while watching James unconscious. But he himself didn't know what that was. So, in the end, he just said, "I was worried about you." And out of nowhere he had to clench his face to prevent tears.

"But I'm basically okay?"

"Oh, yeah, sorry. They said you should be okay now. It's just lucky your dad found you. He'll tell you himself, but he said he had, like, a premonition. Like his parent-sense started tingling. He went upstairs to say goodnight, and you were face down on the carpet. But he doesn't usually come to say goodnight, does he?"

"No."

"I need to text them you're awake. We've been doing shifts."

He let go of James's hand to take his phone from the bedside table, and James missed his touch.

Now that he was awake, the nurses began hustling him to leave. They said he'd get deconditioned if he stayed in hospital too long. They made him walk up and down the corridor and assessed his shakiness. In truth, once his muscles had unstiffened, he wasn't shaky at all. His brain was fuzzy, like the day after a lot of drinking. And his body felt depleted. Even the four steps up to the next stretch of corridor tired his legs. But it didn't seem he was going to collapse again.

The nurses said he could go home once he'd spoken to the consultant. He didn't especially want to leave. Being there was peaceful, out of time, like the recession or those days in school when the teacher was sick and the substitute just had you watch *L'Auberge Espagnole*. Meals arrived regularly. The nurses came to check he'd been to the loo. He was just inputs and outputs.

At night, when he was alone in the over-warm, humming, beeping, never-fully-dark hospital room, under the thin sheet, he smiled. It had been years since he went on holiday. As for the diabetes, he read on the NHS website that it was manageable. And management he could do. Blood-sugar readings. Insulin. Keep the blood sugar in the safe range. He'd have the best-managed diabetes in England.

Only once, unable to sleep, sweating by himself in this institutional box, with nothing colourful or human but some flowers his mum had brought and a bag of his clothes, did he start to feel low. So much striving – he'd given his twenties, in full — and this was where he'd got to. He remembered the night in a Milton Keynes hotel room when he'd got his finals results. More than ten years since then and still nothing accomplished. In his weakness, he wished he were back in education, where the mark scheme was printed out, and all you had to beat was other people.

In the morning, he felt the first stirrings of a need to get back to work.

His family and Roland came in turns, like the sequence of shows on daytime TV. He and Cleo hadn't spoken so much in years. Her husband Rogier had moved from the university to the Red Bull Formula One team, doing data science. She said, "He's being quite spiky with me. But the actual worrisome thing is that, even though right now he's finding it really stressful and difficult, I kind of suspect he'll start getting addicted to the stress." She raised her eyebrows at James.

"What?"

"I don't want him in here, too."

"You think this is stress-related?"

"Isn't it?"

"Actually, it seems there's a genetic component. Could be you in here next."

"Oh, yeah? Did you get that off Wikipedia?"

"Seriously. Nobody knows the triggers. Could be anything."

She said, "You're the expert," as if to suggest that she wouldn't fight him in his enfeebled condition.

When his parents came, his mum told him to scooch over. She slid onto the bed beside him, resting her back against the wall. A flash of recollection: bedtime stories; she and him sitting on the floor in his room, their backs against the radiator, him cuddled into her side, and the book with its magic symbols open on her knees.

His dad was too annoying to tolerate. He moved nervously from chair to window, from window to opening the cupboards, bombasting about his parental intuition. "I've never believed in extrasensory perception, but I suppose I have to now. I haven't come up to wish you goodnight in, what, a *decade*? I *sensed* that something was awry. There's that Roald Dahl short story about a yogi who trains a man to look through playing cards in casinos. Perhaps I could use my gift for something like that. Something lucrative."

And all the while, he looked so scared, and so old, that it hurt James to see him. James tried to calm him down. But he himself was still fuzzy and fatigued. It cost him so much energy that, eventually, an understanding passed between him and his mum, and she took Arthur away.

Roland was the most restful visitor. Instead of hanging around for hours, he came by two or three times a day, to bring lunch or be present for test results. He brought a phone charger, tracksuits, boxers and T-shirts from Uniqlo, and minor company business he claimed to need James's help with. He appointed himself the supervisor of James's care, drinking tea with the nurses and asking them to chivvy the much-delayed consultant.

He became pleasingly angry when Alan sent some flowers with a box of Maltesers. He rang Alan, overriding James's half-hearted instructions not to do it. James watched indulgently as Roland broke with his usual friendly deference. "Hiya. I'm just in the hospital. Did you, um, did you send James a box of Maltesers?"

There was a pause in which Roland nodded and nodded, his mouth bunching up. He said, "But we're not doctors, are we? Maybe it's not, but maybe it fucking is. I mean, Jesus Christ, he's got *diabetes*, and you're sending him chocolate. We might as well give him polonium biscuits. What do you think happens to the company if the CEO's killed by a box of chocolates?" James laughed from his bed.

The only time Roland moved quietly into the background was when Eleni visited with her toddler, George. Roland had only met her once before, at the Red Lion off Jermyn Street when he first came back from Nagaur. He perched on the windowsill and wrote emails on his phone; he'd still be here when she was gone.

She looked different. Her black hair was not straightened but loose, a kinked cascade breaking on her shoulders and straggling into her tanned face. Her features had lost their gym-trained sharpness; her cheekbones had filled in; she looked happy. She also seemed somehow more Greek. Before, she'd been as international as an airport, the Greek stuff no more than local styling — a bowl of tzatziki in the business lounge. But now, with the hair and the skin and the stories about her family, Roland saw that she was not just a shiny Londoner.

She couldn't be still for more than a few seconds. Black-haired little George — his father was French, but the hair had been inherited — staggered around like a paunchy little drunk, lifting his chubby arms as if wading into water. Eleni had to launch from her chair to stop him pulling a tube out of the wall, and again as he licked the frame of James's bed.

She tried to strategise the diabetes — treatments, scenarios, time cost — but kept having to pull a complaining George up onto her lap or push his hands out of her face or rummage in her huge, pink-patterned cloth bag for his carrot puffer sticks, or shush him when he toppled backwards onto his nappy-padded bottom.

She kept forgetting whether James's diabetes was Type 1 or Type 2 and what the difference was. That was unlike her. It was as if she'd graduated into a further stage of life and could only with difficulty keep her mind on the subjects that to them seemed important.

James had thought to ask her for ideas about investors, but he let that slip away unvoiced. Instead, he asked how she was, and the words flowed freely down an evidently habitual course. When she first had George, her parents didn't care that she and Damien weren't married yet, just engaged. But they'd spent the summer at her parents' place on Spetses, and her dad, also George, who was quite old-fashioned, had begun making comments about not wanting little George to be a bastard forever. Which made her so angry she'd cried in front of her parents, which made it worse. At least little George didn't understand yet. She hated her dad speaking like that, but —

Little George tried to put his finger in her mouth. She spat it out like a bothersome fly and said, "I just don't have the bandwidth to plan a three-hundred-person wedding. My parents have completely forgotten what it's like to have a job. You can't just spend six months organising an event. Shell have been great and let me take some extra time unpaid. But poor Damien was commuting from London to Spetses for the weekends. When I finally get it organised, you should obviously come."

She glanced at Roland. "You both should. But if it's, say, next summer, I might want to have another baby before that. I don't have that many years before I'm forty. And if they think I'm going to spend months organising a wedding just to look like a sweaty pig in lipstick, with milk stains on my dress, they can seriously go fuck themselves."

Little George started trying to clamber up the moulded plastic bars on James's bed. Eleni said, "He wants to get in with you," as if that were a powerful compliment. James pretended to be pleased when she hoiked up the toddler like a kettle bell and plonked him down on the covers.

Not knowing what to do with a baby, he said, "Hello, little George. Thank you for coming to visit. If you happen to develop an interest in marine energy when you grow up, I'd be delighted to give you an internship. Mary-Rose will complain that that's nepotism, but I'll just have to let her tell me off." He didn't look at Eleni as he said, "She doesn't understand yet that old friends are very important."

Little George tried to stick his finger in James's mouth. James pushed the pudgy hand away, and Eleni swooped in. "No, no, no, sweetie. Uncle James doesn't want that. We'd better get going anyway." She swung George up onto her arm. "He's getting some jabs this afternoon, so I've got to dose him with Calpol beforehand. It's like trying to tranquillise a bullock. Roland, would you mind giving me a hand with the buggy?"

Once they were out in the corridor, as she kneeled to restrain the wriggling, resistant toddler, she looked up and said, "You've got to keep him in bed for as long as you can. He'll try to just get straight back into it, and he's got to recover. How's the company?"

Roland felt unexpectedly defensive. But James trusted her, so he said, "They're kind of freaking out. They're realising that if James goes down, the person in charge is me."

Eleni said, "Hm." She went to speak but just repeated, "Hm." And then, "But you've been with the company from the start. You must know everything, don't you?"

He said, "*I'm* not freaking out." And, stung by this, he gave away, "Actually I've had a call from the Scottish government. They've noticed the industry is fucked and want to bail it out. But we've bought the whole industry, so they're going to have to bail *us* out. I haven't told him because he'll get too excited."

"That's great! *Roland!*"

He saw her relax.

"What kind of bailout? Loans, equity? What are they thinking? You can't sell the company to Nicola Sturgeon while James is in hospital."

Little George emitted a cry of triumph and they saw that he'd managed to get an arm out of his straps. She bent down to restrain him again, and her hair tumbled into his face. George grabbed two fistfuls as hard as he could. Once Eleni had freed herself, she turned back to Roland and said, "I'm sorry I can't help more right now." She gestured helplessly at little George, who was sucking his thumb contentedly. "I'm actually pregnant as well."

"Amazing," said Roland, unmoved. "Congratulations."

"Thanks. You've just got to hold things together for a couple of months. He's got to recover properly. If he thinks this isn't a stress thing, he's kidding himself."

The consultant was someone Roland recognised. A half Sri Lankan woman with a Bristol accent, she'd been a couple of years ahead of them at Oxford. There was less Bristol in her voice than back then. After a few minutes of "Which college were you in?" and "Does that mean you know Danni Marquez?" she got back on to her professional rails. "So, James. You have Type 1 diabetes."

Roland interrupted. "I've been telling him he needs to do some exercise."

James, for maybe the first time since Roland had known him, looked embarrassed. But the consultant, Payal, said, "It's not correlated with weight. That's Type 2. What's happened is that your pancreas has stopped producing insulin."

"But it would help, wouldn't it?" James let Roland speak for him.

"Ye-es, probably." She looked at her notes rather than at James. "The numbers, I've got them here. Yes, the BMI is 28, which is above the healthy range. And, yes, generally being in good health will help."

"If someone sent him a box of Maltesers, would you say it's practically an assassination attempt?"

She smiled. "If you ate the whole box . . ." And the fun died for her. "I know it's a big change. There's a lot of adjusting after diagnosis."

James nodded. It didn't seem that complicated.

She said, "What was your question? Yes, if you ate a whole box, lying in bed, what would happen? As a one-off, really, not much. You'd have an acute glucose spike. You might get a bit woozy. But if your blood glucose *stays* elevated – really this is more of an issue for Type 2 . . ."

She'd spent too many sad afternoons examining the sugar-blinded and the obese amputees with their stinking black stumps. Sometimes she wondered whether it was too late to find another branch of medicine. So much of this was barely medicine at all – it was about how able the patients were to watch themselves, every hour of every day, always. She wouldn't be there when the patient decided whether to stay healthy or not. But she put the frighteners on him, so he could never say he hadn't been told, "But if your blood glucose is *chronically* elevated – you'll burn out your nerve endings with sugar, which means you go blind, your feet will rot, your kidneys will fail."

James and Roland weren't smiling any more.

"And if you leave an acute spike untreated, and keep shovelling more sugar in, which is basically what you were doing because you didn't know your pancreas had stopped making insulin, you'll go into full-blown ketoacidosis, which used to be almost universally fatal."

Roland wanted to make a joke about how the Maltesers were going to be fatal for Alan if he had anything to do with it but couldn't get there. James said, "That's what my coma was?"

"Correct. But really, for Type 1, now you know you have it, letting your blood sugar go too low is the bigger worry. If you overestimate how much insulin you need, inject too big an amount, and don't have some sweets to bring yourself back up . . ." She sighed. "A hypo. Seizures, collapse, coma, death. That can be very fast."

While they took that in, she tried to pull her own mood up out of its slump. "*However*, with proper management, that should never happen. All of this is completely avoidable. Your quality of life, your life expectancy, should be unaffected, as long as you keep your glucose at the safe level."

James said, "And that's for life, isn't it?"

"Yes. It's for life. Unless you're planning to discover a cure for diabetes."

After James reluctantly left the hospital, Roland constructed and ran an elaborate con all around him, like Paul Newman's in *The Sting*, with fake meetings, fictitious charts, and conversations acted out by a cast of dozens. He coached his talentless actors — Mary-Rose, Alan, Javier and the rest of the team — into Potemkin discussions on the company finances or the latest telemetry from the rotors, in which every problem was soluble, the money was stretching further than hoped, and unavoidable little struggles were rationally overcome.

When he, on an all-hands video call, had explained his plan to keep James safely swaddled in a loving illusion, the team were sullen, restless and unconvinced. Those in Orkney were sitting in a wedge thirty-two engineers deep, to be inside the camera's field. Javier scooted forward awkwardly on his chair to get in range of the microphone. His auburn face filled the screen, blocking the lights behind him and making the video go dark then abruptly adjust.

"We are all very sorry for Yames. But when I had Pelamis, if the engineers have kept secret from me the progress of the machine . . ." He shook his head as if this were beyond the limits of decency.

Roland nodded. "Yes. I get that. I don't like it either." He lied or, rather, told the truth as they would understand it: "The thing is" — he put on a grave demeanour – "James's consultant said if he jumps back in at full speed, full stress, it could, like, actually kill him."

That shut Javier up. But as he went back to his place, he muttered something the microphone didn't catch. The others were murmuring. Alan spoke up from his position in the front row. "Okay, Roland. He's obviously very sick."

"He was in a coma for a week."

Alan grimaced. "We'll obviously help him however we can. But how . . . If he's out . . . There are decisions that need to get made. If we're going to make hydrogen, we've got to buy an electrolyser. That is, if we're still even doing the hydrogen thing. Are we? And an electrolyser would eat most of the cash we have left. It's like, are we going to buy it or not?"

It was a bad sign that Alan was talking about cash in front of everyone. It would make them think this company was doomed like the others. And this electrolyser question was new to Roland, who said, "Okay. Leave it with me, and I'll see if I can figure something out."

"How long's this going to go on for?"

"Two months. That's what she said. A two-month rest. It's not long."

"If we wait that long . . . Roland, it's not like Amazon Prime, where you order an electrolyser and it comes the next day. Have you even looked at the options?"

Roland felt he might lose them. "Okay. Okay, listen. Don't worry. We're not going to do anything drastic. Like, nothing drastic. Just keep things ticking forwards until James is back. In the meantime, with the electrolyser, give me a minute to catch up."

Alan sat back in his chair and folded his arms over his paunch.

Roland thought of playing vulnerable and appealing for help. He could say, I don't know how to do this either. But intuition told him not to. "Actually, there's some good news as well, which we can't tell him yet. The Scottish government have got in touch with, um, me. They want marine energy to develop in Scotland and not in Denmark or wherever. So they're trying to come up with a way of giving us a heap of cash." He grinned. "Not bad, eh?"

More murmuring. The mood lightened a fraction.

"And, don't worry, we'll set it up so that when James is ready he can check it over, make whatever changes he wants, sign the paperwork and, honestly, for once in his damn life, say thank you very much Roland for organising millions of quids for us."

There were some smiles.

"Right now, though, we just need to make sure he's okay. I mean, Jesus, we need him. Without him, Alan would still be at Subsea7, the machine would still just be a little model in a tub, and most of you guys would be looking for a job."

To his relief, Alan took the hint, and helped. "That's true. Not that long ago, my wee model was still made of wood, and the turbines still had three blades." There were laughs among the engineers. "And now we're the number-one marine energy company in the world. I think we can probably look after it for him for a couple of months."

The team acquiesced to his plan for James, but didn't like it. And if they didn't like it, they would screw it up. He fed them their lines for the staged meetings but watched like a director helpless in the audience as they gave the game away time and again with halting dialogue, blatant dissatisfaction or, in the case of Charlie, a wink.

By some miracle, James didn't notice. Perhaps his brain was more seriously fried than anyone but Roland suspected. Another secret to keep. Meanwhile, Roland was having to hustle Charlie onto the back stairs for a private chat. He threw an arm around Charlie's shoulders and, as if laughing, said, "That wink! Jesus Christ! I thought we were so busted. You utter piss-taker." Charlie felt the pang Roland wanted him to: he'd nearly sunk them all.

To coax everyone on the team, each according to their personality, required some cajoling here, some reassuring there, a principled discussion with Mary-Rose, a gag, a story, a hug, a connection for each of them. They needed him to make them feel not spooked and unsteady but affectionate, amused, proud, in on a wonderful act of cherishment.

Never had he thought so intensively about the mood and character of everyone around him. Unlike James, he didn't feel separate, like a captain looking down at a busy deck. Rather, it was as if they were grafted like symbiotes into his side, so that he could sense their hesitancies even as they sensed them themselves. His mood became in part an aggregate of theirs, in an ever-fluctuating double consciousness. As he sat in the cab to the office; as he peed; as he bit, untasting, into his lunchtime sandwich, he rewound through conversations to extract their meaning.

It went both ways: for them to believe, he had to believe. That all things would come good, that everyone would be rewarded, that to be in on the ground floor of what they were building was a great stroke of luck — of good luck. And he *could* believe. He had a talent for it.

He didn't try to reason with them. He took them for intense chats in the stairwell; he walked with them along the docks in Aberdeen, past the industrial ships and the Subsea7 town office; he drank with them in Aberdeen's horrible pubs, severally and in groups; he rode with them on the *California*; he let them tell him about their childhoods, their marriages, the pain of seeing their previous companies fail. He listened to their suggestions for the device, looking not at the diagrams but at them. He heard them; he watched them; sometimes his lips moved as they spoke.

And he insisted with every tool of his personality that they see the situation as he saw it, that they feel as he felt or as he convinced himself he did. As he worked on them, they began to tentatively sense — not as with James, that they were led by a man of admirable vision and ability — but that they were in this together, and that they wanted themselves to succeed.

Roland had never extended himself this far. The faster his thoughts ran, revving towards manic, the more power he found he had over them, a kind of magical felicity, like a hydrofoil that at high speeds begins to lift itself above the water and run faster still. When he saw someone starting to come around, turning from a fearful wobbler into one who would do their work steadfastly and well, who reliably played their part in the meetings staged for James, and whose contagious, destabilising need for reassurance had been transmuted into cautious confidence, Roland felt himself grow stronger still.

He began to appreciate Alan and Mary-Rose, who needed none of this but helped him to rally the others: Alan for the company; Mary-Rose out of instinct, and loyalty to James.

James himself also needed Roland's care. He kept trying to chat about blood sugar and nutritionists. Roland had the team's salary reductions to finalise, the resulting discontent to soak up, a call to make to Nicola Sturgeon's office and a covert trip to Orkney to fit in. No wonder James had been stressed. But Roland had to lounge in the WeWork communal area and listen to James warble on about how carbs converted into glucose. He kept expecting James to snap back to normal, but he seemed to enjoy babying himself for a while. While Roland tried to draft emails in his head, James told him, "I was thinking that I'd get into running. But I just think, before long, I'd be tracking my PBs and all that. I'd just turn it into work."

"Good self-knowledge."

"So my plan is to do sports I can never get good at. And rotate them every six months just in case I get attached. I've signed up for trampolining. And after that I'm thinking Zumba."

Roland said, "Huh" – deadpan – "nice idea." And then, "Also, um, we've decided that for the rest of these two months, you're not going to be allowed in the building outside nine to five. And I'm not going to answer any messages. Like, at all. Obviously, that's going to be hard for you. But the most important thing you can do for the mission right now is recover."

James smiled and said, "I must endure the unendurable."

"Sure."

At least like this Roland could get some work done.

He had a success with the electrolyser. He rang the hydrogen research centre on Eday and offered them free electricity from his tidal machine in exchange for sharing use of their electrolyser. There was reluctance: they hadn't heard of him; they suggested he send an email. But he talked and talked, first to an engineer and then to the boss, bending them, soothing them, making them laugh. He was irresistible.

Once they got familiar with it, his proposal seemed the simplest, most obvious thing. There was no need to overcomplicate it with contracts. A handshake between people who understood each other – not even a handshake – a promise to meet when next he was up. They'd split the hydrogen they generated fifty–fifty.

When he told Alan, Alan said, "Hmm." As if to say: *I see you.*

"What?"

"You're playing a new tune, aren't you?"

Roland blushed. It was like being caught in a costume change. "I don't think so."

"Oh yes you are. Wasn't it you who was saying leave me out of it, I don't want to get in the middle of things?"

"He could die. He could literally die. There's this thing called ketoacidosis."

Alan was patronisingly amused. "Oh, aye, but could he though? Where did this two-month thing even come from? Are you sure you didn't just make it up?"

"That's ridiculous. It's medical. And anyway, we can't let the company fall apart while he's sick. I mean, it's his whole life, the poor guy. And all these people."

"Oh, right. That sounds very serious."

"Yeah, yeah, get fucked."

Alan laughed.

Soon after, Javier asked for a video call and suggested that he, Javier, set up a small "special projects" unit. This would search for breakthroughs outside the main direction of the engineers' efforts. Perhaps this unit should oversee hydrogen as well.

It was like *Game of Thrones* – the princelings becoming restless when the king was sick. *What an interesting idea, Javier. However did you think of it?* Roland said, "Okay. Yeah. Let's have a call with Alan and see what he reckons."

Javier waved a hand in front of his screen. "No need. No need. It's yust a suggestion. Jou do whatever jou think."

"No, no, he's just been texting me. I'll see if he can join. One sec."

While they waited for Alan to join, Roland and Javier looked at each other on video, both well aware what Roland was doing. For Javier, it was awkward. A third window popped up, and Alan appeared. Roland said, "Hey. So just quickly: Javier was saying it might be a good idea to have a kind of special projects unit to investigate the stuff that's too far outside the main flow. Maybe it could oversee hydrogen as well. What do you reckon? Would that be useful to you?"

Alan said, "Hmm," like a teacher hearing a dubious excuse.

Javier had his answer. He said, "It was yust a suggestion."

Alan scratched his fingers through his beard. "Always open to suggestions. But not sure this makes sense, to be honest, Javier. Hydrogen's pretty integral to the work plan."

"Okay. Sure. Sure. Jou guys yust tell me. I'm still the new guy here."

Once Javier was off the line, Alan chuckled and said, "Thanks."

"No problem."

"When he spends his time on the job, he is actually really useful."

"How're the others?"

"Not bad. Getting less ... worried. The electrolyser's given them plenty to get on with. How're you?"

"Erm, heading up to Edinburgh in a couple of days to meet the Sturgeon people. Don't worry, I won't, like, accidentally sell the company."

"Maybe just don't agree to anything while you're there. Come back and we can think about it together."

The meeting was in the Scottish government building, a thousand-window cruise liner made of dirty stone. The soot-blackened walls were decorated with murky reliefs, like something from Gotham. Inside, it was no grander than the administrative floor of a hospital: tough speckled green carpet, IKEA tables in blonde wood, empty expanses of plum-painted wall with, here and there, a framed photograph of the institution in times gone by.

After the offices of London VC funds or Peter Thiel's tech-military complex in California, it seemed constrictive, a series of small rooms, provincial.

The two guys he met were over-caffeinated wonks in lanyards and grey suits, not much older than him. The customary warm-up chat before broaching the matter at hand was an arch, sarcastic back-and-forth about cock-ups and scandals he'd never heard of. They let slip "What Nicola really thinks about it" and "What Nicola said to me is that ..." They seemed to live entirely within the tiny northern court of Scottish politics. Roland pretended to know what they were on about.

He felt powerful enough to not prep for the meeting. Unlike James, who readied himself for hostile interrogations from perfect inquisitors, Roland just turned the conversation back on the wonks themselves. When, getting down to it, they asked how he thought the marine energy sector was looking, he said, "Yeah, good question. Obviously I could talk about that all day. But if it's okay, before I start, like, boring you senseless with stuff you don't want to know, I just wanted to ask, what is it you're interested in here?"

They related a fact they thought was very telling: the first wind turbine ever to produce electricity was built by a Scottish engineer who just wanted light in his cottage. In Marykirk, outside Aberdeen, in the 1880s. As they explained that Scotland really ought to be the centre of the global wind industry, they began competing with each other to know the history better.

Roland stopped listening. He noticed that one had a multicoloured cloth bracelet dangling from under his shirt cuff. A festival entry band. Probably something like RockNess or T in the Park. This adviser, his smooth cheek shaved that morning, his hair parted, wearing his lanyard, tie and grey M&S suit, talking about how people began pursuing industrial-scale wind power after the Arab oil crisis, must have spent a weekend getting off his face in a muddy park outside Perth. And loved it so much he hadn't cut the bracelet off afterwards. Well, Roland thought, don't we all.

This guy said, "And now zero – literally zero – wind turbines get manufactured in Scotland. They all come from somewhere in Denmark."

Roland said, "Esbjerg."

"Oh. You know it?"

"Yeah, it's a crazy place. Like, just more enormous than you can imagine."

"You've been there?"

"Uh-huh."

"Oh, right." With an unconscious gesture, he pushed the bracelet up his cuff and went on. "You'll understand, then, that Nicola doesn't want the same to happen with marine energy. If this industry is going to come out of Scottish ingenuity and geography, of course we want the jobs and investment to be in Scotland, too."

A great surge of self-importance inflated Roland to his very fingertips.

The other adviser said, "Especially because the oil's not going to last forever. And there's climate change, too, right? With the Paris summit, there's going to be much more push behind this."

Roland looked at him but said nothing.

"So it's a bit . . . fucken . . . I don't know . . . *worrying* that practically every marine energy company in Scotland's gone bust."

The two politicos laughed.

"Except us."

They looked at him. "Except you guys. And one or two others, to be fair."

"We're the only ones with a machine in the water."

"And you guys are doing . . . okay?"

Roland performed a wry chuckle. "We've got every half-decent inventor and engineer and everybody's blueprints, so . . ." He didn't want to talk himself out of a cheque. Even the EU money would only keep them above water for a few more months. "But yeah. It's tough. You saw how Pelamis went under."

"I'm sure. I'm sure. Nicola actually met the CEO a couple of times, before."

Roland volunteered nothing, he asked for nothing; he left space for their needs to expand. The one with the bracelet said, "He's working for you guys now, right?"

"That's right."

"And you're Scottish, aren't you?"

Roland grinned and said, "Ha. Yeah. My surname's Mackenzie. And my mum's from near Inverness. But I don't have the accent because I grew up in the Middle East. My dad's in the oil."

The special advisers shared a glance, checking with each other, and the one with the bracelet explained, "So, the Scottish government can't just, like, *give you money*. There are legal issues. There's EU competition law against state aid. But . . ." – they looked pleased with their own cleverness – "we can set up a prize for innovation in tidal energy, with, say, a million pounds" – this was dropped in almost carelessly – "for the most promising tech. It sounds like you guys would win."

Roland grimaced. "Yeah," he said. "Yeah." And then, "You know, I appreciate it. Million quid . . . yeah, great. Always useful. And I know Scotland's a small country. But really, this stuff isn't cheap. Oil and gas in Aberdeen is turning over *billions*. They probably spend a million quid a year on taxis. I think you really want to be thinking more like ten million, to make it worthwhile. It's not a pizza-delivery app we're building here."

The advisers were taken aback, as if they'd taken a chipolata to a dick-waving contest. Roland was delighted with himself. Then it was a cab back to Waverley and the train down to King's Cross. He'd been in Edinburgh about ninety minutes.

Feeling replete, like a grandee after a satisfying dinner, he gazed out the window at the flat grey plain of the North Sea and the ugly little towns flitting by. He was sitting in a cushiony leather chair in First. A Scottish man paid to put on a uniform and a soft, deferential voice had offered him a drink and a pair of mini sandwiches. What a life.

Coming back with a million quid in the bag would settle the team. Maybe the advisers would ratchet it up to a million and a half. Maybe two. He felt so capable of anything that he was tempted to ring and tell them to stick the money up Nicola's arse.

He laughed in his cosy seat about them checking he was Scottish. They were all like that, the fucking Scots. His mum had a tea towel listing

Scottish inventors. It told the story of a fancy Englishman putting on his *mackintosh* and driving on some *tarmacadam*. Then on to phone calls and telly with your Graham Bells and Logie Bairds; then your Dunlops, your Napiers and your Flemings. Nowadays those guys would all move to California and do coding.

He, Roland, who many still assumed was no more than a likeable shambles, was actually, it turned out, a soon-to-be-famous Scottish inventor. He was keeping company with Macintosh and Fleming. And he wasn't fucking about with raincoats; he was in the same line of technological descent as the greatest of them all: James Watt. From him came the steam engine, and thence the Industrial Revolution, the British Empire, the Raj, the railroads into the American West, the decline of slavery, the sudden steep upward curve in life expectancy and living conditions, the transformation of ordinary folk from muddy serfs into consumers with education, the vote and holidays in Thailand. No surprise that the watt was the unit of power. Maybe the unit of tidal power could be the mackenzie.

While he was daydreaming about himself, his phone buzzed with an email from the JET Programme. He'd reached the next round. Of course he had. The admissions coordinator, Midori Stevenson, had written to him personally – *quelle surprise* – to say it was unusual to have applicants from his stage of career. Would he mind providing some more explanation? She added that, in her experience, the absolute best candidates were those from left-field backgrounds. Ah, he thought, 'twas ever thus. For I am a very special sausage.

Impulsively, he clicked reply. He typed: "Dear Midori, I'm very sorry but I won't be able to take this further. I can't leave my employees at what is a very delicate juncture. If I abandon them now, I don't know what will become of them. With my sincerest best wishes and good luck in your search, Roland Mackenzie."

There was relief. Japan – who was he kidding? He could stop trying to bend his surroundings into a shape they resisted. It was like the moments when he gave up on one of his much-hyped drives to quit smoking, and relaxed, as if he were a pig who'd been trying to stand on its hind legs like a civilised human being and could now drop back cosily into the muck. He was what he was, and fuck them all.

By four hours later, when the train slowed and flickered in and out of tunnels, catching its breath as it neared King's Cross, Roland had come down off his high and was sick with instinctual regret. He flinched and tossed in his comfortable seat. Of all the lives he could have led. Maybe there was some other route to Japan. For an insane second, he wondered whether James could have given himself diabetes on purpose, to trap him.

Meanwhile James was trying to recuperate optimally and exasperating Roland with accounts of high-veg meals. He'd never guessed that blood sugar was a question of such fascinating complexity. It was like the oil price of the body. A pint of beer, say, had two opposing effects: the sugar pushed your blood glucose up, but the alcohol pulled you down. The effects were staggered: first up, then down. Inject too much insulin while the sugar was surging, and the subsequent low could be dangerously deep.

YouTube had a rich seam of diabetic content. One school advocated living clean: no carbs, no insulin. The more technically minded set out rules of thumb for estimating the glucose content of food. Some carried a pocket weighing scale.

It was something new to apply this degree of attention to his material self. His sense of where he was migrated from his head to his body, from perception to proprioception. There was a daily round of meals, exercises and readings to work on. The perfectibility of habit, and the habit of perfection.

The readings came from a cream plastic disc stuck to his upper arm. When he pulled it off, every couple of weeks, the underside was manky and greebled, his skin wan and clammy. Its tiny probe, like the point of a drawing pin, had to be pushed through the upper layers of the epidermis. It hurt.

The consultant had asked whether he was planning to discover a cure for diabetes. Cure diabetes! Now *there* was an attractive mirage, beckoning him to walk deeper into a trackless desert. But maybe. Some researchers had tried attaching a small insulin pump, the size of an asthma inhaler, to a patient's arm. Presumably you could connect the glucose monitor and the pump by Bluetooth. Then, whenever the monitor registered that your blood sugar was going too high, the pump would automatically push some insulin into your blood. In effect, an artificial pancreas. A mechanical cure – at least a partial one.

Somehow, the starting gun in his head didn't fire. The research into insulin pumps he skim-read, without becoming obsessed. Someone should start this company, but it wouldn't be him.

Now that the coma had given him time to notice it, he couldn't overlook that, aside from work, his quality of life was shoddy. Food intake: poor albeit improving fast. Culture: meagre. Sex and romance: perfunctory to non-existent. Exploration of the universe . . . ? Before the company, he'd had interests. Emil Zátopek. Stalin and the Great Purge. A solid grounding in Italian cuisine.

He suggested to his dad that they draw up a two-month course in intermediate Italian cooking. Two evenings a week, they fed stretchy, springy pasta dough through a miniature steel wringer, or sniffed stewpots of simmering brown broth, or touched the tips of their tongues to a teaspoon of chicken-liver pâté.

Long-dormant chambers of his brain were activated. When they made the anchovy-garlic paste in *bagna càuda*, first poaching garlic cloves in milk, his mind filled with the sight of a pale-yellow ring spreading outwards around each clove. His dad annoyed him because his thoughts, like a coin on a spiral, kept landing in the same place. He asked, "Is this healthy? I don't know. Fish is healthy, isn't it?"

"It's a dip, Dad. It's not our main source of nutrition."

"Yes, absolutely, good point. I really am glad you're taking such a keen interest in looking after yourself." And, almost managing to have it sound like a joke, he added, "I don't want to go upstairs and find you in a coma again."

"I can show you my tracker data if you like. I'm in the ideal range literally all the time." James stuck his nose deeper into the thick oily stink of garlic and anchovy, like a probe descending through the layers of a gas planet. "The anchovies are almost dissolved. We should have done a control batch with water to see what difference it makes."

Arthur smiled. "You've always had a sadly under-cultivated talent for cooking. Maybe all this will prompt a new phase. You wouldn't be the first. A brush with the Reaper, a reappraisal of what really matters, less time with the spreadsheets and more smelling the garlic. You have to enjoy yourself, you know."

"I'm not reappraising anything. I'm rehabilitating."

"Of course, of course. How silly of me."

But they both understood that, for these months, which were already passing by, James had asked his dad to spend two evenings a week with him. They moved their bodies through the same space. They chewed and tasted, looking into each other's eyes. One evening, James glanced up from shredding capers and said, "Thanks for finding me, by the way."

"Finding you where?"

"You know, upstairs."

Arthur shuddered, and his eyes went wet. But he tried to disguise it and said, "Oh, pleasure. Any time." They were putting the capers into their chicken-liver pâté, for crostini. Arthur said, "When you were a toddler, you were always trying to fall down the stairs or totter into the road. Or indeed, if we hadn't kept feeding you, you'd have starved on thousands of occasions. And, not to put too fine a point on it" – he straightened up from the counter and raised his eyebrows – "I did procreate you in the first place. So you already owed me your life many times over. Once more hardly makes a difference."

"Okay. Won't mention it again."

"I do wish you'd try to enjoy yourself more."

"I'm enjoying myself right now, aren't I?"

He was, but he could already feel himself starting to ruin it. It was hard not to calculate that if they increased their cooking evenings from two to three per week, the learning curve would steepen by fifty per cent. Four evenings would be a doubling; six a tripling. He was having to send a detachment of mental energy to suppress the urge, still weak, to devise a course of study. Foundational theory of cooking. The Maillard reaction; the differences between Maillard and caramelisation. He quelled these thoughts as if they were subversive elements.

But he felt free when he went to the trampolining centre in far north London. It was a very high, echoing sports hall with a squeaky floor and a grid of Olympic-grade trampolines, each separated from the others by netting. The other trampoliners were gymnasts and snowboarders practising flips and pikes; James was learning to bounce up and down without drifting to the side. There was no risk of his ever getting good at it.

The rectangle of white fabric boinged him up, and up, and up. Through the netting he could see the snowboarders executing backflips. Safe from ambition, he just bounced up and up, grinning into the high space around him, with his feet landing again and again on the cross in the trampoline's centre. Perhaps, in all his striving towards satisfaction, he'd overlooked the pursuit of joy.

James's evenings began filling up. As news spread through their little industry that his machine was now the front-runner, he started getting invitations from people he didn't know. Mostly they were for energy conferences in supersized expo halls on the outskirts of Reykjavik or Barcelona. He generally said no. Zhejiang province in China invited him to see a new tidal array in the Zhoushan Islands. Roland said he had to go; he *had to*. It wasn't until the summer.

At the start of December, with the high-end hullaballoo of the Paris climate summit drawing attention to green energy, the invitations began to come from further afield. Even though the papers complained that the Paris Agreement was vague and unenforceable, those whose profession was to notice any shift in the prevailing wind – money men, politicians – suddenly wanted to speak to him.

These weren't conferences but dinners, almost always in London. James said yes. He went to members' clubs with silk wallpaper and portraits of long-dead dukes, to the private rooms of famous restaurants, to tables set up in buildings of historical interest: the wine cellars under Berry Bros, the top floor of the St Pancras clock tower; by candlelight in the John Soane museum, with a pre-prandial gander at the sarcophagus. James was being invited into the outermost ring of the London society that revolved around power. At the tables with him were bosses of medium-sized companies, journalists, ambassadors from unimportant countries, and the kind of government ministers who didn't often get on TV.

At one, he met the energy minister Andrea Leadsom, who was like a cheery, implacable granny, wearing specs and a fun pink jacket. She'd just banned onshore wind turbines. The table of energy people objected, but she swept straight over them. With an encouraging smile, she said, "Of course I absolutely understand your point. But it simply can't be the case that top-down central government inflicts noisy and destructive eyesores onto local communities who don't want them. And, I can tell you, nobody wants them. So, let's move on, shall we? Now, *offshore* wind . . ."

James found her maddening.

Also with him were up-and-comers in the grand investment houses, and the founders of small ones. Many of these small founders, when he had Mary-Rose google them, turned out to be the new incarnations of the landed nobility. These friendly, self-effacing guys who introduced them-selves as Charlie or Freddie proved to be baronets and marquesses. Their families had made the leap from collecting rent on fields and villages to collecting a return on capital. The estate had shifted from smelly cattle and recalcitrant tenants to the clean and odourless abstractions of invest-ment portfolios.

James experienced a need to beat them in arguments. He resented feel-ing that, by contrast with them, he too came from a particular stratum – the professional class. It inhibited him, boxed him in, constrained him with its prejudices. He usually thought of himself as beyond Britain's class system. Of those he argued with, some were clever, some thick, but all were doing well. Since 2008, Ben Bernanke and Mario Draghi – and Ben's successor – had held interest rates down very low to sustain the fragile economy. Low rates meant investors could, with little risk, borrow money and put it into stocks, tech and property. With money flowing in, the price of houses kept going up, as did stocks and the value of tech companies. Every time James heard about a hundred million being invested in flying taxis, he wondered how to make their own machine more intoxicating.

James's entry ticket to these dinners read: youngish person doing something left-field that might turn out to be relevant. He was always seated at one end, where the place settings were squashed together, rather than in the centre, which was reserved for the stars.

Older men, disappointed not to be sitting next to someone more significant, inflicted patronising chats on him. He let them talk, listening, sifting for anything useful. He'd grown far more patient since arguing the toss about the Jesuits in Kitzbühel.

At some stage, the dinner's compère would say, "Um, James, I wanted to come to you on this . . ."

The two rows of heads turned towards him.

"Let's leave aside the inconsistencies in Paris for now; you *do* believe there is going to be a rapid shift away from oil and gas, don't you?"

Then James would start to talk, calmly, factually; a gathering, irresistible flow of data and arguments, ticking by in bullet points and paragraphs. He didn't try to convince anyone, which was convincing. He didn't try to win debating points or sound clever. Other men soon grew fidgety; they hadn't come to listen to some unknown youngster sounding off. But often, as the dinner broke up, someone would come to speak to him.

One evening, he was in the modernist white restaurant above the National Portrait Gallery. Through the bank of windows was a nighttime cityscape of domes and belfries. Big Ben was in the middle distance. Poking up in the foreground was Nelson on his column. James could see the back of his stone tricorn hat and his stone epaulettes. He went closer and peered down into the bright canyon of Whitehall, where he could see the entrance to DFID. A formula offered itself: I've made it from down there to up here. But actually, anyone could come to this restaurant. It wasn't even very good.

He took his seat at the foot of a long table. To his left, their cutlery touching, was a woman about his age who was an up-and-comer at the investment house BlackRock. On her place card, James read the name Alice Winsloe. It didn't seem momentous at the time.

He'd learned that it was polite to speak to the person on one side during the starter and to the other during the main. Both Alice and the man to his right turned away from him, so he sat at the end, looking down the long table, and concentrated on the unpleasant taste of his cold slimy gravlax.

For the final dish of his self-taught apprenticeship in Italian cooking, he was going to make a Sicilian *timballo*: a warm golden dome of pastry, stuffed to excess with macaroni, veal, two types of eggs, béchamel, ham and chicken hearts. His dad kept telling him to read a book called *The Leopard*, in which the characters apparently ate one. James hadn't read a novel since university.

Alice turned back to him and said, "Hi, sorry you just got stranded there. I hope you like salmon."

"Mmm." James didn't want to complain; to lie smoothly wasn't in him. Finally, clunkily, he said, "I didn't come for the free food."

"Oh, what did you come for?"

James was still off balance. "Umm. Ultimately, because I have nothing better to do, and it might be useful. Why do you come to these things? Surely BlackRock doesn't need to look for clients."

"God, no. Far too many already, if you ask me."

"So why *do* you come?"

"Oh, it's just part of it, isn't it? I go to Wimbledon, too, which obviously you can't grumble about even though it just reminds me how shocking I am at tennis. And sometimes I go to just really quite *astonishingly* tedious conferences. But somehow I don't really mind that they're tedious. I sort of think if you want fireworks, you should join the circus."

"What do you do at BlackRock?"

"I don't really do —"

The waiters came to bring the main course: small, thick roundels of fatless beef fillet on a little gravy-soaked assemblage of cabbage and potato — food for people who ate out every night and didn't want to gain weight.

The host, who was head of a consultancy touting for business, stood up and said a few ingratiating phrases about what an insightful discussion it was. When he finally stopped, James said, "Sorry, you were saying what you do at BlackRock."

"Oh, I was just saying that I don't really do anything. That's the whole thing about passive investing. There's not really anything *to* do."

This strategy had risen to dominance since the financial crisis. Since low rates meant all stocks were going up, you didn't try to pick the best ones; you just bought a share in everything. It was called passive investing. The old-fashioned stockpickers couldn't beat it. Together with two sister-rivals, called Vanguard and State Street, BlackRock was now the biggest shareholder in more than half of American corporations.

"My job is to say to people, 'Oh, so you want to invest the pensions of all these, I don't know, civil servants? Well, have you heard of this thing called the S&P 500?' Seems far too obvious, really. I honestly don't know why they bother paying us."

As she talked, James was noticing more about her. She was quite stringy, sinewy, like a weasel, but he wouldn't have said unattractive. Her blonde hair, artificially brightened, was pulled into a sporty ponytail that stood out against her black dress. He could see her lean, muscly arms and simple, unostentatious earrings that, once he spotted them, he thought were probably diamonds.

Watching her, he had the impression that she was showing him a series of preset attitudes: humour, self-deprecation, mockery — always tending away from his earnestness. Her real thoughts must be separate and unseen. You didn't get to be an up-and-comer at BlackRock by saying "How about just buying the index?"

He wanted to know, so he pressed her. "Is that what you want to do with your life? It doesn't sound like you find it very challenging."

"With my life? Yikes. No idea. Are you a life coach?"

James laughed, something he usually only did with Roland. "No. Actually, I can show you what I do." He took out his iPhone and flicked through the videos. "Just a sec. Almost got it." She ate some beef and glanced up the table. "Here it is." He put the phone in her hand, both careful not to touch fingers, and pressed play.

A fixed camera showed an industrial room. A technician's hands were inflating a red balloon from a gas canister. The balloon inflated until its skin went taut. Then the hands tied a knot and let the balloon go. It wobbled in the air and floated upwards, accelerating out of shot.

Alice looked at James's grin. "So what, you're a party balloon innovator? You're disrupting kids' birthdays? Every four-year-old in England knows your name?"

James laughed again. "That's not helium in the balloon; it's hydrogen. That we —"

She spoke over him. "Like the *Hindenburg*?"

That was what Roland said.

"Yes, it's —"

"You believe climate change has created a market for the airship? The zeppelin's time has finally come?"

"No, no. It's just a demonstration. The hydrogen is to go into rockets. It's rocket fuel. We generated it from a tidal turbine. I've got another video here where they blow it up."

"Wait. Are you those guys up in Scotland who just bought the rest of the industry?"

"That's us. That's my company. Mine and my friend Roland's."

"I read something about you in the *FT* . . ."

"The one that said marine energy hasn't lived up to its promise, the tech's not ready, everyone's going bust, and we're going down with the ship."

She made the emoji awkward face. "Yeah, that one."

He smiled with pleasure and thought of Christopher Columbus.

A few days later, he and Roland were at WeWork, and it was nearing five o'clock. Roland asked if he felt like going bowling.

"Bowling?"

"Yeah. There's a hotel in Fitzrovia that's got a bowling alley in the basement. I've booked a lane." Roland seemed anxious. "Unless you're doing your cooking tonight?"

"We're taking a few days off before we do the final dish."

"Oh, wow. What's that going to be?"

James had already told him earlier. "A *timballo*. It's like a pie but stuffed with macaroni and béchamel and some other things. In the shape of a kettledrum."

"Wow, mate. That sounds amazing." Roland's grin was clearly artificial.

"Have you fucked something up?"

"What?" Roland blushed.

"Are you going to, like, take me bowling and give me some bad news? This isn't you moving to Japan?"

"Ugh, you ass." Roland had wanted the bowling to soften him up. "It's good news."

"So, you're not going to Japan?"

"No. If you must fucking know, I missed the deadline by about ten years this time."

James smiled and raised his eyebrows, making the exaggerated surprised/not-surprised expression that his dad did. "Well, now. Was that the news or is there something else? Can you just tell it to me?"

"Can you not look happy, please? And no, we're going bowling. I've already paid for it."

James was smirking. "Okay. Okay. Let's go. Why bowling?"

"Don't you remember we did it that time in Aberdeen?"

"Did we?"

"At the pleasure beach. You loved it."

"Did I?"

"Yeah. You were mad for it. You were saying it must be psychologically brutal at pro level because you should be able to play a perfect game. So you can never get a positive result; it's about who fails first."

"Oh, yup. That does sound like me."

"Okay, great. Let's go."

On the walk over, along pavements beside slow-moving lines of black taxis like processions of beetles, James thought: No Japan. I waited. I held true to my strategy of delay. I was like Kutuzov letting Napoleon's invading army exhaust itself on the march. And I've won.

Roland asked, "How was that dinner the other night?"

"Bit boring. Had a chat with a girl who works at BlackRock."

"Oh, like a girl girl?"

"What do you mean?"

"Like, was she hot?"

"Yeah, she was good-looking."

"Did you get her number?"

"No."

Roland shook his head. "Amateur."

The bowling alley was in the basement of a hotel for prosperous hipsters – ad execs and TV producers. The vibe was trainers and negronis. A waitress took them downstairs and switched on the lights. There were two lanes and a bar done up as a pastiche of fifties Americana. The bar itself was the hind quarter of a pastel-blue Cadillac, its retro-futuristic tail lights still blinking. The waitress turned on a Wurlitzer, which began playing croony, harmonious rock 'n' roll. They let you wear your own shoes.

The waitress seemed unsure what they were doing there. She said, "Usually it's events. But if you just want to play . . . Do you want drinks?"

James said, "Oh yes." He skimmed the menu. "Can we please have the nachos with everything, two hot dogs, fries, two Blue Moons. And a bottle of champagne."

Roland murmured: "Are you allowed that stuff?"

James laughed inappropriately loud. He shook his head at the waitress, and said, "This guy . . . I think we're going to bowl quite a few rounds, frames – is that what they're called?"

She made a faux-patient face and asked, "But do you want the stuff you said?"

"Oh yes. Yes, please. And could we keep the menu."

Once she'd gone back upstairs, James sat on a moulded plastic seat and said, "Okay. I'm ready. So, no Japan, eh? Keep talking. More news like that please."

"Can I at least bowl first?"

"Okay."

Roland lifted one of the marbled spheres from the rack. At the other end of the lane, the white pins waited. He sprang forward and, like in the movies, side-spun the ball so it would arc into the pins and smash their formation with a clatter. Instead, the ball rumbled straight off the side, bobbled heavily in the gutter and rolled out of sight. James thought: Typical. He could definitely beat Roland with a strategy of low-risk moderation. No need for strikes. Just keep hitting the target and let Roland take himself out.

Roland picked up another ball. "But let me finish before you start going mad, okay?"

"I thought this was good news."

"It is. But ... Okay, while you were in hospital, the Scottish government got in touch and basically said they want to give us some cash. I didn't tell you because you were sick." James jumped to his feet, his face contorting. Roland lifted the ball between them. "Wait. Just wait. I haven't fucked it up. They're going to create a marine innovation prize, and we'll win it. They said a million quid but I'm trying to get more."

For James, it was like being a parent who comes home to find that his child has turned on the hobs and cooked dinner. The house was not noticeably on fire; the child was not noticeably burned. "It's a prize? So we don't have to give them anything?"

"Exactly. They just want to promote Scottish stuff."

"Do they think you're Scottish?"

Roland grinned. "What are you talking about? My surname's Mackenzie. Of *course* I'm Scottish."

James was getting so happy he was losing inhibitions. "You know what, I *knew* you wouldn't go to Japan. I fucking *knew*. I delayed you and delayed you until eventually – fuck, *eventually* – you saw sense."

"Don't be a dick."

"How long were you going on about that bullshit?"

"Why don't you go bowl and simmer down."

"Oh, I will. I will. I'm going to whup you now. And I'm not even going to beat you the easy way either. All strikes. And you can thank me for not sacking you when we were at DFID. You could actually say that I've mentored you, I've nurtured you – an unpromising weed – into someone capable of finally making good decisions."

"Buddy, DFID was my idea. And now you're out of action for a couple of months and the cash starts rolling in. Do you think that's a coincidence, you ass? Why don't you say thanks for running everything while you've been off making bloody spaghetti Bolognese?"

The waitress pushed open the door with one hand; on the other, she was balancing a round tray with two bright-yellow glasses of some Louisiana beer, a bottle of Moët and two flutes. All three of them were silent, hearing the music, as she carefully put the tray down on the counter. She got it into place and then said, "The nachos and hot dogs will be a few minutes."

James said, "Thanks so much. I'm going to thrash his ass now."

"Umm, okay."

"At bowling, I mean."

Her cynicism about the stupid rich customers cracked, and she laughed. "Good luck, then. Good luck. I'll be back soon with the food."

She left and James said, "What a day."

As they bowled and drank the refills the waitress brought, their talk gradually shed its banterousness. They spoke about the team's primitive fear of James, as if he might bring death within reach of them, about Roland's only trip to Tokyo – the illuminated Rainbow Bridge through the night-time skyline and the Kiwi girl he shagged in the hostel dorm. She was probably someone's mum by now.

James, with inept drunken fingers, demonstrated how he injected insulin into the fat on his belly. Roland crouched and watched with transfixed disgust as the hair-thin needle pushed smoothly into the bunched-up blubber. And lastly – because once they reached this subject, they stayed on it – Roland said what was preoccupying him about the company. The

Javier problem. Sturgeon's money. Corrosion around the rivets of the hull. The insatiable need for money.

James was wonderfully content. He'd always had to cajole Roland to participate in the company's puzzles, as if trying to make him play a game of chess, and usually ended up playing against himself. Now the thoughts that accompanied him day and night, like worry beads, counted alone for so long, were shared at last.

XI

Alice only saw James's LinkedIn message more than a week after he'd sent it. She'd only logged in because her boss had asked her to share his quite sweetly dorkish post about impact investing.

The message was a welcome little pick-me-up before lunch. It was funny to be asked out on LinkedIn, which must be the most unerotic form of communication ever invented. But she was used to it. The men in finance were such nerds. They imagined themselves as alpha-type, hard-charging, rule-breaking handsome bastards, like the devilish dukes in the bodice-rippers she read at school. But really most of them had maths degrees, and their chat was about buying property or their triathlon regimes.

She didn't remember a lot about James, but she liked the propriety of his message: "Dear Alice, I enjoyed meeting you at dinner in the National Portrait Gallery. I found what you were saying about passive investment very interesting. Would you like to go for a drink one evening?"

It wasn't exactly Leo DiCaprio in *Romeo + Juliet*, a being so perfect it hurt to watch him. But you should say yes to dates with apparently suitable, non-repulsive boys who go to the trouble of asking you. That James seemed clever was a plus. She'd been half-heartedly seeing such a nice boy who – it wasn't his fault – he ran an ad-buying agency – good honest enterprise – backbone of the economy. But it was getting increasingly difficult to ignore that what he talked about was quite, to be just utterly blunt, well, *inane*.

To limit herself to clever boys felt narrowing – what about the devilish dukes?! – and most of the clever boys she knew were finance nerds or just appallingly full of themselves. But maybe that was better than listening to poor, well-meaning Gareth do the best he could. He wasn't even that well-meaning. She suspected that at work he was quite a shit. Oh God, it was time to ditch him, wasn't it? Such a pain, because she'd already spent so much time culling the worst of his outfits and behaviour. But it seemed inevitable. He *was* funny. But still. Goodbye, Gareth, I hardly knew ye. There'd be a period of decent mourning and then, after lunch, she'd say yes to James, who'd better take her somewhere nice since he'd just cost her an almost-boyfriend.

As it turned out, James, with an inkling that a stale Soho pub wouldn't do, took her to the bar at the Connaught. It was discreet, velvet-hushed and heedless of price, arranged into many small nooks for a clientele used to private rooms and personal jets. Talking *sotto voce* at the other tables were ex-KGB men turned minor oligarchs, Libyan colonels living on the last of the pre-war oil revenues, and Americans just over to pick up an estate in the Cotswolds.

She thought it was a solid choice – a bit work-flavoured maybe; she'd been there for meetings. But delightful that he seemed to understand she didn't want to eat in front of him, wielding giant cutlery at some under-sized table and trying not to talk with her mouth full. And she liked that he came properly dressed: dark-blue jacket, light-blue shirt, grey trousers. Not spectacular, but no complaints. The shoes it wouldn't be a tragedy to replace. Overall, much better than most founders she met, who thought it was cool to dress like the IT guy.

As they spoke – about BlackRock, marine energy, the economics of decarbonising – she developed a pleasing sense of his confidence in being who he was and not being what he was not. Cockiness she'd had more than enough of. But unlike most boys on dates, he wasn't trying to present himself from a particular angle. He didn't pretend to know about things he didn't. She didn't have to worry about him getting touchy or nervous if she strayed away from his safe topics or his safe mode of talking.

And he was quick. Even though she did try, unsuccessfully, to nudge the conversation away from their jobs, he saw at once the tensions and contradictions that poor Gareth, bless him, never quite got his head around. Also, really, it would have been difficult to live with the name Gareth for years and years. *Hello, this is my husband, Gareth.* Of course she could have stuck it out. Her family would have felt for her, which would have been incredibly annoying. Her mum had spent decades, literal decades, putting on a brave face at parties to say, *Yes, that's right. Lionel is very committed to his tango dancing. No, I'm afraid I'm such a stick-in-the-mud I don't join him. I ought to really, just once, as he never tires of reminding me.* Next to that, *Gareth* was nothing.

James showed her more videos of his hydrogen filling up balloons and of the long yellow tidal machine itself. She pretended not to have already seen them on his website. After he'd been explaining for a little longer than she needed, she said, "Can I just ask something?"

"Of course."

She gave him a warm smile, to remind him that she was on side. That should have been apparent anyway from her short dress and her bare legs crossed one over the other. Not the greatest legs ever — an extra inch or two wouldn't hurt — but good enough, and unarguably they were a girl's bare legs, waxed immaculately at Strip, so near he could have reached out to touch them.

But she smiled, to remind him, and said, "I just wonder, you know, yes, you can generate some hydrogen. You can probably guess what I'm going to ask: commercial scale. One balloon isn't going to pay for all your engineers."

James was pleased. "Very fair question." He'd answered it many times, in many different ways. Recently, he and Roland had found themselves talking about James Watt. So he tried: "Okay, the very first steam engine, which started the Industrial Revolution, the Newcomen engine, could only convert less than one per cent of its energy into work. The other ninety-nine per cent was lost as heat. The engine in a Prius manages to use forty per cent of the energy you put in, so nearly half. In a Tesla, it's about eighty-five per cent. Almost nothing to roughly half to almost everything. That's the trajectory. And we haven't even built our first full-scale machine yet."

Alice smiled again. "Yes, but when was the Newcomen engine? Two hundred years ago?"

James was deep in his comfort zone. "Three hundred."

"Sorry if this is a bit, well, *gauche*, but isn't this what people with new tech always say? As in, they all think they've just invented the car. But maybe they've invented the zeppelin."

James hadn't enjoyed a conversation this much since . . . he couldn't remember. "Yes, that's what people with new tech always say. But some of those people are right."

"And what makes you think it's you?"

"That's the life. Everyone thinks they're the one, but only one person actually is. And isn't figuring out who's right actually *your* job? I'm just an entrepreneur toiling in my niche. Aren't you meant to look across all the niches and see who's going to make it?"

Not cocky, but confident. Handsome, too. Black locks cut short. A big, heavy, serious, grown-up's face, with darkness under the eyes. A head like a bull's. His easy confidence made her more willing to believe in his machine. And it felt real, what he was doing. Her own job she considered pretty much pointless in the grand scheme. Well-paid, high-status, which was nice for her, and interesting enough as jobs went, sometimes quite fun in its way, but ultimately neither here nor there.

James's endeavours felt to her like something from a more grandiose century; the heroic age of civil engineering; perhaps a folly or mud-caked navvies digging a canal through the malarial jungles of Panama. There was a romance to it. Which there wasn't to, say, forex trading. He also seemed to have a lot of hobbies. He spoke to her with excessive detail about making some kind of Italian garlic sauce and then about trampolining. Which was unexpected.

But it was no good trying to stop men boring you when the anorak came out. With her dad, if it wasn't tango, it was the Thirty Years' War. Given half a chance, he'd start crashing on about Richelieu and the King of Bohemia. Even after suffering through this dozens of times, she still wasn't even sure when this had all happened. Or what had happened. And for Christmas he always just wanted more books about it. More petrol on the fire. Last year she'd given him just the dullest-looking tome, recommended by the woman in Foyles. It felt somehow wrong to give your own father such an awful Christmas present, but the poor soul seemed genuinely thrilled by it.

So, in the James scenario, she'd probably have to hear more about cooking and trampolining than she ever wanted. But still. At least it meant he could cook. And surely there wasn't that much you could say about trampolines. Either way, it was probably for the best that he had these things, and wasn't just another workaholic.

Their third date James had to reschedule because he and Roland were going to Orkney. The European Space Agency, in Paris, was sending a Monsieur Gerard Lacombe to see their hydrogen.

It was James's first visit since the coma, and he experienced a minor shock at how many engineers were crowded into the plainly inadequate warehouse. There weren't enough desks so some were sitting sunken into giant beanbags, with their laptops on their knees — a repetitive strain injury case waiting to happen. Others were in the nooks between Alan's rows and columns of equipment. This kit was ordered and labelled like a collection of zoological specimens, each type in its own heavy-duty crate: steel cables like giant tapeworms, green circuit boards, orange survival suits, until, in the far back corner, you reached the limits of categorisation: "miscellaneous electronics", a jumble of adapters and charge cables.

Leaned against the wall were double-ended rotor blades, like biplane propellers, each the height of a person. Their anodised aluminium coating made them look like massive gold. Above them, James had had Alan paint a slogan from JFK's moon speech, in a draughtsman's black lettering: "That goal will serve to organise and measure the best of our energies and skills."

Since the coma, James could sometimes be induced to wax philosophical about how every goal was arbitrary. Tidal energy was no different from trying to get into the Guinness Book of Records for the most pogo-stick somersaults or the longest time balancing blindfolded on one leg. It was all artificial. But without the bar, you'd never jump that high. He'd started buying back issues of the Book of Records for the office.

The workshop, despite being so densely packed with people and machinery, was quiet. Alan's rule was that he had to be able to hear the radio on his desk: usually Talksport, with callers phoning in to denounce the unforgivable profligacy of Brechin's strikers or elucidate the new dead-ball tactics at St Mirren. The engineers spoke at library volume.

Alan's desk hadn't moved since he was the only person in here. It was on a carpeted strip at one side, the supposed office area. Close behind his chair were tubs of water with metal rods sticking down into them from miniature gantries. The water around the rods appeared to be simmering.

These tubs were electrolysers. In them, electricity was dissolving the chemical bonds of H_2O molecules; these split into oxygen and hydrogen. This water, heavy and drinkable, separated into two invisible gases that bubbled up and away. Each tub held a prototype, trying to extract more hydrogen with the same amount of electricity. The magic of design.

The company's shortages of money and, hence, electricity were forcing them to come up with something entirely new. The most sophisticated models, instead of just being two rods, had a submerged 3D lattice of perforated wafers. When you switched on the current, the water around the lattice turned white with fizzing.

Mary-Rose kept complaining, rightly, about the cost. They were spending a fortune just on purified H_2O, and they were blowing out the fuses on this building almost every day. The landlord was turning against them. Really they needed a custom-built workshop with an industrial power supply.

But even now they must have every prominent marine energy engineer in Europe in this room: inventors, monomaniacs, the kind of people who took jobs at moon-shot start-ups rather than Shell. James had an inkling of how the queen bee must feel, having got the colony started practically on her own, when she sees her teeming legions and, beyond them, the ghosts of greater legions still to come.

Thiel had said they needed three thousand engineers. Well, they'd gone from three to a little over thirty: 10x rather than 1,000x. For a second, he let himself fantasise, as he once had about becoming the youngest-ever partner at McKinsey: if we carry on growing 10x every two years, we'll reach three thousand by 2020. But it was only for a second.

He knew Roland worried about having so many dependants. Apparently, the team had more than forty children. There were dozens of mortgages to pay. Even with everyone on subsistence salaries, the cash from the Scottish government would cover only ten months.

James didn't worry. What greater purpose could these people find? And with so many minds applied, the pace of improvements to the machine was accelerating into another order of magnitude. He wasn't having to shove things forward any more; the company was moving of its own accord. It was like seeing the first moving pictures, the still images of a horse coming faster and faster until they flowed together and the horse began to gallop.

In the car from the airport, Alan had handed him a rumpled Tesco's bag wrapped around two overstuffed folders of equipment requests — roughly six hundred pages, just of wish lists and technical explanations. It delighted him. His mechanical dragon had fire in its belly. Not that they could afford any of this stuff for now.

Some of the engineers he'd barely ever spoken to. He recognised them only because he'd memorised their CVs. Maybe before digging into Alan's folders, he'd just say hi to everyone and see if they had suggestions. A few minutes into the first chat, he stopped doing a smile and started taking notes. The suggestions were going to be another folder: sea anchors for the turbine, a way of detaching the power cable without having to send down a diver, a new chemistry for the electrolysers, a different arrangement on maternity leave for an engineer who was having a baby.

Most asked when salaries could be lifted. And tentatively, but implicitly, whether his diabetes was a risk to their livelihoods. He unbuttoned his cuff and pushed up his shirtsleeve to display the cream disc on his arm. He showed them how he took a reading with his iPhone. Then the short, transparent insulin needle and the pack of Haribo Tangfastics in his breast pocket. On salaries, he told them frankly there would be no increase until the next funding round, when they would conjure the tens of millions needed to build the full-scale machine. But since the Paris climate summit, he'd begun getting WhatsApps from VCs again. The zeitgeist was catching up to them, like a wave rising behind a hard-paddling surfer.

By the end of what became a whole day of talk, his brain was woozy and sensitive, his to-do list hundreds of points long. As Roland drove them to the Kirkwall Hotel, he sat back in the car seat, eyes closed, absorbing. He hadn't even looked at Alan's folders. He understood with something like fear that he wasn't going to have enough time — physically, there was not enough time, even if he stopped sleeping — for him to think through every request at the necessary depth. He'd probably never be able to again. He was never going to learn electrolyser chemistry.

Maybe it was okay. After all, Napoleon didn't personally inspect the hooves of every horse in the *Grande Armée*. Ten years earlier, James would have sincerely taken Napoleon as an exemplar. Now the comparison was self-satirising, mock-heroic. And it was sad, too: he'd been caught up in the productive optimism of the workshop and would have liked to be part of it, rather than away in some campaign tent, giving orders to his marshals.

That evening, after a team dinner in the high, cold dining room of the Kirkwall Hotel, elbow-to-elbow with the shades of Victorian whalers and fur-traders, James went with Roland to his room. The window had been dark for hours. Roland lay down on the bed and took off his trousers. He said, "You're getting thinner and I'm getting fatter. Right. It's decided: I'm not eating fish and chips again on this trip."

James, sitting in the armchair, took off his shoes and socks. "Mary-Rose told me she wants the packed lunches to be vegetarian. She says the younger staff agree, and she can run a course to educate the older ones."

Roland laughed, still lying down. "Oh, that's good. Please let me watch her try to educate Alan or Javier."

"And she told me it's not my fault I don't get it; I'm a product of my time."

Roland sighed. "Isn't everyone?"

James snaggled his phone out of his pocket. Roland noticed that James wasn't talking and peered at him. "Who're you texting? Is that . . ." – he put on a deep, seductive Marvin Gaye voice – "*Mmmm. Alice.*"

James laughed. "It is actually."

"Mmmm Alice, I want you to arouse my interest in index investing. I want to dock my turbine in your industrial port." Roland was amusing himself. "Text me a schematic of your erogenous zones."

"Roland."

"Won't it be weird if – no offence – you get a girlfriend and I'm still just getting thumb cramp on Tinder."

"That is quite offensive. But yes, it would be weird. Although, I suppose, maybe it makes sense now you're busy running the company. Maybe we're turning into each other."

Since he'd been fully back, James had kept talking up how much Roland was still jointly in charge. He didn't want Roland's high-spirited motivation to fade, but it *was* fading. Roland said, "We do have to be quite careful with her though, Mary-Rose. She's a fanatic, like you. We should deal with this before she persuades herself we're betraying the mission by, like, supporting the meat industry."

James thought: The human element. "She told me the other day I've got to stop comparing us to the East India Company."

"I mean, mate, she's right. You should stop doing that. How are we ever going to sell anything to the Indians if there are videos of you going on about . . . the yoga place. Mysore. Tipton tea, the terror –"

"Tippoo Sultan, the Tiger of Mysore."

Roland laughed. "You're so middle-aged."

"You're a month older than me."

"Yeah, yeah. Want to have a joint party again this year?"

"Let's."

A few mornings later, they were out on the ocean before sunrise. It was around nine a.m. They were in the lighted plywood box of the *California*'s cabin. Her headlamps illuminated a small patch of choppy, jostling waves, and the boat shuddered and juddered as the angry water barged around it. The wind yowled, and cold veils of brine flopped on the front windows.

The sunrise itself wasn't visible, but it was as if God slowly turned up the dimmer switch. The total black turned to very dark grey. Objects detached themselves from the background: the low island of Eday, the cluster of buildings at their hydrogen station. A border formed between the ocean and the land, as in the first days of creation.

Gerard Lacombe, from the European Space Agency, was more relieved than he would have admitted. Some primitive chamber of his brain had begun to fear that dawn would not come, that they would sail into the void forever. This was despite his priding himself on not being some timid pencil-pusher. He was a rocket-builder who'd realised that, to build what he wanted, he had to reach for the more powerful tools of administration. He'd done eight years in the Guianese jungle, in Kourou, the French former penal colony where the ESA launched its rockets. The perimeter was guarded by the Foreign Legion. A bus of Creole prostitutes was driven onto the base every Friday. He'd seen a knife fight once, outside a corrugated-iron shack in Cayenne.

But this cold didn't suit him. And he'd wrongly assumed the boat would be heated to a professional standard. So he was wearing thin clothes and a light-duty puffer jacket. Alan had found him a beanie stamped with *Linklater Freight Services*, which sat incongruously above his black rectangular glasses, and for which he was grateful.

As the morning established itself, James showed him the strait along which the sea and ocean emptied into each other. The wind was running contrary to the tide, and the waves were whipped up like meringue into white crests and peaks. They broke onto the long yellow machine with terrible regularity, each a great wet blow on the machine's back. The salt water would be searching for weak spots in the weld. In Guiana, merely the humid air had been an ordeal for the equipment. But this . . .

James enjoyed seeing him look grim, and said, "It's like this from November to March."

"It can survive this treatment?"

"Yes. And you can see now why it floats. If something breaks, we can tow it back to Kirkwall to fix. Imagine doing maintenance in this. And it'll be dark again in six hours."

"It's savage up here."

James was pleased. "Oh, yes. There's an island in the Pentland Firth that's full of man-eating pigs."

While James pointed out the hydrogen station, Gerard considered the pigs. This must be a story intended to shock the new person with how horrible things were. A strange kind of boast, and one he recognised. He'd told enough stories about the jungle. Roland brought out something that looked like a thermos. He said, "This is for you, Gerard. It's, um, a flask of hydrogen we've generated."

Gerard smiled and came out of himself, as they intended. "Oh, that is, that is . . ." His English failed him. He inclined his beanie-topped head. "Thank you." Weighing the flask in his hand, it felt empty. At Kourou, there were huge white hydrogen tanks, millions of litres of explosive liquid chilled far below zero. The tanks gathered condensation in the heat. He took a cheap plastic cigarette lighter from his pocket, cocked the bottle and said, "May I?"

A test. James loved a test. "Of course. We can give you another one."

Gerard and Roland stood close together on the swaying floorboards, and Roland slightly unscrewed the lid while Gerard readied the lighter. Gerard nodded. Roland pulled the lid off, Gerard scraped the lighter's rotating flint – and a jet of flame leapt up out of the bottle, scorching the low ceiling. It only burned for an instant. But in the steel circle formed by the flask's nozzle, they saw the fire catching in the empty space, just like the thrusters of a rocket. Gerard laughed with pleasure. "Oh, oh, oh."

They shared the delight of a trick coming off – the right card appearing, a coin floating above a magnet. They'd made fire from the ocean.

Gerard said, "Oh no. The ceiling."

James touched his fingers to the scorch mark. The varnish was warm. "Don't worry. It's our boat."

James wanted Gerard and the ESA to become their first customer. Launching an Ariane 5 rocket from Guiana required more than a quarter of a million litres of liquid hydrogen. The demonstration had loosened Gerard up, and he said, "Guys, this is very cool. When you are ready, in some years, I hope you will be able to supply us."

James said, "We're ready now. I know we can't supply the whole amount yet."

Gerard laughed at what he thought was self-deprecation, and Roland brought up the other side of the pincer movement. "Didn't you say you needed a way of generating hydrogen without carbon emissions?"

Gerard shooed that away. "Yes, yes, they are in my ass about this now. Because the climate summit was in Paris and the ESA, if we are honest, is a French organisation." He smiled at them. "But frankly, guys, it is not so easy. The other suppliers are companies like Airbus." He pronounced it *Airboos*. "It's not selling pencils. This is the European Space Programme. It's not . . ." He searched for a comparison.

James said, "It's not Pets.com."

"Exactly." Gerard shrugged in the French style. "Your hydrogen isn't even compressed, I imagine?"

"We can figure that out if it's going to help."

Gerard wished he was young again and willing to casually throw himself at such mountainous problems. They'd never be able to do this cheaply enough. But maybe once they'd gone bust, their technology would live on at Airbus or Statoil. There was no need to be cruel; he was here to keep himself informed, not to dispense business advice. He said, "It's not easy to sell to the state. We need to be sure you won't go bankrupt before you deliver what we've paid. When you have been producing for five years, seven years, then, guys, I really hope we can buy from you."

They sent Gerard another thermos of hydrogen to show his colleagues in Paris, just in case it helped. James didn't believe, as he once would have, that signing up a space agency would be a transformative breakthrough. It was just another obstacle to be picked apart.

*

Then, after one flight, one shower and five minutes of dithering over near-identical outfits, James was in the Royal Academy with Alice, taking an intelligent interest in the pictures. She wouldn't usually have been there either. Which she knew made her a philistine. Obviously the pictures were lovely.

They were in front of an early painting of Monet's, who was apparently keen on gardening – the theme of the exhibition. The picture showed some flowers in a basket and some more arranged on the ground beside it. Alice thought: Okay, it's a picture of flowers and it looks like some flowers. God I am such a heathen.

She came up with, "They look so fresh, don't they? Even though they're not in water so they're probably already on the turn. But that's flowers, isn't it? Fleeting, transient, all that." Embarrassing. Awful. Like being back in GCSE English: the flowers in Ophelia's hair symbolise the ephemeral nature of existence. Ten marks A-star thank you can we go now please.

James said, "Mmm. And it's interesting how he's done the chiaroscuro, so these ones at the top are quite dark and these ones here have the light on them." She didn't believe for a second he cared either way, but it was a sign of something that he could produce a passable comment. James went on: "Do you want to look at some more, or shall we go and have a drink?"

With a rush of gratitude, Alice said, "I don't mind. What do you prefer?"

"Umm." James searched her face. "It is a good exhibition."

"So good."

"But I think we've seen the main ones."

"Yes, I think that's right."

On the way out, they agreed that the show had been very interesting, and gladly forgot about it. More pressingly, there was information to learn about each other. How was Orkney? Where did they go to university? Alice thought she would laugh when he asked whether she had siblings, but actually, yes, fair enough, it was something a person might like to know.

They went to a quiet bar Alice suggested above a restaurant in Soho. At the entrance, she concealed that it was a members' club. The people on the door said, "Hello, Alice, great to see you." And on the way up the stairs, James asked, "So you must really come here a lot?"

"Far too much apparently. Bit shaming."

Once they'd found two armchairs, Alice ordered white wine and said, "Boring, I know. But you should have something fun if you want it." James had switched his usual drink from wine to vodka martinis: fewer calories per unit of alcohol. She kept the attention on him and off herself. Gulping her wine, she realised she was nervous.

James, being looked at by her, saw himself a little more. He told her about his first important teacher, a bearded, storytelling Irish communist called Mr Healey, who taught them the Russian Revolution. It had stuck with him: the fascination of trying to construct an ideal society, like SimCity on a world-historical scale; and the harshly comical dissonance between utopian ideal and gory reality. Even now, he still thought of company strategy as Five Year Plans and praised the engineers for "exceeding their quotas".

Alice thought: Thirty Years' War. Men loved reading about disaster. It made them feel cosy. "Sounds like you were very precocious."

James didn't know that in Alice's idiom "precocious" was a synonym for "annoying child", and said, "Oh yes, very."

As he talked, Alice compared him to her friends' boyfriends and husbands. Yes, husbands. Among her friends, getting married was no longer a wild, radical, probably doomed young escapade. So far it was still mainly the obvious ones: those who'd been together since Oxford, and the Christians. But they were the early adopters, the small beginnings of the bell curve.

Some of the boys her friends were marrying . . . It was a tragedy. There was an obvious structural mismatch in the quality of men and women. At every party there were masses of attractive girls: not at all bad-looking, nicely dressed, clean and coiffed, who also happened to be clever and fun, with good jobs. And these boys they were with. The amount of help they needed. Ghastly clothes. Their chat blundering and egotistical, not noticing anything, spoiled by their mums into believing they were charmers. And plain as planks, for the most part. Hair ominously thin. Pudge gathering beneath the shirt. Everywhere she looked, she saw incredibly accomplished hotties coaxing these inadequate boys, like toddlers at a children's party, into the role of fiancé.

Her theory was that this mismatch came from when women weren't allowed to have jobs and had to develop attractions to get boys to choose them: hair, figure, piano-playing, a personality. Men hadn't had to. To have value in the marriage market, all they'd needed was an income. But now women had jobs too, plus they could still look nice and play the piano and take an interest. Lots of men were quite small and sad and self-aggrandising.

It was galling that her teenage acquaintances from the boys' school, whom she and her friends had refused to let touch them, were now considered a catch. As if those smelly boner-wagglers, now in the guise of barristers and bankers, were the best on offer. And all the while, her own value in the marriage market was depreciating. Loathsome spin class meant she was so fit she could practically have joined the Marines. But she was thirty-one and on the down curve. Still near the top of the slide, but sliding. It was enough to make you livid.

James, though, was not a toddler in a suit. He was a grown-up. Not obviously an egomaniac. He was unusually attentive to what she thought, to how he came across. She could tell he was one of those guys who'd never retire; he'd be tinkering with machines and businesses till he dropped. When he was lying in the bath, his mind certainly went – not like hers, to just the most fatuous rubbish, like jewellery and trying to be the funniest on her WhatsApp groups – but to engineering puzzles and Britain's energy mix.

And this sense of direction he had. It was like a lorry thundering past and sucking you into its wake. She was just floating around really. She assumed she'd be a big cheese one day. An OBE at least, surely, or a dame. But he was on this Earth to accomplish something, and it gave him a bearing against which to measure everything else. She couldn't imagine him ever shirking or ducking or not conscientiously, frankly, like a strong loyal shire horse, pulling his allotted load.

As she conceptualised in this way, she felt herself warming up. She hadn't had any dinner. One of the problems with dating was that, because you wanted to look easy-going, you had to eat at strange times or go without. And the spin classes made her hungry. Instead of food she was on her third glass of lovely refreshing white wine. The distance between her and the moment she was in was narrowing. After a while, she was no longer watching herself be on a date; she was simply on a date, laughing, telling him about herself and hoping he was a good kisser.

With his usual thoroughness, James constructed a date-suggestion matrix. He collated and cross-referenced critics, TripAdvisor reviews and hitherto unconsulted publications like *Time Out*.

In the glass cube of their office, Roland looked over James's shoulder and said, "Aren't you meant to be working?"

"Do you think a walk along the South Bank is good or is that only really in summer?"

Mary-Rose turned round on her swivel chair. "A romantic winter stroll. That's so sweeeet. She'll love that."

Roland said, in an East End accent, "*Carm off it*. It's a manky concrete park next to a brown river, in the cold, with the stalls boarded up. It's not exactly Winter Wonderland. And then, just when she thinks it can't get any worse, she'll have you lunging at her." He mimed a zombie, arms out, moaning, "Mmm, Aliiiiice. I want to eat your faaaaace."

James slapped away Roland's outstretched hands and felt very loved.

For Mary-Rose, it was like being let into the bosses' locker room. The part of himself that James showed the company – a person of sober striving and impersonal duty – was peeled off and hung up like a costume. The idea that James, of all people, would spend office hours googling restaurants . . . She dared to say, "You know, the Horizon 2020 people are still waiting for those documents. They're not going to write themselves."

James put his face in his hands while Roland gave her a high five. They were right: he was meant to be working. But since the coma, his stress didn't feel as existential as it had before. On his desk he kept a jagged chunk of metal, steel shot through with torn copper fibres, from when the cable burst. Even that shattering day had been followed by another morning. Never again would he ascend to the saint-like pitch of concentration at which he'd lived before the first machine was launched.

Alice's attitude, which he was comprehending piecemeal by observing her, was that your job was merely one element in a well-lived life. To be doing it right, you also had to go on great holidays, wear clothes that suited you, have fun at parties and many things more. Maybe she was right: maybe there were levels of sophistication higher than single-mindedness. Maybe you could rise above your own ambitions. It was an idea that had never occurred to him.

Sometimes it did seem he'd missed out. Had he ever been to South America? Did he know the nightclubs of Mykonos? Had he, given his interest in Italian food, ever eaten at the River Café or Bocca di Lupo, only a couple of miles away across London? No, no, many times no. The automatic theoretical riposte was that these were the costs of devoting your apportioned hours to one great cause. There was no glory in going to restaurants. But certainly, when lying in Alice's amazingly comfortable bed in her stylish flat near Gloucester Road, with his hand resting on her arm, or his foot keeping contact with her foot, he felt he'd long been lacking precisely this. He disguised his slight hurt each time she mumbled, "Too hot, too hot," and he had to let go.

In March, Roland moved out of his parents' place in Maida Vale. They gave him a few hundred grand for a deposit and, with his unreduced salary, he got a mortgage on a flat a little further out in Kensal Rise. His mum told him to count himself lucky he was an only child; otherwise he'd have only got half the money and had to live in Watford.

James invited Alice to come see it and finally meet Roland. He and Roland had been wonderfully in tune recently, enjoying it whenever they had time alone together – something that had once seemed infinite.

James was careful not to be triumphalist around him. Roland could no longer use the prospect of Japan to distance himself from what he found mundane. Nor did he have a girlfriend. So James let him have his way on small decisions. He tried to re-enthuse him about the company, to have him re-immerse himself as totally as when James was away. And he played up to a less successful version of himself – not a visionary, but a nerd.

Alice told him to get a housewarming present. Not used to gift-giving, he found himself searching for an object of unforgettable specialness and meaning. His budget expanded out of control until, finally, he ordered from Kyoto a print of a brush-and-ink painting. It showed a typhoon, the wind made visible with colour, wrecking some wooden ships in a bay. As Roland messily ripped off the brown paper, enjoying acting like a child, he glanced at Alice and said, "This must have been your idea."

"No," she lied. "It actually wasn't."

When Roland saw the picture, it knocked him out of his fizzy playful mood. "Mate. That's so thoughtful. A little corner of Japan to keep forever. Wow. Thank you."

James knew he would never learn to read the calligraphy: this typhoon was the divine wind, the kamikaze, keeping foreigners away from Japan's shores and safely home in Kensal Rise. A small, crazy, vengeful voice thought: Fuck you, Roland, for putting me through that.

The flat was the upper floor of a Victorian terrace. West London was good; Roland and Alice would have that in common. The more they could have their own friendship, the better. They would be a trio.

Roland had brought his stuff in a rucksack, some open fruit crates and half a dozen black binbags. James said, "Do you want me to help you unpack? I'll do it if you want, and you guys can get to know each other."

Roland and Alice made awkward faces.

James was opening the necks of the binbags. "How have you organised these? By room or by function?"

Roland caught Alice's eye again.

James said, "We've been looking at flats as well. Alice has rightly pointed out that I'm too old to live with my parents."

Roland said, "Wow. You're looking at flats?"

She made a *yikes* face. "Uh . . . *no*. James is looking at flats for himself, and I've been helping him."

"Right. I guess he needs it."

She shook her head in unfeigned amazement. "Like you wouldn't believe."

"What's he doing? He must have some kind of insane master plan."

"Exactly. He wanted to buy in one of those commuter developments halfway to Essex. They have own-brand iPads built into the wall next to the door."

James fed the joke at his own expense: "The block has its own smart grid so you can use energy at low-demand times. And if we want to make a quick ten million, we should —"

Alice interrupted. "But you have to live in a new-build retail park in E-two hundred, and everyone near you is a wide-eyed lawyer who's just moved to London from the North."

Roland said, "Shame you can't convince Arthur and Mary to downsize and let you have their house." He read her expression. "Have you not been there yet?"

"No. James says it's beautiful though."

"It is. It is. And Arthur and Mary are the best. They let us run the company from their kitchen for years. Arthur cooked us lunch every day."

"Sounds dreamy." There was a pause. She answered the unvoiced question: "I just don't want to meet them as I'm coming downstairs in the morning from their son's childhood bedroom. It would be embarrassing for them."

James chipped in. "I keep saying it wouldn't be. They'd love it."

"I completely believe that that's what you believe."

Roland said, "They're very friendly."

"I'm sure they are. But can you imagine anything worse than sitting there eating your toast when some girl comes tottering down the stairs from your son's bedroom in last night's clothes with her make-up still on and her hair in a bush? There's only one thing worse: *being* that girl. *Non*."

From everything James had told him, Roland had imagined her as duller. A clever girl who did finance and probably wrote her notes on different subjects in different colours of ink. Nor had he realised she'd be good-looking. Her yellow hair stood out against her black clothes. He could see the shape of her body. She would definitely smell good – of the classy scents he only encountered in women's flats. Her face was quick-moving, full of expressions, exaggerating or counterpointing all she said. He wondered what her resting face was and whether anyone ever saw it. Presumably James did.

Roland suddenly felt left out.

Alice looked into binbags without touching the contents. She hated unpacking. None of her own actual friends had ever asked her to do this. But making a relationship go was about being game. At least Roland was easy. With no risk of sexual tension, and a great desire to like each other, their chat soon became safe, warm, intimate, almost sibling-like. It was as if they already had the depth of years. And yet each of the other's jokes and anecdotes was fresh. Alice found she was unexpectedly having fun.

She asked about Japan and, out of habit, he told the story of how he'd ended up in Nagaur. He wished he hadn't started. These days it was more shameful than adventurous. He winced as he told her. "I missed the JET application deadline, like a twenty-one-year-old idiot, and so I got a teaching job in this little town in Rajasthan instead. I took all these Japanese books with me, and I seriously believed I was going to teach myself Japanese." He shook his head.

"And what happened the next year?"

"I missed the deadline again."

They both laughed.

"Actually, I didn't even apply. I didn't have the . . . I don't know, the just, like, *bloody-mindedness* to get it done. Pretty bad, isn't it?"

"No, no."

Roland waved his chin at James, who was busying himself in the hallway by reprogramming the boiler. He'd found the miniature instruction booklet and was matching the booklet's diagrams to the control panel. Roland said, "If I'd been the feckin' Terminator over there, I'd be a professor at Kyoto University by now and teaching the Japanese how to improve their own language. But I've been trying to learn for like a decade, on and off, and the only thing I can say is *Hello, my name's Roland*."

"If it helps, I did French for seven years, got an A star, and all I can say is *Je m'appelle Alice*, and last year I went on holiday to Paris."

He smiled. "You remember what you got in GCSE French?"

"It's quite easy to remember when all your grades are the same." She looked dead at him, daring him to react.

"Ha. No wonder you and James like each other."

Alice didn't want to consider herself a James-style juggernaut; she wanted to be present in all boxes and confined to none. So she said, "I don't know. It was pointless really. Just circus tricks. Balance a ball on the end of your nose. A-squared plus B-squared equals C-squared. *L'année dernière, je suis allée à Paris*. And I don't even really like Paris. I just keep thinking, wouldn't it be better to be in London?"

Once Alice left, feeling she'd been a real champ, James came over to Roland. "I just wanted to say, I can see it might be difficult that I've got this great new girlfriend and you haven't got one."

Roland rolled his eyes so hard his head described a circle. "Urrrrrrgh."

James persisted. "I want you to know, you're still my most special sausage."

"Yeah, yeah."

"Still love you, buddy. Don't you want a hug?"

Roland closed his eyes. "Fine."

James hugged him while Roland kept his arms at his sides.

"Thanks again for the print. It's very thoughtful of you."

"Congratulations on the new flat."

"I might not have a girlfriend, but at least I don't live with my parents."

James thought of mocking him back but didn't.

In the next months, James and Alice tried each other on, like walking around the shop in new shoes. They invited Alice's friends for dinner, with James opening the wine and Alice getting scratchy and self-critical about the cooking.

She began to edit James's clothes. After he'd put on his jacket, she sometimes stood in front of him, tweaking and pinching the shoulders and lapels until it sat as well as it could. She said, "We're going to have to get you one made at some point."

When the bin in her kitchen was full, he took the bag outside, and they both saw a lifelong division of labour opening up to them. The stereotypical shapes of grown-up existence were there to be inhabited.

Neither found it difficult. Both were still quite young, undamaged and rationalistically willing to prioritise this developing bond between them. Both were used to delaying gratification, to subordinating their spontaneous preferences and desires to the larger project of making something work. Just as they'd made successes of school and careers, so they made the efforts and small sacrifices required to have their relationship run smooth. After all, what could be so complicated? They were intelligent and attractive and confident, and they liked each other's company.

Of course there were collisions, the ephemera of strong personalities bumping into each other like two gases mixing. Once, when she came out of the shower with heavy wet hair, he told her, with what he thought was affection, "You look like a drowned weasel."

Her eyes went flashy, she drew herself up – and caught herself in time. "I know you meant that as fun teasing. But I'm not Roland. I'm your girlfriend. If you want banter, go talk to him."

And, with repetition, it began to annoy Alice that he never brought any kind of small little token gift for her flat. Of course he wasn't a house guest exactly, who should definitely bring something, but nor was the flat his, and they were usually there because he still lived with his parents. He was not one thing nor yet another, in this awkward period of becoming. After she raised this, James, though he knew it wasn't quite right, set himself a calendar reminder to bring flowers/miscellaneous every ten days.

Personally, he thought her dinner parties – which she insisted were not dinner parties, nothing that old-fashioned, just fun gatherings of friends — were a waste of time. She spiralled herself up to a high pitch of stress, and then didn't eat. Later, before getting into bed, she'd open the fridge and gorge through whatever was on the palely illuminated shelves.

He asked, careful to be constructive in tone, "How come you tend to not really eat anything when we have people over? I thought it was delicious. You're a very good cook."

She twitched her shoulders as if scratched. She'd have preferred not to speak but reluctantly said, "I know it's stupid. I kind of think eating in public is gross. You know, just chomping and masticating like some great troll with grey bits of meat falling off your teeth." She shuddered.

James had just eaten in public. "But then why do we ask people to come round for a meal? We could just have a drink with them."

She slightly shook her head. "You can't invite people over and not feed them. I'm sorry, but you just can't."

James was bewildered. In fact, you could do whatever you wanted. Like that dictum of Keynes's about nations, *Anything we can actually do, we can afford*. Whatever we can physically do, we can choose to. She said, "Look, I know men enjoy telling each other that women are irrational." Now James was getting a little offended. It was late and a wine headache was coming on. "But it's *perfectly* rational. Giving people dinner is the culture we live in, and not giving it to them will make them feel uncomfortable and they won't be able to enjoy themselves, which, unless I'm missing something here, is the entire bloody point."

So they continued to have dinner parties, at which Alice was stressed and didn't eat, but which allowed her to feel that she was living like a human being. James accepted this as a given parameter, and helped her achieve it. They managed with no real rupture to do everything that they thought two such people as themselves, starting a relationship, would do. As an arranged marriage, it would have been perfect.

Their best time was Saturday morning in Alice's calm, sunlit flat on her quiet street near Gloucester Road, where the houses were iced with white stucco. Sex was pleasantly accomplished, unwinding them. Alice went back to sleep while James took her keys, without asking, and walked to the coffee shop. At first, he would drink his flat white in the kitchen, unfolding the *FT Weekend* across its marble surface. But he felt too far from her. So he tiptoed back into bed and browsed the paper till she woke up.

For her, it was very peaceful to sip her tepid coffee and tilt her head backwards to look at the sky through the window. It was the one time of the week her thoughts were not intent on something. Instead, they floated, with long clear gaps of nothing. She remembered disconnected incidents, like the time her brother Charlie, aged four or five, hit a cousin's dog with a rake. The dog made a sound like crying. She'd never liked dogs since.

All too soon, her thoughts began to knit themselves together, like the relentless self-organising impetus of basic proteins. She and James began to talk, in fragments and then in flow. Curiosities in the newspaper – events that week – and, as James grew deeper in trust, his in-progress thoughts on the company. Even Roland's opinion he rarely asked for until he knew his own.

He began to let himself think out loud. His problems now weren't engineering and finance but man-management – not his element. He was trying to train himself in it. Roland seemed bored again. Javier kept trying to stake out his own fief. Mary-Rose needed a path to promotion.

Alice could think of more fun things to talk about on a Saturday morning than HR. But, like when a guest speaker came to school, she asked questions that showed she'd been paying attention. James was pleased. It was as if they were together in their campaign tent, studying the map and deciding where to deploy their regiments.

Alice had to stop her eyes flicking to the ugly beige plastic disc on his upper arm. It didn't give her the ick, exactly. Everybody knew that if you were with someone you might eventually have to wipe their arse when they got decrepit. It just seemed a bit soon for that. Not that he was decrepit.

Very early one Friday morning in June, with unwelcome sunlight already glowing through the thin orange blind, James rang Roland on repeat, letting it ring out and pressing call again until Roland finally answered. Alice could hear his sleep-slurred voice coming out of the phone: "What?"

"They've fucking done it. We're out of the EU. We've Brexited."

There was quiet at the other end. Then Roland said, "Mate. I'm so tired. Did you really have to wake me up to tell me that?"

Alice rolled closer and, still undressed, spoke to Roland on the phone. "Hi, Roland. He did it to me, too."

"Ugh."

"At least you can hang up on him." Sometimes it was as if James were a grown-up, and she and Roland silly children.

Roland said, "Does this mean we don't get the rest of the EU money?"

"I think they still have to give it to us because it's already been allocated. But our chances of getting more are basically zero. The European Space Agency isn't part of the EU, so hopefully that's still an option."

"Urgh. Do you ever get the feeling that, like, since the financial crisis, all the news has been bad news? Like, it's just one crisis after another."

Alice said into the phone, "That's the spirit, Roland. Up and at 'em." She heard him laugh, and then James started talking about whether being outside EU rules would make it easier for the Scottish government to give them money.

When James reached the calendar notification that his six months of trampolining had passed, he regretfully gave it up and switched to Zumba.

Alice tried to persuade him to take up something less patently unattractive. He could do spin, maybe, somewhere other than her. She didn't quite believe that spin carried such a horrible risk of obsession; or rather, she didn't believe that a spin obsession was so very terrible.

The Zumba class he chose was the nearest one to his parents' house, in a community centre. The other dancers were overweight middle-aged ladies who didn't like the gym. They seemed to find it funny that James was there, dressed in technical fabrics. The instructor, a tanned young Australian woman in a crop top that displayed the effort she'd invested in her abs, told him, "This class. It's not, like, the most intense workout."

But when she put on her playlist of Latin American music, and they saw James, stiff with concentration, trying to notice the beat and move his limbs accordingly, they stopped finding him incongruous.

It was like opening another new chamber in his brain, neural pathways being blazed into the black space. And it *was* funny to look down at his limbs jiggling and writhing. Afterwards, he talked to Alice about the interesting differences between salsa and merengue, and she thought: Thirty Years' War, Thirty Years' War. Get me out of here.

His BMI sank to 24.8, within the healthy range and trending down. His blood-glucose readings were stable. Alice was evidently wrong about Zumba. But he hadn't expected how much her unabated hostility to it threw him off. All her moods affected him, for better or worse, as his must her, the gravity of each continually pulling the other off their axis, like twin suns in a complex double rotation.

He told his dad this one evening when they were putting their dinner plates in the dishwasher. Arthur beamed like a Zen master whose pupil has achieved a leaping spark of insight. He melodramatically put a hand on James's shoulder and said, "Yes, m'boy. Now you're getting it. *Now* you're getting it. With your mother, for instance, I haven't bothered having my own feelings for, oh, about forty years. I just ask her what she's feeling and feel the same."

His parents seemed to be brimming over with sentimentality. His dad kept clapping him on the back and calling him "m'boy" or "Jim lad". His mum frowned when she looked at him and said, "I remember when you were not even the height of my hip, and you'd waddle around this kitchen, trying to peer into the fruit bowl and saying "appuh, appuh". What happened to that sweet perfect little angel?"

"Thanks."

"Oh, come on. I'm just your ancient old mum who loves you very much."

Aside from these moments, they strangely ignored him, as if they had better things to do. They were full of improbable plans: his dad was talking about buying a motorbike. His mum asked whether Roland would know where to buy pot. They seemed to have been released from some chronic responsibility. A task completed. A long-standing fear had been allayed. He would not name it, but he knew what it was; he'd feared it too.

SEPTEMBER 2016

James and Alice caught the Thursday afternoon Eurostar, rushing sweatily from their offices, for a weekend in Paris. In lovely quiet peaceful Business Class, the other passengers were older couples or French bankers. Alice would have preferred Rome, but it was an extra hour of flying, while Paris meant they could work online from the train.

They got in quite late, exacerbated by the time difference. The room in the hotel, a boutique place Alice had been recommended, was noticeably small but maximalistically decorated with a gold-framed mirror and crimson wallpaper. Tall double doors opened onto a shallow balcony. It felt very Paris.

They hurried to change out of their office clothes, not showering, and took a slightly-too-long cab ride, at night now, to the restaurant they'd booked. French classics – veal pâté en croute – for a clientele in their thirties and forties. If they'd just walked to it, around the corner, they would have liked it more, but it suffered in the cost–benefit analysis from all the travel.

As they ate and glanced around at smartly dressed couples from the French equivalent of their own education and background, they struggled to shake off the feeling of hurried forward motion, of the need to press on. They drank fast, and Alice felt like a Brit abroad.

James tried to engross his attention in where they were; to be in it. On his plate he had a confit duck leg. The skin – stiff, crinkly and caramel-brown – kept slipping off the smooth meat below. He said, "What *is* confit?" He decided not to take out his phone and google it; they were conversing. Alice thought: We can't become people who talk about the food. She mildly panicked about how to fill the forty or so hours of weekend.

The prospect of joining the sad, slow chain-gang shuffle through the Louvre... *Merci, non.*

The thing to do in Paris, basically, was shag in the hotel. If you did that, you'd hit the minimum standard for success on a Paris mini-break. No shags, and you probably shouldn't have come. When they got back to the room, tired and drunk, Alice roused herself to put the moves on James. She did a bit of kissing and heavy breathing, and he got the picture. She summoned up the determination that her school had drilled into her and told herself that anything these sex-mad Parisiennes could do, she could do better. So, she went down on him as if nothing could thrill her more. James was flattered and turned on. His confit conversation hadn't been that good. Must be Paris.

He fell asleep cleaned out and content. But as the hours passed, his sleep grew uneasy. He dreamed he was at university, walking around the luminous green quad and chatting to smoky, drifting shades of his tutors. Big Eddie was there, his gorilla-like build overfilling a scratchy tweed jacket. James was happy to see him, but something didn't fit. Eddie was reticent, embarrassed, as if there were something he wasn't mentioning. Something was wrong.

James gasped awake in the hotel room knowing what it was: he didn't belong there. He wasn't that young any more. He was a thirty-two-year-old company owner. In a couple of weeks, he'd be thirty-three. Another couple of years, and he'd be as close to fifty as he was to twenty.

In the morning, he was groggy and hungover. The night-time lucidity had denatured into static. Room service brought him a *pain au chocolat* and a coffee, which he ate at an unsteady circular table on the balcony. Through the gauzy white inner curtain, he could see Alice still asleep. Traffic noise slowly made him alert.

Their plan was that, before the romance got fully under way, he would just nip out very briefly to the European Space Agency. He'd annoyed Alice by asking several times whether she was sure that was okay. They'd agreed it was a good opportunity. It would be as if he'd just come by while in town, a friend of the agency rather than a travelling salesman. He was relieved to have a reason to get out and about, to stride quickly down the street before the tiring dawdle of tourism began. Alice would enjoy the weekend. She liked hotels and being in chic places. She'd probably want to go to the Louvre. There must be some kind of priority lane.

Once he was gone, Alice kicked off the duvet and spread out. It wasn't that she was anti-James; it was just quite nice to have a single moment to yourself. And after last night, he'd have wanted to shag again, which she wouldn't — and then she'd have felt guilty about doing a bad job of Paris. He really was a good guy. And this machine he'd built really was something, the golden rotors spinning even now beneath the shifting blue-black surface of the North Atlantic.

Yet as she lay starfish-like in bed, before her thoughts had arranged themselves into their official positions, a single flake of truth drifted up unstoppably from her subconscious. She thought: Our relationship is quite lukewarm. Immediately recognising the danger, she tried to repress this word. But it would not be repressed: *lukewarm*. Half-hearted. Tepid, not torrid. A tepid affair. Not impassioned but pragmatic. A pragmatic romance. Well-priced, with their respective values in the marriage market. All at once, she felt lonely.

No, no, absolutely not. She hurried out of bed, snatched up the nearest object — the hotel phone — and pressed for room service.

A Frenchwoman's voice: "Bonjour, Madame Winsloe. Can I offer you the breakfast in the room?"

"Yes. Yes." Blocking. Blocking. "Tell me what you have."

"On the menu?"

"Yes." Good idea. "Read me the menu. I'll say yes or no for each item, and at the end we'll go back through the shortlist."

A silence and then, "Of course, madame."

Alice could feel the hostility, could imagine this Frenchwoman telling her friends about the ridiculous fucking princess at work today. And this was good. It brought out an imperious response in herself. She made the Frenchwoman read out every type of berry — straw, rasp, blue — with the animosity stirring up her blood and clouding her thoughts.

*

Alice hustled them back to London on an earlier train. She fled from that destructive word. She blocked it out with a flurry of gifts, dinners, city-breaks to Edinburgh and Copenhagen. She had a jacket made for him and, as he was being fitted, ran her hand proprietorially down the side of his ribs, demonstrating how she wanted the cloth to fall. As she did it, she felt as if she were acting. Unspontaneous, inauthentic, fake.

She invited her parents for a dinner, cumbersome with meaning, at Scott's, their favourite restaurant, where in 1979 they decided to get married. Her dad and James jumped into a deep conversation about Napoleon's role in breaking the siege of Toulon, which made it quite difficult to imagine ever sleeping with him again, which she knew she would tonight. Her mum beamed away like Mrs fucking Bennet. Even as she was inviting them, on the phone to her mum, Alice had known she would hate it.

Sometimes James would be over at hers, watching a football match on the sofa so he could talk about it with Roland in the morning, and she'd find herself thinking of topics. "Do you think you're closer to building your own electrolyser, or how long will you keep using off the shelf?" You could fill a whole evening with these essay questions. The more she did that, the more the feeling of fakeness grew.

Sometimes, when they went out for a dinner she'd suggested, she for minutes on end could not think of any words at all. Once, she caught sight of their reflection in the plate-glass window beside them. They were dressed too smartly for the place, a girl in finance and a guy in business, with money for fancy clothes and restaurants but nothing to talk about. Hollow people. Empty people.

It was actually her own fault. Even the ditziest wellness guru on Insta could have told her: when someone shows you who they are, believe them. Almost the first time they met, James talked about the Newcomen engine and how it converted energy into work. That was James. Energy into work. Everything else – *bagna càuda*, Zumba, Alice Winsloe – was just the portion lost as heat. Wastage. Inefficiency.

If they hadn't happened to meet in the two months, out of a lifetime, when he was idling, they'd never have got together. It was practically false pretences. She didn't know why he even wanted it. Just for shags and someone to have around when Roland was busy? That unfair thought brought out its own contradiction: she knew why he wanted this. It was the same reason he was so attentive to what she thought of him. They'd never spoken about it, but every page of his personality was watermarked with the memory of loneliness.

That made her feel for him. And he was good. There was no doubt he was good. And maybe, in fact, when you thought about it like a grown-up, that need in him, and that goodness, were forces powerful enough to keep a relationship impregnable for decades. It was like when you were hiring: drive was more important than qualifications. You wanted them hungry. They would become what you needed.

Maybe she'd been catastrophising. Maybe it was all okay. Sometimes there were evenings when for whatever reason it was all free and open, as if being together were the most natural thing in the world.

Roland saw her tightening up like a golfer with the yips. James didn't seem to have clocked it. On the contrary, he seemed to think this part of life was settled, and he could get back to work. His capacity for working had changed since the coma. He was not at the high clear pitch of elation he'd been at when they started the company, no longer a fresh young blade, but blackened and tempered, less finely made, more able to strike and strike and keep striking.

Sometimes Alice stopped by WeWork to pick him up for the evenings she organised. While James just finished one last thing off, Roland drifted out to the communal space to keep her company.

Once, she came dressed in a knockout gold sparkly jumpsuit and waited, blazingly out of place, on the corporate-hipster sofa. As she saw Roland coming over, she said, "I know, I know. I look like a diamanté lemon."

Roland laughed. "Maybe more like some kind of amazing Power Ranger."

"If Power Rangers did vajazzling."

Roland dropped himself into an armchair shaped like an upright egg. The gold jumpsuit looked even better close up. It clung to her; she was clearly in banging good shape. Lucky old James.

Roland apologised for him: "He'll just be a minute. He thinks we're being overcharged on magnets, and —"

"It's okay. He texted. I said it was easier to wait."

He saw that her make-up had taken a long time. "You guys are going to the V&A, right?"

"The theme is gold and sparkly. I'm going as a traffic cone."

"What's James wearing? Did you get him a gold jumpsuit as well?"

"I think the answer to that is, what's he wearing now?"

"Ah." Roland watched her. "He shouldn't keep you waiting."

"Outrageous, isn't it?" The high-handed style felt thin. "But we'd be early if we left now, and I *loathe* being early."

Her face was cycling through its expressions: high-handed, self-deprecating, long-suffering. None quite landed. Being with James seemed to have weakened her. And, as whenever Roland sensed a need in someone, it seemed so straightforward to plug the gap himself. "If he takes too long, I could go with you. I'm probably more fun anyway."

"You? Are you interested in the V&A?"

"Are you kidding? I'm much more interested than he is."

She resisted their default of talking about James, and said, "That's very sweet. But shouldn't you be out meeting fun young single girls?"

James came hurrying from a glass-cased meeting room, wearing the blue jacket Alice had bought him and some grey trousers. "Hi, Alice. You look fantastic. Sorry about the delay – this guy claims his prices are what they are, but they did it for Pelamis so they can do it for us. But we'd better go, right?"

Roland stood and, before heading back to their office, gave her a silent wave.

Then it was James's birthday. Alice never told the story of that evening, not to her school friends, not to anyone.

For weeks beforehand, she obsessed unproductively about what to lay on. Maybe a black-tie dinner at the Beefsteak Club for James and forty friends? Her cousin Freddie could get them in. But James only had three friends: Roland, Mary-Rose and this Eleni. So maybe an elegant vintage watch, engraved with . . . what? His name? Her name? "With love from Alice"?

She couldn't ever remember where the eventual idea came from – some subconscious mishmash of adverts and movies – but once she had it, she clung to it. She would make him a romantic dinner with her own hands, *but*, for a showstopper, she would build him a literal champagne pyramid, a glass tower of coupes with Bollinger cascading down in fizzy extravagance. How could he not feel spoiled?

It was a Thursday evening. The lights she'd tweaked up and down until she couldn't tell what was better. Fresh flowers stood on every surface. The dinner, a meal kit ordered from Bocca di Lupo – although personally she found Italian food a little *rustico* – sat ready for final prep. The fridge was racked with heavy wide-bottomed bottles of champagne. On the kitchen island, Alice had several boxes of coupes.

Just in her best black bra and pants, so as not to overheat, she began unwrapping the glasses from their crepe paper and lining them up. There were so many. To make the pyramid, you had one at the top, then four on the layer below, then nine, sixteen, twenty-five. Square numbers, to make squares. Duh. Five layers meant fifty-five glasses. But even five layers wouldn't be that high. She'd imagined something spectacular, and it might just look like one of those sad desktop Christmas trees.

Her confidence in the plan wavered. She stood there in her knickers, looking out over a sea of scrunched-up crepe paper. Maybe she was utterly unhinged, and this was the instant of realisation. She flinched back and forth. Then she texted Roland. "Starting to think this may be complete insanity. Can you let James know we've broken up, and we can all just pretend we never met."

He texted back. "Do you need some help?"

She hesitated then bashed out, "That would be amazing. Thank you so so much."

Before he arrived, she put on a new very short black dress that she'd had to cut the tag off without looking at the price. Her shoes, black with a high sharp heel, waited by the door. When Roland came in, his eyes ran over her, and he said, "You don't *look* like a mad person."

"And yet, it really does seem that I am one."

As they unwrapped the last of the coupes, he became aware that she was nervous. Her attention kept slipping off the pyramid, and she wavered with armfuls of discarded paper. It was not the girl he'd first met. This was James's fault. This was the effect that closeness to him had had on her. Roland became very gentle. Wordlessly he collected the empty boxes she kept forgetting around the room, and stacked them out of sight in a cupboard.

Alice put down a grid of four coupes and then another on top. He said, "Here, let me. I think we should probably put the whole bottom layer down first."

"Oh, yeah, of course. Sorry, I'm being stupid."

"No, no. What are you talking about? Don't forget, I run an engineering company. This is, like, my special subject."

"Roland. Don't be sweet to me. I'll cry."

He understood and put on a businesslike tone. "Okay. Then let's get this thing done. First off, if we mark out the corners of the base layer . . ."

It calmed Alice to be directed, to mindlessly arrange the five-by-five grid, with the thin glass screaking when pushed too tight. Roland did the corners, and the pyramid rose from waist-height towards eye-level. For the upper layers, they stood on chairs to lower each glass into position. Roland held out the last coupe for her, but she said, "You do it. If I broke it now, I'd kill myself."

Roland clambered onto the chair and, like putting the star on a tree, finished the pyramid. "Ta-da."

Alice nodded, pursing her lips. The many glass curves caught the light in glints and shadows. Maybe it would look better with candles. "Do you think this is – now that you see it – actually quite shit? Do you feel like you're on a cruise ship for retired dentists?"

Roland took that seriously. "Maybe a bit. But James will be into it. It'll make him feel very loved."

"Do you think it's even going to work? What if, when you pour in the champagne, it just runs down the sides and onto the counter?"

"We can test it. There's loads in the fridge."

"Okay, yes. Do it."

Roland pulled out one of the heavy bottles, the cold dewy condensation wetting his palm. He unpeeled the gold wrapper from the neck and grinned. "I feel like I'm the steward on the cruise ship."

She almost smiled.

Roland twisted out the cork and said, "You should do it. Unless I've misunderstood the plan, I'm not going to be here for your date night."

She took the bottle. The top glass was at eye-height. No need for the chair. She lifted the champagne and, as she tipped it sideways and began to pour, the heavy wide wet bottle slid horribly out of her grip. Her fingertips tried to clutch but couldn't. The fat black bottle plunged. Roland saw it for an instant in the gap between Alice's hand and the glinting pyramid.

Then it smashed down through the delicate layers with a crunching, splintering and bursting. The pyramid imploded and a wave of shards skittered outwards. The bottle clonked against the granite worktop, didn't break and rolled towards the edge, gushing sticky liquid. Roland stopped it automatically and set it upright. For a second, he laughed.

Alice took a step forward, yelped in surprise, and snatched a bare foot off the floor. As she hopped, losing her balance, Roland grabbed her, and her body fell against him. He moved her backwards around the coffee table, still hopping, until she could plump down onto the sofa. Now she began to cry, mainly out of rage. She clenched her jaw and tried to squeeze the tears back down their ducts. Roland said, "You're okay, you're okay. Let's see your foot."

The lighting was too romantic to make anything out, so he turned the dimmer up to full. The overheads shone on the laminated floor and the low wasteland of broken glass. Roland sat on the edge of the coffee table and picked up her injured foot. Her skin was warm and dry. A curved shard was stuck into the underside.

Her foot twisted slightly as he held it, the sole wrinkling and a thin crimson leak spreading between the ridges. Before he could overcomplicate it with reasons not to, Roland, with steady tension, pulled the bloody fragment out of her foot. He put it down on a two-year-old edition of *Vanity Fair*.

Alice reflexively said, "My hero."

"Sure."

She slumped back into the sofa as if giving up.

He said, "It's not your —"

She held up a hand. She was coming back to herself. "Let's at least have a drink since it's open. Use the spare glasses that are still in the box."

"Okay. Um, your foot's dripping onto the floor."

"Honestly, what difference does it make?"

While Roland hunted around for the spare glasses, she said, "You know, I've put in so much bloody effort."

Roland hesitated — whether to pretend she was talking only about this evening. Then he said, "You know I love him. But in some ways he's a very difficult person to be close to."

She gave him a warning glare but let it stand. Roland found the glasses and, crunching back across the floor, brought her one. He sat at the other end of the sofa, and they both sipped. After a while, just as Roland was thinking he should find the dustpan and brush, Alice said, "I really have tried, you know."

Roland leaned forward on his knees.

She said, "It's not like there's anything wrong. And at least he's got you. I think it was just —"

"You should tell *him* this stuff, not me. Or at least you should tell him first."

"Right. Yes. You're absolutely right. I will. But I can't this evening; it's his birthday."

"Okay." A sadness for his friend settled on Roland. After some more quiet, he said, "Your foot's still bleeding. Do you have any plasters?"

"In the bathroom. The cupboard behind the mirror."

When he came back, bringing the bottle of champagne as well, she said, "Thank you for being here."

"It would be a *bit* harsh to just leave you here bleeding with glass everywhere." He perched again on the edge of the coffee table and took her foot in his hand.

"I've really fucked this evening up, haven't I?"

"Oh, yeah. Oh, totally."

Alice laughed with the lightness that comes after collapse. The strain of holding things up was released. What she'd dreaded was here, and she was still alive, and the life force surged in her. With the blood and the champagne, she was a little higher than she realised. Her appetite sharpened. And the slim cutaneous outline separating her from the world had already been punctured. Roland was still holding her foot. His fingers were warm on her instep.

A charge ran through her. What had been inert, like brother and sister, carried some new potential. Roland felt it. He looked at her lying back on the sofa, her very short black dress riding up her thigh, her shield of mascara smudged, her expression for once not mobile and changeable but fixed on his, alert, adrenalised, expectant. An answering jolt ran through him. He was already touching her; his fingers were already on her skin. His vision narrowed.

But he put her foot down, still bleeding, stood up; blinked several times and said, "I'm going to go. It's him you should talk to."

Alice's outstretched legs retracted, curling back under her abdomen. "Of course. Of course." She slipped back into her polite voice: "Thank you so much for coming to help." Roland gestured helplessly at the shattered pyramid and the glass strewn around it. She said, "Oh, don't worry. I'll tidy up." He should leave.

"Okay. Well." He searched for something to say. "See you."

She said, "Maybe."

And he went.

*

When Alice broke it off with James, she tried to communicate her sincere regret that they hadn't fitted each other as well as they'd both hoped. They were not part of the same puzzle after all. Somehow it all came out as unconvincing clichés.

He took it with stiff decency. He said frankly that he was hurt and disappointed. But if it didn't work, what options were there? He shook her hand, which made her want to cry.

Roland waited a month. Then a few more days, so it wouldn't be obvious.

He went with James to a quiet restaurant near their office, one of James's favourites. It was in a brick-built former warehouse and had double-high ceilings, which James liked because it meant that sounds were dispersed. He was starting to be uncomfortable in noisy rooms. There was a long mauve banquette along one side and a corner table as far as possible from anyone else, which he used for afternoon meetings.

They ordered coffees, and he talked to Roland about the funding round. His sense of the financial momentum, like a sailor feeling the breeze shift and freshen, was that it would soon be time. Soon they would bring in the industrial quantity of cash needed for a full-scale machine. Not a prototype any more. Real power.

The coffees came and nudged his thoughts into a different dossier. "We're spending so much on flights, it might be better for us to move up there for a while."

"To Orkney?"

"Mm. I've found an Airbnb in Stromness that the owner will let us rent longer term. Even if we fly down for meetings, it would be a big cost saving. And it's beautiful, actually. It's an old fisherman's house on the harbour, with its own jetty. There are three bedrooms, so Mary-Rose or whoever could stay when they're up."

Roland tried to keep the smile on his face. "Move up to Orkney? It sounds so fun."

"You could rent out your flat, which would more than cover the Stromness house and give you some spending money. We could – I don't know – catch fish and barbecue them on the jetty. You'd love it."

To Roland, moving to a remote fisherman's house in the subarctic, just as winter was coming, didn't seem the product of rational cost-cutting. But he didn't want to press James on that. Instead, his pulse fluttering in his fingertips, he said, "It sounds great. Let me think about it."

James nodded.

"But listen, there's something else I wanted to ask you about. And you can totally, absolutely, say no. I know it's an unfair thing to ask. But I just wanted to at least have asked. Because you only get one life, don't you, and you can't know how things are going to turn out."

James expected something absurd.

"It's about Alice."

"Alice?" James sat back away from him.

"Yeah. I was wondering if it would be okay for me to, like, ask her out. And obviously, obviously, if that's too weird, just say the word, and it's done, I'll never mention it again."

In James, an abyss opened. "Wait. Did you two . . . ?"

"No. No, no. Absolutely not. But I do get on well with her." Roland blushed. "And I just thought, if you two aren't together . . . But like I said, if it's just too fucked up, then let's forget about it."

James was suddenly, utterly, exhausted. He should have foreseen this. Everyone loved Roland. James loved him. For the first time since their trip to Lochnagar in the purple Lamborghini, he felt himself to be alone in the world. Nothing had changed since he was a teenager. He hadn't, after all, left himself behind. Slowly, he reasoned his way through the matter at hand. Perhaps if he'd been less reasonable, he'd still have her. "Well, if Alice and me didn't match up, that doesn't mean you and her shouldn't try. It's a question of compatibility not . . . possession. It's not like I've got any claims on her."

Roland let out some breath. "Okay. Great. That's, like, really, really generous of you. Thank you, pal."

James thought: I've got claims on you, though, pal. And then: I'll always remember this moment; these mauve banquettes, this white tablecloth with creases where it was folded, Roland looking guilty but like he's got what he wanted.

Roland said, "It'll probably come to nothing anyway. I just feel, like, you should give it a go."

James nodded. This was how things were done in the Old Testament: when someone died, his widow would remarry his brother.

"So, it's okay? You're sure?"

"Yes."

"Definitely?"

"What do you want from me? I said it's okay. Do you want me to be happy for you as well?"

XII

JUNE 2017

Roland was underwater with his eyes closed, in a deep old tub, with the worn enamel touching his bum and his sandy hair floating around his forehead.

He pushed up into the afternoon sunlight and rubbed the water from his eyes. Alice was lolling in a wicker armchair, reading a John le Carré. These books were unadulterated pleasure for her, with no risk of learning something useful. She'd come upstairs to keep him company in the bath. He looked along his slight, pale body refracted through the liquid pane. His cock must be less dense than water; it floated upwards like a buoy on a rope, its tip bending the surface from below. "Do you want to get in?"

"No, thanks," she said and pushed a page over.

They were at her friend Neesh's parents' house in Hampshire for the weekend. Alice and Neesh – Venetia – had both pulled him aside to say they knew how ugly it was. He didn't understand; to him, it was . . . he didn't even know the right word for it. A mansion? A manor house? Ridiculously massive anyway, standing by itself in the countryside, with lawns and trees around it and one of those hidden ditches to stop sheep coming up to the garden.

He'd never been in a bathroom with a carpet. It was a sun-faded pink and probably older than him. Even now, the sun was blazing in through the dormer window, heating up the carpet in sections.

He felt as if he'd descended far below the surface of England. Bright green sward in the sun. A lone oak in the field, its big head in leaf. A river flashing at the bottom of the hill. He noticed for the first time in years that he hadn't grown up in this country.

Alice and Neesh had known each other since the first day of senior school, two decades ago. Of Roland's friends from Cairo, only one lived in London, a lawyer called Melvin, whom he'd last seen when still at McKinsey. The others were in places that attracted rootless internationals: Abu Dhabi, Zurich, Singapore. "Citizens of nowhere," as Theresa May put it. It was sad to be called that.

When he was at school, it seemed sort of wonderful, like a United Colors of Benetton dream of the future. In each class there were kids with football strips and weird foodstuffs from dozens of countries, sitting next to each other as if it were the simplest thing in the world. Every term, someone's parents would switch job, and they'd be away. A couple of months later, the class would get a letter, a standing invitation to visit and some photos from another expat compound, now lush instead of dusty, the background faces black not Arab.

Here in Hampshire, the boyfriends and husbands were not quite as homogenous as the girls; sexual attraction had had a randomising effect. The species propagating itself through combination. The kaleidoscope of genes. New blood.

They had lunch outside, getting too hot with the Chablis and the sunlight. It was strange to him that they didn't eat in the shade – a foreigner's thought. As the group relaxed, they began, cautiously at first, to tease him and Alice about James. He understood that it was a sign of welcome; that they thought he was going to stick around.

Somehow they got on to terrible exes, and Neesh, who was being mocked for a boyfriend they called the Fat Controller, said to Alice, "At least I don't just work my way through a whole company one by one." Everyone laughed, and a few glanced at Roland to see how he would take it.

Alice said, "What can I say? I'll do literally anything to get close to tidal energy."

Roland quickly said, "It's just so amazingly lucrative."

Everyone laughed again, and liked him. Soon he was spinning self-deprecating tales of turbine mishaps and eccentric Orcadians. Even that traumatic day the cable shattered in the tidal strait, he succeeded in transmuting into laughter. For them at least. He'd performed this dance a lot when younger, but now he felt a tinge of grubbiness, as if showing too much skin. Then again, if people wanted to welcome you, it would be churlish not to give of yourself.

In the carpeted bathroom, Alice asked, "Was that weird for you? At lunch?"

"Nope. I get it. Otherwise, they'd just be talking about it behind my back."

"Exactly. *Exactly*." She nodded. "You didn't say anything disloyal."

"I know."

"It was nice of you to tell them your jokes."

"Oh." He shook his head, dismissing that.

"I wish it wouldn't keep coming up though."

Him neither.

"It's even — don't freak out — if we ever get married, I just know someone'll mention him in the wedding speeches. And I'll have to pretend to be a good sport about it."

"Maybe not."

"Hm?"

"He'd have to be the best man."

The lazy pleasure of the sunny afternoon was draining away. Back came the low eczemal itch of guilt. They'd done everything properly, and still it was there. Alice was beginning, just a little, to resent being made to feel this way. For Roland, it was worst up in Orkney, when he visited James in the house on Stromness harbour.

The two of them tapped at their laptops in the long evenings, watching Champions League without talking. Each time Roland arrived, James made sure to ask how Alice was, not letting that subject slide into taboo. But it was like when some supplier asked: how's the family.

James was deep into his negotiations with investors, now also including the sovereign wealth funds of Norway and Saudi Arabia, but he wasn't exhibiting the zeal that Roland hoped for. He wasn't twitching and drinking and waking up crazily stressed in the middle of the night. Instead, there was a kind of cold relentlessness. If anything, it seemed to make him more effective because his negotiating was devoid of nerves.

Roland's instinct was to love-bomb a way through to him: to get him drunk, to throw himself on the floor, to beg, to kiss, to force James to forgive him. But he couldn't do that to him as well. So he was considerate, and their conversation never went beyond the company or the football.

Alice said, "I really wish I'd met you first."

"Me too."

"Do you think he'll be okay?"

Roland slipped mostly under, so the water stopped his ears and only the dense sensory array of his face was still in the air. "Mmm. I don't know. And his parents are hurt. I don't think they'll ever . . ."

He stopped. It would be pathetic to feel sorry for himself. "I just need to find him something to get excited about."

Alice said something that sounded like mumbling. He pushed up again and said, "What?"

"I said I've got great single girls coming out of my ears if he wants to meet someone."

"It's still too early for that. And it can't come from you."

"What about Mary-Rose? Would that be such a bad thing, really? Everyone gets together with someone at work. And the way she dresses, he's already seen her cervix."

Roland laughed. "People always think that, but it'll never happen. He thinks of himself as her mentor."

It struck him that he used to speak about Alice with James, and now he spoke about him with her. For a long time, he'd assumed, without even realising it, that James was the big relationship in his life.

Midsummer that year fell on a Wednesday. Mary-Rose nagged James into inviting everyone for a barbecue on his stone jetty. It might cheer him up.

There weren't enough cars to move the team the fourteen miles from Kirkwall to Stromness. Someone would have to go back for the rest. James kept having to repeat that the company couldn't afford a couple of minivans right now, and kept having to thank those who'd brought their cars up. With no money around, minor annoyances regularly led to muttering and criticism. One of his tasks as leader was to absorb dissatisfaction. He monitored the level: humans had a fatigue limit just like steel. If you overloaded them, they broke. But they weren't there yet.

Once they were at his cottage, the irritability lifted. The engineers crowded onto the flagstone jetty to gaze out over the harbour and to set up the disposable barbecue trays on its low perimeter wall. The fires were lit, and charcoal smoke mixed with the tang of seaweed.

A huddle of engineers peered at the blue plaque drilled in next to the door: "There lived here ROBERT GREIG, LIFEBOAT COXSWAIN, awarded the RNLI Silver Medal for 'supreme gallantry' shown in rescuing the crew of the trawler *Shakespeare* wrecked at Breckness on 11th December 1907."

A self-appointed team of grill-men carried James's kitchen table outside and set up a serving station: mounds of sagging raw pink sausages; patties separated by peelable squares of plastic; bags and bags of soft, floury morning rolls. There wasn't really enough space, but it was a party after all.

The shadows of Stromness stretched out across the sheltered water. At this time of year, the sky didn't get fully dark. The sun rested just below the hills like an actor in the wings. The engineers speculated on the few boats going in or out: the huge box-like NorthLink car ferry to Thurso, with a blue Viking painted on the side; sturdy workboats chugging in from the oil platforms; fishermen heading out to try their luck.

Once everyone had something to eat, Mary-Rose said to James, "You should do a speech. People like to know what's going on." He might talk himself into one of his old everyone-follow-me-to-the-future-type moods.

"I'm in the workshop every day. How could anyone not know what's going on?"

"They want, like, an overview."

"If I give a speech, everyone will have to talk about the company all evening."

"Fine."

In the workshop, there was so much to fill up his mind with. That day, he'd been helping draw alternative shapes for the anti-turbulence tips on the rotor blades. You drew them on paper and scanned the shape into an iMac. The computer modelled how the water would flow over your shape, braiding and whirlpooling out behind. They had two years' worth of these improvements waiting to be manufactured and tested, once they had the cash to pay for it.

Mary-Rose said, "Have you signed up to that modern dance class?"

"I haven't yet. But —"

"You have to, though."

"I will, I will. But listen. I'm getting the sense that the ESA are coming round. They said they're getting more pressure to decarbonise. We could be a demonstration project for them. Green rocket fuel."

"Okay."

"And when they say yes, that's our signal to go to investors."

Mary-Rose knew he was distracting her. And talk of investment made her defensive. To ask for cash still felt like charity. James had told her many times that it wasn't; the investors expected to end up with more than they put in. But in her gut, she didn't believe it. At the visceral level, she felt that the people giving them money were fools, the victims of a scam perpetrated by someone high-minded and innocently self-deluding. She preferred funding from the government.

He said, "I've realised we're going to do what we always do: build momentum with scale. Instead of raising money for one machine, we're going to build three at the same time."

Mary-Rose wanted to ask what amount of money that would be, but it felt indelicate. "How is that going to work, though? The engineers have got too much to do already."

"We can get more engineers. That's what the money's for."

"But if we rush it —"

James saw Alan nearby, drinking a can of fizzy lager while sending a text. James said, "Alan, Alan," and, when he came over, "I was just saying this company has always advanced by expanding the scale of its ambition. Like with hydrogen, and buying the other marine companies."

Alan checked Mary-Rose's mood. He wouldn't take James's side against her. He looked forward to her visits. It was like having a bolshy, back-talking adult daughter but with none of the responsibility. He said, "You're better off getting used to it. I tried to fight him on the hydrogen, and now look where we are."

"He's saying he wants to build three full-size machines at the same time. And I guess our own electrolysers as well." She glanced at James, who nodded.

Alan slapped a strong hand onto his heart and staggered backwards, pretending to have an attack. Then he said, "Me and James do sometimes talk to each other. Much more so since James's coma." James had heard how Alan helped hold the company together. Alan said to James, "You not drinking?"

"I don't want one."

Mary-Rose said, "I was telling him to sign up to that modern dance class at the Pickaquoy Centre."

Alan nodded judiciously. "Oh, aye. It's very good exercise. I'm thinking of taking it up myself."

James said, "Yes, ha-ha, very good. Why don't you two make some jokes about it. I'm going to spread the news that we're getting closer with the ESA." He moved into the crowd. He wasn't signing up to modern dance. He'd dropped all that. Instead, he'd taken up running, up over the brow of the small hill behind the village and then along the coast. Tonight, he was running intervals, like Emil Zátopek. Hence no beer. He'd run after the barbecue ended, like Zátopek climbing the fence into the Prague athletic stadium to train at night.

He was impatient for the barbecue to end. He'd found a way to export the data from his blood-sugar monitor, which he cross-referenced with charts of his running speed and heart rate. You could see the sugar level dropping as his cells burned it for fuel. There was an optimum to be found, a perfect match of the curves describing blood sugar and exertion.

All this was a destructive vortex, but he was doing it anyway. He was tired of resisting these impulses. And he was getting very fit. The muscles in his thighs were swelling closer to the skin. The veins were becoming visible, like blue shadows. Soon the expanding muscles would push them right out, a Braille map of his blood supply.

Alan and Mary-Rose watched him edge his way through his employees. Mary-Rose said, "Poor guy."

"It's a shame for Roland too, though." Since James's coma, Alan had thought Roland never got enough credit.

Mary-Rose jerked her chin at James. "He's not drinking because he's going for a run afterwards."

"He told you that?"

"No, but I'm pretty sure."

Alan shook his head. "He's lonely without him. I actually think that's worse for him than what she did."

"You know her and Roland are in Rome this weekend? I bet they're going to get engaged."

"It's not her fault either."

"Yeah. But it would be simpler if she just fucked off though, wouldn't it?"

Alan chuckled into his beard. "You should have seen the pair of them when we started. They lied to me about how old they were. They were living in a hotel in Aberdeen like a pair of orphans. And the first time I met them, they were trying to get me sacked."

Mary-Rose had heard this one before but didn't mind. There was something fascinating about it, like stories about your parents from before you were born.

OCTOBER 2017

James found that, no matter how much had changed, the work was still there, undiminished, patient, ready to fill his minutes and his weeks. It could absorb him whole and give him the purpose that belonged to any turning cog.

With the funding round drawing closer, he began regularly WhatsApping Peter Thiel. Now that Donald Trump was president, with Thiel, practically alone, having bet on him, Thiel had acquired the dark glamour of an evil genius. His instinctive contrarianism was now seen as a pitilessly accurate reading of the times. A further investment from him would move many other millions in James's direction.

Mary-Rose kept saying things like "Oh, by the way, do you want me to ring those graphic designers and see if they can make our logo into a swastika?"

James let her vent.

These days he sometimes found the conversation with Thiel slightly boring. It was always China and state interference and liberal groupthink. James just wanted the money. He wasn't a petitioner any more. He had the world's leading marine energy company.

Thiel liked that James was talking to the new climate minister, Claire O'Neill. She was the third he'd met and the first he could work with. Her mind, like his, had been trained on rationalist problem-solving utopianism. She was an alumna of McKinsey. And if green industries were going to be the gold mines of the future, the government wanted them to be British. James was persuading her to guarantee an inflated price for the electricity he generated. A subsidy, like for other renewables. With that, and three new machines, it might be possible to break even, to heave themselves over the steep ridge that separated the red figures from the black. To reach the end of every month and have more cash in the account rather than less ... accumulation not depletion. It would be a different world.

Thiel approved of this, although he grumbled about state overreach, as he did about the ESA. Gerard's bosses had announced that the agency would be a leader in green propulsion. Research projects were urgently needed. For them, James's green hydrogen was as obvious and easy a win as sending an email. Gerard still had James's flask sitting on his desk. The ESA wanted it to be a grant, not a purchase, because it was administratively simpler. But James stonewalled until Gerard gave way. Drayton–Mackenzie Ltd became an accredited supplier of rocket fuel. Roland wanted to celebrate, but James had thought this would happen.

Once the deal was complete, Thiel texted, "You should meet w Elon. SpaceX tested hydrogen fuels but decided not to pursue. Perhaps you can convince otherwise?"

A few weeks later, James was told that Musk, a man whose tweets were reported by newspapers and who could buy Drayton–Mackenzie Ltd out of his current account, would be in an office block in Shepherd's Bush, a never-gentrifying neighbourhood of chicken shops and motorway flyovers. The third floor of the block was rented by a company called OneWeb. It was trying to manufacture hundreds of small satellites that would orbit the Earth as a human-made constellation and beam internet down from space.

When James and Roland arrived, a secretary told them they could wait on a sofa at the edge of a large open-plan room.

It was too warm. The windows probably didn't open. Eventually they took their suit jackets off, laying them over the sofa's arms so they wouldn't crinkle. Roland grew fidgety. He stood up to look across the top of the room, which was divided by partition boards into cubicles and meeting areas. He sat down again and said, "Actually, Alice was asking the other day if you might like to, you know, come round to hers for dinner one time. Obviously not if it's still a bit weird."

James had been running through the comparative merits and demerits of hydrogen, liquid methane and kerosene. He broke off a thought and said, "Thanks, but honestly I don't want to."

"Oh, okay. Yeah, no, totally get it. Just an idea."

"Tell her I appreciate it. But it might actually make me quite unhappy."

"Okay. Okay, yeah, I will." Roland fidgeted more, then said, "Things are going pretty well between us."

James stared at him with irritation and astonishment. "Good for you. But, pal, I'm trying to concentrate."

"Sure, sure. Totally."

They'd been there more than an hour when Musk finally appeared along the corridor. He was flanked by a much smaller, gym-built, middle-aged guy in a tight black T-shirt. James recognised the OneWeb founder Greg Wyler. Following them was an entourage of a dozen people.

James and Roland flicked upright, pulling on their jackets. Musk saw them and, realising who they were, pointed at them with both hands, like a lame dad doing finger pistols. "Greg. I just remembered I want to talk to these guys for a minute."

He was much larger than James had expected. Maybe six-three and beefy, with thick arms and a solid gut. He was wearing an unzipped blue SpaceX windbreaker with badges sewn on. Its two halves were pushed to the sides by his white-shirted bulk. His collar pressed into his jaw. On his bottom half he had on black school trousers and comfy trainers. With his slight South African accent and his blocky, square, handsome head, he looked like an ex-rugby player.

James thought: Musk by name . . . He suddenly felt like an idiot – all his running had just made him weedier.

Musk hovered awkwardly, glancing behind himself to check how close he was to the wall. The entourage and Greg Wyler waited and watched. Musk was evidently used to meeting people in front of an audience. He said, "So, Peter told me about your company. Tidal energy. Very cool. And you're using the electricity to generate hydrogen. Tell me how I can help."

James said, "What drives the turbines is actually the orbit of the moon, pulling the tide through the rotors."

"Nice."

"And we're selling the hydrogen to the European Space Agency."

"So using orbital energy to power launches into space. Neat. I like that." Musk checked his watch.

James felt he was losing him. "You've got the most exciting space company and —"

Musk interrupted. "We, uh, did some tests with hydrogen but initially went with RP-1 refined kerosene. Obviously RP-1 provides a lower specific impulse than hydrogen, but you can store it at room temperature and it's not as likely to blow everything up." Musk grinned.

James had time to say, "Yes."

"But it's certainly worth discussing the possibilities. I can put you in touch with our fuel engineers." He glanced into the entourage. "Josh, could you arrange that?"

James said, "Thanks."

"Okay, it's been great to meet with you. What you're doing is very cool. Predictable, zero-carbon electricity. It'll never beat solar though. And the maintenance must be hell. Salt water. You've got no idea what we went through on Omelek." He checked his watch again. "Okay, I've gotta go."

James said, "Okay. Great to meet you."

It was strange — embarrassing even — to know so much about Musk that Musk hadn't told him. James had read about the SpaceX launches from the Omelek atoll, and the problems with corrosion. He even knew that Musk had read the same space books as him and Roland growing up: Asimov, *Dune*, the *Hitchhiker's Guide*.

Roland rushed to say, "We're about to start a funding round. Maybe you could give us a shout-out."

Musk smiled with what James read as condescension. "Sure. I'll do a tweet."

*

On the way down in the lift, even before they walked out of the poky foyer, James fell into a slump. He'd met a far superior version of himself. Before this, he'd actually started to believe he was a big deal. "World-leading company" . . . humiliating.

Roland was saying something inane about Musk's jacket. But all at once, James could see that their machine was really no more than a crude floating dynamo. It negated as many carbon emissions as — what? — *one* of Musk's cars? Less than that? And how many cars had Musk produced? In a thousand years, when historians recounted the human race's greatest ever collective endeavour — intentionally changing the composition of the atmosphere itself, to lower its carbon content and reduce the planet's temperature — when that history was written, Elon Musk would be namechecked on page 1. James would not be mentioned. It was crushing. Even Musk's side-project was space flight.

This was what it must be like when the winners of some shitty trophy in Slovenia qualified for the Champions League and came up against Real Madrid. It was the sheer embarrassment of having taken yourself seriously. The feeling of trudging off after forty-five minutes, undone, outrun, outclassed, and knowing you'd have to go out again for the second half.

What had made him think his life should be about tidal turbines, of all things? It was difficult to see where he'd turned off into this technological cul-de-sac. The mistake must have been to work on the problems that happened to be in front of him, and not to seek other, more promising ones. He'd been sucked in by the work itself, by his capacity for it.

Musk must somehow have been able to see more astutely, not just to toil but to choose — no, Musk must have followed the same mixture of impulse and circumstance, but his had led him to computer science and California, while James had gone to the sticks. James's trajectory was similar to Musk's, but just not as high.

Musk was only thirteen years older. Even if James went back to university tomorrow to study physics or engineering or computer science and then moved to California, his brain didn't have the elasticity of an eighteen-year-old's. Gauss had finished his *Disquisitions* by the time he was twenty-one. James was too old to start again.

It didn't even seem as if Musk had had to sacrifice. While James hemmed himself in with the logic of responsibility — the need to do whatever the situation dictated — Musk gave his projects jokey names like the Boring Company or Ludicrous Mode. He crashed rare sports cars and shagged Hollywood actresses. Musk had marriages, children and a life on the biggest stage, among people who were the best at everything.

All James had was a rented cottage in Stromness and a spreadsheet of running data. He couldn't even course-correct. It was too late.

The day after the meeting, they were in the egg-shaped armchairs at WeWork. Roland said, "Check it out" and showed James his phone screen. On his Twitter feed was a post from Musk: "Recently met very cool company @DraytonMackenzie. Tidal turbines generating zero-carbon hydrogen. ***Predictable output*** This technology has a major future."

James groaned, and Roland said, "What's with you?" James's phone buzzed. Already there was a starry-eyed message from a VC guy. Roland said, "What?"

"We're never going to catch him."

"What are you talking about?"

"I'm sorry I got you into this. We've given this our best years and accomplished nothing."

"Mate, he does cars, remember? We're literally the number-one marine energy company in the world."

James hid his face in his hands. "Please stop. Maybe I should have climbed the ladder at Shell and then, I don't know, used that as a platform somehow."

"Where is this coming from?" Roland swallowed another dull helping of guilt; they weren't close enough right now for him to be inside this. "Everyone thinks you're amazing."

"Ha. My mum thinks I'm special? Eleni was right all along. This whole thing was a trap."

*

But what was there for James to do other than carry on?

He officially opened their funding round on a Tuesday morning in February and closed it at Thursday lunchtime, having done the haggling in advance. He brought in £54 million, including another investment from Peter Thiel. It was enough to build three full-size machines plus their own electrolysers; to lift everyone's salaries out of the zone of discontent; and to distribute a few million among the early shareholders. If the machines ran as they should, and Claire O'Neill came through on the electricity price, that would mean more income, more machines, a self-accelerating cycle: financial lift-off.

James thought of the day their cable shattered in the tidal strait, and how for those few seconds before the cataclysm he'd believed that they'd made it. Now, he didn't yet know from which quarter the next emergency would assail him, but he was sure it would be along soon enough.

And there was a kind of emptiness. As he'd had painted on the wall of the workshop, a goal served *to organise and measure the best of our energies and skills.* Now they'd been organised and measured, and it was all so unimportant.

At Roland's suggestion, they took Alan to the car park at Subsea7 to give him the news. Alan drove them in his Audi. The black leather seats had worn to a bald grey-brown where his family sat, and the driver's seat was almost white. From the outside, it had begun to look indefinably old-fashioned. Alan, too, was seven years older than when they started the company. In his beard, the twists of grey and white had taken over, and his wrist ached when he used a screwdriver.

They parked in the centre of the empty tarmac, diagonally across a row of berths. A cold breeze was running, and Roland dived back into the car to pull on his sheepskin coat. The pre-fab was gone. The fields had retreated further, to make space for half a dozen new office blocks. At the back of the car park, a burger van was closing up for the afternoon.

Alan grinned. "So, come on then. Is it the funding? We got the money, didn't we?"

James hadn't planned what to say, and spoke straight out. "Yes, we got the money. We're going to build the big machines. Three to start with. Then more. Dozens, then hundreds, then thousands. Your shares at this valuation are worth about twenty-four million and will go up from here. You can tell Catriona it was worth it.

"And more importantly, your name is going to be taught in universities and engineering colleges as the inventor of the tidal turbine. You're the one who's turned that little yellow model into something that's going to power houses and space rockets. You're the James Watt of marine energy."

Alan raised his eyebrows and said, "Jeez *Louise*. Wind it in a bit, would you? I know you entrepreneur London types have got to be all go-getter-y, but fucking hell."

Roland clapped him on the shoulder. "Congratulations, mate. I know everyone assumes I'm the brains of this operation, but it was your model."

"The machines aren't even fucking built yet."

James said, "But do you still seriously doubt we're going to do it?"

Alan let himself relax into this feeling a little. "Em, no. I guess not."

Soon Roland could see that Alan wanted to be away from them. He mentioned that he and James were going to walk back into town.

Alan said, "See yous later," got into his Audi and drove a sweeping curve to the exit. On the road home, with Talksport chattering incomprehensibly, he found it strangely difficult to keep driving. His hands and feet were losing coordination with the car. He bumped a kerb and, trying to accelerate away, revved the engine high into neutral.

He saw a lay-by and pulled over. He got out, and drizzle began attaching itself to his hair and beard. There was a wooden fence, a bin for dog poo, an oversized map with pictures of birds and squirrels, and a path into the pinewoods.

He began to walk but had only just gone out of sight of the road when he stopped and turned his face upwards. The pinpricks of drizzle pushed his eyes closed. He could hear the breeze whooshing through billions of pine needles and a car swish past on the A93. Under his feet, the orange-brown needles were infinite, and around him was a great biomass of living things, ferns, bracken, trees, the forest drinking up the rain. He gave in to an impulse and, smiling, lifted his palms to receive this water from the heavens.

After a minute or so, his arms began to get tired, and he laughed, imagining a dog-walker seeing him like this. He dropped his hands back to his sides, feeling wonderfully light, as if he'd been rinsed out and left empty and clean. He walked back to his car, a little damp. Then he wiped the drizzle off his face and beard and drove to the jeweller's on Union Street.

James and Roland trudged back along the long straight road into town. Occasionally, the sunshine came on for a moment, like a floodlight with a loose connection, and projected their shadows onto the pavement. Traffic passed constantly. The road led alongside more fields and business parks and on into a fancy neighbourhood, with granite villas and muddy gardens.

It was comfortable at first to walk together. But, as neither said anything, and then couldn't think of anything, it gradually became awkward. Roland grew more and more restless until he couldn't take it any more. "Do you want my coat? We could alternate."

"I'm fine. If you don't want to walk, we can just call a cab."

"No, no. It's great."

"Mm."

"Alan seemed happy."

"Did he?"

"Okay, more shocked. But I'm sure that under that he's really, like . . . like you said, it was worth it. I'm glad we gave him that."

"Now we've just got to build the things, and make them run properly, and then and then and then."

"What?"

James shrugged. "It's just another step, isn't it?"

"So what, it's good enough for Alan to be happy about, but not good enough for you? Don't be a douche."

Annoyance crossed James's face. "What more do you want from me?

If I remember right, your other life plan was to be a beach bum in Goa."

"Oh, I should be grateful?"

"Shouldn't you?"

Roland didn't argue; he didn't want James to bring up Alice.

The drizzle was turning the shoulders of James's blazer a deeper blue. They waited at a crossing and, once the signal changed, James spoke – a peace offering. "What are you going to do with your cash?"

Roland crossed the road, then stopped on the next strip of narrow pavement. They were beside a high blank wall running to the next junction. The traffic had picked up, and tons of steel were rushing past close by them. He said, "Listen, there's something I've got to tell you."

"I thought so."

"What?"

"No, no. Go on."

"What do you think I've got to tell you?"

"Mary-Rose guessed that you and Alice got engaged."

Roland blushed under his sandy hair. "I didn't want to tell you till after the round was closed."

James, his voice flat, said, "Congratulations. It's great news." Then he softened. "Actually, I did think you guys could use some money to ... I don't know, set up together. Get a dishwasher. What do I know? That's why I cashed in some stock for us."

Roland grinned. "Really?"

"Yes. Really."

Roland grabbed him into a hug. "Thanks, buddy. I know it's weird. It's so weird. But maybe we just have to lean into the weirdness."

"Okay, okay. Get off me."

"What? You're worried the Aberdonians will think I'm one of your boyfriends?"

James laughed. Their faces were very close together. "Okay, okay."

Roland didn't let go.

James softened a little more. "I'm happy for you."

"Happy like you are about the funding round, or actually happy?"

"Actually happy."

"You sure?"

"I'm sure."

"Okay. Good."

They started walking again, both smiling. Roland found he was close to tears. He said, "Also, there is one more weird thing. No pressure, but . . . best man?"

James was suddenly angry. "Of course I'm going to do it. Who else is going to? One of your dumbass uni friends? No way."

"Okay. Great."

"Does Alice want me to do it?"

"Oh my God, she won't stop going on about it. She says it's like she's a scarlet harlot, and if you and me can't sort it out she won't be able to live with herself."

That did sound like her. "Okay."

"I know it's weird. But that's never stopped you before, has it?"

"Ha."

JUNE 2018

The day before the wedding, Alice was at her parents' house in Berkshire. She was trying to resist the tendency of everyone around her – the florists, her friends, her parents – to be carried away into a kind of light-headed wedding waltz. It was as if they were being lifted off their feet by some inaudible music, swaying, swelling, until they were in a wonderful whirl and practically useless.

People kept sweeping in and out, gabbling nonsense, waving outlandish objects like a floral arch or a selfie booth, and then sweeping out again with nothing resolved or decided, sure to appear again later waving something else, or to vanish completely with one of the few actually necessary props, like the rings – the rings, where were they? James must have them. She sent Neesh to find him, not expecting to see her again.

The one person who remained level-headed was the wedding planner, Hugo. Short, amiable, the middle-aged younger son of an ancient English family, his manner was professionally light and humorous. But, like a bodyguard, he stayed by her, intercepting caterers and aunts, blocking their questions, and sending them either to their duties or to drink champagne in the walled garden, which served as the holding pen. Alice had never seen such wonderful sangfroid. If you can keep your head, etc. Maybe she should be marrying Hugo.

Around lunchtime, when Alice felt she'd been awake for several days, Hugo spoke not to an underling but to her. Very neutrally, as if this situation might well be what was intended, he showed her some place cards. An overzealous lunatic at the calligrapher's had evidently googled the guests and added titles. Neesh's read: "The Hon. Venetia Smith". Hugo said, "I just wanted to check this was what you had in mind."

"Oh God. No. This is awful."

Hugo was relieved. "Right."

"What are we going to do? If we ditch these cards, then only those people won't have one. And if we ditch them all —"

Hugo cut her off. "It's not a problem. I've got an emergency calligrapher in an Uber. She'll arrive" — he glanced at his phone — "in just over an hour. We've got spare cards; the ink is the same. The style won't be a precise match but very, very close."

"Incredible. Okay. Thank you."

"I do just have to tell you that the person who noticed this — I hadn't done my table check yet — was your mum."

"Oh fuck."

Hugo left that uncommented.

"I know this is really unfair to ask, but can you keep her away from me?"

Hugo smiled genuinely for the first time that day. "I'll do what I can." He retired a short distance to arrange a crisis in the holding pen — a shortage of chairs, an urgent query about the flowers — that would require her mum's attention.

It was a small mercy — disappointingly small — that since Roland was now loaded, her parents weren't paying for the wedding. She and Roland were splitting it. Purely arithmetically, she could have afforded it alone, but that would have been too tragic, like paying for herself to have a princess party.

She'd assumed that paying would mute any commentary from her parents. But it hadn't. Her mum kept saying things like "I know you'll decide this however you prefer, as of course you absolutely must, but if you want my opinion . . ."

Alice didn't want it.

Or "I'm sure you'll think this is terribly old-fashioned, but . . ."

Mummy certainly would not believe that these place cards didn't, like a campaign gaffe, reveal that Alice was secretly bent on embarrassing herself.

Even her sweet, beloved, perfect dad, who, despite his crashing hobbies, never criticised her and whom she'd worried about hurting when she asked him not to pay, had seen her after the spray tan and said, "Dear Lord, you can't look like that."

Alice was so enraged she couldn't answer. She said to Neesh, "Can you explain." And while Neesh laid out the stages of the tan process, Alice went up to her childhood bedroom. Despite being a grown woman who was paying for half her own wedding, she cried with frustration. She must be more wound up than she realised. Before coming back down, she spent an hour replying to work emails, just to settle herself.

As Hugo prepared his garden crisis, Alice heard the metallic crackle of a supercar pulling up outside. She looked out of the stupid small leaded windows her parents weren't allowed to change. Outside, between the house and the old stables that were now her dad's absurdly long office, was a parking area of honey-coloured gravel, crowded with delivery vans. What had pulled up was a flashy low-slung garish purple racing car. Its engine cut out, the door opened, and James clambered from the driver's seat. She had to admit he was beautifully dressed, in a light blue-grey suit, a white T-shirt and sparkling white trainers. Someone must have picked that for him.

Alice said to Hugo, "Do you know what kind of car that is?"

Hugo peered. "Mm. I want to say . . . Maserati? Not really my field, though."

Alice, in this instant trusting Hugo more than anyone alive, confided, "That's my ex-boyfriend. He's the best man."

Hugo said, "Ah."

"He's recently made quite a lot of cash."

"I see."

"I was sort of hoping no one would notice him."

As they watched, Roland appeared from the house. He and James began laughing. They hugged, and then James ceremonially held out the key, dangling it from the chain. Alice breathed, "No."

Hugo glanced sideways at her. "These things break down constantly.

They're always in the garage being repaired." But even Hugo couldn't make this go away.

She went outside to where they were grappling each other like schoolboys. When Roland saw her, he said, "Look at this! Isn't this crazy?"

"Yes, it is. Hi, James. Good to see you. You've made a small boy very happy."

They stepped towards each other and paused. Kiss? Handshake? They defaulted to a clumsy hug, their torsos not touching. She noticed that James was getting better looking, ageing into his face. Roland began telling her about some legendary trip they'd taken together. Strangely enough, seeing James was not fraught. There was no charge in the air. A sense of bruising, yes, but no danger. They were just standing outside her parents' house, all knowing each other quite well.

Some conventional part of her kept insisting that, not so long ago, James had been touching her foot with his as they lay in her bed and – carried by the day into being less euphemistic than usual – she'd been giving him BJs in Parisian hotel rooms. But the cognitive dissonance this implied, the grinding mismatch between that situation and this, just didn't take. Yes, they'd seen each other naked; they'd shagged. So what? Life wasn't tidy. It probably just meant – poor Roland – that he was never going to get a BJ in Paris. Which was absolutely fine by her.

And yet, what Roland wanted – for them to be a trio – she didn't want. She and Roland were getting *married*. To find some kind of tangled three-way friendship interesting was something for French people and students. It was bad enough that she was now honour-bound to take James's side in everything always, so as never to come between them. Of course marriage was a beginning, but it was an ending, too; Roland should understand that. And if, even once, even for a second, they made her feel like some slapper they'd passed between them like a sloppy dooby, it might be quite hard to stay married, for all she knew.

Roland was still talking about this day trip in Scotland, wanting her to see how funny it was. She smiled at James. "I'm glad you're here. There's so much to do. And this is *such* a generous gift. Why don't you two go ride around in it for a while? You could drive it up to the White Horse and have lunch."

Roland and James looked at each other, grinning like morons. Roland said to her, "Are you sure? There's still so much to do."

"Honestly. You've got to eat. And —"

"Sorry to interrupt," said Hugo, who'd been waiting. To James: "I'm Hugo, by the way." And to Alice: "I'm sorry, but before anyone sets off, the vicar's here and would like a word with you both." Hugo shrugged very slightly, as if to suggest that people simply couldn't be trusted to behave as they should. "I've pointed out that you've already been through it all, but he's adamant and, ultimately, it's his venue."

Roland and Alice looked at James, who said, "Don't worry. Do what you have to do. I'm just here to help."

Roland said, "Sorry, pal. It'll just be a few minutes, I'm sure."

Alice said, "If you want lunch, there's heaps of food in the walled garden." A pang of guilt. "Actually, no, don't go there, it's full of my parents' boring friends." *Forgive me, Uncle Simon.* "Go in the kitchen. There's some lunch laid out for us. Just help yourself."

Already Hugo was guiding them off to where the vicar was waiting. They glanced back at James, who was standing on the gravel next to the purple Lamborghini. Roland said, "It'll just be a couple of minutes."

"Don't worry."

James watched them go into the house together and wished he could go with them. For weeks, while he found the car online, while he took the train up to collect it from a dealership in Chester, when he had it waxed to a purple shine, he'd been imagining what Roland would say when he saw it. And now he'd seen it.

Someone close by said, "Is that yours?"

It was a girl from the florist's, younger than him, and cute in her uniform green polo shirt. She was looking at the car.

"It was. I just gave it to Roland."

"You *gave* it to him? Like a wedding present?"

For him these days, there was no shortage of attention at least.

SEPTEMBER 2018

In one of the grand houses of North Oxford, bitterly coveted by dons in less lucrative disciplines, Big Eddie – aka Professor Lawton – was watching the six o'clock news. The chimes of its intro music were his signal to stop writing for the day – his factory whistle.

This book he was jokingly calling his *Politisches Testament*, à la Hitler in the bunker, written with the Russians at the gates, in hope that the Nazi party would one day rise again. The faculty was trying to elevate him to Professor Emeritus, to rank him as a professor on the grounds of meritorious service rather than through mere banal possession of a so-named post. In other words, Please piss off and retire already. Oh, he'd still be allowed to use the library and hang around the college like the retired dons who'd never thought to cultivate a life on the outside. Politicians liked to say there's nothing so ex as an ex-MP but, right now, ex-professor felt pretty close.

His source material – stacks of his own diaries, calendars and emails printed off by his research assistant – teeteringly occupied the entire coffee table, like the blocks and towers of an Italian hill-town. There was a gap at the front where he could put his laptop or, when the TV was on, his feet.

At six, he closed the laptop, let himself fall backwards into the cushions, relieving his aching spine, and put his feet up. Margot had suggested he might like to try something more ergonomic, like this new-fangled contraption called a desk. But he held mulishly to the unvoiced belief that if the sofa was good enough when he was in Downing Street with Blair . . .

That felt like another era. *Was* another era. He'd been wrong about an awful lot. Chiefly his naive belief that Western politics had evolved beyond the ideological bloodbath of the twentieth century. That they'd progressed to find a pragmatic third way between left and right. Textbook teleological fallacy.

Everything his generation had done was now being undone. Instead of ever more, ever faster international exchange, the dismantling of barriers to movement and trade, American phones being made in China, T-shirts from Bangladesh, the entire old East Bloc joining the EU, a big bang of global prosperity, hundreds of millions rising out of poverty, anyone marrying anyone – instead of that, the borders were going up again: tariffs, protectionism, foreigners out, the mirage of autarky, "British jobs for British workers."

He was still shocked that Gordon had stooped to that. Or rather, that Gordon was the first to understand, out of everyone, even as the financial crisis was still unfolding, that that was where things were heading. It ran so totally against Gordon's nature that he couldn't really capitalise on it. As a political force, it was perhaps at that point still too inchoate to be harnessed. But it was Gordon who sensed it first, despite everyone deriding his political abilities. The blind man had seen the future. Very Greek.

Now there was no more of the confident magnanimity that came from abundance. Instead, politics was tacking back the other way: shrinking incomes, lower prospects, the hospitals deteriorating, the pie getting smaller and, with that, the politicians getting nastier, angrier, as each faction tried to grasp what it could. The nationalists' drums were again beating their intoxicating tattoo, even here in sensible old England. The hammer-and-sickle brigade had performed a coup on the Labour Party, and the whole bloody carousel was creaking back into motion. He sometimes thought he'd wasted his life.

But at least he'd seen how politics could be. With this book, he was burying a few thoughts for when the madness passed. By then he would be too old to help.

On the news, the prime minister's party was praising her for being "tough on the Europeans". In her querulous voice, as if raising a pedantic complaint at the AGM of a provincial golf club, she said she demanded "respect". Oh God.

He'd been inflicting a supposedly humorous, provocative riff on guests at high table: speaking as a political scientist, he'd concluded that the main cause of Trump, Brexit and the new nationalism was himself. He and his cohort hadn't seen it coming, had failed to prepare, when in fact it was classic Hegel: their political era brought its own antithesis into being. A wave of globalisation created a generation of nationalists. When he said this, everyone had an opinion, even the neurologists and chemical engineers.

Now the prime minister was visiting some British manufacturer. It was always manufacturing now. Another fantasy. As if *services* weren't what most British people actually did. He must make sure not to become a cantankerous has-been. Just a benign has-been.

Suddenly he jerked upright. But with his straight legs counter-levering, he fell back into the cushions. He swore and wrestled himself to a stand. As he watched, a smile opened. The two business leaders standing politely behind the prime minister while she warbled on about Great British industry were former students. James Drayton – Eddie remembered him perfectly. A wonderful student. So he hadn't squandered his talents after all. What was this company? Tidal power? A climate thing. Splendid. And the other one – Richard? Roland! A likeable wastrel. He hadn't realised they were friends.

The PM said something about "global Britain leading the world" and, over her shoulder, Eddie distinctly saw Roland roll his eyes. He laughed with surprise. In delightful haste, he fumbled for the remote and paused the TV. A large light-blue circle appeared over the frozen PM. He bounded to the door and yelled up the stairs. "Margot! *Margot!* You've *got* to see this."

XIII

MARCH 2019

Roland's forearms ached from gripping the steering wheel so hard. Dry-mouthed, with his chest beating its tom-tom, he flicked his gaze to the rear-view mirror, to the wing mirror, to the road. Threats everywhere. A building site was pushing oncoming cars into his lane. A Crossrail lorry loaded up with rubble, its driver probably exhausted, unlicensed, wired with speed. The tension itself might tire out Roland's arms so badly they'd quaver and plough the car into a wall.

He was driving Alice and their newborn home from the hospital. It was crazy to leave the lovely safe warm maternity ward, teeming with midwives and paediatricians who could be summoned with a button. Now they were in the outer darkness, on their own, like random civilians handed suits and guns and told to protect a miniature, defenceless president.

Seventeen more minutes until they were home and under the supervision of Beatriz, a Brazilian maternity nurse whom he'd only met for a half-hour job interview but who now seemed to him like a safe haven in human form.

The traffic came to a stop, and a wild impulse urged him to just pull out onto the wrong side and bulldoze any smaller cars out of the way. He was suddenly so grateful, so moved, that Alice had insisted they buy this Range Rover.

"Babe! Babe!"

Alice looked up from where she was bent over the terrifyingly complex car seat. "Is everything okay?"

"You were so right about getting this car."

Alice smiled, her wan, bloated face wrinkling around the eyes. "Okay, sweetheart, thank you. Keep your eyes on the road."

They arrived, and, with sweat now running down his arms and sides, he manoeuvred the Range Rover into the parking space without a crash. A panicky fumble with the baby seat. Why was it so fucking complicated? Then up their steps. The key?! But the door was opening from inside. Light spilling out. Beatriz. Thank God. They handed over the package, and Roland went upstairs to lie down.

But now that he'd protected his child's life, he had to secure its future. All too soon, he set out on foot, back out into the hostile city, clutching a sheaf of documents in a waterproof folder. Registration forms for nurseries and schools.

Alice and her mum had briefed him. The Willcocks, Iverna Gardens, Pooh Corner. A good nursery would set the baby up for prep school at St Thomas's or Pembridge. Those would get her into senior school at St Paul's or Godolphin, which would get her into Oxford or Cambridge. Or at least give her the option. She should not have less than he'd had, in anything. Though of course, she might do something totally else, like become an Olympic athlete, or a celebrity chef.

Really he should have done this on the day she was born. It was first-come, first-served. If she missed out on a place for the sake of those seventy-two hours... He broke into a jog.

In those early weeks of her life, he constantly looked at himself and asked, What kind of father am I being? It was all abstract: he protected her; he took care of her education; he provided for her – rushing out to Sainsbury's for wet wipes and formula. So many people had bad dads; he would be a good dad. He was always hurrying out or coming in from another errand.

Alice was being indulgent to him, as if he were also a child. She herself was in a blissed-out sleepless daze. To speak to him, she had to emerge from a tight private female world that consisted of her, Beatriz and the baby. Pumping milk. Nap routines. Special teas.

When his mum made some snippy remarks about Alice having a maternity nurse, he defended his family. Lorna said, "I don't really see the need to have someone there twenty-four hours a day. She's just a baby."

Actually, it was only twenty hours. Every morning, Beatriz had a four-hour sleep break in which the minutes wouldn't tick and Roland's fear steadily rose.

He and his mum were in the kitchen while Alice, Beatriz and the baby were upstairs in the bedroom, which annoyed his mum. She'd come to see her granddaughter. Roland said, "It's better for her if we have a professional showing us what to do."

"I'll show you how to wipe a baby's bum! My goodness. Do you really need that explained? I thought you were supposed to be clever."

Roland let that pass. His mum was thirty-five years out of the game. She didn't understand the intricacies of modern child-rearing. The baby's schedule had already been updated twice.

Lorna added, "A bit of money in your pocket, and you start behaving like some fancy Dan."

"Oh come off it. How many people did we have in Heliopolis? Five?"

"Rubbish! We never had a lot of help, unlike some others I could mention."

Roland felt he'd won this exchange.

Lorna muttered, "And a brand-new car as well." She shook her head. "I ask you."

"Yeah, I've parked it next to my purple Lamborghini."

Lorna let out a growl of rage then laughed and pretended to box his ears. "How's my granddaughter going to turn out if she's waited on hand and foot from the day she's born and driven around in Lamborghinis?"

"Beatriz isn't waiting on her. She's helping *us*."

"And it would be a shame to fritter it all away. Just because James has given you one big cheque doesn't mean there's more."

"He hasn't given me shit, Mum. It's *my* company."

He felt like a very important, powerful father, a Tony Soprano, dispensing justice and largesse. But in all this frenetic activity of striking poses and observing himself, he barely noticed little Kate.

For Alice, that was different. Even in the first seconds after Kate was born, rising from between her thighs in the doctor's gloved, bloody hands, Alice felt it: that they were family, that their blood rhymed, that Alice loved her more than anything or anyone.

Roland, however, became tense in the baby's presence. He preferred to be out doing dadmin for her, being a good dad, rather than literally being there on the sofa next to the Moses basket, noticing how easily you might snap her stubby limbs by mistake or feed her the wrong thing or infect her with a cold that carried her off. The tension dropped only when she fell asleep. But then . . . had she been sleeping too long?

Much calmer to be away. Thank God for Beatriz.

He was fifth in the hierarchy of understanding the baby, behind Alice, Beatriz, Alice's mum and his mum. But Beatriz had those accursed breaks. Then sometimes Alice trusted him to hold Kate in the crook of his arm, ever more comfortably, or to coax her into drinking her bottle at the appointed time, which he kept succeeding at.

On Saturdays, Beatriz's night off, a yawning chasm of dread, he lay awake next to the crib, listening to Kate sigh and grunt. He gave the bottle, he cleaned the tiny butt with wet wipes and, his highest achievement, he laid her back in the crib, where she fell asleep. He began to believe that she knew who he was. Unconsciously, he stopped calling her "the baby"; instead, "my baby".

Then, on one of his mum's all-too-frequent visits, she brought photos of him as a newborn. The resolution on these glossy eighties prints was low and, as he held the images up to his eyes, they disintegrated into coloured fuzz. But there was his mum, younger than he was now, her face plump, looking more like him, sitting propped up with pillows in an old-fashioned steel-framed hospital bed. She looked a bit shocked, as if she'd just come through something, and was showing off an inexpertly wrapped bundle of blankets, at the top of which was a smudge of pink grease on the lens: his face.

It was as if something in him cracked open. In his mind's eye, he saw the same scene another generation back: his mum as pink smudge, being held by a nana far younger than he was now. And then the baby nana being held by great-grandma, and so on, back and back through the millennia.

It was like the regular ticking of a clock and each tick a human generation.

He understood, so abruptly it hurt, that he was not, as he'd always assumed, an individual. He was like one of Mendel's peas in GCSE biology, just one of a row of seedlings in which the inherited traits — a nose, a talent, a sense of humour — were recombined and passed forward again. He was like a fish who'd always believed he moved for his own reasons but now realised he was just one iridescent shimmer in the shoal.

He saw now that his sole purpose was to pass forward this fragile torch of life. Not to be the one who let it go out after it had been handed down to him in unbroken sequence by who knew what teenage Highland crofters, through what wars and famines and fatal labours, the trust held, the promise kept, since before there was an England, before even Egypt, since the first people made handprints on the walls of their caves. It burned in him, and now it burned in his daughter. She could carry it forward, ever further and higher, through her own children, until human beings lived among the stars.

He wept and wept, bending forward over himself. His mum rubbed his back and said, "Okay now, okay. You're just a bit wound up." Then, "Oh, jeez, you're going to set me off too."

This flash of understanding faded again with the passing months, but it never went away completely. For years after, he could not bear to look at charity adverts on the Tube with pictures of starving children. Nor could he watch a TV show in which a child was hurt or frightened. Nor really enjoy movies about war or gangsters because he felt too keenly the wrongness of pain and the squandering of lives that had begun in the cradle, and that could have been lived in happiness.

There were days of deep contentment when he did what Kate needed, and then went to the office and did what his colleagues needed, and there was no distinction between them. On those days, he tuned himself in to what was best for his child and his colleagues, and tuned out of his own ego's ceaseless chattering about itself.

*

When James came to visit, Roland talked as if this house had in recent days witnessed acts of poignant self-sacrifice, the pursuit of profound knowledge and titanic struggles to safeguard a fragile new life. To James, the baby seemed fine.

He sat on the sofa and since, as a non-parent, he wasn't trusted to pick up the child himself, it was placed cautiously on his lap. While they peered nervously at him and kept telling him to support the head, he examined the wrinkly pink homunculus stretching out its little limbs. There didn't seem to be much to think about it. They'd expected a baby and, yes, this was a baby. There weren't any health problems.

He'd never felt more distant from any of them. Alice was a stranger. Dressed in her pyjamas and an oversized tracksuit top, she was lolling in an armchair, satisfied and semi-comatose, like an athlete conserving energy between heats. On every surface around her were bouquets of flowers still in the boxes they'd been delivered in, the congratulations cards taped unopened to the outside. Beatriz kept quietly pressing her to have her snacks and vitamins. Alice munched and scrolled on her phone. She'd barely said hi when he came in.

When he asked, purely out of politeness, whether there was anything they needed, Alice glanced up sharply at Beatriz, who said, "We do need some more muslins. That would be so great, thank you. We were going to order them, but this will be so much faster."

"Of course. Just so I get the right thing, what exactly is a muslin?"

Alice said, "Beatriz can show you. But get nice ones. I sent Roland out and he came back with a dishcloth."

Roland coloured. "They're muslins. It literally says so on the pack."

Alice said, "Mm," with absolute indifference to his excuses, and went back to her phone.

Really James wanted to talk to Roland about electrolysers. Their first home-made one was now working and, due to their extreme dearth of money and electricity as it was being designed, it had come out more efficient than those you could buy off the shelf. A pleasing success.

But he could see Roland was still thinking about muslins. He gave up and said, "Did you see about McKinsey?"

Roland was glancing at Alice. "Um, no. I don't think so?"

"They've been caught consulting on how to maximise opioid sales in the US. How to push higher doses and make doctors prescribe more."

Roland *was* still thinking about the muslins, but he gave the expected response. "Oh, wow. That's pretty bad."

"Yeah. We're much better off out of all that."

"Oh, yeah. Much better." Roland paused to see if there was more to be said on this topic, then went on. "Just take a look at this pack. It's from M&S. Okay, it's not the White Company but, like, come on. Alice thinks these ones are sad and institutional and you can't wrap a baby in them if you love it."

Alice could hear all this but plainly saw no reason to explain it again.

It reminded James of when Eleni visited him in hospital and couldn't hold a conversation. Now Roland had joined the same cult. It even turned out that Eleni and Roland had been texting, despite James not having heard from her in more than a year. Roland shook his head like a Vietnam veteran told about a VC ambush and said, "You know she's got *two*."

Roland was not making fatherhood look like something James was missing out on. But nor did James have the old certainty that this was all meaningless animal existence beside his great endeavour. Was it really so wonderful to build a floating dynamo? The question persisted.

Meanwhile, the once-mutable shapes of lives were growing stiffer, like soft clay setting hard. The open field of possibilities was narrowing to a one-way street, and the price of getting off it was ever higher. Roland and Alice were locked into each other, this house, this baby business, for decades. By the time the child reached its eighteenth birthday, Roland would be fifty-three, and within sight of retirement.

In James, this induced a certain restlessness.

JULY 2019

The channel in Orkney looked more distinct from the air; you could see the straight line of water drawn by chance through a dense cluster of sunlit islands. Their boats were crawling over its surface, laying pink buoys to mark out huge rectangles where the new machines would go. The seascape was becoming workspace, like virgin prairie being parcelled and fenced; the ocean itself being domesticated. And beyond the archipelago, the open, untamed, cloud-patched Atlantic, stretching towards America or the North Pole.

James had chartered a helicopter to see the layout from above. He was visualising the maximum number of rectangles that could be fitted into the twelve-mile strait. Alice had told Roland not to get on the helicopter. He was a father; helicopters crashed all the time. But his friendship with James, like a healed bone, still held the shadow of a fracture within it. He couldn't not go. It was like a marriage put back together after an affair; he had to be seen to commit again.

He was surprised by how small and flimsy it was, this claustrophobic glass bubble they were supposed to sit inside. It was like a bathysphere for going not down but up. After the whirring metal contraption hopped weightlessly into the air, his stomach went loose, and he gripped the harness as if it could save him. If he died today, his daughter wouldn't even remember him.

James lifted a heavy, large-lensed camera off his lap and started taking photos. Roland, through his headphones, could hear him directing the pilot to various positions. This must be the Olympian perspective James had always had in mind: the strait like a canal connecting the North Sea and the Atlantic, brightly coloured boats, the machines abandoned by their defunct rivals casting shadows on the water. Those would need to be torn out.

The sun was coming in through the curved plexiglass – it was practically a flying greenhouse – and Roland began to sweat. After he felt he'd held on more than long enough, he said, "Got what you need?"

James sighed. "Yeah, I guess so."

Despite sitting so close, he could only hear him through the headphones. "What's wrong?"

James looked out the window again. "I reckon there's space for – absolute maximum – six hundred machines."

"Six hundred! I thought we were building three."

"We need hundreds, thousands actually, to really change anything. Just imagine how long it's going to take."

Roland could picture it: a power station twelve miles long; hundreds of machines floating in array, like a glinting Starfleet in CGI regularity. "That would be a shit ton of power."

"Enough for most of the houses in Scotland. Or to fire an awful lot of rockets into orbit. But you know what I've realised?"

"What?"

James felt the melancholy of a chess player who's seen how he's going to win; the equipoised hostility of opposed armies disintegrating into a result. He told Roland the secret that had been growing in his mind: "The tidal stuff is a sideshow. The real business here is the electrolysers."

He studied Roland's face to see if he was getting it. "Everyone now wants to produce hydrogen. They want to make it from nuclear, from wind, from gas, from everything. All that hydrogen is going to have to be generated with electrolysers. And because we didn't have enough money or power, we've built one of the most efficient electrolysers in the world. It was a fluke, pure and total. But that means the real opportunity here is to sell our electrolysers to everybody else."

"Okay."

"It's like that cliché about how in a gold rush you want to be the one selling shovels. Well, climate change is the gold rush of our lifetime, and electrolysers are a shovel."

"Right. Okay."

"Roland, I'm saying the electrolysers are a multibillion-dollar business.

And if you like, that revenue can fund the construction of basically unlimited tidal machines."

"Billion?"

"Billions, plural."

"You're sure?"

"Well, of course, it depends — everything depends."

"That's . . . great, isn't it?"

"Of course."

"So what's the problem?"

James looked at him, his expression unreadable. "I suppose, to be totally candid . . ." He turned down his mouth, as if giving bad news. "I think I've reached the end of this."

"Of what?"

"The company. The machines. I think I'm done."

Roland was too astonished to speak.

James said, "You can have it. You did a great job when I was out after the coma, and they all love you."

Really James felt as if he'd made the breakthrough now — electrolysers, then thousands of tidal machines — and the rest was just legwork. He began giving Roland notes on what he would have to do: expand with all conceivable speed, with every pound he could raise or borrow, to get ahead of the established electrolyser companies. Then he'd need factories — James had blueprints and planning permission for one on the outskirts of Aberdeen — then in Vietnam, Poland and Mexico for the Asian, European and American markets. He'd need thousands of employees. He'd need to go public. It would take decades.

The pilot's voice came through their headphones: "Sorry to interrupt. Do you guys want any other angles?"

Roland said, "Could you just, like, do a loop for a few minutes?"

"Just fly in a circle?"

By now, Roland and James were used to giving other people instructions. "Yeah. Please."

The helicopter began a sweeping curve over the coastline of Eday, where a yellow forklift was stacking up coils of copper cable for a new substation they were building. The pilot turned west, towards the Atlantic, with the sunshine bouncing off a wide plain of water. He listened in, grinning at the horizon, as Roland lost his temper.

Roland jabbed James in the upper arm. "I wanted to go to Japan more than anything, and you took that away from me. And now you want to fuck off because you're bored. This thing has never been about the moon or climate change or whatever, just about your fucking ego. You asked these people to follow you, and now you just want to fucking abandon them because you can't be assed any more."

"What's the problem with you doing it? You've got a baby; it's not like you can go anywhere."

"I've got a small baby and I haven't had an uninterrupted night's sleep for months – and you think the answer is for me to start running a company on my own? You haven't got a fucking clue."

James's anger was rising to match his friend's.

"Oh, yeah? *You* fucked *me*, remember?"

"Oh, yeah? How did I do that?"

"You really don't know? Who had your baby?"

"That is such, *such* bullshit. You said it was okay. And you've never stopped making us feel guilty about it."

"I haven't done anything. Maybe you just do feel guilty. What does that tell you?"

Roland said, "Excuse me, pilot? Hi. Can we land, please. I need to get away from this person."

That afternoon, Roland roamed around the drizzly streets of Kirkwall in a fizz of frustration and petulance, trying to distract himself from the craving for a cigarette. He'd only smoked once since the positive pregnancy test. If he cracked now and poisoned his baby's innocent lungs, it would be James's fault. He rang Alice instead and had an argument with her about the helicopter.

But slowly the thought came to him that perhaps James needed to do something exorbitantly selfish to restore balance in their friendship. If James did this, they'd be even. More than even. He felt the surly, resentful release of being let out of the doghouse. James would make his point, then come back. In the meantime, Roland was fine not talking to him.

A few days later, James visited Roland's room in the Kirkwall Hotel and apologised for losing his temper. "I didn't mean those things. You didn't fuck me. Being honest with myself, I suppose it's just that you two are married and settled down, and I'm ready to do something else."

It was a relief for James to have said the unsayable. It passed, like everything else, and brought them closer. Roland nevertheless took the opportunity to emotionally blackmail him into not leaving at once.

James agreed to a transition period. He would go in early summer. Gerard from the ESA had invited them to a rocket launch, down in the former penal colony in Guiana. The rocket was going to use some of their hydrogen for fuel. Only a token quantity, mixed in unnoticeably with the rest. But something. That would be James's last day.

Roland asked him, "What are you even going to do afterwards?"

"Have you ever read a book called *Kon-Tiki*?"

"No."

"It's about these anthropologists who sailed a balsa-wood raft across the Pacific to demonstrate that it's at least technically possible that the Polynesians originally came from South America."

Roland said, "This is my fault. Me getting together with Alice drove you insane. Your parents are right to hate me."

"It's entirely sane."

It was an unmatched feat of adventure in the service of human understanding. Not something Elon Musk had ever done. Of course the *Kon-Tiki* voyage had already been accomplished, but there must be some other feat that James could be first to. The highest jump could always be bettered, but to be first was unsurpassable.

To Roland, it sounded lame and derivative. It didn't have the usual audacious originality of James's schemes. It was more like Richard Branson flying around the world in that balloon or Jeff Bezos cosplaying as an astronaut. Roland thought he should stick to the day job. And even if he did sail around the world, or whatever, what was he going to do afterwards? He'd be back at the company soon enough.

James began taking sailing lessons. At the weekend, before dawn, he made the long drive down to the Kent coast so that he could launch off the beach at first light. Where once he spent Saturday morning with Alice, he was now in the company of paid instructors. The small-town sailing club he alighted upon was bemused by his intensity. He would come in off the water at twilight, exhausted, cold, chowing handfuls of Haribo to stave off hypoglycaemia, and stay the night in a chintzy B&B for romantic weekenders.

To be a good sailor, you really had to go to sea aged twelve, like Nelson. James was decades behind that curve. But you could crash-course the knowledge with application and brainpower. Once you abstracted it, sailing was just geometry.

And there was wonder, too: he learned to see the wind by watching patches of ruffles on the water's surface. To be on the sea at dawn, with the clouds blazing pink and gold, the sky all kinds of blue, the ocean reflecting everything above, as that ball of fire rose above the horizon, was like being inside a painting.

On the Sunday-night drives back to London, seemingly so much further than on the way down, he listened to voice notes from a researcher he'd hired to search for adventures. Perhaps he could sail the Northern Sea Route, from Orkney over the top of Russia and down through the Bering Strait into the warm Pacific. It was being opened up by climate change. Or apparently the ancient Persians had dug a canal through the desert from the Nile to the Red Sea. No one had ever traced its course. The ocean, the desert; one was as good as the other. Shame it was Egypt.

At the company, he found it hard to absorb details or come to any decisions. If he hadn't already decided to wait till the launch from Guiana, he would have just closed his laptop and been done. Roland tried to enmesh him in surreptitiously interviewing potential CEOs to help run the company, just in case that changed his mind. But, unlike Roland, James could not be delayed indefinitely.

JANUARY 2020

Roland was at Monkey Music with Kate. Supposedly he was working from home, but hey, it was his company. So, on this Tuesday morning, while normal people were at their jobs, he was sitting cross-legged on the floor of a church hall with a dozen mums and babies, clapping in time. Kate was sitting between his legs, and while the professionally jaunty instructor waved an orange baboon and tried to lead them in song, she was banging a wooden maraca against his left trainer.

He was annoyed because James had said Kate looked like she'd been released from the Gulag. A short fuzz of hair, as if shaved; a fairly random smattering of teeth; uncoordinated, effortful movements. Roland couldn't unsee it. So he was snappish when James phoned.

"Yeah?"

"Hey. Do you have a minute?"

"Not really. I'm stimulating your goddaughter's brain development."

"Say hi from me."

Roland looked down at Kate's fuzzy scalp. Sometimes he loved her so much he felt an urge to obliteration: to rip her head off. The feeling for her was so strong it jumbled the wiring of his emotions.

"She says hi."

"Okay, great. Do you want me to call back later?" James sounded excited about something.

"No, go on. What is it?"

"Okay, so, you know this virus in China?"

Roland had seen some news about it. "Yeah, sure."

"I've been tabulating the flights that have left Wuhan for international destinations since the start of the year."

"Of course you have."

"There are still flights to London. There's one landing this afternoon, which is kind of insane. Then you consider people travelling from Wuhan to other Chinese cities, and international flights from those."

While James was talking, Roland caught a distinctive whiff and pulled back the waistband of Kate's nappy to glance inside. Just a fart. He hoped she would hold in anything more substantial until he could give her back to Marcella, the nanny.

He said, "So what? They're not going to be able to, like, contain it?"

"Exactly. They're saying Wuhan is going to be locked down, but it's too late."

"Oh, wow. You'd better get right on the phone to Xi Jinping and tell him he's doing it wrong."

"There's not much he *can* do any more."

"Great. Good chat. Thanks for calling."

"No, can you just listen? Once people realise this is going to be a global epidemic, the markets will crash. We can use the company's cash on hand to short the S&P before that happens, and make bank."

Kate waved the maraca dangerously close to Roland's face.

"Mate, if this is you getting loose, I don't like it."

"I'm not loose. I'm so not loose about this."

"If we need more money, we can raise more. Are you trying to eff everything up before you quit?"

"Just . . . Wouldn't it be great to be so right about something this big?"

The whiff from Kate had developed into an unambiguous pong. It was much worse since she'd started eating real food. The instructor, who now had a mini disco ball going, was giving him angry eyes for being on his phone.

"Okay, fine by me. But don't eff it up. If you do, you can't quit until you've fixed it. Okay?"

"Okay."

"And don't bet everything, okay? And don't tell anyone."

"Understood. Maybe a million or two. Just so it's for real."

"Jesus, James. Listen, I better go. If it goes wrong, I'm going to pretend you didn't ask me. Deal?"

"That's ridiculous. But okay."

MARCH 2020

Roland and Alice fled London during the days of crisis. As the government wavered, the TV showed untidy heaps of black-bagged corpses round the back of an Italian hospital. WhatsApp was full of forwarded rumours that London was going to be sealed off by the army. Video snippets on Twitter showed crowds of poor Indians setting out on foot for their home villages; a reporter standing alone on the deserted Piazza San Marco in Venice with a flock of white pigeons clattering into the air behind her; an emergency briefing at the White House with a health expert instructing the public not to touch their eyes, nose or mouth, and then licking her finger to turn the page.

Roland and Alice escaped to her parents' house in Berkshire. Kate's nanny, Marcella, came with them rather than take her chances in the city. They packed the Range Rover as if leaving forever: Alice's jewellery, Roland's share certificates, the deed to their house. On the M4, they saw other cars like theirs, jammed with clothes, children, cans of food; bulging duvets pressed up against the windows.

But once they reached Berkshire and pulled up on the honey-coloured gravel, with no other houses in sight, it was as if they'd entered a well-stocked refuge from the misery outside. Force majeure compelled them to take up the simple life. Their worries shrank to the practical business of bringing in supplies and passing the time.

Alice's mum, after a hiatus of decades, began to practise the piano again. Roland watched hours of TikTok. Both of Alice's brothers were there, too, and, since it was a sunny, dry spring, there was a family walk in the woods at the end of every afternoon. Over dinner, Alice's dad told stories about when his own mum, as a child, was evacuated to a farm in Suffolk during the Blitz.

It was awkward having to eat with Marcella and make conversation with her about how the pandemic was going in Romania. But it heightened the feeling of all being in it together. James, taking the piss on a Zoom call, said it was like Shackleton in the Antarctic, temporarily suspending the mess separation of officers and men.

Roland and James zoomed several times a day, seeing each other's heads loom in the box on screen. James had cleared just over four million pounds shorting the American stock market. He suspected there were further drops to come but didn't intend to fall into the classic trap of thinking he couldn't lose. So he cashed out, having proved himself right.

Since they produced electricity, everyone in the company was classified as an essential worker — essential to the nation in this time of emergency. Roland would have liked them to be issued special cards, or badges maybe. At dinner time, he told Alice's family, "Just another hard day doing my essential work." He could tell that James was enjoying it, too.

Nevertheless, they let most of the team work from home. A skeleton crew was up in Orkney, practically unreachable: there were no flights from London. James was thinking of driving up in Roland's Lambo. Roland often thought afterwards that James probably would have, had it not been for complications about how to get him the keys.

Then, as they started a Zoom towards the end of March, James immediately said, "Guess what?" and coughed.

"You've got it?"

"Yes." And coughed again.

It was horrible and fascinating.

"How do you feel? Is your sense of smell gone?"

James, too, was fascinated. There was some nervousness. It was disquieting, like being pickpocketed — where and how had it been done to him without him noticing? — but mainly it was astonishing to have, in his own body, a small fragment of this world-historical event. These multiplying germs had been passed from person to person in a human chain stretching from some wet market in Wuhan to him. World history was now in his bloodstream, spreading through his delicately branching bronchioles, the rising and falling seaweed forest of his lungs.

While they were poring over his symptoms – headaches, not too bad; some shortness of breath – Roland abruptly said, "Shit. Mate. You've got to be careful. Isn't there a thing about diabetes?"

"Technically, yes. It's a co-morbidity. And actually quite interesting. There's a reciprocal effect." As he spoke, he kept coughing, a bone-dry *hack-hack*. "Diabetes weakens your immune system. And on the other hand – *hack* – part of the immune response to infection is to – *hack-hack* – is to pump sugar into your bloodstream. And – *hack*, just a sec." James drank from a glass of water, his eyes streaming. "Yuk. Okay. So diabetics –"

Roland interrupted. "Mate, are you going to be okay? Do you want to come here? Oh no, you can't. Or actually essential workers are allowed to travel."

James laughed, setting off the hacking again.

"You could live in Alice's dad's office. It's massive. We could bring you food. I could come pick you up if you can't drive."

"Thanks. But I don't really want to spend the next couple of months locked up with Alice's family."

"Okay, but –"

"Honestly, the risk is mainly for – *hack* – fuck's sake – people who don't manage their blood sugar properly. And I preordered an oximeter." James couldn't speak with hacking so held his index finger up to the screen. On the end was a bulky grey clamp, like some medical clothes peg. "I can – *hack* – I can track . . ."

He began hacking and hacking, water again running from his eyes. He typed, "I'll call you back later."

"Okay, mate. If you change your mind about coming here, just say."

Over the next few days, James was coughing too frequently to do Zoom calls. He and Roland typed their conversations instead. He didn't feel too bad, but the intercostal muscles around his ribs were beginning to ache from all the coughing.

Meanwhile, the ESA, as expected, cancelled their launch schedule. It wasn't as if James or Roland had any chance of getting down to Guiana anyway.

Then, when Roland woke up one Thursday, he checked his phone in bed and found messages James had sent at 2.48 that morning, rendered in the cheery bubbles of WhatsApp: "Ambulance coming to take me to hospital. Blood ox dropping too far. Sugar levels going crazy. Woke up going into ketos. Insulin helping. Will text where they take me."

And, several hours later, far longer than any ambulance journey in London should take, at 5.24, just the words "London spine centre".

With clumsy fingers, Roland googled "London spine centre". A private hospital in St John's Wood. He pressed call. It rang and rang. Maybe it was too early for anyone to answer.

It was as if he was both in this moment and not in it. It was like being in a room where everything was normal and the fittings made sense, but the room was actually a cabin being flung around by some hellish fairground ride. The mundanity of the details disguised the dislocation of the whole – a kind of surreal normality, in which blanket, telephone, bedroom were unchanged but nothing felt the same. Part of him was able to do what was obvious – call the hospital – while part was already freezing stiff.

A receptionist picked up and said, "London Spine Centre."

He gratefully said, "Hi. Good morning. Thank you. I'm just calling – do you have a James Drayton there?"

"I can't give out patient information. Sorry, who is this?"

"My name's Roland. Roland Mackenzie. He texted me in the night to say he was going there in an ambulance." He told an inspired lie: "I'm his next of kin."

"Oh, okay, sure. Just a sec." An agony of waiting. "Yes, he arrived early this morning. He's in one of our rooms."

"Is he okay?"

This conversation had gradually penetrated through the layers of sleep in Alice's brain. She sat up, trying to clear her vision. Their eyes met.

"Um, I don't have his medical notes. But" – the receptionist's voice changed, softened, lost its professionalism – "if he's here, I'm sure he's okay. This is a very good hospital. I can ask one of the doctors to give you a call later."

"Okay. Yes. Thanks. Thank you. But I don't understand. Why's he there? What's happened to his spine?"

"Oh" – her voice brightened – "probably nothing. We're doing this thing with the Royal Free where they use our beds as overspill. Is there any chance he's got covid?"

"Oh, yes, yes," he said with the relief of explanation. "Yes, he's got it."

"Oh well, that'll be it. If you don't hear from him in a while, one of the doctors can call you."

"Oh, that would be amazing. Thank you. Thank you so much."

Alice, sitting up in jungle-patterned silk pyjamas, a tropical fantasy of black and Amazonian green, told him to ring James's parents.

"Can't I have breakfast first? I'm kind of freaking out."

Outside their door, they heard Kate burbling as Marcella carried her downstairs.

"No, my love. You've got to do it now. Then we can go down; I'll make you breakfast myself. What if they don't know?"

He called Arthur. Roland had seen them and Cleo at the wedding, to which Alice had insisted they be invited and James had insisted they come. At the reception, Arthur, controlled and formal, as if delivering a negotiated statement, said to him, "I accept that this wasn't what you expected. Mary and I wish you well." No mention of wishing Alice well.

When Arthur answered, his frostiness was quickly superseded. They hadn't known. Why the Spine Centre? Were visitors allowed? They would ring and ask. He's probably still asleep. If either of them heard something, they would call.

At breakfast, a noisy affair with Alice's parents, her brothers, plus Kate and Marcella, Roland couldn't really hear anything.

The noises from outside were muffled. Alice, trying to cherish him, put down a plate of scrambled eggs on toast, touching him on the shoulder. He noticed that, because she never did this, the eggs were overdone, like in a hotel buffet. He took a bite mechanically and chewed for a while before forgetting about it.

By when should he have heard from James? How would the receptionist know he hadn't heard? She would help him, he knew, but she couldn't ask the doctor to phone him if she didn't know that James hadn't been in touch. She hadn't taken his number. It must have been on her screen. But what if it wasn't? What if she'd forgotten, and she was wanting to ring him at this very moment, as he was thinking about her, but couldn't. Or maybe James would text right now and just be absolutely fine. Right now. Right now.

He sat unmoving and absent amid the family tumult, his face slack, as if a black light were pouring out of his eyes.

Alice's family glanced at each other beneath the upbeat hubbub they were keeping going. Alice encouraged him to eat. He flinched into motion, took a bite, and again came to a stop.

A few hours later, his phone vibrated. Messages. One from James. "Hey mate. I'm in the London Spine Centre."

Roland wrote straight back. "Hey I know. How are you?" After a few seconds, he tried ringing, but James didn't pick up. Roland called the hospital. His receptionist was no longer there. Someone else answered, and Roland explained. "Hi. I'm James Drayton's next of kin. I was expecting a call from a doctor about how he's doing, but I haven't heard anything. He just texted me but now he's not picking up."

This new stranger took his number and promised that a doctor would call, just as the last one had.

Alice walked him around the woods. Once they got back to the house, he couldn't remember if they'd already walked or not. The only thing that reached him was Kate. She tried to crawl towards him on the chequered black and white kitchen tiles. She hadn't yet figured out how to coordinate her limbs so found herself moving backwards, bum-first and away. She laughed at this bizarre occurrence and crawled away faster, until her little naked feet touched the skirting board. Roland's mind could hold on to this.

That evening over dinner, he drank down glass after glass of wine, but it didn't seem to have any effect. Alice's family asked him kind questions about James, which he couldn't answer, and told him they were sure James would be fine. The mood had come down a long way since breakfast. They talked about how the virus was only dangerous for old people.

Drinking fast suddenly made Roland feel like James. In the months before their prototype was launched, James was so stressed he drank every day, just like this.

The next afternoon, the London Spine Centre finally called him back. He had several stories ready in case they questioned him about being next of kin. But the voice on the phone just said, "Roland Mackenzie?"

"Yes."

"My name's Stephen Harrison. I'm one of the consultants here."

"Okay."

"I'm sorry it's taken me some time to ring you. You can imagine how things are."

"No problem. No, totally."

"I'm sorry to have to tell you Mr Drayton is very unwell. The virus is interacting with his diabetes and that is making it hard for his immune system to cope."

Roland felt waves of cold and heat. "He said there's, um, a double effect. Sugar in the bloodstream. I'm sorry, I can't remember exactly."

"That's right. That's exactly it. Now, he's lucky. His diabetes seems to have been well managed. And we happen to be excellently stocked with ventilators. Many patients with spinal injuries need mechanical ventilation at some point."

"He's going on a ventilator?"

"Yes, we've started ventilation."

"It's started already? No one told me."

"Oh. Well, I'm sure you can understand the hospital's extremely busy. But he's got very good chances. He's young. He's seems to be fit."

"Yes. He runs a lot."

"Good. Good. His oxygen level appears to be controllable. But ventilation is hard on the body. It's a long recovery." The doctor, fulfilling his obligation to state this message, said again, "He is very unwell."

"Okay. Okay. Thank you."

"I'm sorry, I have other patients to see."

"Okay, thank you . . . Wait."

"Yes?" The doctor, task complete, suddenly sounded weary.

"Can I visit?"

"I'm afraid not. But one of the nurses may have time to hold up a phone for a video call, if you'd like to say something to him."

Another evening, another dinner, more wine. This time there was no conversation. The family broke up quickly, to watch Netflix or speak in other rooms.

The next morning, Roland was wrenched from sleep by his phone going off beside his head. He'd left it on loud. Groggy and clumsy, his head aching, he slid the answer bar across and put the phone to his ear.

"Mr Mackenzie?" It was the doctor again.

"Yes." Fear yawned open in Roland's heart.

"I've just come on shift. James is very unwell." Why was he calling him James, and in that sympathetic tone? "I've spoken to the nurses, and, if you'd like, we can make it possible for you to visit."

Roland started to cry. "What does that mean?"

"His immune system is not coping. I'm sorry to say his oxygen levels are dangerously low."

"I'm coming. I'm on my way."

Roland was shaking and Alice saw he wasn't safe to drive. She'd take him. Before they left, she made him eat, putting in his hand toast, eggs, bacon, as many calories as she could. She would not let him leave until he'd finished, even though he cried and kept saying, "We have to go. We have to go."

While she was telling Marcella she didn't know when they'd be back, Roland took the car key, walked alone to the Range Rover and drove away.

He could not have Alice with him. If she did just one thing to interrupt him, if she needed to stop to pee or wanted to wait a minute for a coffee, he could never forgive her. And what if Kate got sick and they, because they were both in the car together, had to turn around and go back?

Alice phoned him, her name appearing on the car's screen. He hesitated but then did press the button to answer. She spoke very calmly. "My love, you don't have to go on your own. If you wait, I'm only a couple of minutes behind you. One of the boys can drive me to where you are."

Roland couldn't really speak. He managed to say, "No. No." And then, "Please stay there with Kate."

"Kate? Kate's absolutely fine. She's playing with her caterpillar. You don't need to worry about her."

"Nobody in or out of the house. No trips to the butcher." Roland was gaining momentum. "Your brothers can't go and chat to their mates in the village."

"Okay. Okay. If that's what you want. I'll tell them."

"And can you ring Arthur and tell him. I can't while I'm driving."

There was silence. "I will if you want me to. But I don't think they want to hear this news from me."

"Okay. I'll do it. I'll do it."

"Sweetie, I can do it if you like."

"No. It's fine. It's fine. I've got to go."

Thank God Arthur didn't pick up and Roland could leave a message. To stop Arthur calling him back, he said he'd text when he got there.

The drive made him feel better. He was moving forward. And being on the empty motorway into London was pleasantly uncanny, like driving into a deserted radioactive zone. Without cars, you could see how broad the tarmac really was, the wide road already looking like a remnant from some collapsed empire.

Roland drove down the middle at a steady seventy-five, never needing to brake or change lanes. He and the few other cars he saw seemed to acknowledge each other, a little warily. He rehearsed his story in case there was a police roadblock.

The feeling grew stranger as he crossed into the outer districts of London, now just a vast, low-built plateau of brick and concrete, riddled with streets. On the Westway, he saw no one at all. It was a bright blue cloudless morning and the city looked decluttered of people, like an architect's drawings. On the overpass near Paddington, an elevated road between glass office blocks, he imagined photophobic zombies lurking in the deep shadow underneath.

As the big green road signs began to mention St John's Wood, he wished he weren't there already. Far better to do another lap of London, savouring the strangeness.

But a receptionist had explained very clearly how to find the London Spine Centre and where to park. There was its sober blue sign in a classy font. There was the brick-arched alley he was to drive into. And here at the back was a small car park. Next to the tarmac was a strip of soil planted with shrubs and ferns. On the other side of it was a row of doors and windows blocked out by blinds – rooms from which patients could be wheeled out for fresh air. James was in one of them.

Roland glanced around his Range Rover's cabin for something he'd better do before going inside. But there was nothing. He submitted and rang the reception. A few minutes later, a door opened and a human figure came out, dressed as if for an alien planet. Over purple scrubs, she was wearing a disposable white-plastic apron. Plastic gloves. A blue paper mask over her mouth and nose. And over that a full face-shield, kept in place by a band around her forehead. She was carrying a chair on which was more of the same, for him. She called over: "Hi. Is that Roland?"

"Yes."

"Put this on and come inside when you're ready."

As he came forward, she retreated back indoors, maintaining the distance. He rubbed alcohol into his hands and wrapped himself in the layers of plastic, beginning to sweat. It was eerie not to hear any traffic. There was a laminated card explaining the correct order for putting on gloves, masks and apron, to avoid contaminating yourself. He'd done it wrong. It was gloves last, not first. There was a stab of despair, then he thought: It's not going to make any difference; he's already got it.

His peripheral vision obstructed, breathing into the mask, he went in. The nurse had taken up position in the far corner. The room was like the one James was in during his coma: moulded plastic, wipe-down surfaces, the hard floor speckled to disguise stains. There was an adjustable hospital bed and some tall machines on wheels, each with a screen at eye-height, standing beside the bed like bony mourners.

James himself he could not look at.

The nurse said, "You can bring in the chair from outside to sit on."

"Okay."

"And you can stay as long as you like. Obviously just don't come through into the clinic."

"Okay." A pause unfolded. "How's he doing?"

Her tone became respectfully mild. "I'm sorry. He's very sick."

Roland began to cry, filling up his mask with heat and condensation.

She said, "I'm sorry. How long have you been married?"

Roland yelled with laughter and relief. He squeezed a finger up under his face-shield to wipe his eyes, and said, "Oh, he would love that. We're friends. We run a company together."

She was relieved too. "Okay. If you need anything, just press that button. We'll be in to check on him in a couple of hours."

Fortified by the joke, he could now bear to look at James. He was unconscious, flat on his back. Crouching on his face was a tentacular mass of yellow-white plastic tubes. A thick tube pushed disgustingly into his open mouth. The rest of his body lay corpse-like, irrelevant but for the lungs. They'd stripped him. Even though he was under a sheet, you could see at his shoulders that the patterned gown didn't wrap all the way round.

Roland was afraid to get close, but he dragged the chair over, hearing it screak on the floor. He saw that James was not asleep: there was no twitching or snuffling; he was in the slack, knocked-out oblivion of a chemical coma. Like a lump of inert meat with one organ, the internal bellows, being artificially moved up and down.

Imitating what he'd seen in films, Roland held onto James's hand. Another warm lump. The texture he felt was just the inside of his glove. The plastic bunched around his fingers when he bent them. They seemed to be internally coated with talcum powder.

He said, "Hey, mate, it's Roland."

No sign that this had penetrated to the pilot light deep within.

Roland began to cry again. Memories came to him vivid and disconnected: the night they decided to quit McKinsey and walked around Aberdeen in the dark. The percolator coffee at the airport hotel when they went to California to meet Peter Thiel. The night sky on the boat ride from Belfast to Orkney.

He spoke these memories out loud and, as he talked and talked, the dominant note became guilt: he apologised about Alice, about being cruel to James at DFID, about so often being lazy at the company. He confessed, he confessed, he confessed. He turned himself inside out for James to hear. It was a bit like falling in love.

Once it had all come out of him, he felt better. James seemed unchanged. Roland yawned and rubbed his eyes and waited for something to happen.

Some hours later, the door that led into the clinic opened. A walking bundle of rustling plastic introduced himself as Mr Harrison, and suggested they go outside.

It had clouded over, but Roland's eyes squinted in the muted brightness. Mr Harrison said, "If you stand a few metres away, you can take off the PPE. It's probably time for a new set anyway."

With sudden haste, Roland pulled off the face-shield and the paper mask, drawing in an unrestricted lungful of air. His ungloved hands were shrivelled and clammy. The apron he couldn't untie and ripped off. Mr Harrison pointed out a bin. Roland twirled his hands in the fresh air a little, letting them dry.

He'd been having a reasonably contented time, keeping James company and playing with his phone. There were some messages from James's dad that his mind slipped off without reading. Nothing seemed urgent. But now the dread was on him again.

Mr Harrison pushed his own face-guard up like a welder's mask and pulled the paper down under his chin. This revealed an exhausted, taut man in his sixties. He must be a marathon runner or something. But the skin under his eyes was purple.

Roland couldn't take it and said, "How is he?"

There was no preamble any more. "His blood oxygen level keeps slipping. We're also now dealing with sepsis."

Roland could feel himself going sweaty. "So what does that mean?"

The doctor sighed. "He's a lot younger and healthier than everyone else in this hospital. So he's got a chance. But the diabetes — actually, even the diabetes should be fine. But," he shrugged, "if there's a one in a million chance of something going wrong, and you have a million patients, then one *will* be unlucky. People never understand that."

Roland talked as if he were still a management consultant. "What probability would you give him? Percentage-wise?"

"Well, if his lungs . . ." The doctor shook his head and, with an effort, retained his professional demeanour. By now, it was all that was holding him upright. They both clung to their roles. "Honestly?"

"Honestly."

"Honestly, I think the fair thing is to tell you . . . you can never really tell and watch me get this completely wrong. I hope I do. But my opinion is that he is not going to pull through. The blood-ox levels keep dropping, and they're already below the level that starts doing permanent damage."

The only part of Roland capable of speech was rationalising, practical. "How long do you think?"

"It's impossible to say. I understand that's not helpful. But it is impossible. The body is now under all kinds of different strains. Low oxygen levels, sepsis, which means kidney injury and cardiac problems, potentially septic shock. We've got respiratory failure, and the heart's straining more and more to push oxygen around the body."

Harrison was so tired he let his frustration slip out. "I'm not even a specialist in respiratory illness. I do spines. I'm pretty good at them." The disorder of it all. "But from observing the other patients . . . Basically, things are breaking down. I'm sorry. He might yet pull out of it. You never know."

Roland put on a fresh layer of plastic, and they went back inside. The doctor went on through the internal door, and Roland followed him to it, as if walking him out. He could see the corridor through the thin vertical window. There was a whiteboard with James's name on it in red marker. James Drayton. It was one of a dozen or so. Margaret Boyd. Kari Lindholm.

Roland sat back down. It did not seem that James was really in there. Roland held the hand again. Then he peeled off the glove. What difference did it make? Skin on warm skin. Some thread of connection.

The door opened. A nurse. She glanced at his bare hand and said nothing. Then, "Have you eaten anything, sweetheart?" A Welsh tinge. "We're doing lunch in a minute. Do you want some?" Roland began crying at this kindness. He managed to nod and rasp out his thanks. She said, "I'll bring some tea as well, will I? I'm sorry, you'll have to pee in the garden. Let me know if you need the bathroom, and I'll see what I can do."

Later – Roland had lost his sense of time – he noticed a black stain on James's fingertips. Weird that he hadn't spotted this before. He bent forward to examine it. There was no longer any compunction about inspecting James's body. The stain wasn't dirt or ink; it seemed to be inside the finger, like a smoker's yellow.

He sat back in his chair and picked up his phone. There were messages coming in steadily: from Mary-Rose, from Alan, from his own parents. He opened those from Arthur. "They're saying James is only allowed one visitor. But we've decided we want you to stay there. It's you he would have wanted to be with him." This was self-evident and barely touched him. He couldn't reply. He was so far away from them that he wouldn't have known what words to use. The only person he could write to was Alice. It was as if she came to the edge of where he was, and he whispered to her.

He read a *Guardian* article about how to make the perfect pasta alla norma, and on impulse read it out to James. He watched some TikTok. It wasn't unlike waiting for Kate to be born.

When he noticed the black stain again, it had spread from the tips up James's fingers, as if he'd dipped them in something. It was past the first knuckle. Panicking, he pressed the big green help button mounted on the wall. After a stressful wait – why hadn't he called when he first saw it? – the Welsh nurse appeared in the doorway. Roland backed off to the other corner of the room.

She picked up James's fingers and looked quickly, as if seeing something expected. Delicately, respectfully, she lifted up the end of James's sheet. His toes were black. She said, "I'm sorry, love. His circulation is starting to go. The blood's not getting to the extremities any more. And see how he's sweating." How had Roland not seen this? There were pearls of sweat rolling down James's temple. The hair was wet. How had Roland missed it? "You see? That's his thermostat starting to go wrong." She opened the window a crack. "It won't be long now, love."

She said this and left him alone with James. Fear rose in him, as if this room were going to be visited by something. He watched the black stain in horror. He couldn't see it moving, but it must be. Imperceptibly, it spread up James's fingers until they were entirely black. It would spread up his hands and arms until they were black, and when it reached James's heart, he would die.

Already on James's face there was a developing sallowness, a waxiness, a yellowness, as if the flesh were changing its nature, becoming dead flesh. Roland used some Kleenex to wipe the sweat off James's temples, and when he touched the skin he shuddered.

Later, much later, it began to feel companiable again. He plugged in his phone and watched old episodes of *Frasier* on the tiny screen. Maybe James could hear it, could hear him laughing. It was almost like they were watching together, back in the Aberdeen Mercure late at night, watching movies while James fell asleep in the armchair.

The Welsh nurse came back and said it was the end of her shift. Roland, almost cheery now – the gallows lightness – nodded at James and said, "How long do you reckon?"

"Oh, it could be anything. Some people, you think it's over, and it goes on for weeks."

Weeks! He was still thinking of that when she asked whether he was going to go home for the night. Yes, yes, he would. He'd go home to his empty house. It would be fun. He'd have a long sleep alone between the cool sheets. Suddenly he was in a rush to get away. He clutched James's hand, saying, "See you tomorrow, pal." And, just in case, "I love you."

On the way out, he wanted to wave to the nurse, like someone who's won a reprieve, and peered through the familiar thin window in the door. He saw the same whiteboard; all the names bar James's had been wiped away. He fled before this could touch him.

Outside, he yanked off the PPE. By now he had a red patch on the bridge of his nose and raw red lines on his cheeks, where the mask chafed. The scratches hurt in the fresh evening air.

He bombed the Range Rover out of the alley and away, away, along the street. Traffic lights. Shops. The world of the living.

But the roads were empty. It was something of a surprise that the pandemic was still going on. He'd only been there one day. He could call Alice. He would have a shower.

He was almost home when a call came through from a London number. He pressed the button to answer. A new voice, strict, unhappy: "Mr

Mackenzie, this is Erica from the London Spine Centre." He hated her. "I'm the head nurse on the night shift tonight. I've just been in to check on Mr Drayton and he has deteriorated. If you want to be with him, you should come as soon as you're able."

Roland pulled a broad U-turn right across the empty double lanes of Queen's Gate and drove back the way he'd come.

Back to the London Spine Centre. Into the alleyway. Car park, strip of garden, now at night. Apron, mask, face-shield, gloves, already routinised. The mask rubbing his cheeks.

Inside, James, still flat on his back, still out cold, the plastic tubes still squatting over his mouth. The hateful nurse saying, "His heart became very unsteady. It's stabilised again for the time being, but he's close now."

Back onto the chair. One glove off. Holding James's hand. It was as if James wasn't there. Just his body. The short black curls hanging away from his waxy forehead. The eye sockets deeper somehow, as if sinking. His expression very stern.

His hands! Somehow Roland had forgotten them. But the black rot had risen no further; it had not gone past the fingers.

He rang Arthur. They were beyond awkwardness. Roland pointed the phone at James so his parents could FaceTime him. He tried to shut his ears. He did not want to hear the sounds James's mum was making. Nor what Arthur and Mary said to their dying child. Then he did it again, with Cleo. The tears came hot and painful, his jaw and stomach clenching as if something were being ripped out.

After a few hours, his alarm receded. James didn't die, just lay there, present but not present. The nurse seemed put out and defensive that she'd been wrong. Roland hated her more than he'd ever hated anyone.

He watched an episode of some Viking show on his phone. Actors with undercuts and ponytails. Dragon boats. Oaths to reclaim the usurped birthright. Again, it was as if he and James were watching together.

At first he tried to sleep in the chair but couldn't. He put the cushion on the floor and stretched out. Still in the mask and shield. His legs were trembling and tense, as if he'd been running all day. He passed out, snatching himself back up from sleep every few minutes.

In the morning, aching, his clothes greasy, James still there, he felt as if he'd survived something. A new nurse was on, a lean black woman with an African accent. She brought him coffee and a breakfast of beans on toast. When he'd arrived, only yesterday, he'd been subordinate to the nurses, but now she treated him with some new deference, as if he were closest to what was happening, the interpreter of James's state.

Drowsily, blearily, Roland drank the hot sugary instant coffee. He remembered so many things. James's looseness in his first months with Alice. More guilt. The time they talked their way into the Lehman building and looked out on Canary Wharf in the belief that civilisation was crumbling.

A doctor came in, a new one, and began talking in the mild, sympathetic tone that Roland now recognised. He was struggling to follow. Oxygen levels. Brain damage. Some battle fought deep inside James's organs was being lost. Roland did not really believe that anything would change. They wanted to take James off the ventilator. A tactful hint that other lives could be saved. Perhaps Roland would like to step outside while they removed the tubes. They could clean James at the same time.

Outside in the car park. Surprising sunlight. He pissed behind his car. Messages. Many messages. Tears again. Too many tears. He kneeled down and put his forehead on the rough tarmac, squeezing his teeth and his fists. Then stood up again when it passed. Messages from Alice. Inconsequential. Asking how he was. He could not return back up to that level.

When he went back in, James had changed. The tubes were gone. His mouth was raw – red and marked where tape had held the tubes in place. But worst was that Roland could hear and see him breathing. Short fast painful gasps. Strained sips of air. As if trying to breathe through a straw. His chest jerking. James's face wincing now, the forehead lined with effort. It looked like agony.

Roland gazed at the doctor, who said, "I'm sorry. I know this is distressing. But he's thoroughly sedated. He isn't feeling it."

For the first time, Roland thought: Let this be over. There was the inevitable guilt. And still the terrible gasping went on.

He sat in the chair and, when the doctor left, he spoke to James. Just saying anything, a flow of words, so that if James were in there, alone and terrified, he would hear a voice. Everything he'd never told him. That he hadn't been rejected by the JET Programme. Once he came to the end, he just meaninglessly repeated, "I love you."

After some time, even this became normal. James continued to gasp. Roland wiped his eyes. The messages he was getting had become incomprehensible. He and James stood together on the brink.

James's shoulders began to judder. His body twitched. It was almost as if he were trying to sit up. His face creased with exertion.

Now Roland felt him clearly. It was as if James were trying to rise into consciousness. As if he could dimly understand that he was asleep and was trying to float upwards towards this voice. He was below the surface and the surface couldn't be broken. But James bumped up against it, and Roland felt him. He said, "I'm here. I'm here."

Later still, when James had subsided back to the gasping, the African nurse came and asked if Roland needed to rest. It was a good idea. He would rest for a few hours. Just to be on the safe side, he squeezed James's hand and said, "I'll be back in a few hours, mate. Just need some sleep. Love you."

Outside. His body already crashing. The car door. An age to tilt the chair fully back. And he was out.

What felt like immediately, someone rapped on the window. He snatched himself awake. It was the Welsh nurse, in mask and shield and apron. She took a few steps backwards, out of infection range, as he opened the door. He was glad to see her. She said, "I'm sorry, love. He's gone."

The current of grief that had been flickering through him now surged, blowing him out. He went limp, sliding down until he came to rest on the tarmac. The tears couldn't flow fast enough to relieve the pressure in his chest. He sobbed like hiccoughing, his body in spasms. The nurse, who'd stayed at her distance, saying gentle sounds, told him, "You don't need to feel guilty. They often do that."

"Do what?"

"They wait until they're alone before they go. It means he knew you were there." Roland howled, and she went on: "I hope it's not disrespectful to say, but animals do the same. When I was a girl, I grew up on a farm, and the animals would go off on their own when it was their time. It's not that you weren't there, love. It's an instinct."

And while Roland half-sat, half-slumped on the tarmac, she, in her wisdom, told him all about her childhood, soothing, comforting, like telling an overwrought child a long and aimless story to settle him down. As she spoke, his mind could not fill itself entirely with grief; in one illuminated corner there were sheep and low green hills and the early-morning mist rising off the fields in spring.

XIV

In the hour after James died, Roland could feel his presence everywhere. Weakly in the streets and terraces, and strongly in the sky. The gauzy light-blue afternoon air was so full of James it was throbbing, as if James had shed his earthly form and shot upwards. But this presence faded, and, the day after James died, there was another day. Kate had to be fed; his bladder had to be emptied into the toilet; the food that was placed in front of him had to be chewed and chewed and chewed.

There were far too many phone calls and messages to read, let alone reply to. Investors, engineers, Eleni. Unwanted condolences, like gifts at a cancelled wedding. And under their supposed distress or delicacy, he could imagine what they really cared about: what it meant for their jobs. And beneath even that, they wanted him to explain what James had done wrong; to reassure them that they were not in danger.

Roland shoved it back in their faces. In his first Zoom announcement to the team, he told them with hostile candour, yes, it's possible the company will fall apart; and yes, it was horrible: he died in agony. The engineers groaned or gasped or cried on the screen, and Roland watched impassively. The only ones he didn't punish were Mary-Rose and Alan, because he believed their grief ran deep enough.

He had Mary-Rose organise a conference call of the investors. Peter Thiel was in one of the on-screen boxes, seemingly in the back of a limo, with palm trees going past the window. The Statoil guys and VC people were dressed down in shirts and gilets, dialling in from farmhouses and places they had in the country.

At the start of the meeting, some of them interrupted to show off that they were such decent people – humans after all and not just money machines: sorry for your loss; how is everyone? The usual pre-business warm-up chat was, this time, about sympathy. Roland let them talk for a minute or two, then said, "Okay, I know there've been some questions about whether I'm going to take over the CEO job or get in someone more experienced. Well, I'm going to do it. And, as of today, we're changing direction. We're now an electrolyser company. Got it?"

The little faces were like an array of carved stone heads, each with its own expression: gobsmacked, appalled, furious. The audio kept chopping and cutting out as they spoke over each other, and Zoom kept trying to adjust. It was boring to listen to. Everything they said was so predictable: not the right time – understand that emotions are high – company needs stability.

James had said to him that the switch to electrolysers would make Drayton–Mackenzie a legendary, career-making bet for the investors, like when Thiel was the first person into Facebook. If they were too stupid to see that, he wasn't going to explain it to them. He didn't mention that this was James's plan, nor that James had expected them to earn a fortune. Watching them, there was a glimmer of satisfaction, a malicious glimmer. He wanted them to be angry. He hated them.

There was an article in *The Times*. "Star Entrepreneur, 36, Dies of Covid". World-leading tidal energy company. Visited by Theresa May. It said how fit he was. Total crap. They didn't even mention he was diabetic. The commenters underneath expounded ignorantly on the course of covid-19.

Roland was so angry he began creating an account in order to reply. But fortunately he couldn't find his credit card and gave up in disgust.

Dozens of people sent him the article.

One Sunday morning, it was his turn to get Kate up and give her breakfast. Alice kept annoying him by offering to take over. But he'd said he'd do it, and he would.

Everyone else was still upstairs sleeping. He and Kate were alone in the big quiet kitchen. After breakfast, he set her down in what had become her end of the room: an expanse of squidgy multicoloured plastic tiles, a jumble of plastic caterpillars and a playmat where she could lie on her back and paw at dangling forest creatures, which she was already too old for. He looked at her short brown fuzz of hair: the Gulag.

He sat on the tiles beside her, and she started banging two sections of caterpillar into each other. The sections were supposed to interlock so that if you twisted one, the whole caterpillar moved up and down as if wriggling. She didn't get it.

Without knowing he was going to do it, Roland tipped forwards and put his forehead on a yellow plastic tile. His body relaxed one degree, and from deep within him came strange inarticulate animal sounds, like a cow bellowing in distress. Kate was delighted. She thought they were playing a game. She giggled and slapped her fat little palms against his wet cheeks, wanting him to do more.

The heavy black curtain that had descended around him was lifted at the bottom for a few seconds. He saw her laughing face; the pitiless, empathy-free egotism of the small child; the fast-growing replacement for himself. Today, she could crawl; tomorrow she would walk; and one day, when her parents died, everything they had would be hers. This was the true nature of things, and she was the only one admitting it. Once she was eighteen, he would be free to die as well. Roland put his head by Kate's feet and sobbed gratefully while she pulled his hair.

In the next months, Roland drove the company forward with cold relentlessness — like James in the months after Roland took away the only girlfriend he ever had. It also felt very James to announce that their electrolysers, of which they'd never sold a single one, had to become the global gold standard.

The pandemic opened a gap for them. While their rivals were dismayed and distracted, Drayton–Mackenzie Ltd could surge ahead. It was like accelerating away from the lights while the others didn't even know they were racing.

Roland began spending big and fast: he hired electrolyser engineers who'd been sitting at home idle, and bought start-ups who had good technology but were going bankrupt in the pandemic. The accountants sent him cautiously worded warning emails, which he ignored.

Soon a group of investors began the process of suing him for misuse of their funds. This was the only thing he enjoyed. Instead of doing them the undeserved favour of explaining his plan, or explaining that it was James's plan, he channelled the guy James always did: an American general called Stonewall Jackson – inflexible, absolute, conceding nothing, giving no ground, no compromise, no quarter, never, on nothing. He told the company's lawyers to fight for every bullet point, regardless of expense.

Thiel didn't join the lawsuit. On the contrary, he sent a message saying he could see the play. He knew some people in this space; he could make an intro. Roland didn't reply.

The investors wanted the board to replace him as CEO. But they couldn't. It turned out that James, while waiting for the ambulance, had written a will. Roland could see him bending over his kitchen table late at night, alone and afraid, gasping, sipping air, writing out those few sentences. Thank God it had gone so shockingly quick; some of the nurses had talked about weeks. Beside that suffering, the desire to say goodbye was frivolous.

In the will, ten per cent of James's assets went to his sister Cleo; ninety per cent to his goddaughter Kate. Apart from the purple Lambo, he hadn't spent any of his riches. Until Kate was eighteen, her shares would be voted by Roland. With these and his own, he needed no one else for majority control. Alan would always vote with him anyway. The board could fuck themselves. Realising that no one could stop him, he sacked Javier. He felt like Michael Corleone at the end of *The Godfather*, settling all family business.

On a Zoom call, he told Javier, "You're one of the most inventive and original engineers we've got. But it's not worth it to have you always trying to take things over. The cost–benefit equation is wrong."

Javier gesticulated like a footballer at a referee, miming pulling out his coppery hair. "But what is this? I don't understand. What has happened? Nothing. Nothing has happened. We are all so, so sorry Yames is passed away, but this is . . . this is insane."

Roland nodded to show he'd understood. But this was a blood sacrifice. "Okay, I'm just going to remind you that anything you've worked on while you've been an employee remains our IP, as does anything from Pelamis, since you sold it to us. James also had the foresight to put a two-year non-compete in your contract, so if you start any kind of related company, I'll sue, and that new company will become ours as well."

"You're fucking crazy. This is –"

"Javier, Javier. Listen, because I have another call in two minutes, and then after that you'll need to pay some lawyers if you want to talk to me. You still have your stock options so you'll still get rich when the time comes. Take two years off and enjoy yourself. Then find something else to work on."

He hung up satisfied that he'd made an enemy.

Sometimes when he was on a Zoom call, his mind would slip onto another track and he would see James lying dead in the wipe-down room. The nurse had said that in some ways it was a shame he wasn't seeing James tomorrow morning. After a few hours, the dead began to smile. The muscles of the face contracted as they stiffened, pulling up the corners of the mouth. It sounded horrible.

Rather than smiling, James had looked stern, as if he'd seen beyond earthly concerns. To say goodbye to a dead body seemed contrived and schlocky. You might as well say goodbye to a side of pork. But he said it anyway. What else was there? It was as if James had been bundled out of life while no one was watching. His final message? I'm in the London Spine Centre.

As for Alice, he remembered that James liked her, and so Roland had sex with her sometimes because it brought less of her attention onto him than avoiding it would have. He closed his eyes and short-circuited his thoughts with sheer physical stimulus, fearing that if he relaxed or slowed down, he would go soft.

As the summer approached, she suggested they go on holiday. The past few months hadn't exactly been the time of *her* life either.

The lurches in the financial markets had triggered a frenzy. Everyone kept saying this was a once-in-a-career bonanza. She was at her laptop in her parents' guest bedroom from breakfast till late in the evening. Her child hardly saw her, even though they spent all day in the same building. Her only regular breaks were childcare and dealing with Roland. Her eyes were sometimes blurry from too much screen.

She could do with some heat, some sunshine, rosé over lunch, naps in the afternoon. A villa, a boat, she didn't care. Maybe Greece. The Mediterranean countries were opening up faster. She would have to fill in pages of paperwork, but, essentially, they could do it.

Roland said no. He was aggressively hiring hydrogen specialists and forcing the engineers back to the workshop to finish a more intricate lattice for the electrolyser. Renouncing holidays felt very James. He sometimes felt as if James's ghost were possessing him.

Alice didn't argue. She took her fortnight off in the house where she'd spent every day since March. At least it meant lots of time with Kate. But she needed at least just one thing that was purely trivial. She took up fantastically detailed online shopping. Making her eyes even worse, she read thousand-word blogs by swivel-eyed American tiger moms about the comparative merits of different brands of welly boot for toddlers. Those from Polarn O. Pyret had a more rugged sole, while those from JoJo Maman BéBé were lighter and hence less tiring for infant legs. The question of which boot was best could expand into hours of detail, and she found she didn't even need to buy anything at the end of it.

SEPTEMBER 2020

As the first phase of covid passed, with offices reopening, one of the engineers quit. No one had ever resigned before. It was Charlie – Alan's first hire, who'd been with them since before they had a machine. He was on the boat when they towed the prototype up from Belfast – one of what James called the Old Bolsheviks, those who'd been with them since before the first revolution. Charlie was taking a job at Statoil, now renamed Equinor, that would pay him far more than the company could afford. He apologised and said he needed the money. He was getting married.

Roland in no way believed that someone would abandon them for something so meaningless. He would descend on Aberdeen like a righteous avenger, bringing a fiery sword. On the evening before his flight, Alice, cautiously, neutrally, from the other side of the bed, asked whether he'd packed everything.

"Yes. Why wouldn't I?"

Alice absorbed that in silence. "You know, sweetie, it's great you're so engaged in the company, and driving it so hard. But you don't need to be like him. He loved you as yourself, not as a version of him."

"Yeah, so?"

"Okay." She held up her palms. "Okay."

Maybe he had gone a bit too far. He relented a little, and let her see one of the thoughts he kept clenched tightly to his chest. "He actually turned everyone around him into a version of himself."

"But not on purpose, my love. That just happened because people admired him. *You* admired him."

He thought another secret but didn't tell it: *I want to turn into him.* "He was an egotistical prick most of the time."

"Was he? Is that true?"

If they carried on like this, there was a risk that Roland's sustaining anger would dissipate like mist. He reminded himself that Alice had actually fucked James, and said, "I've got to get back to it."

Roland flew up with Mary-Rose, whom he hadn't seen in person since the start of March. Her hair was still a red wave, but in lockdown she'd ditched her short skirts for the opposite: shapeless jeans and fleeces. There must be something behind this. Mental health? He'd ask her later.

Alan picked them up in a huge black Mercedes SUV. They drove to a field on the outskirts of town, where the construction firm Balfour Beatty was digging the foundations of the company's first factory. Alan and Mary-Rose chatted on the drive. The pale-blue sky seemed further away up here, impossibly high and distant. Roland remembered flights to Aberdeen with James, back when they were at McKinsey.

The site was screened off with wooden hoardings. Signs announced that Balfour Beatty was a considerate constructor. Stamped here and there was "Drayton–Mackenzie Ltd". Mary-Rose noticed the name, too, and glanced at him. He'd get it changed. Mackenzie Ltd.

Roland was given a hard hat, like a politician at a photo op, and shown around. It looked like an archaeological dig: an orderly pattern of trenches cut into the turf. Yellow machinery hulked at the edges, like builders stopped for a fag. Behind the nearest digger was a parallel trail churned into the grass by caterpillar tracks. The architect and site manager, older men with florid cheeks and big paunches under their checked shirts – they probably drank together – vied to explain their progress to him. They wore paper masks despite being outside.

Roland didn't bother. They probably thought he was a wanker. Baby-faced young guy up from London in a blue blazer and grey trousers; English accent; telling them what to do. It had been like this at Subsea7. The Millwall chant: no one likes us; we don't care.

While he interrogated them, he stopped listening to the conversation he was in. James would have loved to see their very own factory – to start mass-producing their own descendant of the Newcomen engine, that first ancestor. It was not nothing, what they were building here.

After the site visit, Alan drove him and Mary-Rose to a pub on the coast. No one spoke in the car. They went down a long, straight, single-track road between fields. At its end, the land reared up into a low cliff overlooking the sea. On top was the Creel Inn. Below it was a perfect crescent of sand. They were allowed to sit at picnic tables placed far apart on the pub's clifftop lawn. There were no menus, which could spread disease, just a tall blackboard leaned up beside the entrance. A waitress in a mask came and took their orders from a few feet away. The breeze fidgeted with Mary-Rose's hair.

Even like this, it lifted them out of themselves to be with other people, with warm sunshine on their faces and backs, being served food they couldn't make at home. Scampi and chips. Everyday pleasures.

Roland started to cry. To hide it, he gazed out over the North Sea to where it went flat in the distance. Big squat oil tankers crawled along the horizon.

Once Alan had eaten, he said, "So. Charlie."

Roland said, "Yeah." And what he'd planned to: "We've got to root out what's really going on."

Alan frowned at his pint. "To be honest, I doubt he'll be the only one."

"What?"

Alan glanced at Mary-Rose, who picked this up a little too fluently: "Yeah. I think a lot of people are feeling, like, quite unsettled."

This was an ambush; they were pincering him. But somehow he couldn't rouse himself to fight.

Alan carried on. "See, I'm not saying it was wrong to get rid of Javier. It makes no difference to me. Actually, I always thought he was a dickhead. But with him gone, and James gone, this electrolyser business" – Alan shook his head – "and the investors suing us . . ."

Roland caught a fright. "You really think more of the team want to leave?"

Mary-Rose said, "I wouldn't say *want to*. But, like, it's kind of obvious that they're asking themselves 'Should I get off before the ship starts sinking?' It's always easier to get a new job while you still have your old one."

"Why would we sink?"

"This electrolyser stuff. I don't think everybody gets it. And they feel kind of burned out. The pandemic's been hard on people. I can admit it's been hard on me. Especially with James dying."

Alan shifted as if to put a hand on her shoulder, thought better of it, and said, "Yup. Yup. Mary-Rose is right. You've been cracking the whip a lot."

Roland looked out at the sea again, endlessly mutable. Okay. He would let out another of his secrets. He unclenched, which brought swiftly passing pain, and said, "It was James's plan." He turned to them. "Before covid even. Me and him laid all this out. The world needs a lot more electrolysers than it does tidal machines. James reckoned it would make us a multibillion-dollar company. Then we can build as many tidal machines as we feel like."

He hadn't expected that their reactions would make him happy. Smiles, relief, optimistic questions. Alan asking, "Why didn't you just say that at the start?" The high tension of being alone slackened.

He didn't mention that James had planned to abandon them – never mentioned it, in fact, until decades later, when it didn't matter any more. Even then, he only told Alan, Mary-Rose, a few others he trusted. Never in public.

To the business journalist who wrote a biography of him – of Roland – he said only that he should be writing about James. "What he would have said, if he could see what's happened, is basically that he was Lenin and I'm just Stalin. It all came from him." The journalist-biographer nodded and took notes. Maybe there was an interesting origin story here. Though it was all kind of unsurprising. Drayton's mum was an industrial economist; his sister did solar panels. The apple hadn't fallen far from the tree.

That afternoon in the Creel Inn, with the high blue sky far above him and the sea everywhere on his right, Roland began to let himself back into some less absolute modes of feeling. Alan and Mary-Rose were now saying he'd been kind of a dick lately. He made an *eek* face, shrugged, and said, "I also may have spent a bit too much money."

Alan said, "Fuck's sake, Roland."

"It'll be okay. Probably."

Mary-Rose said, "How much did you spend?"

"Doesn't matter. I only bought useful stuff. Well, maybe I shouldn't have spent so much on the lawyers." He pre-empted their interruption: "But listen. Listen" – he put up his hands – "I hear what you're saying. I'll explain to the team and to the investors."

Mary-Rose said, "Good. Great. I think they'll be very receptive. They're just, like, their minds are blown and they need some reassurance."

"Oh, don't worry. I can play the team like a fiddle: 'I'm sorry, everyone, for being a dick – I was just cut up because my friend died. But actually James left behind a plan for us all to get wildly rich. Now I just need you to help me do it.' They'll be lapping it up."

There was a flash of contempt, but that, too, was fading. Suddenly there was a deep aching in his chest, as if his ribs were being spatchcocked. He said, "I just really miss him." Mary-Rose couldn't speak, and Alan's face had gone stiff. Alan lifted his pint and said, "James." They touched their glasses, an inadequate gesture.

He and Mary-Rose were staying in a country-house hotel on the edge of town, a mock baronial mansion with tartan carpets and giant American redwoods in the garden.

That night, he dreamed he was in the Mercure. He and James were standing in the lamp-lit corridor before bed, talking about the company. James looked like he had on the last day before lockdown, fit from running and dressed in his usual blue jacket. It was so normal that Roland forgot James shouldn't be there.

As they talked, James began to walk unhurriedly down the corridor away from him. After a few paces, Roland had to louden his voice. But they carried on speaking, shouting now, reduced to shoutable phrases, as James continued ever further along a corridor that was stretching into infinity. Soon James passed out of earshot, but they could still see one another. Roland waved, signalling, and James waved back. And then James was too far away to wave to, still walking, a distinctive blue blob far off, a dot, a speck, a single blue pixel. And then he was gone.

In the morning, crying again in the hotel bed, he WhatsApped Alice. "Morning, babe. Miss you kiss you. Pls send me some pictures of the little monkey if you get a minute. Love you xxxx"

SPRING 2021

Kate walked unsteadily across the kitchen to where Roland and Alice were eating breakfast. Roland stuck out a leg as protective barrier – her curly head kept colliding with the table. She clung onto his shin and glared at him crossly. She looked at the toast in his hand and said one of her phrases: "Me first. Me first."

Roland said, "You little rat. Okay then." He held out the toast at mouth height, and she bit into it, then grabbed the slice in her fat fists. She gave him another warning glare and, through a spray of crumbs, told him, "Me first." He laughed.

Roland expected Alice to tell him off for spoiling her, so retreated towards the toaster and put in more bread. When he turned round, Alice was gazing at him strangely. He said, "What? Okay, you're right. She's meant to say please – aren't you? Say please, sweetie." Kate carried on chewing.

"No," said Alice. "I was just thinking, that's the first time I've heard you laugh since James died."

Roland's eyes started squirting out tears again. He still couldn't stop this happening. It was like the washers on his tear ducts were broken.

It must be a year now, or more than a year. He couldn't hold on to the date it happened, and didn't try to. Everything from the London Spine Centre was blurring fast. The body was protecting itself: deleting memories, destroying records. He didn't interfere.

A couple of weeks previously, he'd cleared out James's desk at WeWork. They were moving to a bigger office. He gave some things to Arthur and Mary, who invited him to take whatever he wanted from James's bedroom. They'd had both their jabs and chatted with him in the kitchen like in the days before Alice.

There wasn't much in James's room. The Seoul National University baseball cap and the dragon dressing gown he left to James's parents; these belonged to a time before Roland knew him. In his backpack he put the random objects he found: a christening card from the pregnant girl at Subsea7, Eloise, saying that little Angus was ever so grateful. The torn hunk of steel, shot through with copper fibres, from when the cable snapped in the tidal strait. One of James's back issues of the Guinness Book of Records. A small assortment of flotsam.

What did it mean? Did it mean anything?

Lastly, a photo he didn't know James had, printed out but not in a frame, taken on the boat as they'd towed the first yellow hull from Belfast up to Orkney. They were at the stern, and you could see the machine following along behind like a faithful sea monster. He and James had an arm around each other's shoulders. James was dressed for an Arctic expedition, in a fluorescent survival jacket and rip-proof trousers; Roland in a hoodie and jeans. They were both squinting into the sunshine, screwing up their faces as someone took the picture.

And that was all there was.

Epilogue

TWENTY YEARS LATER

Roland's plane landed on the cargo runway at the Scotland National Spaceport. On the short walk to the launch station, the breeze tousled his thin sandy hair and played with his tie like an annoying child. He'd got dressed up.

Beyond the edges of the rigorously flat compound, he saw the summer landscape blooming in purple and green, and, beyond that, the open sea. He didn't have much reason to come to Scotland any more.

The head of the spaceport met him outside the lobby and said, "Welcome, Sir Roland." He'd given up correcting people. Every now and then some minister discreetly sounded him out on whether he'd like to become a sir, or maybe Lord Mackenzie of Gloucester Road – the longest-serving chief executive in the FTSE 100. Crazy, really. It had all taken so much longer than he and James imagined.

But these ministers were just soliciting donations. One fee for a knighthood, another for a peerage. And he didn't need their stamp of approval. His mum would like it though; maybe he would accept while she was still around to see it. Maybe not.

While people talked at him, he was led up to the viewing gallery, a long loud room crowded with his guests, clutching champagne flutes and paper napkins. A corporate banner said *Welcome Drayton–Mackenzie Ltd*.

He'd invited as many people as would fit. Assorted politicians and CEOs. Some journalists. James's friend Eleni, glamorous and forbidding, elegantly wrapped in cashmere and diamonds. They'd been almost close for a few years when they both had small children.

And, most important, the Old Bolsheviks. Alan was there, looking slim, leathery and wrinkled, like human biltong. He and Catriona had retired to a palace outside Malaga and were out on one of his boats most days, getting sun-damaged. Mary-Rose was there alone. It irritated Roland that she was wearing her dog collar. It was faux-humble peacocking – a guarantee that everyone would ask her what she did. Surely even vicars had days off.

James's sister Cleo was there, looking more and more like her mum in a dowdy-formal work suit. James's parents hadn't made the trip. Arthur said he was too unwell; he probably just couldn't face it.

Roland found Kate, who was chatting to a star-struck engineer. Even though she was dressed like a student, her hair shone and swished, and these days Roland could tell that her ripped jeans were understatedly expensive. It still surprised him sometimes that he had a rich girl for a daughter. He approached, the engineer was greeted and politely moved away, and he said to her, "Why didn't you fly with me? I could have picked you up."

"I don't know." She shrugged. "It seemed easier."

He rolled his eyes. "Where's your brother?"

"He said he couldn't make it. He's got an essay crisis."

Infuriating. It was nothing to do with essays. It was that Kate had inherited a major chunk of the company from James, and Leo had not. Kate had been on the board since her eighteenth birthday. She had a private office of three people to look after her investments and screen the continuous influx of invitations. She'd just been in Japan for a summit. Leo had none of this. All he had was a rich dad, which he could maybe try being a bit more grateful for.

Roland had decided to give Leo his own share – Roland's share – of the company. That was the only way to make things even. Doing so would make every day after that more complicated for himself. He would be called a lame duck. He would be suspected of wanting to retire. His decisions would be questioned. But what was being a parent if not making your own life harder for the sake of your kids.

This plan wavered whenever Leo was being a bolshy little ingrate. And if he told Leo the plan, of course Leo would be on besties until he got what he wanted. But Roland wanted him to behave well without expectation of reward.

He said to Kate, "Tell him from me that if he – oh, forget it. How's your mum?"

Kate avoided reporting on either to the other. She said something he must know already: "They've asked her to be on this new innovation commission."

"That's never going to work. They've got completely –"

Kate's face went blank. "Talk to her about it."

He made a noise of irritation. "Why is it that no one in this family will do what I want?"

"Is Mum still in your family?"

"Of course she is. Jesus."

Kate patted him on the arm. "Come on, Dad. Don't stress yourself out. Try to, you know, relax."

"I *am* relaxed."

"Maybe have a glass of champagne, and let's go look at the rocket."

"You're right. You're right."

Roland downed two glasses of champagne. Why was he nervous?

He and Kate went over to the bank of windows. Down there he could see it, pointing up like a sundial. It was a larger, heavier rocket than they'd had here before. Not just making the short hop up into polar orbit, but carrying a telecoms satellite into orbit around the moon.

The engineers thought it made no sense to launch from here. They kept saying it would be better to launch from near the equator – Guiana, for example. But what was the point of owning the company if you didn't sometimes just do what you felt like.

Painted vertically on the rocket's side in retro red lettering was the vessel's name: SS *James Drayton*.

Roland blinked, and Kate leaned a little so her shoulder touched his upper arm. He said, "You know, he never saw the first launch. It was meant to be an ESA mission from Guiana with, I mean, literally a *teaspoon* of fuel from us. But it was postponed by the covid pandemic."

Kate had heard this several times before and just nodded.

About half an hour later, the head of the spaceport gave an unctuous speech that Roland tuned out. Then they switched on the speakers, and he could hear mission control counting down the launch sequence. Fire erupted from the rocket's base, pale and transparent in the sunshine. Before they had time to take in its wholly unnatural motion, the craft pinged upwards. Launches only looked slow from far away. Already they were seeing the rocket from below: a blowtorch of flame emerging from a flying pen.

Roland watched it ascend. James had now been dead longer than Roland ever knew him. He'd stopped ageing much younger than Roland was now. He would still be the age Roland was when he took over the company. Many times since, Roland had wanted to do something else with his life, but he could never quite convince himself that the company didn't need him. His debt of loyalty had been paid in full.

As the rocket disappeared, he remembered being young, before James, not bound to anyone, irresponsible, full of hopes, and free. Onto his retina, his mind projected a wisp of fluorescent pink – all that remained of a night out in Tokyo, long ago.

The rocket itself hurtled upwards, accelerating even faster as the ground rapidly collapsed into a distant, multicoloured pancake. The sky's high wide blueness deepened to indigo, to navy, to black. Far below, the pancake was curving, gaining edges, becoming a ball. The rocket, like a flying needle, pierced the vault of the sky, and escaped Earth's gravity.

There was no atmosphere up here, no sense of rushing, just space stretching out in every direction. The rocket drifted, adjusting itself, and cast off the last of its boosters. Then it went on with its lonely work, towing the payload to its position among the stars.